RAGE OF DESIRE

His eyes were smoldering. "Let you go?" he breathed deeply. "No, I think it is too late for that...I think perhaps you have used me," he said darkly.

Samantha watched his face take on a look of sheer rage. It frightened her. He had changed from the laughing, handsome man she had felt so safe with, to a dark, menacing stranger.

"A lady does not trifle with a man as you have trifled with me. So, if you are not a lady, I need not treat you as one..."

He unbuckled his gunbelt and dropped it to the ground. Then his hands moved to his belt buckle and Samantha's eyes grew enormous with comprehension. He caught her wrists and threw her down. He unbuttoned his shirt and gazed down at her, fire glowing in his gray eyes.

"I can't let you," she whispered.

Other Avon Books by
Johanna Lindsey

CAPTIVE BRIDE
FIRES OF WINTER
GLORIOUS ANGEL
PARADISE WILD
A PIRATE'S LOVE
SO SPEAKS THE HEART

Heart of Thunder

Johanna Lindsey

AVON
PUBLISHERS OF BARD, CAMELOT, DISCUS AND FLARE BOOKS

HEART OF THUNDER is an original publication of Avon
Books. This work has never before appeared in book form.

AVON BOOKS
A division of
The Hearst Corporation
1790 Broadway
New York, New York 10019

Copyright © 1983 by Johanna Lindsey
Published by arrangement with the author
Library of Congress Catalog Card Number: 83-91100
ISBN: 0-380-85118-0

First Avon Printing, November, 1983

AVON TRADEMARK REG. U. S. PAT. OFF. AND IN
OTHER COUNTRIES, MARCA REGISTRADA, HECHO EN
U. S. A.

Printed in the U. S. A.

WFH   10 9 8 7 6 5

Thanks, Mom,
for falling in love with
Hank and making this one possible.

Chapter 1

February 8, 1870, Denver, Colorado

SAMANTHA stopped pacing as she caught sight of herself in the large oval mirror over the fireplace. She was standing across the room, far enough away from the mirror to see almost a full view of herself. Samantha's eyes glittered. She didn't see how provocative she looked in the stylish two-piece dark-green-taffeta suit trimmed with black velvet. All she could see was that her hair, which she had spent an hour arranging artfully, had fallen into complete disarray because of her furious pacing. Two of her silken auburn locks hung all the way to her slim waist.

Samantha gritted her teeth and stomped across the large hotel suite she was sharing with her friend, Jeannette Allston. Jeannette was not at home, but even if she had been, Samantha wouldn't have tried to hide her anger. Usually, she did keep her temper in check around the petite blonde girl, but just then she was too furious. *Furious.*

She halted her angry stride and stood directly in front of the oval mirror, hands on hips, glaring at herself. Large emerald eyes flashed back at her.

"See what you've done now, Samantha Blackstone Kingsley?" she hissed at the mirror. "You've gone and let him upset you again. Look at you! *Estúpida!*" She often cursed in Spanish because she knew it as well as she knew English.

Viciously she poked the loose curls back into place, not really caring anymore how she looked. Her green velvet hat would hide the coiffure anyway. She would put it on just before leaving. *If* she left. *If* Adrien ever got there to escort her to the restaurant.

An hour late—an hour! Her stomach growled with hunger, and that increased her fury. Why had she told Jeannette she would wait there for Jeannette's brother? She should have left with Jeannette. But, no, Samantha wanted the chance to be alone with Adrien. It seemed she was never alone with him.

She loved Adrien, she adored him, and how could she let him know it unless she could get him alone for just a little while? But Adrien was late. He was always late, and this time she was furious about it.

This one time she had had a chance to have Adrien all to herself, but he had spoiled it by being late, and he had put her in a temper because of it. When he came, *if* he came, she was just mad enough to let Adrien Allston know what she thought of him! The nerve!

Why had she chosen *him* to fall in love with? Sophisticated Adrien. Handsome—no, beautiful. He was simply beautiful. Not too tall, but so muscular, so virile looking.

He was going to be her husband. Of course, Adrien didn't know that yet. But Samantha had known it from the moment she met him, two years before. He was the man for her. And Samantha always got what she wanted. Ever since she had come to live with her father ten years before, when she was only nine, she had had everything her way. She was used to getting what she wanted.

And Samantha wanted Adrien. So she would get him, one way or another—if she didn't alienate him completely today.

She really had to calm down, because she couldn't afford to vent her anger on Adrien. He wouldn't expect it at all. She had always managed to be the sweet, gentle lady he thought she was. From the moment Jeannette had confessed that her brother couldn't tolerate emotional disturbances of any kind, Samantha had never raised her voice in his presence. She was always calm, even demure. What an effort! She who was always so quick to fly into a rage, so temperamental.

Spoiled, her tutor had called her, spoiled and selfish and willful. But he didn't understand what she had gone through during her first nine years, living with her grandmother in England. So he didn't know that, once she had tasted freedom, she couldn't get enough of it. She was determined to forget the rigidity of those first nine years, determined to do whatever she wanted. And if she had to show a little temper at times to get her way, and if she was spoiled, what of it? She got her way. Always.

Maria, the Kingsleys' housekeeper, who was the closest thing to a mother Samantha had ever had, was more kind than the tutor. Maria called her *pequeña zorra*— little fox. "You are wily like *la zorra, niña,*" Maria would scold whenever she saw that determined gleam in Samantha's eyes. And one day she had added, "You are wise enough to handle your papa, but someday you will meet a man you cannot handle. Then what will you do, *niña?*"

But Samantha had scoffed and replied confidently, "I will have nothing to do with a man I can't handle. Why should I? I'm not ever giving up my freedom."

That had been... how long ago? Nearly three years. Right before she went East to finishing school. But she still felt the same way. And she would be able to handle Adrien, she was sure of it. Sure enough to marry him.

But he didn't know about her plans. Why, Adrien hardly knew she was alive. It was a wound to her vanity, for if Samantha was anything, she was beautiful.

It was her good fortune, yet she took it for granted and had never given it much thought—until recently. Because, for all her effort, for all her endeavoring to improve what the good Lord had given her, Adrien still didn't notice.

Hers was almost a classical beauty, and she had vivid coloring, hair that gleamed almost crimson in certain light, and eyes like the brightest of emeralds. A fine, slim figure. And remarkable features that demanded more than one look from anyone. But did Adrien look? He seemed to see right through her, to look, yet not to be looking at all. It was maddening.

Samantha's belly grumbled embarrassingly loudly and shook her out of her reverie. She glared at herself in the mirror once more and then suddenly, in a fit of temper, ripped out the pins she had taken such pains with and let the bright reddish-brown locks fall over her shoulders and back in an abundance of unruly waves and curls.

"That settles that," she said petulantly, spiting herself and her gnawing hunger. "Now I can't go even if you *do* show up, Adrien."

Too late, she realized she was hurting no one but herself. Adrien wouldn't care. In his typical emotionless way, he would serenely ignore the possibility that she might be angry because of his tardiness. Then again, he might not show up at all. The lunch hour was long past. Was Jeannette still waiting for them in the restaurant with the chatty widow they had met on the bumpy stagecoach ride from Cheyenne to Denver? Mrs. Bane had taken it upon herself to be the girls' unofficial chaperone. Or had Adrien gone straight to the restaurant because it was late? Had he just forgotten about their luncheon engagement?

"Damn him," she swore softly. She was alone, and no one would hear the shocking breach of etiquette. "If I didn't love him, I'd kill him."

The knock on the door startled her. Her eyes narrowed, then widened in dismay as she remembered what she had done to her hair. Oh, why couldn't he have come five minutes sooner, before she gave in to her temper?

"Go away, Adrien," Samantha called reluctantly. "I have decided to forgo lunch today." Would he be disappointed?

The knock sounded again, and she frowned as she started toward the door. "Didn't you hear me?"

"Yeah, I heard you, Miss Kingsley, but why don't you open up anyway?"

Samantha stopped. It wasn't Adrien. She would recognize that voice anywhere, though. Tom...Tom...She couldn't remember his last name, but the man had been at the stage depot last week when they arrived. He had taken an instant liking to her—a disagreeable liking at that. The man was downright rude. He was ignorant, as well, for he had followed her around all week, talked to her whenever he could, and would not accept her hints that she was not interested in him.

He was handsome, in a rugged sort of way. A young man, he was prospecting in Denver, trying to strike silver, like so many others. Gold had dwindled in the Pikes Peak region, but silver had only just been discovered the year before.

But Tom held no interest for her. In fact, he'd begun to frighten her, with the intimate way he spoke to her when no one else could hear, and the way his eyes roamed over her, as if he were trying to imagine what lay beneath her clothes and was doing a good job of imagining. But what disturbed her the most, what angered her, was that the man actually believed she was attracted to him despite her having gone out of her way to show him otherwise. The last time she had passed him in the hotel lobby, refusing even to glance his way, he had pulled her aside and warned her to stop playing hard to get! He had said he was running out of patience.

She had been so shocked that she hadn't known what to say when Jeannette asked what was wrong.

And now he was at her door. *Why?*

He had the audacity to pound then, a loud and insistent pounding. "Come on now, Miss Kingsley, open up the door for me."

"Get away from my door, do you hear?" she ordered angrily. "I'm not going to open it, so just leave."

It was quiet for a moment, quiet enough to hear the doorknob turning. Samantha gasped. The nerve! Worse, the door was not locked. It opened slowly, and the tall young man stepped into the room. He grinned, quickly closing the door behind him.

Samantha was speechless—but only for a moment. "Are you crazy?" she demanded, her voice rising on each word. "Get out of my room!"

He just shook his head, amused. "I aim to stay, Missy, least till we've had a little talk."

She threw up her hands. "Lord, you *are* crazy." And then she drew herself up stiffly and attempted a calm approach. "Look, Mr. . . . whatever your—"

He cut her off with a narrowed look and said sharply, "Don't pretend. You know my name. Tom Peesley."

Samantha shrugged. She had never heard the name before, but she seemed to remember everything else he had ever said to her. It was because of him, and the way he stalked her, that she wouldn't leave the hotel alone. He was always in the lobby, always, as though waiting for her.

"I don't care. Can't you understand? Why won't you leave me alone?"

"I hear what you're sayin', Miss Kingsley, but I know better. When are you gonna stop pretendin'?"

"Just what is that supposed to mean?"

"You know exactly what I mean," he growled. "You like me, but you gotta keep pretendin'."

Samantha held her tongue. Was he angry? So far he had been a very exasperating man, hardheaded, persistent, but not really threatening. Yet he was huge, tall, and brawny, with enormous arms and shoulders, hard-muscled from working in other men's mines when he wasn't looking for his own stake. She remembered him telling her about that, that and the reason he stayed in Denver. He liked the excitement of a large city, and Denver was large, almost Eastern in its prosperity. Unlike most towns that had started with the gold rush, Denver had survived, and the town continued to grow.

"Well, Missy?"

"What?"

"You didn't answer me." He ran a large hand through reddish-gold hair in a show of impatience and then pinned her with light brown eyes. "When are you gonna stop pretendin' so we can get down to some serious courtin'? It's time for some honest talk 'tween you and me."

"You and me?" she snapped. "There *is* no you and me. Why can't you get that through your head?"

"Stop it, woman!" he shouted. "I warned you this mornin' that I was runnin' out of patience. You either start actin' more friendly, or I ain't gonna be responsible for my temper."

Samantha stared, aghast, but held her tongue. His outburst made her wary. He was such a large man. He made her feel much smaller than her five feet four inches. And she could well believe he was capable of violence. What chance would she have of defending herself against him? And what on earth had she ever done to make this man think she wanted to court?

He was glowering at her, waiting for her to answer him. She frowned. How could she get rid of him? Oh, Lord, why didn't Adrien come? He could stop this.

"Mr. Peesley—Tom—why don't we discuss this on the way down to the lobby?" Samantha smiled warmly, hoping he would not be suspicious of her sudden change in attitude. "You can escort me to the restaurant where my friend, Miss Allston, is waiting for me."

But he shook his head stubbornly. "We're stayin' right here until we get this settled."

His obstinacy infuriated her, and she forgot to be wary. "How can we settle anything when you won't *listen?*" she asked heatedly. "The plain truth is that I don't like you. In fact, you have pestered me so much that I'm actually beginning to *dis*like you intensely. Is that clear enough for you, Mr. Peesley?"

In two long strides he was towering over her. Samantha gasped as he grabbed her shoulders and shook her. Her head flew back, and she found herself staring up into his angry eyes.

"You're lyin'," he growled ominously, and shook her again. "I know you're lyin'. Why?"

Tears stung her eyes. "Please. You're hurting me."

He didn't loosen his hold. "It's your own damn fault."

He brought his face close to hers, and she thought he was going to kiss her. But he just looked into her eyes, shining then with tears. He seemed to be willing her to say what he wanted to hear.

Less harshly, he said, "Why can't you admit you feel the same way I do? I knew you were for me the moment I saw you. I've had my women and left 'em. I never wanted to marry any until I saw you. Is that what you've been waitin' to hear, that I want to marry you?"

"I..." She started to deny it, but thought better of her temper—and his. She pushed at him, struggling to get out of his grip, but he didn't budge. "Let go of me!" she demanded.

"Not until you answer me."

Samantha wanted to scream, to swear, but ladies didn't swear. That had been drummed into her during the last few years. Ladies might swear in their minds, or, if they were alone and it was absolutely necessary, they could utter a mild curse. But never, ever in public. It was a pity, because Samantha had a few choice names for this oaf. She knew some pretty shocking words, words she had picked up from her father's *vaqueros* on the ranch. They had spoken freely, unaware that the English miss was quickly learning Spanish.

Most of their words had meant nothing at her young age. Once she had asked Maria what a *puta* was, and Maria had slapped her. She hadn't spoken to Maria for a week after that, and she never asked her the meaning of a word again.

Later, she went to an Eastern school, where the girls talked openly and descriptively about sex and men, when an adult was not around. They were quick to answer all her questions and not at all shocked—well, maybe only a little—by Samantha's vocabulary of words forbidden to ladies.

This man was making it very difficult to remember that she was a lady. She would give anything for a gun, she told herself. But her derringer, which was in her purse on the writing desk, would do no good. With only one bullet, it was suitable for city travel, where a single shot would bring help. No, she needed the gun in her bedroom—her six shooter.

"I'm waitin', Missy, and I'm gettin' damn tired of waitin'," Tom growled.

Samantha took a deep breath to keep from shouting. "You want answers, then you give me one first. Whatever did I do to make you *assume* I cared for you?"

He frowned. "That's a fool question."

"Humor me."

"What?"

"Just tell me!" Samantha said, exasperated.

"Well...you know. The moment you seen me you was all smiles, battin' those pretty green eyes at me. You were the most beautiful gal I'd ever seen. I knew right then you were for me."

Samantha sighed. Lord, she would never smile politely at another man again.

"Mr. Peesley, a smile does not necessarily indicate affection," she said. "I smiled at everyone that day, simply because I was overjoyed not to have to look at another stagecoach for at least a few weeks. I was delighted that the journey was over. I smiled at *everyone*. Do you understand?"

"But your smile for me was special," he protested doggedly. "I could tell."

Damn. She would have to be blunt.

"I'm sorry," she said tightly. "But you were mistaken, Mr. Peesley."

"Call me Tom."

"No, I won't," she snapped. "How can I make you understand? I have no wish to know you. I am in love with someone else, the man I came here with. Mr. Allston. *That* is who I am going to marry. *Now* will you let go of me and leave?"

Instead of being outraged, Tom Peesley laughed. "Now I know you're lyin'. I've seen you with him. He pays more attention to his sister than he does to you."

That hurt, for it was absolutely true. "That is none of your business. It is him I love."

Her insistence was making him angry. "I'd kill him if I really believed that."

And then, finally, came the kiss. Samantha was unprepared for the brutal assault. Crushed in his arms, she tasted her own blood where he bruised her lips against her teeth. The scream of outrage that tore from her was trapped in her throat.

And then he suddenly set her free, but for a moment she was too numb to realize it.

His tone was icy. "I can be a tender lover, or I can make you suffer. I almost killed a gal once who got me riled. And that's what you're doin', Missy. You're gettin' me riled with your teasin'."

She should have been frightened, but she wasn't. She was furious. She had never been treated that way before, and she would not stand for it any longer. She slapped him, using enough force to send a lighter person flying across the room. It didn't move Tom Peesley, but it did stun him. It was the last thing he had expected, and it left him standing there open-mouthed with shock as she whirled around and ran into her bedroom.

Samantha slammed the door. There was no lock, though, and she didn't know whether Tom Peesley would give up or follow her. Dashing to her dresser, she dug through the top drawer for her revolver. In a moment, with the pearl-handled weapon gripped firmly in her right hand, she felt herself in control at long last.

She could use the gun. Oh, how she could use it. Manuel Ramirez had made certain of that. The oldest of her father's *vaqueros,* and Maria's husband, Manuel was stubborn—often reminding Samantha of herself. When, at twelve, she had insisted that she no longer needed an escort, that she could ride the range alone, no one had been able to persuade her otherwise—except Manuel. He had threatened to shoot her beautiful white mustang if she dared go out alone without first learning to shoot. So she had learned to shoot, not only a handgun but a rifle, as well, and she became expert at both. After that, no one worried when she took off for a whole day, or even spent the night on the range. They knew she had all the protection she needed in her swift horse and the Colt she wore strapped to her hip.

Unfortunately for Tom Peesley, he had decided to follow Samantha. He opened the bedroom door, and his eyes widened at the sight of the Colt revolver pointed at his chest.

"Just what the hell do you think you're gonna do with that, Missy?"

"Force you to leave."

"You think so?"

"I'm sure of it, Mr. Peesley," she said very calmly. "In fact, I can swear to it."

She grinned for the first time. She was in charge again, and it felt wonderful.

Only Tom Peesley didn't know it yet. "I'm only gonna tell you once, gal. Put that gun down."

She laughed, moving the gun playfully, flexing her

wrist so that the barrel made several half-circles, drawing a wide target from his left shoulder, down his belly, up to his right shoulder, and back again. Her laughter echoed in the large room.

"I am quite a good shot." Samantha's eyes were bright with laughter. "After what you've put me through, I really would like to show you."

"You wouldn't," he said with total confidence.

Her amusement faded. "Why not? I should shoot you for mauling me. Or for being in my room without an invitation. But I won't. I'm going to advise you nicely just to leave. Of course...if you don't *take* my advice, then I'm going to take a chunk of skin off your inner right thigh."

Her matter-of-fact tone threw Tom Peesley into a rage, and he took a step toward her. But he got only as far as that one step before the gun exploded.

He bent to clutch at his inner right thigh, just inches from his groin. Blood squeezed through his fingers. The bullet had struck right where she said it would, going through him to imbed itself in the door. He stared at her in disbelief, then lifted his hand to stare at the blood.

"Do you need another demonstration before you leave?" Samantha asked softly.

Acrid smoke burned her eyes, but she held her gun steady, pointing it at Peesley. He hadn't moved from his aggressive stance.

"Perhaps your left thigh now, only a little higher?" Samantha continued.

"You god damn—"

The weapon cracked again, and Tom howled with pain as the bullet tore the tender flesh high on his left thigh.

"Do you understand that I am quite serious, Mr. Peesley? I want you out of my room. And out of my life. Or would you rather bleed more first? Maybe you would like to keep one of my bullets as a memento? Say, in your right shoulder?"

He glared at her as blood poured down both his legs, spreading darkly over his light gray pants and down into his boots. She could see he burned to get his hands on her, and thought he would probably kill her if he did.

"I'm losing patience, Mr. Peesley," she said coldly.

"I'm goin'," he replied gruffly, and turned away. He left the bedroom, stopping at the door to the hallway. She followed him from a safe distance, the gun trained on his limping form. When he continued to stand in the doorway, she said, "Do I have to escort you out of the building?"

His back squared stubbornly as she spoke, and he swung around to face her. Bullet number three slammed into his right shoulder and threw him back against the door.

"Now!" Samantha shouted above the echo. Her eyes were running with tears from the smoke, and she was furious that he had made her go so far. "Go!"

He did. Finally he was ready to retreat. Samantha followed him down the hallway, oblivious to the commotion there. Guests had gathered at the sounds of gunshots. She marched behind Peesley, past the guests, to the back of the hotel. The back stairs were on the outside of the building. She waited impatiently for him to open the door, and while he fumbled with it, she got too close to him. As he started down the stairs, he swung his left arm backward and tried to knock her down. But before his fist could touch her, she put her fourth bullet through the thick muscles of his upper arm.

Though the rest of his face was contorted with pain, there was black rage in his eyes. His hand stretched out toward her, blood dripping on the wooden landing. There was no strength in the wounded arm, but the fingers still reached for her.

Samantha grimaced and stepped back. "You're *loco!*"

she gasped, her stomach turning at the sight of all the blood seeping from his arm, his shoulder, his legs. He stood there, a big ox who didn't have sense enough to give up.

"I didn't want to hurt you," she whispered urgently. "All you had to do was *leave me alone*. Damn you! Will you go? Will you just go!" she pleaded.

But the stubborn fool took another step toward her and his outstretched fingers touched the front of her taffeta jacket. Her gun exploded once more, and she choked back a sob. The fifth bullet entered his shin. She didn't know whether she had been able to miss the bone or not, her hands were trembling so by then. He stumbled backward, then lost his balance on the edge of the stairs and tumbled down the long flight.

Samantha stood at the top of the stairs and looked down at Tom Peesley as he landed in the dirt. She held her breath, waiting. Would he move? She didn't want him dead. She had never killed anyone, and she dreaded the notion.

He moved. He even managed to pull himself to his feet and stand up, wavering a little and staring up at her. He knew as well as she did that there was only one bullet left. Was he wondering whether he could stand another bullet? Would he follow her back into the hotel and try to kill her? She guessed what he was thinking.

"You fool!" she yelled down. "Don't you know I could have killed you at any time? With only one bullet left, I will be forced to. This last bullet is for your heart. Don't make me use it!"

He stood there for an eternity, debating. Finally he turned and limped away along the back of the buildings.

Samantha didn't know how long she waited there after he was gone from sight. Though it was not cold, she began to tremble. At last she stepped back into the hallway, turning red when she saw all the people facing her at the end of the corridor. With a small cry of shame, she ran back to her suite, slamming the door on their curiosity.

She rushed into her bedroom and threw herself on the bed, pouring out her frustration. "Damn you, Tom Peesley. I hope you bleed to death!" she cried, completely forgetting that she didn't really want him to die.

But Samantha would have been even more mortified had she known that a tall, dark stranger had witnessed the scene on the landing.

Chapter 2

THE hotel where Samantha Kingsley had her suite was in a new part of Denver, on the edge of the city, where constant expansion was the rule. At the front of the hotel was a street crowded with stores, several saloons, two restaurants, two smaller hotels, a meat market, a bank, and even one of the new theaters. But at the back of Samantha's hotel was open country, land still waiting for Denver to claim it.

Hank Chavez rode slowly toward the hotel from the south, hoping that the size of the building did not mean the rooms were expensive. He wanted to stay there rather than search farther for his lodging.

He had pulled up his mount under a cottonwood tree when he saw a man and a young woman step out onto the landing behind the hotel. In the bright afternoon light he could see that the man was bleeding. Wounded by the young lady holding the gun? It was hard to believe, yet Hank grimaced as the man reached for the woman and the gun was fired.

Hank stared in rapt fascination. The woman—no, she could be no more than a girl, seventeen or eighteen—was very lovely. A young girl, but she had a woman's body. Lovely hair floated down her back and shoulders, dark hair that shone fiery red in the sunlight.

Leaning forward, Hank rested his forearms on the pommel of his saddle and watched the scene. He would have given anything to know what they were saying, but he was too far away to hear. Soon the man fell down the stairs and then limped away. Hank's dark gray eyes flew back to the girl, staring at her intently, willing her to look his way so that he could see all of her face. Was she as lovely as she seemed?

But she did not turn toward him. And after a moment she was gone, back into the hotel, and as quickly as his desire to meet her had come to him, it was gone, as well. The lady with the gun. No, he did not want to meet her. He had important business here, perhaps even killing business, and no time for getting entangled with vixens.

It had taken months to get to Denver from Dallas, months of pushing himself, of getting lost, of back-tracking, always avoiding towns where he might be tempted to rest. He might have caught up with Pat McClure, who had left Dallas only a few days before Hank had found he was gone. But after reading Pat's note, Hank had been so furious that he had wrecked his hotel room, proceeded to the nearest saloon, and wrecked that, too. Unable to pay for the damages, he had gone to jail for a month.

He might have got the money from Bradford Maitland. After all, Hank had once saved Maitland's life, and Maitland was rich. But Hank had been too proud to ask. Maitland had won the woman Hank had wanted, and while Hank had conceded graciously, there was still a resentment deep inside. After all, she was the only woman Hank had ever asked to share his life. But he had never really had a chance with Angela. When Hank had met her, she had already belonged to Maitland, body and soul. Of course, Maitland had been too pigheaded to know that. If only he had continued to be pigheaded, Hank thought again wistfully.

No, he would never ask Maitland to help him, or Angela, who had her own wealth. He had already taken money from her, actually taken it, when he had robbed the stagecoach she was traveling on.

That was how he had met Angela Sherrington. Hank

hadn't been able to forget her, and he had gone to find
her and give back half of what he had stolen from her.
She had been furious of course—oh, such fury—until
she saw the jewels he was returning. Later he had used
the excuse of returning her money in order to seek her
out again. But, by that time, Maitland had come.

Hank had asked Angela to go with him to Mexico.
She had refused. She was a woman who would love only
one man in all her life, and that man was Bradford
Maitland. Hank admired that. Yet he had waited in
Dallas for her to change her mind, hoping Maitland's
cruel treatment would kill her love. She was a woman
well worth having, even if she had loved before. But
when Maitland had come to his senses, Hank had known
he had lost her forever.

His partner, Pat McClure, had joined him in Dallas,
willing to go to Mexico with him to help Hank get back
his family estates. But Pat had found a pretty little
señorita and had moved into her adobe house on the
outskirts of town, while Hank stayed at the hotel. So
Hank had been unaware that Pat had left for Denver
until he finally had gone to find him and the *señorita*
had given him Pat's cryptic note, the note that told
Hank nothing and everything. Hank could have killed
Patrick McClure right then, no matter how close they
had been. For Pat had taken not only his own money,
but the money he had been holding for Hank, as well,
the money meant to buy back Hank's family's *hacienda*
in Mexico.

All Hank Chavez had lived for those many years was
that dream. Since the day in '59 when a band of Juárez
irregulars had come to the *hacienda* and massacred his
family, Hank had dreamed of vengeance. The men were
bandits, indulging in killing and pillage for profit, using the revolution as their cover.

The leader of this band had claimed the Chavez lands
were church property, which everyone knew to be un-
true. But that hadn't mattered. Since Juárez had de-

clared that the church was to be stripped of its property because of its support of the conservatives, "church property" had been a ready excuse for plundering anything in Mexico.

Hank could never forget seeing *vaqueros* he had grown up with shot for resisting conscription into the army. Their wives and daughters had been raped. His grandmother had died from a heart attack after watching her son, Hank's father, killed for trying to bar the gang from their home.

There had been survivors. Though a few women had died fighting rape, most had survived, as had their children and the old men not useful to the army. Hank, seventeen, had survived, though many times later he had wished he had not.

After the horrors he had seen, he had been struck from behind and had woken up to find himself in the army, forced to serve or to die. He had been told that his lands were no longer his, that they would be sold to help the revolution.

All that had been in the name of revolution—but, hell, it had been all for private profit. And there had been nothing Hank could do. He couldn't even blame Juárez, blame the revolution, blame an oppressed people trying only to better themselves. He could do nothing except try to get back what was his.

For a year and a half, Hank had fought for the liberals, fought bitterly, unable to reach Juárez to demand justice and unable to escape. It had been a galling, bitter time, and he had become obsessed with getting his land back.

Two others of his family had survived, only because they had been away from home at the time of the attack. His grandfather, Don Victoriano, had taken Hank's sister Dorotea to Spain to meet the Vega side of the family, and they had stayed on when Don Victoriano became ill. Word had reached Hank that his grandfather was dying, and he had rebelled at being prevented from going to him. He had spent almost two years in prison because of that rebellion. While he was in that stinking prison, his grandfather had died and his home had been sold. He could not have hoped to buy it back, not even when he escaped from prison. He was poor.

No one knew his true name was Enrique Antonio de Vega y Chavez. The many *gringos* in prison had called him Hank.

After his escape, he had left Mexico. There was always the chance that he might have been hauled into the army again. He had worked in Texas until he had had enough money to get to Spain, to his sister. But his sister was no longer in Spain. She had married an Englishman and was living in England. So Hank had gone to England. But Dorotea, who had her own family, did not really need Hank anymore. He had felt useless. And there had been that terrible desire to reclaim the family lands. For that, he needed money, a lot of money, money he didn't have. He had returned to North America late in 1864. He had been educated very well in his youth, and there were many things he could do, but none would bring him the kind of money he needed.

Then he had met Patrick McClure and some other men who were making money easily. They were stealing it.

Becoming an outlaw had gone against everything he believed in, and he had compromised by robbing only people who could afford to lose a little. He would not steal from the miners in the Midwest, as Patrick and his gang had been doing, for those men worked hard for their gold and what they carried was usually all they had. Nor would he rob banks, which meant taking the savings of innocent people. But he had robbed the stagecoaches that crossed Texas. Passengers on stages did not carry all their money on them. It had been important to Hank that he not leave a man destitute. He had even returned money a few times, when someone convinced him that what he was taking was all he had.

His new profession had been profitable if not likable. Amassing money took a long time because a single stage did not produce a great deal and everything had been split with the other men. But after five years, much, much sooner than it would have taken otherwise, Hank had had enough to return to Mexico and buy back his land.

He ought to have been there now, his dream realized, he thought bitterly. Instead he had had to ride hundreds of miles to track down his partner. He could only pray that he wasn't too late, that Pat hadn't spent all his money. If he had, he'd kill Pat, so help him he would.

A quick word at the desk in the large lobby and Hank knew he'd have to find other lodgings. He had only ten dollars left, and that would not even give him one night in the fancy hotel.

He found a stable for his horse, then moved on down the street looking for a cheaper hotel or a boarding house. He hoped for a bath, too. His clothes were no longer black but brown, they were so covered with trail dust. And he needed to see a barber. He'd grown a full black beard in the last months, and his coal-black hair was several inches past his shoulders, making him look like a saddle bum.

Hank passed a barbershop, made note of its location, then moved on past a restaurant and an ice-cream parlor. Then he saw the sign, MRS. HAUGE'S BOARDING HOUSE. On plain white paper tacked on the bottom was the word VACANCY. He got the room for a dollar a day or five by the week, taking it by the day. He wasn't planning to stay long. His saddlebags slung over his shoulder, he declined Mrs. Hauge's offer to show him to his room and just asked for directions.

It was a new two-story house, and his room was upstairs, at the end of a long hallway, on the right. As Hank moved down the hall, he found himself following a trail of blood, blood still wet. He heard voices coming from a room where the door stood open. The path of blood ended there at the door. As he drew nearer, the voices became distinct.

"I'm just glad your new house ain't finished yet, Doc, so you're still here. I don't think I could've made it any farther than this."

"Nonsense," came a crackly reply. "You've lost a lot of blood, but you aren't that bad off, Tom. Now lie still."

"How the hell can you say that? I'm dyin'."

"You are not dying," was the firm reply.

"Well, it sure feels like I am," the deeper voice grumbled. "I'm hurtin' all over."

"That I don't doubt."

Hank moved to the open doorway and peered inside. Tom was stretched out on a long, narrow table. A short, older fellow stood by his feet holding a knife. Neither man noticed Hank. He forgot his fatigue and watched as the Doc cut away Tom's pant leg and began examining one of the wounds.

"I've never seen anything like this, Tom. How did you get so shot up?"

"I tol' you, this fellow jumped me by Cherry Creek," Tom replied testily. "And don't ask me why again, 'cause I just don't know. He just kept firin' and firin', and I couldn't get out of his way in time. He was crazy."

The doctor shook his head as if he didn't believe a word. Hank wanted to laugh. He supposed Tom didn't want to admit the truth, and he sympathized.

"It's those two wounds between your legs that have me puzzled," the Doc continued thoughtfully. "They're mighty close to you-know-what."

"I *know* how close they are!" Tom snapped, his face reddening.

"I just don't understand. If your legs were closed, and a single bullet sliced between them, that would have been a strange shot. But the two wounds aren't from one shot. You were shot twice there. The wounds are identical, an inch of flesh out of both thighs. The fellow was an expert shot. For Christ's sake, Tom, were you just standing there letting him use you for target practice?"

"Will you stop yammering and get me fixed up?"

"I can only work so fast," the doctor grumbled. He moved alongside the table, studying each wound in turn. "That lower leg wound is as clean as the one in your arm. The shoulder is the only one I'll have to dig into."

"Yeah, she—he—said he'd leave me a bullet as a memento," Tom muttered.

The Doc raised a brow. "You said 'she.'"

"Did I?" Tom stammered. "Well...the guy had a woman with him. The green-eyed bitch enjoyed every minute of it!"

The doctor handed Tom a bottle of whiskey, shaking his head. "Enough talk. Drink some of that before I take the bullet out. You realize, don't you, that you won't be able to go back to the mines for some time? Neither arm is going to be much use to you for a while."

"Hell," Tom growled, and took a drink.

"I wouldn't complain. You count your blessings instead, Tom. It's remarkable, but not one of your wounds is really serious. No bone is shattered, not even in the shoulder. Out of five wounds, you've just got a lot of torn muscle and cartilage. You're damned lucky, young man. If that fellow *was* an excellent shot, then he didn't mean to do you any permanent damage." The doctor ran his eyes over the length of his patient. "I just don't understand it," he said softly.

Hank moved on to his room, still unnoticed. His curiosity was thoroughly aroused again, yet he knew that Tom would never admit to being shot five times by a slip of a girl. Ah, well, it wasn't Hank's business. And he was not fool enough to question the girl. He would ask no questions of a lady who could shoot so well—or so badly. And it might have been either one. Either she had aimed way off while trying to hurt Tom, or she'd been a superb shot. Hank shrugged. He'd probably never know which it was.

Chapter 3

SAMANTHA was still crying into her pillow when a deputy of the law knocked on her door. She wasn't at all prepared for Mr. Floyd Ruger, not in her emotional state. A man with a much-too-serious face, he threw one question after another at her without giving her a chance to think before she answered.

"Your name, Miss?"

"Samantha Blackstone Kingsley."

"That's an unusual middle name."

"Well, it was my mother's family name. I didn't even know my father's name until—"

"It doesn't matter," he interrupted. "Where are you from?"

"Back East."

"Where?"

"Is that any of your business?" Having been rebuffed, Samantha wasn't going to offer any more information.

Without batting an eye, Ruger repeated, "Where?"

She sighed. "I was attending school in Philadelphia, if you must know."

"Philadelphia is your home?"

"No. I only went to school there."

Ruger sighed pointedly in turn. "Your home is where, then?"

"Northern Mexico."

He raised a brow. "But you're not Mexican." He seemed startled.

"You noticed, did you?"

He ignored her sarcasm and asked, "Will you be staying in Denver?"

"No, Mr. Ruger, I'm just passing through on my way home," she replied impatiently. "And I don't see the need for all these questions."

Again he ignored her. "It's been reported that you shot a man. Is that true?"

Samantha's eyes narrowed. She had known what he was there for.

"I don't think I'll tell you."

Floyd Ruger gazed at her intently. "You don't think you'll tell me? Now see here, Miss Kingsley—"

"No, *you* see here!" she snapped. "I haven't committed any crime. And I'm in no mood to answer ridiculous questions. I would like it very much if you would leave, Mr. Ruger."

At that moment, Jeannette Allston walked into their suite, followed closely by Adrien. Jeannette had a look of concern about her, but Adrien simply looked shocked. Samantha had known he would be.

It infuriated her, and she glared at him. "So! You finally decided to get here."

"They said downstairs that you have shot a man," Adrien said, incredulous. "Is this true?"

She could see Mr. Ruger watching her keenly. It was too much. It really was.

"I'll explain later," Samantha said stiffly to Adrien. "As for you, Mr. Ruger, I have no more answers. If the man I am supposed to have shot dies, then I will be happy to answer your questions."

"I insist on his name, Miss Kingsley, at the very least," Ruger returned.

"Who says I know him? Perhaps he was a stranger."

"Or a close friend," Ruger insinuated.

Samantha's eyes flashed emerald fire. "I don't shoot my friends, Mr. Ruger. If it will put an end to this, I will tell you that the man forced his way in here and wouldn't leave me alone. I was protecting myself. I was all alone."

"Protecting yourself by shooting him five times?"

"Five!" Adrien gasped and fell into a chair.

Samantha shouted at the deputy. "I've had enough! You have no business here. Good day!"

After Floyd Ruger left, there was utter silence. Samantha stared at Adrien. He seemed to be in shock. What kind of man was he to react that way? He was ridiculous. He should be comforting her, she thought, not sitting there looking like he needed comforting himself.

"Ah, *chérie,* what you must have gone through," Jeannette said gently as she put her arm around Samantha and led her to the sofa.

Samantha thanked God for Jeannette. She and her brother were both decidedly French, though born in America. Their mother was French, and their American father had died when they were children. The father had left them comfortably well off. Their mother had not married again, so they had had no influence except hers. Perhaps Adrien had needed a man's influence. Lord, he was acting like a faint-hearted woman.

"Did you really shoot someone five times?" Jeannette asked.

Samantha sighed. "Yes," she answered simply.

"How terrible!"

"For him," Samantha said bitterly.

"You are not upset?"

"Oh, I don't know. I was so furious. I still am. The man just wouldn't *leave,* not even after I got my gun. I guess he didn't think I would use it."

"But after you shot him the first time, surely—"

Samantha laughed shortly, cutting her off. "You would think he'd have gone, wouldn't you? But after that first shot he was mad, and he wanted to get his hands on me. He would have killed me if I had given him a chance."

"Mon Dieu! So you were only protecting yourself, just as you said."

"Yes. I finally got him out of the room and made sure he left the hotel by the back stairs. But even then he wouldn't give up. He tried to knock me down, so I shot him again."

"How could the man live after all that?" Adrien broke in suddenly.

"I didn't mean to kill him, Adrien. I knew what I was doing. I gave him five harmless wounds."

"Harmless? Harmless!" Adrien gasped. "You can talk so calmly of shooting a man! I thought I knew you. I have traveled across this country with you, but I do not know you."

Samantha was enraged. "What was I supposed to do, let him hurt me? He had already attacked me before I finally got hold of my gun. And he *was* able to walk away. He will live, I'm sure of that. And I would like to point out that none of this would have happened if *you* had got here when *you* were supposed to. Where were you, Adrien? Did you forget we had a luncheon engagement?"

Adrien nodded his head. She had deftly turned the tables on him. But Samantha got no satisfaction from his weak answer.

"I did forget."

"Oh, Adrien, how could you?" Jeannette said the very words Samantha had been about to say, though Samantha's tone wouldn't have held mere disappointment.

"Do not look at me so, Jean," Adrien replied with a little more gumption, his shock lessening. "I simply forgot. I made an important decision this morning and acted on it promptly. I only just finished."

"Only just finished what?" Jeannette asked with sudden surprise.

"Buying supplies," he said almost defensively. "I am going to Elizabethtown."

Samantha frowned. She hadn't expected Adrien to leave Denver. She had assumed she would have at least another month in Denver to work on him. In a month she would leave for Santa Fe to meet her escort from the *hacienda*.

"Elizabethtown? Why?" asked Jeannette.

"To find gold, of course."

The girls gasped. Jeannette spoke first. "But why, Adrien? You came here to open a law office."

"Others are getting rich here, Jean. I never dreamed what it would be like," Adrien replied, excited now. "We shall be rich, too, and own one of those fine mansions like the wealthy miners are building."

Samantha laughed suddenly as the realization struck her. "He's got gold fever!"

Jeannette looked from Samantha to her brother, thoroughly bewildered. "But why go all the way to Elizabethtown? There is silver here—tons of it, if the reports are true."

"I agree, Adrien," Samantha added soberly. "You could stake a claim right here. There's no need to go running off to New Mexico. Haven't you heard of the Indian trouble they're having there?"

"Ah, that is nothing." Adrien waved a dismissal.

"You've never seen an Apache, Adrien. You don't know what you're saying if you can scoff at the danger of fighting Indians."

"That is beside the point. If I could mine silver here, I would. But I cannot do that until I can afford to buy equipment for reducing ore. Panning for gold is much easier."

"Oh, Lord." Samantha sighed in disgust. "You're going to pan for gold there in order to come back here and mine silver? That's ridiculous, Adrien."

"I have made my decision," Adrien replied stubbornly. "And it is not ridiculous. I am not the only one who cannot afford the equipment it takes to mine the silver. There are many others going to Elizabethtown.

Gold can be picked up off the ground. Silver must be refined. I have bought a very good mine already. I need only a smelter."

"You bought a mine!" Jeannette cried in growing alarm. "What did it cost?"

He shrugged. "It was very reasonable, since the owner was faced with the same problem as I—no smelter."

"How much?"

"Only a few hundred."

"Adrien!" she gasped. "We could not afford to spend a few hundred!"

"We could not afford to let this opportunity go by. In a year we will be able to afford anything."

Samantha was embarrassed. She had thought the Allstons did not have to worry about money, as she did not.

"How much would it cost for this device to process the silver?" Samantha offered.

Adrien turned to her hopefully, but Jeannette snapped, "We are not reduced to borrowing, Adrien. If you must do this thing, you will do it yourself."

"I was thinking of it as an investment," Samantha said quickly. "Not as a loan."

Adrién shook his head. "Thank you, Samantha, but no. Little Jean is right. We must do this ourselves."

"Very well. When did you plan to leave? We might as well all go together, since I must go south anyway."

"The day after tomorrow," he said readily, glad that Jeannette had made no further fuss. "We wait only for the stage."

Chapter 4

IT took Hank four hours of hard riding to reach the Pitts mine. When he got to the site, he found six men working in the hot sun, digging rock from the earth, grunting and muttering as they sweated. Seeing a large tent set up by a stream, he rode toward it and dismounted, keeping a watchful eye on the tent.

Hank entered silently. Inside were two long wooden tables, bedrolls lying along the edge of the tent, and an old potbelly stove. That, and the cooking utensils around it, meant a permanent setup. There was only one man in the tent, and he sat at the long table to Hank's right, a tin of coffee beside him, working a column of figures on a sheet of paper.

"*Hola*, Pat."

Patrick McClure's head shot up, and he started to rise, but stopped halfway and sank back into his seat. The voice was the familiar voice of old, but the face was very different. Gone were the laughing gray eyes Pat knew so well. In their stead were eyes of steel. He had been afraid that this might happen, that Hank wouldn't understand.

"Now, laddie, you've no call to be lookin' at your old *amigo* like that," Pat began uneasily, his voice cracking.

"*Amigo?*" Hank walked slowly forward. "You call yourself *amigo?*"

Hank didn't wait for the answer. Pulling back his right arm, he shot his fist straight into Patrick's jaw. The chair—with Patrick still in it—toppled over backward. Patrick was an older man, and his body had gone soft, but he was on his feet in a moment. Very slowly, he backed away from Hank.

"I won't fight you, laddie. At least not till you let me explain," Pat growled through his throbbing mouth. "After, if you still want to have it out—"

"I want just one thing from you, Pat—my money. Hand it over, and I will leave it at that."

"Didn't you get the note I left you?"

"Perdición!" Hank swore between clenched teeth. "Do not change the subject!"

"But I told you about this mine," Pat continued, undaunted. "We're going to be richer than we ever dreamed, laddie."

"Then give me my share now, and you can keep all the rest. I have no interest in mines, Pat. You know my dreams. I have waited more than ten years. I will not wait any longer. I must go home to Mexico."

"But you don't understand, Hank, me lad. Sit down and let me explain."

"There is nothing to explain. Either you have my money or you don't."

"I do not. I spent nearly all of it on a smelter," Pat said quickly, and stepped farther back.

Hank grabbed hold of his shirt front and pulled him closer, nearly lifting him off the ground. There was murder in his eyes.

"I think I must kill you, Patrick," he said in a deadly calm voice. *"Sí,* I must. You knew what that money meant to me. You knew how I hated what we did to get it. You knew...and you spent it anyway."

"But, laddie, you will have enough money to buy a dozen *haciendas,* two dozen," Pat pleaded. "I tell you we will be rich."

"How can you know?" Hank demanded. "When you have yet to process the silver?"

"I have had it analyzed. We have top grade ore here, the best, and so much of it! It's only a matter of processing it as soon as the smelter gets here. Of course, that will take a little while."

"How long? A year—two years?"

"I cannot say, laddie. I sent to England for the newest and best equipment."

Very suddenly, Hank let go of Pat and turned away. The older man sighed in relief. Hank was a much taller man, and stronger, lean yet well muscled. Angry, he could easily kill Pat with his hands.

"How could you do this to me, Pat? I trusted you. We were *amigos*." Hank's voice was barely audible.

"We still are," Pat protested. "See reason, will you? I have made you a rich man."

"Riches that I do not see cannot help me now," Hank growled.

Pat eyed Hank warily. He had known Hank Chavez for a long time, but he had never seen him like this. A darkly handsome man, usually dressed in dark clothes, Hank had always looked dangerous. At first glance, he appeared to be a gunfighter. But the warmth and amusement in his eyes dispelled the image quickly. The young man could find humor in almost any situation, and his genuine love of life despite the tragedies in his past made him remarkable.

Pat tried again. "Hank, me boy, can't you see this from my side? This was my one chance. We had plenty of money, but you know how I am. I would have lived it up for a while and soon had nothing left."

"You could have bought a business or a ranch, Pat. You could have settled down."

"That's not for me," Pat replied, hope rising. At least Hank was listening. "I'm not one for workin' at anything steady."

"You are working here," Hank pointed out.

"Work? I'm payin' others to break their backs splittin' rock."

Hank's eyes narrowed. "With what are you paying them, Patrick?" he asked softly.

"Well, there was a little left over. A thousand or so," Pat admitted reluctantly, sorry he had trapped himself. "I thought I'd save time by gettin' all the rock ready so we could get right to work once the smelter gets here."

"I will take what is left, Pat."

"Now, laddie—" Hank started toward him again, and Pat conceded quickly. "All right, all right. I suppose it won't make any difference." He saw Hank relax slightly and believed there would be no more trouble. "Tell me, what took you so long getting here? I expected you to be right behind me."

Hank tensed. "I was in jail."

Pat frowned. "Not...?"

"No, it had nothing to do with our robberies," Hank said bitterly. "I ran up a few damages after reading your note and getting drunk."

Pat grimaced. "I'm sorry. But you do see why I had to do it that way? I'd won this mine in a card game, and I knew how valuable it was by the way the fellow was actin' after he lost it. Took it real bad. He had been on his way to south Texas to borrow money from friends for a smelter. I knew I couldn't buy the smelter on my own, so I borrowed your share, laddie. I had to do it." Pat hesitated. "What will you do now?"

"I will get drunk again, and most likely destroy another saloon or two," Hank said darkly.

"All is not lost, laddie. You've had fair remarkable luck with the cards. You could double, triple your money easily that way."

"Or lose it all."

"There are other ways."

"I am through with stealing!" Hank growled.

"No, no, I wasn't going to suggest that. There was a big gold discovery down in New Mexico a few years back. Thousands of men have rushed to that new settlement, Elizabethtown."

"You think I should pan for gold?" Hank snapped. "I might as well wait for this mine to produce. Either way will take too long. My lands are there, and I burn for them. For years, I burn. I cannot wait any longer."

Pat grew uneasy again. "You always were hotheaded about your land. You never would listen to reason. You should have found out a long time ago just how much you would need to buy back your land. Did you ever consider that you might not have enough?"

"I had enough—until you stole it."

"Now, laddie, you don't know that for sure. You could have got down there and found out the owner wanted twice what you had, or even more. You just don't know. Why don't you find out *now?*" Pat cried with sudden enthusiasm. "That's what you can do! Go and find out exactly what you'll need. Hell, by the time you get back, this mine of ours will be producing and you'll have whatever you need. You said you don't want to wait. Well, this way you won't have to. You'll be doin' something *now* to get your land."

"What you suggest is a waste of time," Hank said brusquely. "Yet, because of you, I have time to waste and nothing better to do. So be it." Then he smiled, his eyes crinkling in the old familiar way. "But the money you have left, *amigo*—I will take that."

Hank left Denver the following day, riding directly south. He would be crossing most of the Colorado territory and the whole of New Mexico, a large area that was not at all safe for a lone traveler. But Hank was adept at avoiding people, including Indians. He had learned well after his escape from prison, learned how to hide in the mountains or on the plains. His senses, always keen, had been honed sharp after his escape and during his outlaw days.

Hank had seven hundred miles of unfamiliar terrain to cross just to reach the Mexican border. Even at a grueling pace, it would take him more than a month, but he had already decided not to push himself. Not this time. There was no hurry, thanks to Pat. He was

furious over the new delay, yet he could do nothing to
hurry matters along except steal again—and Hank
would not do that.

Damn Pat and damn his silver mine!

For the next few days, Hank brooded on his luckless
life. By the fourth day, his mood was so dark that he
became careless. He was riding the base of the Rocky
mountain range, pushing his horse cruelly, trying to
ride off his anger, when suddenly the horse floundered
in a hole. Hank was thrown several feet. He twisted
his ankle, but, worse, the horse had broken his foreleg
and could go no farther. He had to be shot.

Hank found himself without a horse, filled with remorse over the accident, and stranded a long way between towns.

Chapter 5

IT was stuffy in the stagecoach. Two of the passengers, a woman and her young son, had left the coach in Castle Rock when the son got sick. No one had taken their places, so there were only four passengers in the coach. But there would be many more small towns and many stops before Elizabethtown, so the stage would undoubtedly fill up again.

Even with the roomier arrangement, the coach was still warm and stuffy. Mr. Patch, riding with Samantha and the Allstons, insisted on keeping the window shades drawn shut because it was an old coach and the windows were all broken. Patch had said he had a condition aggravated by dust. The man shouldn't be traveling in the Southwest if he wants to avoid dust, Samantha thought to herself in annoyance.

She wasn't really annoyed with Mr. Patch, though, not even when they were forced to light a smoky old lantern for light. No, it was Adrien who had her miffed. It was always Adrien. Sometimes she wondered how she could ever have fallen in love with such a man. After all this time, all the traveling together, he still remained distant. Why, he wasn't even talking to her just then.

Of all the childish ways for a man to act! It was something *she* might do in a sulk, but a man of thirty? And all because he had been reminded of Tom Peesley.

She could thank Mr. Ruger for that. Hearing that she was leaving Denver, he had come to the stage office just before the coach departed and had had the gall to ask that she not leave until he was sure no crime had been committed. He couldn't insist, however, and they both knew it. Tom Peesley had not made a complaint against her, and Samantha knew he never would. He didn't dare.

She appeased Floyd Ruger by telling him where he might find her if necessary. But there had been no appeasing Adrien.

She just didn't understand Adrien. She couldn't even put his behavior down to the fact that he was an Easterner, for other Easterners weren't so...so childish. She had complained to Jeannette about him, but the petite blonde had sympathized with her brother.

"He is sensitive, *chérie*," Jeannette tried to explain. "He just cannot abide violence."

"But this is a violent land he has chosen to come to," Samantha pointed out.

"Oui, and he will get used to it in time. But it will take time."

How long would it take for him to get over Tom Peesley? Samantha wondered. She was coming to the conclusion that she would have to do something drastic. She considered making Adrien jealous. After all, she had rebuffed all other men since meeting Adrien. He really had had no competition. Perhaps he needed a good shaking up. But Mr. Patch, with his nearly bald pate and heavy paunch, was the only man available just then, so she had to dismiss the idea for the time being. The trouble was that when they reached Elizabethtown, Adrien would be busy.

What was she going to do? She wouldn't give up on Adrien. She had decided that he was the man she wanted, and she always got what she wanted. She dreamed about him, imagining him holding her, kissing her, making love to her in the way the girls at school had described. Yes, Adrien would be her first man.

She had never even been held by a man, not tenderly, for she didn't count Tom Peesley and his bruising em-

brace. But Peesley was the first man ever to kiss her
with passion. She prayed that such brutal kissing was
not typical, and that the kiss of Ramón Mateo Nuñez
de Baroja, from the ranch nearest theirs, was also not
typical. Ramón's kiss had been a brotherly peck, given
to her before she left for school.

There had to be an in-between kind of kiss, something that would stir her, make her faint, as she had
read about in the romantic novels that were smuggled
into school. That was the kind of kiss Samantha dreamed
about, the kind she knew Adrien would give her—if he
ever got around to it. There *had* to be something she
could do, some way to give him a little push in her
direction.

They had been bouncing along in the coach for five
days, a miserable way to travel. The train ride from
Pennsylvania to Cheyenne had not been so bad, but
after her experience on the stage to Denver, Samantha
had almost considered buying a horse and riding along
beside the coach. But then she wouldn't be near Adrien,
so she had rejected that idea.

Her father had been appalled to learn she was coming home across the country instead of traveling by
ship, as she had gone. She had known he would be
furious, so she had waited to telegraph him until they
left Pennsylvania. His reply caught up with her a week
later, telling her how furious he was. He would send
an escort to meet her as soon as she let him know that
she had reached Cheyenne. But she didn't wire him
again. She was giving herself more time with Adrien.

Her father had cautioned her not to use her full name
as she neared home and had telegraphed her other fath-
erly advice, or, more specifically, orders. Hamilton
Kingsley worried about his daughter, but she didn't
begrudge him his protective attitude, not anymore.
There had been too many years when he never scolded
because she was so new to him. He couldn't deny her
anything. After all, she hadn't even met him until she

was nine years old. It had taken so long for him to get her away from her grandparents in England. And he never did get her brother, Sheldon.

Her grandparents had been so strict that Samantha hadn't known what a normal childhood was like. From the time she could walk and talk, she had been expected to act like an adult, but without the privileges of an adult. She hadn't known what it was like to play, to run, to laugh. All of those things had been strictly forbidden by her grandmother, and, if she was caught acting in an unladylike manner, punishments were swift.

Her grandfather, Sir John Blackstone, hadn't been so bad. It was Henrietta who had been a terror. Henrietta Blackstone had hated the American Hamilton Kingsley for marrying her only daughter and had contrived to separate Samantha's parents after the children were born. Ellen Kingsley had come home to the Blackstone country estate with her two children and had taken her own life a month later. Samantha could never blame her mother for killing herself, for she knew what it was like living with Henrietta. And she never once had doubted that Henrietta's harping was what had driven her mother to suicide.

When her father threatened to take the Blackstones to court, since they wouldn't even let him see his children, Sir John had talked his wife into letting them go rather than face scandal. Samantha had jumped at the chance to leave Blackstone Manor, but Sheldon had refused to come. Henrietta's influence over him was strong, and Hamilton had had to settle for only one of his children.

Samantha had been so afraid, afraid that her father would expect the same things Henrietta had expected. When he gave no sign of doing so, Samantha had slowly started doing all the things she had never been allowed to do, balking at anything that had to do with being a lady. She had tested her father in their first years together, taking advantage of his love and his joy in finally having her with him.

She felt terrible about that now, even going so far as to follow some of his directions. She used only half her name once they began traveling into the area where people knew of Hamilton Kingsley's wealth. She would not make it easy for someone to get a lot of money by kidnapping Kingsley's only daughter. Kidnappings were common, and the kidnappers were hardly ever caught. So she would have a large escort to take her the rest of the way home, even though that would leave the ranch short of men.

Samantha sighed and looked across the coach at Adrien sitting next to Mr. Patch. She no longer balked at being a lady. In fact, she was trying her damnedest to remember everything her grandmother once had forced her to learn. Adrien wouldn't take anyone for a wife except a lady. She *would* be that lady. She *would* be Adrien's wife.

Her long lashes were lowered so that he couldn't tell she was watching him. Samantha unfastened the top button of her white silk blouse. The mulberry-blue jacket that matched her skirt was on the seat beside her because the coach was so warm. She could use that warmth as an excuse to undo another button, then another. The ruffles up the front of her blouse fell slowly to the sides, baring her throat after the fourth button had been undone.

Adrien did not look her way. She tapped her foot on the floor in vexation and unfastened two more buttons. She felt cooler, but she fanned herself briskly anyway, to see if that would draw Adrien's attention. It didn't. She got Mr. Patch's full attention, however, and bristled silently. She wanted to scream. *What* would it take?

The coach slowed suddenly, and Adrien opened the shade nearest him. Mr. Patch started coughing.

"What is it, Adrien?" Jeannette asked.

"It appears we are taking on a passenger."

"Have we reached a town?"

"No."

Adrien watched as the coach door opened and a tall man climbed inside. Adrien moved over to make room, and the stranger took the seat next to him. He tipped his wide-brimmed black hat to the ladies, but didn't remove it. Samantha nodded briefly but moved her eyes away from him quickly. A saddle tramp, she assumed, and dismissed him, her eyes resting on Adrien again. But Adrien was looking at the stranger curiously, ignoring Samantha.

"How is it you came to be out here without a horse?" Adrien asked in a friendly manner.

The man did not answer readily. He studied Adrien before he spoke in a deep, curt voice. "I had to kill my horse."

"Mon Dieu!" Adrien gasped, and Samantha sighed, disgusted by his unmanly reaction.

The stranger's eyes were drawn to Samantha on hearing her sigh. She felt compelled to ask, "Your horse was injured?"

"Sí, he broke a leg. I have injured mine, as well. It seems I will go to Elizabethtown after all."

He chuckled then at some humor that escaped the rest of them. Samantha looked at him more closely. The top portion of his face was hidden by the shadow of his hat, but the lower half showed a strong jaw faintly covered with black stubble, a firm mouth quirked up at one corner to reveal a dimple, and a narrow nose, straight, but not too long. It was the promise of a handsome face.

He slouched in his seat in an almost cocky manner. Or perhaps he was just tired. His long legs spread out before him took up a good portion of the aisle and nearly reached Samantha's knees. The hands he folded across his middle showed long, tapered fingers, almost graceful, which surprised Samantha. He took care of his hands. There were no calluses, so he probably wore gloves when he rode.

At first glance he looked like an ordinary cowboy, dusty, a little rakish in his dark clothes. But, on closer inspection, she began to wonder. He was dirty, yet there was nothing really unkempt about him except the stubble on his chin. His ebony hair only just reached his shirt collar, and his clothes fit him well and were of good quality. His dark brown shirt was chambray linen, the bandanna around his neck was silk, and the black vest was a superior grade of Spanish leather. So were his boots.

Samantha was slowly growing curious about the man she had dismissed so quickly. It was the first time she had felt an interest in another man since meeting Adrien, and she was surprised.

His body was lean, but his chest and arms were well muscled, as were the long legs in tight black pants. Samantha mentally compared him with Adrien. The stranger was young, vital, in superb condition. In fact, blond Adrien paled beside the cowboy, looking almost sickly.

Adrien was studying him curiously, just as Samantha was, but the man was looking at—whom? Jeannette or herself? She couldn't tell, unable to see his eyes clearly. But he was probably looking at Jeannette, she told herself, for Jeannette had a classic beauty. Petite, she was the type of woman men were drawn to, inspiring protectiveness, making them want to cuddle her. Though she was neither ungainly nor too tall, Samantha felt downright awkward next to Jeannette.

The silence lengthened. Mr. Patch continued to cough until Samantha took pity on him and closed the shade. In the ensuing quiet, she grew uncomfortable. Jeannette had closed her eyes in boredom, as had Mr. Patch, but Samantha could not. She had to know whether the stranger was watching her or not.

Annoyance gathered until, finally, she asked bluntly, "Do you never take your hat off?"

Adrien gasped at her rudeness, and she blushed. The stranger grinned and, removing his hat, smoothed his wavy black hair.

"Your pardon, *señorita*."

She found herself staring into slate-gray eyes that crinkled at the corners. Laughing eyes, Samantha thought. His eyes actually seemed to be laughing at her!

"You speak Spanish, *señor*," Samantha said impulsively. "Yet you do not look pure Spanish. I would guess...half American?"

"You are very observant."

"Samantha, really," Adrien interrupted in a scornful voice.

She turned her green eyes on him, and her brows rose slightly. "Oh! You are speaking to me again, Adrien?"

"I really shouldn't," he answered peevishly. Then, turning to the stranger, he said, "You must forgive my companion's rudeness, Mr....ah...?"

"Chavez. Hank Chavez." He nodded at Adrien. "But there is nothing to forgive such a lovely lady."

Samantha smiled at his gallantry. "You are kind, *señor*. But I really was rude—and I wasn't even right. Your name is Mexican."

"*Sí*, I have Indian blood, as well."

"But not much," she surmised.

"You are correct again, *señorita*."

Adrien quickly broke in with introductions, before Samantha could embarrass him further with her bluntness. She settled back then, and listened to Adrien make small talk, explaining why he was going to New Mexico. She closed her eyes and let his voice, and then the deeper voice of Hank Chavez, lull her to sleep.

A jarring bounce woke her, and she opened her eyes to find Hank Chavez's gray ones on her. Or, more exactly, on the deep V she had made at the top of her blouse.

Samantha glanced down. Her breasts were revealed, just a little. She had never exposed so much of herself before. And it hadn't even worked. After all that time, Adrien still hadn't noticed. But Hank Chavez had.

Her eyes met his. He was smiling. She wanted to die. A flush spread up her neck and turned her face bright pink. She didn't know why she should be so embarrassed, but she was. Perhaps it was because he was such an attractive man, or maybe it was the way his eyes assessed her. Whatever the reason, she was utterly mortified. And she couldn't do anything about it. If she quickly buttoned up her blouse, that would only make things worse.

Adrien was still talking, oblivious, and finally Hank Chavez turned to him. Samantha wasn't listening. She raised her fan to cover the front of her blouse and surreptitiously fastened one button. But she got only as far as that before those gray eyes fell on her again. She lowered her hands to her lap. Only he knew what had happened, and his gaze moved to where her cleavage had been, then back up to her eyes. He seemed to be chiding her for denying him the view he had so admired.

Samantha grew warm under his continuing gaze and closed her eyes. She would sleep, or she would pretend to sleep, but she wouldn't look at Hank Chavez again, no matter what.

Chapter 6

DUSK was gathering, but the coach rambled on, the next stop still several miles away. Hank leaned his head back on the seat. Adrien Allston had finally stopped talking. Hank's ankle throbbed, and he ached to take his boots off, but he would have to wait until they stopped for the night.

He had had to limp more than a mile, toting his saddle, in order to reach the stage line. Another ten minutes and he would have missed it. He wondered whether he should go all the way to Elizabethtown and give his ankle a chance to mend, or try to buy a horse in the next town. As he looked at the woman across the aisle from him, he decided to wait.

What a fascinating woman she was, even in sleep. The blond was undeniably beautiful, but the dark-haired one was a vision of loveliness. She reminded him of the girl in Denver, the one with the gun. The hair, a dark reddish-brown, the slender form, the pert nose, all seemed familiar. But he had seen that girl only at a side view and from a distance. This one was much more mature, her hair elegantly coiffed, and she looked older. He guessed she was twenty—a woman full grown.

Her creamy white skin made him think she might be from the East. Or perhaps she just didn't like the sun. Yet she knew something of Mexico, having guessed right about his bloodlines. His mother, an American, had had ancestors in England. It was she who had named him Hank, his father later changing it to Enrique and adding considerably to the name. His father had been a Mexican Spaniard, though very little of Mexico had run in his veins. Hank's great-grandfather had been half mestizo, had married a Spanish *doña,* and their son Victoriano had married into the Vega family, newly arrived from Spain.

Hank didn't dwell much anymore on his ancestry: everyone who mattered was dead except for his older sister. But Samantha Blackstone had brought his family to mind. What a curious lady she was! The talkative Adrien Allston had certainly been shocked. Hank did not mind, though. He admired a woman who was not afraid to speak her mind or satisfy her curiosity.

He couldn't take his eyes from her. Long brown lashes fanned her cheeks, and, as she slept, a short stray curl fell on her temple, shining red in the lamplight. He recalled with relish her embarrassment when she caught him admiring her full breasts. He had enjoyed her embarrassment, and liked making her blush. She was not indifferent to him if he could make her blush.

He was certainly not indifferent to her. In a way, she reminded him of Angela, though there was no physical resemblance except perhaps for the shade of hair. He had made Angela blush easily, too. He remembered her face turning bright crimson when, robbing her stagecoach, he had searched inside her bodice for valuables. She had slapped him soundly, and he had been compelled to respond to the slap with a kiss he had wanted never to end.

For the first time in his life, Hank truly wanted to rob a stage—this one, just so he could search the dark-haired woman across from him. Just looking at her made him want her, and he had to place his hat over his lap to hide the stirring there.

What was wrong with him? He had never before reacted so strongly, so physically to a woman without even touching her. Not even Angela had aroused him so quickly. And the woman was only sleeping. She wasn't even influencing him with her eyes!

Hank shut his own from the sight of her, hoping to cool his blood. But it didn't work. He couldn't stop dreaming about her.

It was going to be a long way to Elizabethtown.

Samantha was the last one out of the stage. Jeannette had had to wake her, chiding that she wouldn't get any sleep that night. Samantha didn't care. The journey was so boring, and there was nothing to do but sleep. And then she remembered Señor Chavez and was instantly wide awake.

But he had gone with the other men. They were at a dismal coach stop, the only building for miles around. There was a barn where extra horses were kept, and a house, really just one large room. There, passengers could get a hot meal and bed down on benches for a few hours' sleep.

Samantha followed Jeannette inside. She wouldn't sit down. Her backside was numb. The food wasn't ready yet. It was late at night, and the old man had to be wakened to fix them something.

Only Jeannette, Mr. Patch, and the old timer were in the large room. The others had gone out back to wash up. Samantha walked, stretching as much as possible without being unladylike. Jeannette sat down in the only high-backed chair near the fireplace. She was tired and looked it.

The driver and Adrien came in the back door, but Hank Chavez was not with them. Samantha wished he would hurry so she could wash at the well. It wouldn't be proper for her to go outside while he was still there.

Adrien saw to his sister's comfort, and when the food was ready he brought her a plate. Samantha bristled. He was still ignoring her. The old timer offered her a plate, but she declined, wanting to wash first. She felt grime from the stage all over her. She would have changed clothes, but the luggage was not unloaded for this short stop, and she didn't feel like asking anyone's help in getting one of her cases down.

When, at last, Hank Chavez came into the room, Samantha couldn't help but stare at the remarkable change. He had shaved and was even more handsome without the beard. He had changed into a dark gray shirt with mother-of-pearl buttons, which matched his eyes.

As soon as those slate-gray eyes fell on her, Samantha looked away. She walked past him without a word, picked up the lantern he had set down, and went out into the back yard. By the well was a stone ledge on which sat an empty bucket and a large tin pan of dirty water from the others who had washed there. Samantha put the lantern down there and emptied the dirty water, then poured in fresh cold water from the well. Using the handkerchief from her purse, she bent to wash her face and hands, her throat and neck, and between her breasts.

She laid the handkerchief out on the ledge to dry, then briskly fastened her blouse. She wouldn't repeat the mistake of leaving it unbuttoned! She grew uneasy all over again remembering the hot eyes on her.

A footstep made Samantha swing around, gasping. Hank Chavez stood a foot away. The back door to the house was closed, she saw, which meant that they were alone in the yard. Samantha could feel her heart pounding wildly, but she moved back a step and tilted her head, looking as calm and in charge of the situation as she could. His eyes weren't laughing. The crinkles were gone, and that frightened her even more.

At last he spoke. "I forgot my hat."

"Oh," she sighed. "Well, you certainly gave me a start, coming up behind me so quietly."

Lord! How long had they stood there looking at each other without speaking?

"I did not mean to frighten you, Señorita Blackstone, but you should not be out here alone."

"Nonsense." She laughed, her fear receding. "I am close enough to the house. Besides, the passengers from the stage are the only ones here. And I trust all of them."

"But you should not, *señorita*. You do not even know me."

He said it so seriously that she stepped back and reached for her purse, taking it from the ledge. She could easily get to her new double derringer if she had to. She had bought the Remington model soon after Tom Peesley had harassed her. A two-bullet gun was better than the old model.

"Are you saying I shouldn't trust you, *señor?*" she asked smoothly.

"I am saying only that I am a stranger and you should not be so trusting of strangers. But let me assure you now that you can indeed trust me."

She grinned at him. "Considering your advice, assurance from a stranger is no assurance at all."

He laughed heartily, a deep, warm laugh. "Ah, *la señorita* is not only *bella,* but *sabia,* as well."

Samantha tilted her head to the side, deciding to pretend ignorance. "And what does that mean?"

He reached out a hand as if to touch her cheek, but quickly thought better of the intimate gesture. "That you are wise as well as beautiful."

"Well, thank you," she answered, smiling to herself because he hadn't lied. She knew Spanish very well.

It was a game she played with people who did not know she could speak the language fluently. It was a sure way to test a person's honesty. Hank Chavez had passed the test.

She had admitted to herself some time before that she was drawn to him. His virile magnetism affected her strongly, but she wasn't sure exactly why. He was handsome, of course, but she had known other handsome men, and his appearance was not the only attraction. There was something different about Hank, a dangerous quality. A touch of the forbidden, perhaps? For all his smiles and his laughing eyes, she had seen the other side of him. Wasn't she a little afraid of what she saw?

"Will you allow me to walk you back, *señorita?*"

"Yes, thank you. I'm finished here."

He put his hat on at that rakish angle and, picking up the lantern, took her arm. His hand on her elbow was warm. His shoulder was nearly touching hers, and the nearness of him was unnerving.

"El hombre Allston, what is he to you?" he asked abruptly. The bluntness of it stunned Samantha. She wasn't really affronted, though. And, after all, hadn't she questioned him as boldly in the coach? But she didn't know how to answer. She didn't want to tell him about her feelings for Adrien.

"He is my ... escort, he and his sister. I went to school with Jeannette, and we became very close friends."

Hank was too much aware of his desire at that moment to notice Samantha's hesitation and the note of evasion in her voice. She had not answered him, not really, for a betrothed could also be an escort. A lover could be an escort. But he did not consider the fact. He could think only of how much he wanted this woman.

She was so close that he could smell her hair. It smelled of roses, and, if he leaned just a little closer, he could—

What was he thinking of? He had only just met her that day. She was a lady and would expect to be treated like one. Ah, if only she were not a lady, I would have her on the ground in two seconds, Hank thought devilishly.

Too soon, they were inside, and he had to let go of her arm. He could not even have that innocent touch anymore.

She walked away from him to get a plate of food, and Hank quickly followed her, then sat across from her at an empty table. The others had eaten. Jeannette

Allston was sleeping in a chair by the fire. Her brother and Mr. Patch were stretched out on benches, and the driver was in the front, seeing to the horses.

Hank was alone with Samantha Blackstone—yet not alone. He wanted to know about her. He wanted to know everything. *Por Dios!* What was the woman doing to him?

"I know why Señor Allston and his sister go to Elizabethtown," Hank remarked as they ate. "But why do you go there?"

Samantha kept her eyes on her food, afraid that if she looked at him again, she wouldn't look away. "I'm just going along, you might say. For their company. I don't like to travel alone."

"Will you stay in that gold town?"

"Not for long. And you?" she asked slowly.

"I have business farther south."

He became aware of her evasive manner. Either she wasn't used to talking very much or she did not want him to know where she was going. But he wanted to know.

"Where will you go when you leave the Allstons?" he asked directly.

"To Santa Fe. My father is sending some of his *vaqueros* to meet me there."

"Vaqueros?" he asked in surprise.

She looked up at him then and grinned impishly. "Yes. My home is in Mexico, *señor*. Did you really think I was from the East?"

"Yes, I did." He grinned back at her.

"Well, now you know better."

"We have that in common, then. Yet you are certainly not Mexican."

"No, I am American and English."

"I have a sister in England."

Her brows rose, and she laughed. "And I have a brother there. Another thing in common, eh?"

She was relaxing, and they talked of incidental matters. Now that she was over her nervousness in being near him, she found she liked Hank Chavez, liked him very much. She felt at ease with him. With Adrien, she had to be forever on guard, forever checking her temper, always behaving in a ladylike manner. With Hank she felt comfortable. He made her laugh. He was charming and witty, yet a gentleman at all times.

Why couldn't Adrien be that way? Why couldn't he sit there and talk to her, show such an interest in her? He hadn't even told her good night or made sure she was all right before he went to sleep. Adrien didn't *care*, that was the plain truth. But she cared about Adrien. That was the problem. She would have to do something to jolt him into caring.

And then it hit her again, the idea she had had earlier. She would make Adrien jealous. She had just the man for it—Hank Chavez. But did she dare use him in that way? He had shown an interest in her. She needed only to cultivate that interest.

The girls at school had taught her the techniques of flirtation, though she had yet to actually flirt with a man—Adrien had never given her the chance. She could practice on Hank. Only a *little*, however. She didn't want to encourage him, just hold his interest... just show Adrien.

She was excited. It would work! It had to.

"Your eyes are sparkling," Hank remarked softly, his gaze admiring.

She gave him a weak smile. "Are they? Oh dear, I'm so tired." She pretended a yawn. "I don't know how I'll sleep on these benches. I would be too afraid of falling off to get any sleep."

"I have a bedroll on top of the coach," he offered. "Would you allow me to get it for you?"

"Would you? Oh, that would be so nice. I was considering sleeping in the coach."

His eyes twinkled. "I could keep you company there."

"No, no! The bedroll will do nicely," she said hastily, a blush rising.

Was he a gentleman or not? She wondered, uneasy then. He had better be. She wouldn't be able to do what she was planning if he wasn't. A gentleman would have to concede gracefully to the better man. That was the way it *had* to end. She would make Adrien love her, and Hank Chavez would go on his way. That was what would happen.

He returned with the bedroll and gallantly kissed her hand, bidding her *buenas noches*. Then he moved off to a bench far away from her, and she relaxed once more. Yes, he was a gentleman. When her plan reached its conclusion, there would be no hard feelings. She was sure of it.

Chapter 7

FOR three days Samantha and Hank carried on the only conversation in the coach. Mr. Patch joined in occasionally, but Jeannette felt excluded unless they were talking of the East. And they did for a while, when Samantha told Hank about her experiences there.

They talked of many things. Samantha didn't let Hank know who her father really was, or where she lived. She deftly avoided the particulars, and he didn't press her.

They spoke of England, and he told her of Spain, and of France, where he had gone to school. At that point, Adrien joined the conversation.

It was working! Adrien frequently looked at her oddly, and she sometimes caught him glancing at Hank with almost a smoldering look. And Hank Chavez did not lose interest in her. He was solicitous, helping her in and out of the coach at rest stops, bringing her meals. It was just what she had planned.

The coach pulled into Trinidad in the early evening of the eighth day. They had already traveled nearly two hundred miles and there were still another seventy-five to go.

Adrien and Jeannette elected to stay at the stage depot. They were conserving money in any way they could. Adrien had spent so much on his mining supplies. Samantha offered to buy them rooms for the night, but they refused, too proud for that. Samantha shook her head. She had known they would refuse. There had been a strain between her and Jeannette ever since the three of them had talked about money. Jeannette was easily offended by the subject, and had become rigid about paying her way. Samantha was exasperated. Didn't Adrien realize that, once he was married to her, he would be wealthy? Didn't his sister's comfort matter to the man? Jeannette was not used to scrimping—or to sleeping in stage depots.

Her father's ranch was huge, thousands of acres in Mexico and thousands more across the border in Texas. He had more land than he could handle, but he did use a lot of it. Besides ranching, he grew crops in the fertile valley east of the West Sierra mountains, and his two copper mines were making him richer every year. If only Adrien knew all that. But she didn't talk of her wealth, so it was possible that he didn't know. All the Allstons knew was that her father was a rancher in Mexico. Perhaps they didn't equate ranching with wealth. Adrien would be surprised when they married and she was finally free to tell him.

Hank walked Samantha to the hotel. "Will you dine with me this evening?" he asked before leaving her at the top of the stairs. When she nodded, he caught her hand and squeezed it, then let it go. "I will call for you in an hour." He went to his room.

Samantha soaked for a long time in a too-small wooden tub, brooding on that intimate gesture. It was something she would have liked Adrien to see, but it had made her uncomfortable because she and Hank had been alone.

She hoped that Hank was only amusing himself with her. It wouldn't do at all for him to become serious about her. She liked him, but she loved Adrien, and she was not so fickle that she could change her feelings easily— not even for such a handsome, gallant man. For more than two years she had dreamed of becoming Adrien's wife, and marry him she would.

Hank was at her door precisely at six o'clock, as promised. He had bathed and shaved, and he was wearing a suit. The frock coat and trousers were black, but the striped satin waistcoat was in two shades of brown. The ruffled shirt was white. He looked magnificent. Could he have tucked the clothes in his saddle bags? Impossible. He had probably just bought them.

"You look *magnífica,*" Hank complimented as he took in her gray merino dress with the fitted jacket trimmed in black.

Samantha couldn't help smiling. "I was just thinking the same about you."

He grinned, his eyes crinkling, the dimples giving a boyish quality to his face. "Shall we go? There is a small restaurant a few doors down the street."

"Do you mind if we walk awhile first?" Samantha ventured. "Perhaps see whatever there is to see of this town?"

"It is dark now," he pointed out.

"We can stay in the main street."

There was hardly any light, only a quarter-moon and an occasional dim glow from a window. They strolled slowly along the wooden walkway in front of the stores. Samantha just enjoyed the feeling of walking, the chance to stretch her legs.

Lord, how she hated traveling by stagecoach! Only three more days. Only? She was seriously considering sending a message to Santa Fe, asking her escort to come to Elizabethtown. She could be done with stages. The *vaqueros* would be on their way, for she had wired her father.

"What do your close friends call you, Samantha?" Hank spoke softly beside her.

She thought of Adrien and Jeannette and answered, "Samantha."

"You are always called that?"

She looked at him sideways, amused. "Why? Don't you like my name?"

"It does not suit you," he said frankly. "You are more

like a Carmen, a Mercedes, a Lanetta. Samantha is so... Victorian."

She shrugged. "My grandmother *was* Victorian, and she chose my name. Still, you're right, it is rather formal."

Then she grinned. "At home they call me Sam, or even Sammy."

Hank chuckled. "Sam! No, you are certainly no Sam. Sammy is not so bad, though I could still think of better names for one so lovely. Do you mind if I call you Sammy?"

"I don't know." She hesitated. "It's a bit..."

"Familiar?" He shook his head. "You do not consider me your friend, then?"

"Of course I do," she quickly reassured him. "Oh, I suppose it will be all right. It will just sound funny coming from you. I'm called that only at home, and I've only known you for a few days."

"But you have agreed we are *amigos*."

"Yes, we are friends. And here I am taking advantage of our friendship." She had noticed that his limp was getting worse. "Here I am making you walk with me, when your ankle isn't healed yet."

He took her arm and steered her back toward the restaurant. "I assure you, it is my pleasure to walk with you... Sammy."

She grinned impishly. "Even when you are in pain?"

"I do not feel pain when I am with you," he answered smoothly.

"How gallant! But you really should tell that to your ankle," she teased.

They reached the restaurant, and his hand slipped from her arm to her waist as he escorted her to a table. As she felt those strong fingers clasping her side, something happened to Samantha. She grew warm all over, and was sure she was blushing seriously. Yet she was not embarrassed.

They ate a quiet meal. It was hard to pretend indifference toward Hank, as she had meant to do. He was just too attractive, and she enjoyed his company very much. She found herself glancing at him often during the meal, only to find him glancing at her. He was probably used to having an effect on women, and it thrilled her to have the same effect on such a handsome man.

They walked back to the hotel slowly, reluctant to part company just yet. But it was late, and the stage would be leaving early the next morning.

Hank took her to her room, and Samantha waited in breathless anticipation. Would he try to kiss her?

She didn't expect him to be so forceful. When she turned to bid him good night, his right arm gripped her waist, drawing her to him. His left hand went to the back of her head and held it so firmly that she couldn't turn away. She didn't want to. He was going to kiss her, and she wanted him to kiss her. Just one kiss wouldn't hurt. She would be sure it was only one.

The force of his lips on hers was shattering, and for a moment she thought she would faint. She felt his body pressing hard against hers, setting her afire. She was no longer herself but a puppet in his arms.

When he let her go, she was plunged into disappointment. She was suddenly cold. But then, as he said good night, the look in his eyes warmed her again.

She entered her room in a daze, leaving her clothes wherever they fell, and crawled into bed, his kiss still burning her lips, her body still trembling.

Chapter 8

THE next morning, Adrien intruded into her thoughts, and she felt guilty. Once she had walked up those stairs with Hank, Adrien had ceased to exist. It was as if she had betrayed him, not by the kiss, but by forgetting about him so completely.

She wouldn't let it happen again. She could wait until Adrien kissed her and made her feel that same excitement. Naturally, Adrien's kiss would be even more wonderful, because she loved him. She *did* love him. She did. So why did she have to keep reminding herself?

Angry, Samantha left her hotel room. She wasn't going to wait for Hank, even though it would give Adrien a chance to see them together. When she got to the lobby, however, Hank was there waiting.

"*Buenos días,* Sammy." Hank smiled.

Samantha couldn't meet his eyes. He said her name so softly, as though it were an endearment. How could things have got so far out of hand so quickly? It was obvious that he was falling for her. It was too much, too soon. Would she have to abandon her plan? She certainly didn't want to hurt this charming man.

"Hank...about last night," she began.

"I have thought of nothing else," he answered quickly, and she knew that she had to discourage him before his feelings grew.

"Hank, you...you really shouldn't have kissed me."

"But you enjoyed it."

"Yes, only—"

"It was too soon," he finished for her, before she could

explain about Adrien. "You must forgive me, Sammy. I am not a patient man. For you, however, I will try to be patient."

She started to protest, to tell him that he had jumped to the wrong conclusion, but he took her arm and led her out of the hotel. She would have to tell him that they could only be friends, that she loved Adrien. How could she find the words? Perhaps it would be better if she showed him. Yes, that was it!

They arrived at the stage office just as the others were getting ready to board. Adrien eyed them coldly. Ah, it had worked so well. He was jealous. But now she couldn't continue the game. She couldn't hurt Hank.

Samantha left Hank's side without a word and joined Adrien and Jeannette. She would have to appear cold and indifferent to Hank. It was the only way. Yet she felt so damned terrible about it.

All that day, Samantha sat in the corner opposite Hank, rather than directly across from him, as she had been doing. And she didn't speak to him or look his way even once. Adrien seemed in a better mood and even talked to her occasionally. He talked mostly with Hank, however.

That night they stopped at a stage rest, and Samantha continued to ignore Hank. At dinner, she sat as close to Adrien as she could and forced him to talk to her. She did not leave his side until it was time for bed.

She didn't sleep that night. She was miserable. She had caught Hank watching her with a curious, almost pleading look. She cursed herself a hundred times for using Hank, as she lay awake all night. He didn't deserve that. She was so sorry. But the damage had been done.

The next morning she was so tired that she could hardly walk to the coach. She slept all day, jolted awake every so often, only to fall right back to sleep. That night, when they stopped at another town, she was wide awake. She would not go to a hotel. She would stay close to Adrien. Hank waited to see if she would leave with him, and when she didn't, he caught her arm and pulled her away from the others, forcing her to talk to him.

"Why do you ignore me, Sammy?"

"Ignore you? Whatever do you mean?"

His eyes narrowed. "You stay close to your friend Adrien as if you were frightened of me."

"Adrien is *more* than just a friend," she said pointedly, then walked away, tears stinging her eyes. She couldn't have been more blunt. Now he would have to understand.

A dark frown furrowed Hank's brow as he watched her walk away. He wanted to grab her and shake her. What was she doing? Why did she suddenly ignore him and give her full attention to Adrien?

And then the answer came to him, and he almost laughed aloud. The little fool! She was trying to make him jealous! Didn't she know how unnecessary that was? He was already completely taken with her. She did not need to make him jealous.

But he would let her play her game, he decided. For her he would have patience. For her he would do anything.

The realization startled Hank. It was true. How could he have become enamored of this woman so soon? She had made him forget about Pat, forget about reaching Mexico. Everything flew from his mind except Samantha.

It confused him. The closest he had ever come to loving a woman was Angela. And that was not so long ago, not so long that he couldn't remember all too clearly the bitterness of losing her to another man. But all of that seemed unimportant now. Samantha was making him forget even that.

He didn't love her yet. He didn't think it was love, not this soon. But he could love her. He could very well give his heart to her completely, if she would give hers to him in return.

But he was certain of one thing already. He was aching with wanting her. There was no confusion there. He had only to look at her to feel his blood race. But she was a lady, so he had to move slowly. And it seemed, too, that she wanted to play her feminine games.

Thinking about those games, Hank shook his head over the absurdity of it. Didn't Samantha realize what kind of man Adrien Allston was? He could not be jealous over Adrien. He was an *hombres puta*. Hank could not understand such a man. Already Adrien had made two advances to Hank, the second of which Hank had ended by pulling his gun, making his disgust understood.

Samantha was as safe with Adrien as she could be with any man, but obviously she didn't think Hank knew that. He would let her get away with it this one time, wait until she tired of this charade, and then he would speak seriously to her. After that, there would be no more nonsense. He would not allow it. Once he asked her to marry him—*Dios!* Yes, he realized that he was thinking of doing just that.

Chapter 9

THE settlement called Elizabethtown had been established in 1868, two years after gold was found in creeks and gulches around Baldy Mountain. Thousands of miners had come to the area in the last few years, and more were still coming. Buildings rose continuously. They were mostly ramshackle wooden huts, but more than a hundred were already standing—stores, saloons, dance halls, hotels, even a drugstore.

The coach had made good time and rolled into town in the late afternoon of February 18th. Adrien was infected by the raw, bustling activity of the place and could not wait until the next day to rent a horse and head out for the Moreno Valley. He left Jeannette alone with all their luggage and the supplies.

Poor Jeannette was dazed. She couldn't understand Adrien's wild enthusiasm, nor was she used to depending on herself, for Adrien usually took care of everything.

Samantha quickly took charge, and Jeannette gratefully let her. Samantha found a cheap hotel and arranged for the Allstons' things to be carted over there. She intended to stay there, as well. She didn't like it, but she wouldn't consider leaving Jeannette alone while Adrien was away.

Before they left the stage office, Hank Chavez approached them. Samantha grew tense, but he surprised her.

"*Señoritas.*" He tipped his hat to them both, then said gallantly, "Your company has turned what would have been a most tedious journey into a pleasurable one."

Samantha nodded. "You are kind to say so."

"Perhaps we will see each other again before I leave," Hank continued, his eyes on Samantha.

"Perhaps," she replied evasively.

He smiled. "If not, I bid you *adiós* now, Samantha. Señorita Allston."

He tipped his hat again and was suddenly gone. Samantha stared after him. She was relieved, yet she felt something else as well, something she couldn't define. He did understand, she told herself. By calling her Samantha, he was saying he understood. And he was completely gracious about it, as she had hoped he would be. In fact, she thought, he had given up a bit too easily.

"He certainly was a nice gentleman—considering," Jeannette remarked.

"Yes, he was."

"And he was certainly taken with you, *chérie*."

"Not...not really," Samantha replied uneasily.

"Ah, you did not like him then?" Jeannette continued. "I do not blame you. He was not a very appealing man."

"What do you mean?" Samantha asked sharply. "He was very handsome."

Jeannette was shocked. *"Mon Dieu!* You are being too kind, *chérie*. The man was much too dark. Too...how can I explain? Rugged looking, too dangerous. He would make a terrible lover."

"Why do you say that?"

"He would be too aggressive, too demanding. The rugged ones are always demanding."

Samantha's eyes snapped green fire. "Do you speak from experience?" she asked cuttingly, angered.

"Oui, chérie," Jeannette replied evenly, then walked away, leaving Samantha staring after her in surprise.

It was late that evening when Adrien returned and

found Jeannette and Samantha at the hotel. He was excited, full of prospects for the next day. He had received a great deal of advice from miners who already had claims staked, advice about where he was likely to find gold. He found no gold the next day, but his enthusiasm was not dampened. On the third day he found a few nuggets of gold near a dry creek bed and immediately staked a claim. He returned to town only to file the claim and to fetch supplies, then headed back toward the valley.

Jeannette and Samantha went with him that day so that they would be able to find him in the future, for he would live out there in the valley. Jeannette was worried. It was the middle of February, hardly a good time to be sleeping in a tent in the open air. But Adrien was determined.

Jeannette was also determined—to visit him each day. Samantha went along every time. It was her only chance to see Adrien.

Except for those rides out to Adrien's claim, Samantha was bored. There was nothing to do in Elizabethtown. She found herself spending a good deal of time in the general store, buying things she didn't even need. But it was an interesting place, typical of stores in the Southwest, and smelled of plug tobacco, leather, fresh-ground coffee, and even pickled fish. There were few luxuries. Basic items and food needed for a rugged life crowded every available space. Even the rafters were hung with hams, slabs of bacon, and cooking pots. The floors were covered with barrels and kegs brimming with sugar, flour, even vinegar. This was where Samantha went, nearly every day, to pass the time.

She had not seen Hank Chavez and wondered if he had left Elizabethtown. There was a month still left before she could expect her escort to arrive. What could she do with all that time?

She began to think wistfully of home. She had not seen her father for nearly three years. The time had lengthened because she had stayed an extra six months to visit Jeannette, mostly just to be near Adrien. But he had paid no more attention to her then than he did now. *Why* didn't Adrien find her attractive? Other men did.

Samantha began to think he might be like Jeannette, his taste peculiar, as hers was. Imagine Jeannette not thinking Hank Chavez handsome! Was Adrien repelled by dark skin? Perhaps she was too dark, too robust, too healthy. She had had a dark, healthy tan when she had gone East and had kept it for almost six months. Though she was pale enough now, perhaps he couldn't forget how dark she had once been. Was this healthy appearance repugnant to him? Or maybe he just didn't like dark-haired women. His mother and sister were so blonde, so petite. Was she perhaps too tall?

Damn! What *did* he find wrong with her? If he didn't so dislike boldness in women, she would simply have asked him. Time was running out. Now she would only be able to see him a few hours each day. She needed help. She ought to have confided in Jeannette long before. Jeannette did not know that Samantha loved Adrien. Perhaps it was time they talked.

They did, that night over dinner in a small restaurant featuring home-cooked meals. It had been almost empty when they arrived, but had filled up quickly, mostly with rough men who came in from the gambling hall next door. They suffered noise and unwelcome attention while they ate.

"Does Adrien have a sweetheart somewhere? Someone I don't know about?" Samantha began.

Jeannette was surprised. "Of course not, *chérie*," she said. "Why do you ask?"

Samantha was embarrassed, but she couldn't stop. "I was just wondering why he doesn't seem to like me."

"Certainly he likes you, Samantha. You are his friend, just as you are mine."

"I don't mean as a friend, Jeannette. Am I so ugly? Why can't he like me as more than a friend?"

Jeannette frowned. She couldn't meet Samantha's too-revealing eyes. "Why would you want him to?"

"Why?" Samantha leaned close to whisper. "Can't you tell I love him? But of course you wouldn't know. *He* doesn't know. What am I going to do, Jeannette?"

"Ah, *chérie,* I am sorry. I had no idea you felt this way about my brother."

"But what am I to do? I will be leaving in a little less than a month."

"Perhaps you should forget him and go home to your papa," Jeannette said gently.

"Forget him? Impossible!"

"It might be for the best, Samantha. You see, Adrien has set a goal for himself." Jeannette tried to explain. "He has sworn to have nothing to do with women until he has reached his goal."

"Which is?"

"To be rich and respected. Before, his goal was to establish a law practice. Now I suppose it will be this silver mine he has bought. Until he is rich, he will not even think of women."

"He is being too hard with himself," Samantha remarked. "What if he were to marry a rich woman?"

"He would not, unless he were equally rich. It is a matter of pride with him."

Samantha became annoyed. She wanted encouragement and she wasn't getting any.

"You are suggesting I give up?"

"*Oui.* It would be best for you."

"Then you don't know me at all, Jeannette," she replied stiffly. "I never give up."

Samantha was too angry and disappointed to say any more. Jeannette fell silent, contemplating her food with a thoughtful frown. They were just about to leave when they were interrupted by a deep voice.

"Ah, *la señoritas*." Hank greeted them cheerfully. "What a pleasure to see you again!"

Samantha nodded, and Jeannette said, "And you, Señor Chavez. We have missed your company. And Adrien has remarked after you."

"How is your brother?" Hank ventured politely. "Did he find a gold mine yet?"

"Not exactly a mine, but he is prospecting in the valley." Jeannette smiled warmly. "I am sure he would like to see you again. Would you care to visit him with us tomorrow? We ride out to see him every morning."

"I would enjoy that," Hank replied, his eyes crinkling with his smile.

"Wonderful. We will see you in the morning then, at the stable. Nine o'clock?"

After Hank had gone, Samantha turned fiery green eyes on Jeannette. "Why on earth did you do that? You don't even like him!"

"But he is charming, and quite amusing."

"But you didn't have to invite him to come with us!" Samantha snapped.

"To be honest, I will feel much safer with a man along escorting us to the valley."

"I am able to protect us perfectly well, Jeannette," Samantha replied indignantly.

"But it should not be up to you to protect us, *chérie*. Actually, I have been considering staying with Adrien, so I will not have to make that ride each day."

"To sleep in a tent? Don't be ridiculous, Jeannette. You would be too uncomfortable."

"But I would feel better, not so afraid." Then she added, "Perhaps I won't have to if I can persuade your friend to escort us each day—until he leaves this town, of course."

"Hank Chavez is not 'my friend'!" Samantha insisted sharply. "And you can go with him by yourself tomorrow. I don't want to see him."

"No, no, I could not be alone with him!"

"You said you would feel safe with him," Samantha reminded pointedly.

"But only if you are there, too. You must come. Adrien would miss you if you do not."

Put that way, Samantha agreed. She was being silly about Hank Chavez, anyhow. His interest in her was surely over. He had not tried to see her since their arrival in Elizabethtown. Their meeting tonight had been accidental.

"Well, I suppose I'll go with you," Samantha said as the two young women rose from the table. "Besides," she added with an impish grin, "it just might make Adrien jealous to see me with Mr. Chavez."

Jeannette sighed. Poor Samantha. If she only knew how futile her efforts were. She hoped for Samantha's sake that Hank Chavez was ardent enough to make her forget Adrien, for loving Adrien would do her friend no good at all.

Chapter 10

ELIZABETHTOWN never settled down. From earliest morning there was great activity, and the bustle and noise continued all night long in the saloons and gaming halls. There were even huge tents for gambling and drinking set up by ambitious entrepreneurs eager to take the miners' gold.

On their sixth day in Elizabethtown, Samantha awoke earlier than usual to the loud morning traffic. At once she decided to take special care with her appearance. She soaked longer than necessary in the too-small tub, and washed her hair twice with her special rose soap. Afterward, she brushed it until the long, thick hair sparkled with fiery highlights. She pinned it up artfully until every strand was tucked away except two short curls at her temples. The effect would be stunning with her pert, narrow-brimmed beige hat. Its six dark green ribbons fell halfway down her back. The hat matched the better of the two riding habits she had with her. Light green velvet, it was of the Eastern design, made for a sidesaddle. She deplored sidesaddles but had been forced to use them. Ladies did not ride astride.

Samantha was still fussing before her mirror when Jeannette came in. They walked to the stable and hired horses, Samantha choosing the gray mare she had ridden before. She was used to the animal already. It was gentle and would give her no trouble. She did not especially care about impressing Hank with her excellent horsemanship.

He joined them after a few moments, dressed nearly as he had been on the day they met, all in black except for a blue silk bandanna and a blue patterned shirt. He looked exceptionally rakish and devil-may-care, and Samantha returned his warm greeting with a happy smile.

They didn't talk as they rode down into the valley. When they reached Adrien's camp, Samantha perceived at once that Adrien was not pleased to see her with Hank. He fairly bristled, and ignored them to the point of rudeness, continuing his digging in the creekbed with barely a civil word even for his sister.

Samantha was embarrassed and stepped away for a walk. Jeannette had gone to sit by her brother. Hank returned to the horses. He didn't consider following Samantha. He would let her stew a little longer. He could wait. He had already let five days pass without trying to see her. She needed to know that she could not toy with him.

He had missed her and had passed the time gambling. Pat had been right about one thing. The luck of the cards was with him. He had done much more than simply double his money. He still did not have enough money to buy his estate, but he felt rich. He had never had so much money. And who knew? If Samantha kept him there long enough, he might continue to win until he had enough to buy his land.

How long would he and Samantha stay? He would not allow a long courtship. He was being patient with her, but he would not be patient forever. This was not Europe, where long courtships were common. This was the West, where a man could meet, court, and marry a woman all in one day. Many did just that.

When they left Elizabethtown they would be married, or else they would be on their way to Mexico to be married there. If she insisted on her father's blessing, he would agree to that. For her, he would agree to almost anything. Within reason, of course.

Finding himself in this exalted state caused Hank no small amount of wonder. He had looked at Samantha once and had known he had to have her. She was a lady, so he could not have her without marrying her. And therefore he had decided to marry her. Just like that! He did not stop to think that he hardly knew her. She talked about her family and herself very little. But it did not seem important. He was letting his feelings rule him—just as he had with Angela. He was letting himself be carried away by love for a beautiful woman.

Before the day was over, he would show Samantha that he had not lost interest.

Samantha returned to the camp a few minutes later, noting that nothing had changed. Hank was sitting against a tree twirling a long stem of grass. Jeannette was several feet away, sitting on a fallen tree trunk. Adrien had moved farther up the creek. No one was talking.

Samantha smiled weakly at Hank before she moved to join Jeannette. "What is wrong with Adrien today?" she whispered, hoping Hank couldn't hear. "He's been rude before, but never like this. I thought at first he was jealous. But he's ignoring you, too."

"I think he is becoming discouraged with his claim," Jeannette replied. "He has found very little gold."

"Do you really think that's all?"

"*Oui.*" Jeannette sighed.

"Have you tried to talk him out of this? He could still make a success of a law practice in Denver."

Jeannette shook her head. "I know this and you know this, but he has his heart set on great riches gotten quickly. He will not give up, not yet. I know my brother."

"Well, we might as well go back to town. Perhaps he will be in a better mood tomorrow."

"You go on back, *chérie*. I think I will stay here tonight with Adrien."

"Don't be ridiculous."

"No, I am serious," Jeannette replied. "Adrien has worked himself sick. He is not feeling well."

"Did he tell you that?" Samantha became instantly concerned.

"No, but I see it. He is pale. He sweats too much. He is running a fever. He will not stop work to see a doctor. I would worry myself sick if I did not stay here to take care of him. It will be easier for me to stay than to worry."

Samantha glanced over at Hank and thought of being alone with him on the ride back. She shivered. "But, Jeannette—"

"No. Señor Chavez will see you safely back to town. You need not worry about me."

Samantha bit her lip, frowning thoughtfully. "I will stay, too."

Jeannette laughed. "There is not enough room in Adrien's small tent for the three of us." She turned serious again and nodded toward Hank. "You are not afraid to be alone with him, are you?"

Samantha's back went stiff. "Of course not!" she said indignantly. "Very well, I will see you tomorrow."

"Oui, tomorrow."

The stiffness left Samantha's manner as she approached Hank hesitantly. "Are you ready to leave?"

"Sí." He stood up in one graceful motion, then looked toward Jeannette. "She is not coming?"

"No. Jeannette insists Adrien is getting sick, and she won't leave him. I hope you don't mind. It will just be the two of us."

Hank grinned, and his eyes danced. "How could I mind...Sammy?" he answered softly.

Hank wanted to laugh. So she was making the moves again! To arrange for them to be alone. She was not as coy as he had thought. She was as eager for him as he was for her.

As they rode away from the camp, Hank was on top of the world. He would not disappoint Samantha. He knew just the spot where they could stop and be alone, far away from any camps. It was below the bluff they had crossed earlier, where a thin stream ran directly beneath it. A large tree stretched out its limbs by the stream. No one from the bluff could see beneath that tree, and there was a grassy bank beside it, a tiny Eden where he could be alone with his woman. Already he thought of her as his woman.

Samantha was getting increasingly nervous, her thoughts running rampant. What did he mean by calling her Sammy? Could his interest in her have returned? It hadn't been her idea to be alone with him. He knew that. What could he be thinking? Why was he being so...so familiar?

Ah, Jeannette, what have you done to me?

Hank rode abreast of her, on her right side. When they came to the bluff, he suddenly swerved left, guiding Samantha's horse off the path and down a small slope. Overgrown with sagebrush, cactus, and trees, the slope was never traveled. When Samantha tried to pull up, Hank caught her reins and rode on ahead, pulling her along with him.

"Hank?" Samantha demanded in a tight voice. "Where are we going?"

Hank looked back at her and grinned. "Only a little way off the beaten path. There is something I wish to show you," he explained.

She fell silent then and let him lead her. What harm could there be? No one with such a winning manner could cause her any trouble. Besides, her purse was hanging securely from her wrist, and her derringer was inside it, as always.

They descended several feet, at the beginnings of the bluff, and reached the stream after only a few moments. It was a very shallow stream, and Hank walked their horses right through it without hesitation. The bluff grew higher and higher to their right. When they were almost under its peak, they came to a huge tree that stretched across the stream, touching the steep wall of the bluff opposite.

The oak spread over them like a tent. Hank stopped and dismounted, then reached up to help Samantha down.

She hesitated, and he smiled. "We will let the horses drink from the stream."

She put her hands on his arms and let him lift her to the ground. The horses moved to the water as soon as they were free.

They were walled in on two sides, for the brush trees behind them grew taller than Samantha. In front was the bluff. And overhead was the tree, blocking out most of the sunlight.

"It's lovely here," she whispered. "Is this what you wanted to show me?"

"No, *querida*," he murmured in a deep voice. "This is what I will show you."

He drew her close to him, and she had no time to wonder before he bent forward and his lips touched hers. His kiss was gentle for a few seconds. Then, very quickly, it grew more intense, more demanding. He cupped her face so she could not escape the kiss.

And then, somehow, she was not standing up anymore. One of his arms had moved behind her back, and he had lowered her smoothly and gently to the ground. His lips did not leave hers for a moment.

The warm feeling spreading through her ran so quickly, so delightfully. She slipped her purse off her wrist so as to raise her hands easily to him. Her fingers moved up through his hair, knocking his hat to the ground. His hair was so soft, so cool, sliding so sensuously through her fingers. Without realizing it, she was pressing her mouth more firmly against his.

She was returning his kiss wholeheartedly, her breathing rapid. And the warmth inside her was turning to a burning heat.

Samantha was unaware that Hank was opening her

jacket. But she came to herself when he began to unbutton her blouse. A small voice told her to stop him. It wasn't permitted for a man to undress her. But it was only a small voice, and it disappeared again as his fingers touched her breasts. His hand seemed made of fire. It covered one firm mound completely, then squeezed deliciously.

Samantha moaned at this new, exquisite feeling and began to squirm, turning toward Hank, wanting to get even closer to him, but he gently pressed her back against the soft grass. His mouth left hers then, and she started to protest until his lips seared the side of her neck. She shivered, delighted. And when his tongue licked teasingly at her impudently pointed breast, she arched her back, offering more, until his mouth closed over her inviting flesh.

Samantha was beside herself. Hank was kneading one soft breast while his mouth tortured the other. She was moaning, drowning, sinking.

Hank's mouth moved slowly back toward hers, leaving a trail of fire across her as he went. From far away she heard him groan, "Ah, Samina, *mi querida, mi bella amor.*"

His mouth closed over hers again, but by then the words had awakened her. Shock took hold. What had she allowed to happen?

She stiffened and moved her head away. "No! You mustn't." She groaned and tried to push him away. "Please, let me up."

He allowed her to push him back just far enough that he could look down at her. Beyond that, she could not budge him. His eyes were smoldering darkly.

"Let you go, *querida?*" he breathed deeply. "No, I think it is too late for that."

"No!" she gasped. She became frantic. "Please, Hank, you don't understand. I can't do this. I can't!"

He smiled tenderly. "You are frightened, but that is

only natural. I will not hurt you, Samina. I will be very gentle with you."

"No, no—no!" she cried emphatically. "You have already done too much. We shouldn't be here. You should never have kissed me. I...I..."

"You let me kiss you, *mi querida*. You let me do much more. If I should not have kissed you, then you should not have kissed me."

"I know," she said miserably. "And I'm sorry. I didn't mean to. I wasn't thinking. I've never been kissed like this before. I've never felt this way. Oh—you wouldn't understand!"

"But I do." He said it so softly. His voice was a tender caress. "I understand very well. You lost yourself to feeling, as did I."

"But I can't let you kiss me anymore or...or do the other things." Her face burned with shame. Why, she hadn't covered herself yet. She did so quickly, but his eyes were on her, and her embarrassment increased. "It's wrong, Hank. You do see that, don't you?"

"It is not wrong. Not for us."

"It's wrong for me," she insisted. "I've never done anything like this before."

He sighed deeply then and stood up, turning around to allow her privacy in which to fasten her clothes.

"Very well, *querida*," he said, his back to her. "I will wait."

Something in his voice made Samantha's head come up sharply. She had been so relieved, relieved that he understood and wasn't angry. She sat rigidly still and stared at his wide back, frowning.

"Wait?"

He glanced over his shoulder. Seeing that she had managed to button up her blouse, he turned to face her. He grinned at her suddenly, shaking his head.

"You have to ask, Samina, when you've known very well what I feel for you?"

"I don't know anything." Her voice rose with alarm. "Why, I haven't even seen you for days."

"That was your own fault. You wished to toy with me."

"What are you talking about? I assumed you had left town."

He shook his head again. "No. You knew I would not leave without you."

Samantha took a long, deep breath. What could he possibly be thinking of?

"Hank, I—"

He cut her off. "Ah, *mi amor*, you wish this to be done *properly*, I suppose? Very well, I will tell you that from the first I knew you would be my woman. I ask you now formally to come to Mexico with me and be—"

"Wait!" Samantha cried, scrambling to her feet. "Oh, God, Hank, this is terrible!"

His smile vanished. "You wish to explain?"

"I like you, Hank, I really do. And I enjoyed traveling with you. But our journey together is over."

"What are you saying?"

She cringed at the sharpness in his voice. "You're a nice man, a very attractive man, and things might have been different if I didn't love someone else. But there is someone else, and I intend to marry him."

Hank's eyes narrowed. "You flirt well with other men, *niña*, when your man is not with you. Where is he?"

Samantha was stung. "He's here, of course. I thought you understood when I told you Adrien and I were more than friends."

"Adrien? *Por Dios!*" Hank stared hard into her face. "Now you tease me?"

"I'm not teasing. I love Adrien. I have for more than two years."

"This is ridiculous, little one," he said softly now. "You cannot possibly."

Samantha's eyes sparked furiously. "How dare you say so! I love him!"

Hank's body went rigid. She meant what she was saying. She really did love that man—a man who would never return her love. But why, then, had she devoted so much attention to Hank?

"I think perhaps you have used me," he said darkly. "You ignore Adrien on the stage and give your attention to me. Why?"

Samantha watched his face take on a look of sheer rage. It frightened her. "I didn't mean to mislead you. I...hoped Adrien would be jealous. But as soon as I saw that your interest in me was growing, I told you about Adrien and me. I didn't mean to mislead you. I told you we were more than friends."

"I know what he is, *niña*," Hank hissed furiously. "I did not believe you would be foolish enough to love him."

"Why?" she demanded. "Why do you talk about him that way?"

"Do you think he will ever return your love? You are a fool, *niña*. But then, I am a fool, as well. Once more, I make a terrible mistake."

He said it so solemnly that she was reluctant to ask what he meant. But she needed to distract him from the things he was saying about Adrien, so she pressed him.

"What mistake?"

His eyes bored into her coldly. "Being fool enough to give myself to a woman who loves another man. At least Angela was honest from the first. I knew she loved someone else, but I still wanted her. You were not so honest."

Samantha smarted. "I never dreamed you would want to *marry* me. How was I to guess a thing like that?"

Hank's pride was badly wounded. He wanted to throttle Samantha for the way she had used him. He would never admit that he had wanted to marry her.

"You flatter yourself, *chica*." He struck out at her with brutal words. "Marry you? That is not what I had in mind."

"But you asked me to go to Mexico with you!"

"I did, and that was a mistake. But marry you? Now you have made a mistake."

Hank laughed scornfully, an ugly sound. His eyes narrowed, and there was a look there Samantha had never seen before, a look that chilled her. He had changed from the laughing, handsome man she had felt so safe with, to a dark, menacing stranger who terrified her.

He continued, his voice rich with malice. "I had no intention of marrying you. I would have made you my woman and treated you well. But a lady does not trifle with a man as you have trifled with me. So, if you are not a lady, I need not treat you as one."

"Meaning?" she challenged, anger overcoming caution.

His grin was not pleasant. "I have lost the desire to take you with me, but my desire to have you is still strong. I need to purge you from my blood, *mujer,* the only way I know how."

He unbuckled his gunbelt and dropped it to the ground. Then his hands moved to his belt buckle, and Samantha's eyes grew enormous with comprehension. She dashed wildly for her purse, but he got there first and kicked it out of her reach. She tried to run after it, for it held the only help she would get. But Hank caught her wrist and threw her to the ground, dropping between her legs, pinning her to the earth.

He knelt between her legs, looking so serious, so deliberate, that she could only stare up at him. Then he unbuttoned his shirt and gazed down at her, fire glowing in his gray eyes. The shirt was open, but Hank didn't remove it. She realized he wasn't going to, and the fact made it all seem even more shameful, somehow.

Muscles rippled above his nipples, and short, dark curls extended to his navel.

Samantha was fascinated despite herself, but only for a moment. As he moved down closer to her, she flailed her fists at him, but he shoved every blow aside. When she raked her nails down his chest, he lost patience and raised his hand to her.

She gasped, cringing away from him, covering her face. She hadn't considered that he might beat her. There was nothing to stop him. She had never felt so helpless in all her life.

When the blow didn't come, she dared to look at him. He was glaring at her, his mouth a hard line.

"I do not want to hurt you, *chica*. Do not fight me anymore."

She moaned softly as his fingers moved to the buttons on her blouse. She caught his hands, looking up at him forlornly.

"I can't let you," she whispered.

As he gazed down at her, his anger softened just a little, enough to remind him of his feelings of only minutes before. Yes, Hank wanted her. But not brutally. She had hurt him, and she had been silly, but he never wished to cause her harm.

She saw his feelings changing, saw the softening in his handsome face, and suddenly the desire of a little while before came back, all in a rush. She wanted him, as she had wanted him before. Her arms reached out for him as he bent to kiss her.

Soon a fire was spreading in her once again. Hank's mouth moved along her neck, biting her gently. She began to moan, to twist. The heat was increasing, driving her onward.

Somehow her clothing was no longer there, nor was his, and somehow it seemed so right. His arms wrapped around her, and she raised herself to take him, taking him all at once and with only a moment's pain before the fire began all over again, building and building.

There was a feeling of exquisite torment, and then a wave washed over her, through her, and she cried out. Whatever had been building in her burst.

She had been told it would be magnificent, but no one had told her that it could be better than magnificent. She had never imagined the wondrous pleasure of it.

It was several long moments before the exquisite throbbing stopped and Samantha was aware of her surroundings once again. Hank was lying beside her, breathing heavily.

He got up without a word, quickly buckled his pants, then began tucking in his shirt without even buttoning it. Samantha moved only to draw on her skirt. She didn't try to cover her breasts. She felt languorous, more relaxed than she had felt in a long time.

Hank strapped on his gunbelt, then picked up his hat. He was standing at her feet, brisk and businesslike again.

"What's the matter, Hank?" Samantha asked sarcastically, suddenly angry all over again. "Do you expect me to cry? Would that make your triumph complete?"

He turned away from her stiffly and stalked to his horse. But before he mounted, he called back to her, "If you convince your Adrien to marry you, he will never know you are not a virgin. You needn't worry about that."

She grimaced. "Damn you, of course he will know!"

"No, *chica*, for he will never come to your bed," Hank taunted, wanting to hurt her. "If you marry Adrien Allston, you will have a fine time trying to keep him away from your lovers."

"What are you talking about?" she gasped.

Hank laughed shortly as he mounted his horse and walked the beast to her side. He bent over, whispering with deliberate calm. "The man you love prefers men in his bed, *querida*."

The shock of his words made her scream before she really understood what he was saying. "You're lying! Bastard! How I hate you! Get out of here! And when you go, you'd better keep right on riding!"

He chuckled. "Will you send a posse after me, Samina? I have run from posses before. One more will make no difference. They never catch me."

"If I ever see you again, I'm going to kill you," she said with furious calm.

He shrugged, unconcerned. "We will not meet again. *Adiós*, Samantha Blackstone." He tipped his hat.

Hank walked his horse back into the stream, leaving Samantha shaking with fury. Her hair had tumbled down, and she pushed it out of the way impatiently. Just then a thought struck her, and she jumped up, looking for her purse.

Hank stopped once to look back. Anger and bitterness were still eating at him, making it impossible for him to regret the manner of his leaving, or the cruel way he had told her about Adrien.

When he looked back, he saw first the fiery hair tumbling about her shoulders and then the gun, which she was raising slowly and pointing directly at him.

A memory flashed through his mind, and Hank spurred his horse, hunching down over its neck. *Madre de Dios!* It was she! The girl from Denver! With her hair tumbling down like that, the sun shining on her, and a gun in her hand, it was the same girl! *Dios!*

Quickly, Samantha fired her only two shots, one right after the other. She didn't know whether she had hit her target, for he was out of sight. Her hands were shaking with anger as she threw the gun down, cursing it for not being her six-shooter. Then she slumped onto the bank, beating her fists on the damp earth.

"Damn you, Hank, for the devil you are! Liar! Filthy liar!"

She began sobbing. It couldn't be true. She couldn't

have been fooled by Adrien, not for so long. She would never believe Hank. Never!

How she hated that bastard, hated him more for his lies than for seducing her. She would go and see Adrien, prove Hank was wrong. Then she would be able to forget this day, and forget that she had ever known Hank Chavez.

Chapter 11

LEAVING the scene of her disgrace, Samantha had one consolation. She found blood on the ground. Whether the blood was from the eight deep, ragged cuts on his chest or from bullet wounds she didn't know. But at least she was assured that he was in pain. It made her feel much better.

It had taken a long time to pull herself together as she sat by the stream, recalling every single thing. She washed Hank's blood from her chest and tried to get it out of her white blouse. It had stained both sides because he had bled so much. She took satisfaction from that. She had scarred him.

With that thought firmly in mind, she rode hard, tracing the way back to Adrien's camp. She had loaded her derringer again from the bullets she always kept in her purse and was in a mood to face trouble, any kind of trouble, but there was none on the way back to the camp.

She had pinned her hair up off her neck again and replaced her hat, and her clothes were only slightly wrinkled and damp, so she believed that she looked herself. She didn't know that her eyes were flashing like emeralds in the bright sun. But Jeannette noticed immediately, noticed that and other things, as well.

"Mon Dieu! What has happened to your mouth—and your neck?" Jeannette gasped after Samantha slid off her horse and stomped over to her.

"What are you talking about?" Samantha stopped in her tracks.

"Blood is smeared from your mouth to your neck! And..." She walked around Samantha. "There is blood on the back of your neck and in your hair. What has *happened?*"

"It is not my blood, so it doesn't matter!" Samantha snapped, and she went to find the canteen of water that was always by Adrien's tent.

Jeannette followed, her face tight with concern as she watched Samantha wipe viciously at the blood on her face. "It is his blood, then?"

They both knew who she meant. "Yes!"

"What did you do to him?"

Samantha's head snapped around, and she stared fiercely at the petite blonde. "What did *I* do?" Her tone was contemptuously cutting. "You haven't asked what *he* did! All I want to know is how you could leave me alone with that bastard."

"Samantha!"

"Samantha nothing!" she stormed. "You knew how improper it would be to let me ride back alone with him. Yet you insisted on staying here. You insisted Adrien was sick. He better damn well *be* sick, Jeannette," she warned darkly. "Where is he?"

"Not far," Jeannette replied, alarmed. "He went up the creek a little way."

"Adrien!" Samantha shouted toward the creek. "Adrien! Get down here!"

"Samantha, please. Tell me what happened."

Samantha turned on her friend, her eyes narrow. "I'm beginning to wonder if you didn't contrive the whole thing."

"What do you mean?"

"*You* were the one who invited Hank along today, and I know you don't even like him. And then you managed to leave me alone with him. Did you do it on purpose? Were you hoping he could make me forget about your brother?"

Jeannette paled and was about to stammer out an

answer when Adrien appeared. "What is all the shouting? Samantha, why have you come back here?"

"To see you, Adrien." She managed a calm answer.

She found she was looking at him in a new light, Hank's accusation taunting her.

"What did you want to see me about?" Adrien asked cautiously, her mood warning him to keep his distance.

"You seem wary of me, Adrien," she said in a deceptively soft voice. "Why do I make you nervous?"

"You don't," he denied, even as he backed farther away. "What has got into you, Samantha?" he demanded.

"Nothing that a little honesty wouldn't help," she replied with calm purpose as she caught his hand, drawing him close to her. "Kiss me, Adrien."

He jumped back, snatching his hand away. "What is the matter with you?" he gasped.

"Nothing," she said evenly, "but if you don't kiss me this minute, Adrien, I'm going to think there's something wrong with you."

He was looking at Jeannette helplessly, when suddenly Samantha grabbed his head and pulled his face down to hers. She had to do the kissing herself. It was a disaster. Adrien was repulsed. He kept his hands at his sides. His lips were stone cold. There was absolutely no feeling in him.

Samantha let go of him slowly, and he stood back, wiping the back of his hand across his mouth. She was not shocked. She wasn't thinking about him. All she could think of was the time she had wasted loving and wanting him.

"You bastard!" she raged.

"Samantha—" Jeannette began, and Samantha turned on her.

"You Judas! If you had just told me the truth! I told you last night that I loved him, and you had probably guessed before. Why didn't you tell me?"

"Chérie, this is not...something we can admit to," Jeannette said helplessly.

"You could have told *me!* You knew how I felt." Tears sprang to Samantha's eyes, and she couldn't stop them. "I would have been hurt, but at least I would still have my virtue. And now I don't—because you had to lie to me and play matchmaker instead. You served me up on a platter to that devil, Jeannette."

"Samantha, I am so sorry," Jeannette said sincerely. "I could not know that Hank Chavez would take advantage of you. You must believe that."

"It's too damn late for either of us to be sorry."

"What is this about Hank?" Adrien finally spoke up. "What have you done to him?"

Samantha started to laugh hysterically. "Oh, God, it's just like you to think I'm the villain."

Adrien pivoted around and stalked away, and at that moment Samantha didn't know which of the two men she hated more.

"Samantha—" Jeannette tried again.

"No!" Samantha snapped, and headed for her horse, throwing back at her friend, "There's nothing you can say that will help now, Jeannette. I'm returning to town, and I sincerely hope I don't see either you or your brother again before I leave here."

Samantha rode off then, her anger and bitterness burning hotter than ever. When she reached town, she changed hotels, moving to the best Elizabethtown offered.

She spent the rest of the afternoon brooding. What could she do about Hank Chavez? She had quickly understood that she hated him more than she hated Adrien. She couldn't let Hank get away with what he'd done, get away with seducing her and then mocking her. No matter how much she might have hurt him, he had had no right to hurt her so badly.

It was not the loss of her virginity that was eating at her, keeping her anger aflame. That had been his revenge, simple and over with. Hank had felt she deserved it for having hurt him, and perhaps she could even forgive him for that. After all, she knew what hurt was. And though she wished it had not happened, she shamefully admitted that she had found pleasure in their union. Somehow, her body had responded.

But Hank's parting taunts had truly shamed her. She could not stand his knowing what a fool she was. Hank knew that she would never have the man she loved.

Had loved. Samantha felt only pity for Adrien now. She was disgusted with herself. That she could be so stupid! That she had belittled herself, always thinking that it was her fault if Adrien didn't notice her.

All that ate at her. That was why she wanted so desperately to get even with Hank. Only she didn't know how. She didn't know the first thing about tracking a man. She could hire someone else to do it, but she didn't even know how to find the sort of man who would hunt another down.

There was nothing she could do except hope that she would meet up with Hank again one day. And there was a way to make that a possibility—by posting a reward. *Wanted, alive.* And she did want him alive, so that she could see him horsewhipped for the despicable bastard he was.

In order to post a reward, she would have to have a reason. Robbery would be the easiest to explain. If the law ever caught up with him, they would hold him until she could identify him. Then she would have him released and take the law into her own hands. A few of her father's *vaqueros* would help her.

She felt better just thinking about her revenge. She had a plan, something she could act on first thing in the morning, so she went to sleep easily...only to dream about Hank Chavez.

Chapter 12

FOUR days later, Samantha and her six-man escort rode out of Elizabethtown in a cloud of dust. She was quite a dramatic sight, a wide-brimmed brown hat perched daringly atop her tightly wound red hair. In a brown leather skirt split down the middle and a matching vest over her white silk shirt she made a stunning picture. She looked just like a female cowboy, right down to her spurred boots and the gun holster clinging to her thigh. Her skirt had been made in order to accommodate it, and to make riding astride easy.

She had thanked Manuel profusely for bringing her riding outfit along with him, and she was just as pleased with the horse he had brought her. A frisky black stallion, El Cid had been just a colt when she left home three years before. Now he was powerful and sleek, and she would learn to love him as she had loved Princesa, her spirited white mustang who had died just before she left for the East.

That first week, Samantha insisted on putting as much distance as possible between her and what she thought of as the place of her shame. But soon Manuel did some insisting of his own and slowed their pace, explaining that he would not bring home *el patrón*'s *niña* exhausted and bottom-sore from hard riding.

They rode only about twenty miles a day after that first week, a pace the horses could keep to easily. They stopped in every town, and Samantha checked each to see if her wanted posters on Hank had been put up. They usually had.

She became jumpy and irritable around strangers. Every time she saw a tall, black-haired man in dark clothing, her pulse raced and her hand moved to her gun. The frequent reminders of Hank didn't help her to forget him. And she had meant to forget him. It wasn't fair! He was supposed to be haunted by her, not the other way around.

The day they crossed the border into Mexico was a day of rejoicing, though they still had a week of riding before reaching Kingsley land. But the days did not seem so long anymore. They were riding on familiar terrain—the flat plains, the rolling hills—and always there were the beautiful Sierra mountains in the distance.

How she loved that mountain range. It was framed outside her bedroom window at home and was the first thing she saw every morning. Seeing it each day now made her feel as if she were home already, and just out riding the range with the *vaqueros* as she used to do. They had often spent nights out on the range, and whenever they camped near the mountains, Samantha went off on her own for whole days, exploring caves and gullies and finding narrow mountain paths traveled for centuries by the Indians, magnificent hidden valleys, old village ruins. It had been a fascinating life.

Samantha sighed. She wasn't so young anymore, and she no longer felt quite so adventurous. She had grown up a lot in her three years away from home. And, she thought ruefully, she had done most of her growing up in the last month.

They arrived at the ranch in the middle of the afternoon, halfway through the second week in April. It was a sunny, warm day. The sprawling one-storied house of stuccoed adobe and stone welcomed Samantha, but her father, standing by the front door impatiently waiting for her to dismount, made her heart leap with joy.

She ran to Hamilton Kingsley, throwing herself into his arms.

For several moments, she couldn't let go of him. Here was safety. No one could hurt her when these arms were around her. This man spoiled her, pampered her, loved her. Oh, it was wonderful to be home!

At last she leaned back to get a good, long look at him. He looked the same, and she found herself terribly pleased by that. Her father was still the broad-shouldered, robust man she had fought so hard at first, yet had come to love so well.

He laughed, but his eyes were filled with tears. "Well, daughter, do I pass inspection?"

She laughed, too. "You haven't changed."

"But you certainly have. You're no longer my little girl. I never should have sent you to school. Damn, but it's been too long, much too long to have you away. I've missed you, *niña*."

"I've missed you, too." Samantha knew she was going to cry. "I'm sorry I stayed away longer than I really had to. I regret not coming home sooner. I regret it more than you could ever know."

"Here now," he said gruffly. "Let's not have tears in those pretty eyes. Come inside." He led her inside to the enclosed patio at the center of the house. "Maria! Our little girl's home!" he bellowed. "Come see how she has grown!"

The kitchen, off the patio, which was planted with flowering shrubs and vines, was where Maria could usually be found. The plump Mexican woman came running from that direction, and Samantha met her halfway, under the large arched hallway entrance. Maria had changed just a little. There was a little more gray in her coal-black hair. But when she folded Samantha in her pudgy arms, she felt just as soft and cushiony as she always had.

"Look at you. Look!" Maria scolded. "You have grown too much, *muchacha*. You come home a woman."

"Prettier?" Samantha grinned, teasing.

"Ah, now I know you have not changed at all. You still try to tease compliments from me, eh?"

"And you still won't give them."

"Not so!" Maria gasped with indignation. "How this girl lies. Is this what they teach you in that fine school?"

Samantha suppressed a grin, as did her father. "Now, now, Maria, you know she's only teasing you," he said.

"She knows, father," Samantha added. "She just has to make a big to-do about it."

"*Ay!* I will not listen to insolence from one so young," Maria said with mock severity.

"So young? And here I thought you said I had come home a woman. Make up your mind, Maria."

Maria threw her plump arms into the air, conceding in frustration. "I am too old for your antics, *mi niña.* Leave an old woman alone."

"I will do so only if you promise to make *arroz con pollo* for dinner," Samantha replied, her eyes twinkling merrily.

Maria looked at Hamilton sharply. "Did I not tell you she would ask for *el pollo?* It is her homecoming, and I cannot even give her her favorite dish—because of that devil," she spat in very real disgust.

"Maria!" Hamilton said in a warning voice.

"What is this?" Samantha asked, frowning. This exchange was unusual. "Aren't there any chickens?"

Maria ignored Hamilton's warning look and answered angrily, "Not a one, *niña.*" She clicked her fingers. "Like that, they are gone."

"Disappeared? You're saying they just vanished?"

Maria shook her head. "Your *papacito,* he gives me dirty looks," she said huffily. "I am saying no more."

Samantha watched her walk back toward the kitchen and then turned to her father. "What was that all about?"

"Nothing, Sammy," Hamilton said smoothly. "You know how dramatic Maria is."

"But how could the chickens disappear—unless they

were stolen? And our workers wouldn't steal from us. Do you know who did it?"

He shook his head. His tone was evasive. "I have only suspicions. But it's certainly nothing to concern yourself with. Jorge will be back any day now with a crate full of new chickens, so you will get your *arroz con pollo* yet. Why don't you go and rest before dinner? You must be tired. We can talk later."

Samantha grinned. In her happiness at being home, the chickens were forgotten. "It's not a nap I want, father, but a bath. I have had so many cramped, uncomfortable baths, that I've been dreaming for months about that heavenly bathtub you bought me."

"It's nice to know one of my gifts is so deeply appreciated." He chuckled.

She laughed. "That one is so deeply appreciated that I can't wait to get into it. I'll see you later, father." She kissed him on the cheek. "Oh, it's so good to be home."

Samantha's high-ceilinged, whitewashed room cheered her, as it always had. It was just as she had left it, roomy, neat, furnished sparingly. The clothes she had left behind in her wardrobe would still fit her if she let out the hems a little. Even so, she had brought a new wardrobe from the East and would probably give the old clothes away, all except her riding habits.

The narrow bed was still covered in the old plaid blanket she liked so well. There was no vanity, just a large uncluttered oak dresser. The tables by her bed held no feminine knickknacks. There was really nothing in the room that identified it as belonging to a young girl, for that girl had been a tomboy, disdaining feminine frills.

Now she would have a vanity put in, and perhaps lacy curtains at the windows, as well as a full-length mirror and even some doilies for the tables. She hadn't changed all that much, but she no longer denied being a lady. She couldn't go on forever reacting against the childhood spent with an overly strict grandmother. Then again, she wouldn't give up her freedom, either.

Dinner was a delight. Maria had outdone herself. There was Spanish rice with thick steaks and peppers, and *frijoles,* the delicious beans mashed and fried in bacon drippings. Maria served *enchiladas* and *quesadillas,* as well, and Samantha stuffed herself on the different *tortilla* dishes. She had so missed Maria's Mexican cooking, and she quickly decided that if she ever left home again, she would take Maria along with her.

After dinner they retired to the comfortable living room off the central patio, Samantha insisting that Maria join them. The old woman was family to Samantha, never mind that she had her own children and Manuel, her husband.

Samantha talked only briefly about school, for she had already written home about so much of it. Maria and her father were more interested in her journey home, and in the Allstons. But Samantha could not speak enthusiastically about her journey, and she gave only a general account of Jeannette and Adrien. Her father asked many questions about them, but she never once let on that her feelings for Adrien had run deep, or that those feelings had been sorely wounded. She spoke of Elizabethtown with distaste, but her father attributed that to the primitive atmosphere of a boom town.

Samantha didn't mention the dark, handsome stranger of her journey. She would never speak of him or of her shame, not unless he was found and she had to explain why she would be identifying him.

Then it was her turn to ask questions, to find out what had been going on at home. There had been a marriage and four births among the *vaqueros* and their families. One of the copper mines was shut down because there had been too many accidents. There had been some cattle missing on the range recently, nothing serious, and only because the ranch had gone short-handed while Samantha's escort was away. There had been building and repairs, minor things, of no concern.

Her father changed the subject.

"Don Ignacio's son has been here often, asking after you, Sammy."

"Ramón?"

"Yes, he's turned into a fine boy."

"You mean man, don't you?" Samantha pointed out. "Ramón is several years older than I am."

Hamilton shrugged. "I've watched him grow up, Sammy. It's the same with you. You're still my little girl. It's hard to think of you as a grown woman."

"Well, I still feel like your little girl. So maybe we can forget sometimes that I'm grown."

"Agreed." He chuckled. "But, as I was saying, Ramón Baroja has turned out to be a fine...man, and I think you'll be surprised at the change. He must have grown six inches since you left."

"And how is his family?"

"Well."

Maria grunted. "*Very* well, considering they have not been troubled as we—"

Hamilton cleared his throat loudly, cutting her off. "I could use some brandy, Maria."

"What trouble?" Samantha asked Maria.

Her father answered quickly. "It's nothing. A few drifters killing some stock. Things like this have happened before."

Samantha watched Maria shaking her head as the older woman left to get the brandy. What was going on? The chickens...the mine...missing cattle...dead stock. Yet her father shrugged it all off. Or did he? Was it really nothing, or did he not want to worry her?

"Ramón will probably stop by to see you tomorrow," Hamilton was saying. He chuckled. "He has been coming every other day. I suppose he doesn't trust me to send word when you arrive."

"Why is he so eager to see me?"

"Well, he's missed you. He hasn't married yet, you know."

"You sound like you're matchmaking, father." Samantha grinned impishly. "I suppose you wouldn't mind at all if I married Ramón?"

"I think he would make a fine husband, yes. But don't get your dander up, Sam," he added. "I'm not about to tell you whom you should marry. I expect you will follow your heart."

"Marriage is the furthest thing from my mind," Samantha said. There was just a touch of bitterness in her voice, but not enough for her father to detect.

"I'm glad to hear that," he replied. "After all, you just came home to me. I wouldn't want to lose you too soon, *querida*."

"Don't call me that!"

Hamilton looked up, surprised by her sharp tone. "What?"

"I said don't call me that," she snapped, and then sighed. "Oh, I'm sorry, father. I don't know what's the matter with me."

She was shocked. How she must have sounded. She was letting Hank Chavez affect her homecoming. Her father wouldn't understand why she never wanted to hear that endearment again, nor did she want to make him understand. He worried too much over her welfare as it was. He would be devastated to know what she had allowed to happen to her. And she *had* allowed it, she reminded herself cruelly. She had let him fondle her, build her to a feverish pitch. She had allowed all of that—and then it had been too late to stop the rest.

"I must be tired. I don't know what I'm saying." Samantha tried to excuse herself for the outburst. "I didn't sleep very well last night because I was so excited, knowing I'd be home today."

Her father nodded. "And I am keeping you up late. Go on to bed, Sam."

"Yes, I think I will." She bent and kissed him.

"I'll see you in the morning." He squeezed her hand before letting her go. "Good night—Sammy."

She walked away, furious with herself instead of happy at being home. She was letting Hank Chavez haunt her. Why, her father had always called her *querida* when saying good night to her. And now he couldn't say that—because of Hank Chavez!

Chapter 13

FROILANA RAMIREZ woke Samantha, bringing fresh water into her room. Maria's youngest daughter was twenty-three, and unmarried, though many men had spoken for her. She was waiting for the right man, "the one who sweeps me off my feet and carries me away," she always told Samantha quite seriously.

"He must be very strong, very handsome. He must make me swoon for love of him."

Samantha had always scoffed at Froilana's fanciful dreams. She had felt that boys were good only for beating at contests. She always beat Ramón and the boys on the ranch, even the ones much older than she. But now, older, she could understand Froilana's dreams.

She lay there listening to Froilana's frivolous chatter. A vivacious girl, pretty, with silky black hair, wide brown eyes, and golden skin, Froilana's only fault was incessant chattering.

"...no longer the *muchacha* and I the older woman. Now we are both women," Froilana was saying.

Samantha suppressed a grin as she pulled her legs over the side of the bed and stood up. "I suppose so," she answered as seriously as she could manage.

From as far back as Samantha could remember, the older girl had thought of herself as a woman. Yet Froilana had been only thirteen when Samantha joined her father in Texas, and Maria and her family had come with them to Mexico the year after. Her father had moved to Mexico in order to avoid the Civil War brewing in the American states. There had been fighting in

Mexico, as well, a revolution, but her father remained neutral there, and they were so far north that the trouble never reached them.

"Now you do not laugh and giggle when I talk of men," Froilana continued, making Samantha's bed. "Now you have an interest in men, eh?"

Samantha yawned, tiptoeing to the small room adjoining hers where her huge four-legged bathtub was kept. Water had to be carried to it, but there was a piped drain which led outside for emptying it. Her morning bowl of cool water was on the towel stand.

"Oh, I don't know, Lana," Samantha called over her shoulder. "Men can be very deceptive. I think I can do without them for a while yet."

"*Ay*, no!" Froilana scoffed.

"I mean it."

"What will you do then when the young Ramón asks your *papacito* to marry you? And he will. He was always taken with you, even though you act like a child. Wait until he sees you now!"

Samantha splashed cool water on her face then grabbed a towel before she replied. "Ramón can ask my father for me all he wants, but I am the one who will have to give the answer. And how can I know what I will say when I haven't seen him for almost three years?"

"You will like what you see, *patrona*."

"*Patrona?*" Samantha called out in surprise. "Lana, you never called me mistress."

"But you have changed so," Froilana explained, subdued then. "You are a lady now."

"Nonsense. I haven't changed that much. You just call me what you always have."

"*Sí*, Sam." Froilana grinned.

"That's better. And as for Ramón and my liking the changes in him, it will not matter," Samantha said as she came back into her room and headed for the wardrobe. "As I said before, I can do without men for a while."

"The prospect of seeing Ramón again does not excite you? Not even a little?"

"Excite me? Heavens no." Samantha laughed. "I'm happy just being home. I don't need any more than that."

"But what then did you think of El Carnicero? Were you not excited by the stories about him?"

Samantha turned around and gazed curiously at Froilana. "El Carnicero? The Butcher? What kind of name is that?"

"It is said he cuts up his enemies and serves them to his dogs, piece by piece. That is how he came by the name," she said breathlessly.

"Lana! How disgusting!"

Froilana shrugged. "I do not believe *that* story about him, but the other things, *sí*. They say he is *mucho hombre*, but very mean. They also say he is very ugly, but that he can have any woman he wants. I wonder—"

"Wait a minute, Lana." Samantha interrupted. "Who are we talking about? Who the devil is this Carnicero you find so fascinating?"

Froilana's dark eyes widened. "You do not know? *El patrón* did not tell you?"

"No, my father didn't say anything about it," Samantha replied.

"*Ay!*" the older girl gasped. "*Mamacita* will take a stick to me for telling you!"

"But you haven't told me anything much," Samantha said impatiently. "Who is El Carnicero?"

"No! I say no more. I go now."

"Lana!" But the girl ran from the room, leaving Samantha confused. "Damn and be damned, what the hell was that all about?" she muttered to herself as she dressed quickly in a jade-green riding outfit of suede and a bright yellow silk shirt.

The Butcher. A man who cut up his enemies. What sort of man would kill people in this time of peace? A general from the revolution, perhaps? There had been many fierce men on both sides. An outlaw, perhaps, or an official of the government? The liberals had triumphed in the revolution, and Juárez was president. But the president could not control the officials in all of his states.

Soon she joined her father for a breakfast of thick corn cakes, ham, and hot, strong coffee.

"Who is El Carnicero?" she asked him.

"Where did you hear that name?" Her father sat back and frowned.

"What difference does it make?" she rejoined. "Who is he?"

Her father hesitated for several moments, then replied, "He's no one you need to be concerned about."

"Father, you're evading. Why didn't you tell me about this man?"

"He's a bandit, Sammy, a man who has gained notoriety farther south in the past several years."

A bandit. "Why is he being talked about here?"

Hamilton sighed. "Because the fellow came north recently. He and his followers are living in the West Sierras now."

"You mean they're hiding out there? Has no one tried to get them out?"

"You know as well as I, Samantha, that if someone wanted to hide out in those mountains, it would be almost impossible to find him."

Everything fell into place suddenly. "Has this *bandido* been giving you trouble?"

"I can't be sure it's the same man."

"The chickens and the cattle?"

"It's possible, of course. Our people say it is, that El Carnicero has declared war on me for some reason. I doubt it, though. It doesn't make any sense. I've never even met the man. And besides, the Sierras are a good three, four days' ride from here."

"And that's why you think he's not the one causing you trouble?"

"Yes. There are other ranches closer to the mountains that he could prey on far more easily. It doesn't make any sense for him to ride so far to forage for food and make mischief here. And then there is another good reason, which the *vaqueros* who insist it is him constantly ignore. This man is supposed to be a cold-blooded killer, yet in all the trouble we've been having, no one has been hurt. And no one has seen him or any of his band. They say that when El Carnicero rides, he rides with all his men, dozens of them. Yet whenever something happens here on the ranch, the tracks of only a few men are ever found."

"Which would indicate drifters." Samantha spoke her thoughts aloud.

"Yes."

"Then why are people so convinced it is El Carnicero?"

Hamilton shrugged. "Having a famous bandit declare war on you is more exciting than drifters passing through. People love dramatic stories. Once it was learned that the famous bandit was in the area, every mishap was blamed on him. They gossip about him constantly, because he has brought excitement and danger, and they love it."

"Is there any real danger?"

"Nonsense," Hamilton scoffed. "Don't you go believing any stories. That's why I didn't want you to hear about this bandit. I didn't want you to be worrying."

"I wouldn't have worried a great deal, father. We've had bandits in the area before now."

"I'm glad you're being sensible about it." He leaned forward again and looked her over carefully. "You're wearing your riding outfit. Were you going out?"

She grinned impishly. "That was always my habit, wasn't it? To ride in the mornings. I'm eager to get back to my old routine."

"I hope your routine doesn't still include going out to work the range with the men?"

Samantha laughed. "Do I detect a note of disapproval? No, father, I won't be working the range anymore. My wild days are over," she assured him.

"You don't know how glad I am to hear that." He grinned. "I know you will have sense enough also to take an escort with you for your rides."

"To ride on our own land?" Samantha laughed. "Don't be ridiculous, father."

"Now, Sammy, you're not a child any longer. A young woman shouldn't go out without an escort."

"Let's not fight, father," Samantha sighed. "I'm not giving up my freedom simply because I'm a few years older."

"Sammy—"

"Why, you old faker." She had heard the alarm in his voice. "You really are worried about this *bandido*, aren't you?"

"It doesn't hurt to be careful, Sammy."

Samantha hesitated, then stood up. "Very well, father, I'll play it your way for a while," she conceded. She turned to leave, then stopped and grinned mischievously at him. "But it won't do any good, you know. The *vaqueros* can't keep up with me. They never could."

Samantha rode in the direction of the south range, racing as fast as she could, leaving her two-man escort far behind. El Cid was a gem. He seemed to fly through the air. Samantha was exhilarated. She hadn't raced like that for years. Her saddle was magnificent, of the best Spanish leather, mounted with silver and fancy with fine carvings and gold braid. It suited El Cid.

She dismounted atop a small hill and stood waiting for the *vaqueros*. She could see for miles, miles of flat plains, with a few hills breaking the monotony. Flat land dotted with cactus and a few lonely trees. But to the west were the magnificent mountains—and smoke.

Samantha stared off into the distance at the spiral of black smoke, her brow furrowing. She mounted immediately and rode to join her escort, pointing out the smoke before she passed them, heading for it. She reached the burned-out line shack in only fifteen minutes, finding just a smoldering pile of rubble. She sat on her horse, looking off in all directions, but there was no sign of anybody nearby.

When the two *vaqueros* finally reached her, she asked, "What could have started this fire?"

"El Carnicero," Luis answered promptly.

Luis, Manuel and Maria's oldest son, should have had better sense, Samantha thought. "Look around, Luis. There is no one here. Do you see any tracks?"

"No, but it was El Carnicero," he replied stubbornly. "The fire has burned out already. He has had plenty time to get away. And this is the second fire here in a week."

Her eyes widened. "You mean this shack had just been built after another fire?"

"*Sí*. It was finished only yesterday."

Samantha frowned. "How many fires have there been?"

"Nine in the last two weeks."

"Nine!" she gasped. "The storehouse? Was that one of the fires?"

Luis nodded. "Such a waste, that fire. So much food and supplies burned to nothing. And so close to the *rancho*. El Carnicero, he dares much."

Samantha said nothing further. She rode back to the ranch in a spirit of hurt and disappointment. Her father had lied to her. He had talked of repairs, when actually buildings had been burned down. Why had he lied to her? And what else, she asked herself, wasn't he telling her?

Chapter 14

WHEN Samantha returned, she saw Ramón Baroja's horse in the stable. She recognized the mustang and the rich silver-mounted saddle, emblazoned with the initials RMNB for Ramón Mateo Nuñez de Baroja.

Samantha was not interested in seeing Ramón just then. It was Manuel she wanted to talk to, the one man she knew would be honest with her, and she found him beyond the branding corrals, where the workers' houses were all located. Manuel was sitting on the steps of his little house, eating a lunch of chili and fat enchiladas in the shade of a porch cluttered with potted plants and bright wicker chairs.

"*Hola,* Sam," he called as she approached. "There is one waiting for you at the house. He came soon after you rode out. Did you not see him?"

"Ramón can wait," she replied, sitting down on the steps beside him, removing her wide-brimmed hat. "It's you I want to talk to, Manuel. You know my father as well as I—at least, as well as I *thought* I knew him. Perhaps you know him better."

"What is wrong, *chica?*" he interrupted, understanding her troubled mood.

"Why would he lie to me?"

Manuel was amused, not shocked. "And what has he lied about?"

"All the trouble we're having. He wasn't even going to tell me about it at first. If Lana hadn't mentioned—"

"Lana!" Manuel's temper rose. "My *hija,* she has a big mouth. If *el patrón* did not want you to know, then you should not have found out."

"Nonsense. With everyone talking about it, I would have found out soon enough. But that is beside the point. Last night, when we talked of the ranch, father told me that the line shacks had needed repairs. Today I found out that they were destroyed by fire and had to be rebuilt for that reason."

"Wait, Sam. Your father did not lie to you. Many repairs were made while you were gone. What year does not pass without repairs?"

"I'll grant you that. But why didn't he tell me about the fires? Even the storehouse burned down. But he didn't tell me that, only that he had built a new one."

"Is this why you say he has lied?" Manuel chided her, grinning.

"He didn't tell me the whole truth," Samantha pointed out firmly. "That is the same as lying, Manuel."

"If he did not tell you, perhaps it is only because he did not think to tell you. He has a lot on his mind lately."

"I don't wonder, with all these fires and thefts and God-only-knows-what-else he's keeping from me."

"But can you not see that he might only have forgotten these things?"

"Oh, I suppose," she admitted grudgingly. "But tell me, what do you think is going on? Do you believe this Carnicero is responsible?"

Manuel shrugged. "How can I say, *niña,* when I have only just returned? There was no trouble when I left for New Mexico to bring you home. I learned of this *bandido* last night for the first time, when Maria filled my ears with all the news."

"I'll bet *you* learned everything," she said bitterly. Maria always knew everything that went on at the ranch.

"Perhaps," he chuckled, knowing her thoughts.

"Well? Is the bandit causing all the trouble, even though he is hiding out so far from here? Or is it just coincidence, so many things happening at once? My father says it could be drifters."

"Drifters? No." Manuel frowned. "For the cattle, *sí*. Maybe even a few of the fires. But for what reason would a man passing through destroy the mine?"

"Destroy?" Samantha gasped at this additional news. "What do you mean, destroy?"

"Luis said there was no doubt that dynamite caused the explosion that collapsed the mine."

"Accidents, he told me. Accidents!" Samantha gasped. "Manuel, another shack was set on fire this morning. I saw it smoldering."

"*Dios!*"

"Never mind calling on God. He's too busy to bother with mischief going on here."

"But you might have been closer to the area when the fire was started. You might even have come upon the men who set it. *Dios*, Sam!" Manuel exclaimed. "You might have been killed!"

"Nonsense. It was probably only one man or two who set that fire."

He threw his arms up in frustration. "Certainly it takes only one man to set a fire, but there still might have been a dozen others with him."

"There was no evidence of many men, Manuel," she insisted. "In fact, I found no tracks at all."

"Luis tells me there is never any sign," Manuel said. "Yet others could have been nearby, watching. The men doing this always seem to know where our men are, and they strike when no one is nearby. But you, *niña*, you ride where you will—you never follow the same path."

"What are you getting at, Manuel?"

"That you could come upon these men. They would not expect a *señorita* to be riding the range, and you never keep to a route."

"So?"

"So? It is not safe for you to go out, even with an escort. I must speak to *el patrón* about this."

Samantha bristled. "Before you do that, Manuel, I want you to tell me everything that Maria confided to you last night—everything. Let me be the judge of whether it's safe or not."

He did, in vivid detail. Samantha managed to hold her tongue, even as the news got worse and worse. Besides the mine explosion, the stolen chickens, the few dead cows, and the fires, there had been two dozen mustangs stolen, and not just a few cattle, but over a hundred head. That was rustling, pure and simple. That Samantha could understand. But the rest—a large initial "C" smeared one night with blood on every outside door of the ranch. Was this El Carnicero's way of bragging over the deeds he had done? Or was it someone else pointing blame at the bandit?

And that was still not all of it. Two messages had been left, one stuck to the carcass of a dead cow, the other stabbed with a rusty dagger into the front door of the house.

"No wonder they say the *bandido* has declared war on my father," Samantha gasped when Manuel was through. "What did those messages say?"

"Only *el patrón* knows, and he has told no one."

"But were they signed by El Carnicero?"

"I do not know that either," Manuel replied.

Samantha shook her head in disbelief. "I find it inconceivable that all of these things could have happened in only the last two weeks."

"I felt the same way. But Maria says something happens every day. And now you tell me there has been a fire today."

"It really does sound as if a war is going on—a one-sided war," Samantha remarked. "Isn't my father doing anything about it?"

"He has not notified the authorities, if that is what you mean. Not yet."

"Don't you think he should?"

"What can they do, Sam, that we cannot do?" Manuel said a little indignantly.

"I suppose you're right," she replied, remembering the last time the *soldados* were called when cattle were stolen. They had not been eager to help the *americano,* as they called her father. "But what exactly is my father doing?"

"He has had men follow the tracks left, but the tracks always vanish after a few miles. He has posted guards at night around the *rancho* since the last time they came here. The cattle and horses are being brought in off the range, closer to home, and men are left with them at all times now."

"Is that all?"

"What else is there, *niña?* We are prepared, but the *rancho* is too large. The *bandidos* strike our weak points, when no one is there. They are never seen."

"You just called them bandits. So you *do* think it is El Carnicero."

"You mistake me, Sam," Manuel said quickly. "There are many *bandidos*—not just this one."

"I wish I could meet this one," Samantha said impulsively.

"*Madre de Dios!*" Manuel exclaimed. "He is one man you must pray never to meet, *niña*. They say he hates *gringos* with a madness and kills them with more pleasure than he does his worst enemies."

Samantha changed the subject. "What else do you know about this man?"

But Manuel stood up. "You keep an old man from his work, *niña*. Enough questions for one day."

"Oh, no, Manuel." She caught his arm and pulled him back down beside her. "You do know more, don't you?"

"Sam—"

"Tell me!"

He sighed. "I saw him once. It was many years ago." He gazed off into the distance. "It was the time *el patrón* sent me to Mexico City to bring back that big trough you bathe in."

"My bathtub?" She grinned.

"*Sí.* On my way back I stopped at a *cantina* in a small town—I do not remember the name of it. El Carnicero had been brought there, captured by *soldados* when he was wounded raiding a village nearby. They were taking him to Mexico City. It was said the *bandido* had massacred everyone in that village, not even a woman or a child was left alive to tell the horror of it."

Samantha had turned pale. "Did you believe that?"

"Why should the *soldados* lie? They were there. They saw it all. But this was during the revolution, *niña.* Such things happened often, innocents killed on both sides by both armies."

"Are you saying El Carnicero was a soldier then, a *guerrillero?*"

"They say he fought for both sides during the war, on whichever side was winning at the time. I do not know if that's true. You can't believe everything you hear."

"But what happened when you saw him? Was he really terribly ugly? Lana says he is."

Manuel shrugged. "Who is to say if a man is ugly? I could not tell. I could barely see him because he was so covered in filth and blood."

"But was he tall? Short? Fat? What?"

Manuel strained to remember. "He was a short man, with dark hair surrounding his face. His body was like a barrel, his arms long and like so." He touched his fingers together to form a large circle. "If a man can be called ugly because he looks like the devil, then *sí,* he is ugly. I have never seen such a mean-looking *hombre.*"

"Was he taken to Mexico City?"

"No, *niña.* He would be dead now if he hadn't escaped

that very day before my eyes, while most of the *soldados* were busy in the *cantina*. Some of his followers had sneaked into town. They killed his guards, and he got away. So he went on to rob and massacre again and again."

"He's not doing that here, though. Killing I mean," she said thoughtfully.

"No, he is not."

Wheedling information out of the old *vaquero* was becoming very wearing. "You're just not going to give me your opinion, are you?" Samantha sighed, exasperated.

"You have not yet given me yours," Manuel countered smoothly.

"Because I don't have one!" Samantha exploded. "I haven't really thought about it."

"Nor have I," he replied. "You forget we have both only just returned."

"Oh!" She stood up to leave. "At least *you* had Maria to tell you everything. I had to pry the truth out of you—which was not easy! You *have* told me all of it, haven't you? You didn't leave anything out?"

"No, Sam. You know as much as I know."

"Well, I intend to find out one thing more—what was in those messages. It's time my father started being more truthful."

With that thought in mind, Samantha strode determinedly toward the house, passing the corral and stable and entering the house through the side patio, which led from the stable. But two steps inside, she collided with a figure of medium height in a short bolero jacket and bell-shaped pants, the chamois leather of the suit intricately embroidered with white braid.

It had been a long time since Samantha had seen a typically Spanish outfit, and she knew without even seeing his face that the owner of the costume could be only Ramón Mateo Nuñez de Baroja. She had completely forgotten that he was waiting for her. El Carnicero had pushed him out of her thoughts.

Samantha tilted her head back to see his face. His appearance surprised her. There was a thick blond mustache added to the adult Ramón, and there was also a marked masculinity in his face, which had not been there before.

"Ramón, *mi amigo.*" Samantha spoke at last.

She hesitated, greeting him, as she had always done, with an innocent sisterly kiss on the cheek. This new Ramón was imposing, a stranger. This was not the boy she had once teased, calling him the white sheep of his family because he was the only fair-haired one.

"Samantha." He said her name softly, wonderingly. And then he gave her a brilliant smile. "Samantha! I had forgotten how truly beautiful you are. And now—"

"Yes, I know, I know." She cut him off with a laugh. "I've grown up—I'm a woman now."

"Not just that," he assured her, taking her hands, spreading her arms so that he could look her over. "Now you are even more beautiful. And where is my greeting?"

Without giving her a chance to answer, he pulled her forward for a kiss. He captured her mouth with his. There was nothing brotherly about it.

The kiss lingered, but when Ramón started to push his tongue through her closed lips, Samantha drew away abruptly. "You never used to do *that!*"

"You never would have allowed me to." He grinned. His grin was infectious.

"I suppose not." She gave him an impish smile in return. "I would have laid my fist to your cheek and told you to go home."

Ramón threw back his head and laughed. "You do not say, as a woman would say, that you would have slapped me. You say, as a man would say, that you would have punched me." And he added with mock severity, "I think you did not stay at your Eastern school long enough, Samantha. There are still things I must break you of."

Samantha stiffened, and her eyes flashed angrily. *"Break me! I—"*

But Ramón quickly put his finger to her lips. "Forgive me, Sam. I was only teasing you." He coaxed her with that charming smile. "I know as well as anyone does that no one can break you."

"I'm glad you understand that, Ramón. I may look more like a lady now, but I will never think the way ladies are supposed to think. I tried, and it..."

Samantha turned away, repelled by the turn of her thoughts. She had almost told Ramón too much. She had given so much effort to acting like a lady for Adrien that the effort had blinded her to what he was. Could that also be why she had misjudged Hank Chavez?

"What is it, *niña?*" Ramón ventured quietly, turning her around to face him again. "You are looking so miserable."

Samantha rubbed her forehead. Lord, couldn't a day go by without that devil popping into her thoughts? She needed a distraction, and Ramón supplied it.

"Niña?" Her vivid green eyes narrowed, and her hands went to her hips. So you think you are old enough to call me that, do you?"

"Now, Sam..."

"You were no bigger than I when I left here, and not very much older either," she continued in a stern tone. "But now that you are taller, you think you are much older, as well, eh? Is that it?"

"You wound me, Samantha." His brown eyes turned mournful. "I had forgotten this quick temper of yours."

She suddenly grinned. "Now who cannot take a little teasing—*niño?"*

With a gleeful laugh, Samantha mussed his blond hair, then dashed around him and ran into the *sala*. By the time he turned around to touch her, she was gone. He followed her to the center of the large room and found that her carefree mood had gone as quickly as it had come.

"Wasn't my father in here with you?"

"*Sí*, he kept me company while I waited for you—several hours I might add."

Samantha ignored that. "Where is he?"

"He left when one of your *vaqueros* reported a fire."

"The line shack to the west?"

"*Sí*."

"Damn! I wanted to talk to him. Now there's no telling when he'll be back."

"Then talk to me instead." Ramón came up behind her. "I have waited forever to see you again. Come, sit here with me." He gestured to the long sofa.

She let him take her mind off her father and those mysterious messages for an hour. But as soon as Ramón left, her thoughts returned to the problem of El Carnicero. There was something more complicated there than just cattle rustling and a little malicious damage. What was really going on? She was certain her father knew. And she wouldn't let him evade the issue again. There would be no more of his "don't worry, Sam, there's nothing to be concerned about." She knew better.

It was long past the dinner hour when Hamilton Kingsley returned. Samantha was asleep. She had worked herself into such an anxious state while waiting that she had fallen into an exhausted sleep. He did not wake her.

Chapter 15

THE plains were bathed in the delicate pink glow of approaching day. Samantha woke at dawn to see the dark blue sky streak with purple over the mountains beyond her window. She knew that, behind the ranch to the east, the sky would be vivid with reds and oranges.

She did not often awaken at dawn, and instantly, realizing that she was fully clothed, she remembered falling asleep simply because she had rested for a few minutes. She had missed the opportunity to speak to her father.

She would speak to him now, before he had a chance to avoid her again. She would wait outside his door if necessary, just in case he decided to sneak away. She knew he wasn't looking forward to facing her with the truth, not after he had tried to pretend nothing was wrong. No, he wouldn't want to see her.

Samantha rolled off the bed, which was still made but rumpled. There was a chill coming through her open window, but she didn't feel the cold floor, because she was still wearing her soft leather house shoes. Sleeping with her shoes on!

She quickly tore off the green striped linen dress and donned a full beige buckskin skirt. It was split up the middle and fell only halfway down her shins. A saffron yellow blouse of heavy linen was enough even in that chilly morning air, but she also grabbed her fringed buckskin jacket that matched the skirt. Of all the outfits she had designed herself, she liked this one best. It made her feel like a cowgirl. She liked feeling equal to the land, equal to the harsh elements.

Picking up her high leather boots, she carried them over to the bed and put them on. All of her riding outfits and boots still fit. It didn't matter if the skirts were a little short. They had always reached daringly above her ankles anyway, and an inch or two higher was of little concern, because her boots were nearly all knee length. Her waist had not thickened in three years, but her many shirts and blouses were a trifle tight now.

The gunbelt she always wore when she was riding was draped over the foot of the bed, but she didn't need to strap it on yet. She grinned, thinking that it might intimidate her father while they talked—or argued. She would come back later for her gun and hat, when things were settled and she could go out for her morning ride.

Standing, Samantha straightened her skirt, then crossed to her dresser for an ivory-backed brush. A few quick brushes and a piece of leather braid to tie them back was all the attention she gave her streaming auburn locks. She turned to leave her room, which was already bright with the increasing light outside. She took a few steps toward the window first, to see what kind of day it would be. And then she saw the smoke.

There was a great gray-brown wall of smoke rising higher each moment, threatening to hide her beautiful mountains behind it. It was far away, far enough to be...the crop fields!

"Damn them to hell!" she cried, gripping her window sill, wanting to disbelieve what she was seeing.

Instead of staying in one place, spiraling higher, the wall of smoke moved first south and then north, spreading on and on in both directions. After a while she could see nothing but smoke, relentless smoke.

With a cry, Samantha grabbed her gunbelt and hat and ran from the room. She pounded twice on her father's door before she rushed into his room.

"They've set the west fields on fire!"

Hamilton was too stunned to speak. Watching his daughter stomp back and forth in agitation as she buckled on her gunbelt with stiff fingers, his bleary green eyes focused with effort.

"Get up!" she screamed. "It's too late to save the fields, but Juan and his boy are in the field camp. They might be dead!"

It worked. Hamilton swung out of bed, the message finally reaching his sleep-clouded brain.

"I'll get the horses ready and wake the men," Samantha called as she turned to leave the room. "I'll meet you out front. Hurry!"

"Sam, wait! You're not going!"

But she was running down the hall. He knew damned well his order was falling on deaf ears anyway.

Hamilton cursed the day he'd first let those green eyes twist his heart. She had been such a defiant little creature in their early years together. He had spoiled her terribly, his new daughter, the daughter he'd tried for nine years to bring home. After all the time they'd been apart, he'd felt he had to earn her love. He'd done anything she asked of him.

It was his fault that she was so independent, so willful. It was his fault, too, that she was such a little hellion sometimes. He had hoped the Eastern school would temper her, but it hadn't. He grimaced, thinking of his daughter in that buckskin outfit, a gun strapped to her thigh. His Samantha...a better shot than even he was! That wasn't right. She should have no desire to tote a gun, to ride the range on her own. She should wear silk and lace.

Why did she have to be so damned—different? But how he loved her, this unique child of his. Even with her temper and stubbornness, she meant the world to him. He hadn't seen Sheldon since he was a baby. It had caused him years of heartache, but now he considered that he didn't have a son. Samantha was all he had.

She was riding away as he reached his horse. Hamilton mounted and, having selected ten of the best riders to follow, set off after her.

He couldn't afford to take all his men with him, couldn't take the chance that this wasn't a trap, a fire meant to lure them away from the house. He might return to find the house in flames, too. It was just as well that Samantha was with him. He could keep an eye on her. He knew he would die if anything ever happened to that girl.

Since receiving the first message, Hamilton had known for certain that El Carnicero was responsible for everything. That miserable bastard! The audacity, ordering Hamilton to leave Mexico! It was absurd, yet the bandit was making certain that Hamilton seriously considered the ultimatum. No outlaw was going to dictate to him, however. He'd bring in his own army of mercenaries before he'd leave. He'd blow The Butcher right out of those mountains. And now, with this attack, it was time to think of doing just that.

They were drawing close to the field camp, and smoke was heavy. Samantha had been right—it was too late to save the fields. The earth was scarred black and no longer burning, but the small camp of thatched huts where the workers stayed during harvest and planting was still roaring, black smoke belching skyward.

Samantha rode straight to the huts before Hamilton could stop her. She was the first to see Juan, beyond the camp, leaning back under a gnarled tree and holding his head in his hands. His small son knelt beside him, staring up at his father.

"Juan!" cried Samantha as she slid from her horse and bent over the two.

The child, no more than seven, was wide-eyed with terror. Juan himself was crying, holding his hands to his forehead where a deep gash bled.

"Patrona?" he looked up in a daze. "I tried to stop them."

"Of course you did, Juan," she replied gently.

"There were too many of them." He was mumbling now. "One of them hit me with a rifle, but I still tried— until they said they would kill my *hijo.*"

"It is not your fault, Juan. Your life and the boy's are more important."

He seemed to understand. But he was gripped by a sudden fear just then and grabbed her arm, his fingers clenching painfully.

"You are not alone, *patrona?* Please! Say you did not come here alone!"

"Do not worry, Juan. My father is here. We will get you back to the ranch safely."

"No! You must go—quickly. They are still here. They have not gone!"

Before the Mexican's frantic words could sink in fully, Samantha's father was behind her, pulling her out from under the tree.

"Did—did you hear what Juan said?"

"Yes," Hamilton growled. "But I didn't need to. Look."

She followed his hard gaze to a small hill on the other side of the field. Now that the smoke was not so heavy, she could see clearly. There were fifteen men on horses spread out across the hill. Samantha had never seen such a menacing-looking group. They sat watching, sunlight glinting off crossed bandoliers and long knives. Wide sombreros hid dark faces.

Her father pulled her to her horse and helped her to mount quickly. She had never seen him look the way he did.

"Ride, Sam," he ordered firmly. "Get back to the ranch *now.*"

"No." Her voice held defiance, but was as firm as his.

He scowled darkly. "Get out of here!"

"I'm not going without you."

"For God's sake, will you do as I say for once?" His voice rose. "We're outnumbered here."

"Exactly. You'll need every gun."

Hamilton stared, incredulous. "You can just bury that bravado right now, little girl. There could be more men behind that hill. We're not riding into any trap."

She saw the wisdom of it. "Let's go, then."

"You start out now. We'll catch up with you as soon as we get Juan and the boy on horses." He signaled Manuel and Luis to do just that. "Go on now, Sam."

"I'll wait."

Hamilton grew furious. "Don't you realize that every second is precious right now? This is the first time the bandits haven't run from their crime. They're feeling bold, Sam. They could attack at any moment."

"I'll wait," she said again, her mouth set firmly. "I'm not going to leave you here alone, father."

He glared at her, shaking his head, then turned to help the injured Juan onto a horse.

Across the blackened field, the bandits held their ground. They had not moved. They seemed to be waiting for something. But what? To be attacked, or to attack? Samantha could kill six of them before she had to load her gun again, and another six before they came close enough to do her any damage. In a good position, she could pick off every one of them.

She hated to turn tail and run, and was glad that they didn't race away from the area like cowards. Through caution and in deference to Juan's injury, they moved slowly, rifles in hand, prepared to shoot if attacked. The bandits didn't follow. Samantha looked back once and saw that they had not moved from the hill. Was this all just for show?

After what seemed an eternity, they reached the ranch. Juan was taken away to have his injury tended, and Samantha followed her father into the house. He was stiff-backed as he marched across the patio and into the *sala*, and as they entered the room, he turned on her. "That's it!" he shouted. "That—is—it! That's the last time you will defy me!"

"Calm down, father." Samantha spoke gently. "We can discuss this reasonably, you know."

"Now you want to be reasonable? Why couldn't you have been reasonable out there? You risked your life!"

"I didn't see it that way."

"You never do!" he said sharply. "But you're too old to be acting like a child."

"Then don't treat me like one!" she snapped back, adding more calmly, "I was aware of the situation, father. I know very well we could have been attacked at any moment. But I could have taken care of myself—better than you, in fact. I would have shot three men with my Colt before you hit even one."

"That is not the point. You're my daughter, Samantha, not my son. You shouldn't have been in danger at all. I wanted to protect you, to get you away from danger."

"Father, those protective feelings run in me, as well. I couldn't leave you. I just couldn't."

He sighed and sank into a chair. "You just don't understand, Sam. I'm an old man, I've lived my life. But yours is all ahead of you. You're all I have. If anything happened to you...I wouldn't have any reason to go on living. You must not take chances."

"Now stop it!" she said hoarsely, uncomfortable with the way he was talking. "You're all I have, too, you know."

"No, Sam. You'll have a husband and children. You will have others to love. God, I should never have let you leave the house this morning, but I never dreamed they would still be there. When I think of what might have happened..."

"Now don't start blaming yourself."

"I'll blame myself if I damn well please!" He sat up sharply and glared at her. "But that's the last time you'll be placed in danger, my girl. You're not leaving this house again until the trouble is over!"

"You're going too far!" she protested.

"No, I'm not. I'm quite serious, Sam. There will be no more morning rides, not even with an escort."

"I won't stand for it," she warned, her temper on the rise.

"Yes you will, or, by God, I'll put bars on your windows and lock you in your room."

Emerald sparks shot from her eyes as she realized that he meant it. "For how long?" she demanded coldly. "Just how long do you intend to keep me a prisoner?"

"You needn't sound so offended. I'm only denying you your morning ride, and only for the sake of safety."

"How long?"

"A week, maybe. I'll send for the authorities today. But if they can't help, then I'll get my own army in here. We'll see how El Carnicero likes having the tables turned on him."

"At least you're admitting the truth now," Samantha said bitterly. She took satisfaction from her father's expression. He actually flinched. "I'll agree to a week on one condition."

"What?" he asked wearily, suspicious.

"You tell me what was in those messages The Butcher left for you."

To her surprise, he looked relieved. "I'll do better than that." He got up and left the room, returning a moment later with two dirty, crumpled sheets of paper. "Here, read them."

They were written in a crude scrawl, and each was signed with a large "C." One said: *"Go home, Gringo."* The other was clearer. *"Mexico hates you, Gringo. You will die if you stay here. Go home."*

"Manuel told me he hates *gringos* passionately," she said after a moment.

"He hasn't given up trying to evict me. He's grown

bolder. But the last straw was seeing you in danger. The *bandido* will get the war he wants now."

"I'll wait a week, father, I promise. But no more than a week."

He knew she meant it.

Chapter 16

THAT next week was the slowest of Samantha's life. But the trouble seemed to be over. *Soldados* had charged into the mountains. Reports came back slowly. Evidence was found in an old abandoned village that pointed to many men having stayed there. But they were gone. The Mexican soldiers then went deeper into the mountains, but there were no tracks to follow, and no sign of the bandits. It was the general consensus that El Carnicero had returned to his southern territory. Samantha was quick to agree, and soon the week was over.

She was ready to ride again, but her father insisted that she take four *vaqueros* with her.

"But the trouble is over," she protested. "The Butcher has gone."

"We won't know that for sure until more time passes," Hamilton insisted. "Four men, Sam, and you'll stay close to the ranch, as well."

"Why didn't you tell me about all these conditions last week?" she stormed. "You were afraid to, weren't you?"

"Be reasonable. I would really rather you didn't go out at all. Not yet. At least give me the peace of mind of knowing that you're well protected."

Samantha gritted her teeth. "All right, I'll give you one more week—but no more. After that I have my freedom back completely and you stop treating me like a child."

"Agreed—as long as nothing happens in the meantime." She turned to stalk away, but Hamilton added, "And these conditions include your staying with your escort, not racing ahead of them, Sam."

"Oh!"

Samantha was still furious when she stormed into the stable to get El Cid, but Ramón was waiting, and he tried to coax her out of her mood. She had forgotten that he had promised to join her for a ride. Now she would have five men along to protect her—though she would most likely end up protecting them if anything happened.

She waited while her escort readied their horses, and Ramón sat his horse, smiling at her vexation. So much trouble for just a few hours' ride!

Ramón and Samantha had returned to their old camaraderie, and she was grateful for his company, but there was often a difference in his behavior toward her, and she was disturbed by it. There was sometimes a dark passion in Ramón's eyes. Surely he was not falling in love with her, she told herself. She hoped not, for her feelings did not run that way.

He looked exceptionally handsome today in his black leather waist-length jacket and black pants that flared out at the knees. Samantha was wearing soft leather herself, a dark-chocolate-brown skirt and vest embroidered along the hems with fancy gold thread. Her blouse was brown-and-beige-striped moiré silk, with cuffs on the long sleeves and a wide collar opened only discreetly. She wore her hair pinned up under a wide-brimmed brown hat.

She sighed. She had planned to give El Cid a vigorous workout. Now she would have to go slowly, to allow her escort to keep up with her—or would she? As they rode away from the ranch at a leisurely pace, Samantha kept looking at Ramón's gray stallion. It was a powerful horse, nearly as spirited as El Cid. They were riding abreast, heading south, the four *vaqueros* a good twenty yards behind Ramón and Samantha. She looked sideways at Ramón, her lips curling in a mischievous grin.

"Ramón, race me to that far hill at the end of the south range. You know the one."

But he shook his head firmly. "No, Samantha. We are no longer children."

"What does that have to do with it? I want to race."

"No. Your father would not like it."

Samantha's grin deepened. "I'll wager you," she bribed. "If I lose, I'll dance the *jarabe* for you. But, of course, I won't lose."

Ramón's eyes brightened. Only once had he seen her dance the passionate Mexican dances that Froilana had taught her. She had set his blood afire that time, when he was seventeen. He would give anything to see her wear the loose, deep-necked *camisa* and the full red skirt that sparkled with bangles, to see her hair cascading down her back like a cloak of fire, to have her dance, only for him, a dance of passion.

Samantha knew by his sudden change of expression that she had won. As he nodded, she dug her heels into El Cid and shot off ahead of Ramón. But Ramón caught up with her quickly. One mile passed, then two. She pushed El Cid to his limit. She did not look back to see how far behind her escort was trailing. She bent down against the wind, her hat whipping off to bounce on her shoulders, caught by the cord around her neck. She was flying. She was free. She had never felt better.

The hill was just ahead, and she sensed Ramón falling back. The hill sloped gently at least twenty feet upward, and Samantha charged to the top, laughing in delight. She had won. At the top she turned sharply and slid off El Cid to look down the hill. Ramón was only halfway up. She could not even see the *vaqueros*.

"I told you I—"

The words died in her throat as a hand slipped over her mouth from behind her. She jerked, startled. In the next second her hand went to the gun on her hip. But another hand was pulling it out of the holster before she could touch it.

Ramón rode to the hilltop, his eyes wide. Three men were standing there, one pointing a rifle at him. He wore bandoliers across his chest, and long pistols on his hips. Another man in a poncho and a large sombrero was holding the horses, five of them including El Cid. A third man in a brightly striped serape was standing behind Samantha, holding her own weapon on her, his other hand covering her mouth.

Seeing Samantha's wide eyes staring up at him, Ramón went a little crazy. He wasn't sure whether it was fear or anger in those green eyes he loved so much, but he was sure she was beseeching him for help. He went for his gun, but a rifle exploded before he reached it. The blast, at close range, whipped him off his horse, and he tumbled halfway down the hill before he could stop his fall.

Samantha came out of shock and bit the hand over her mouth. She was suddenly free then, and ran down the hill screaming Ramón's name. He was trying to sit up, but the effort was too much, and he fell back, spent. There was a big, gaping hole in his shoulder. Samantha caught her breath.

"Ah, Ramón, you were so brave! But you shouldn't have done that. You will be all right, though." She was talking through tears, talking just to hear the sound of her own voice, to ease the sickening turning of her stomach. "I swear you will be all right. I will take you home and tend you myself."

"You will not take him, *señorita*."

At that moment, Samantha realized that they were not alone. Somehow, she had forgotten her assailants. She turned and looked at the two men who had followed her down the hill. It was the first she had seen of them, and the color drained from her face. *Bandidos!* She prayed quickly that they were only after money, but she knew full well how foolish that was.

"Of course I will take him home," she said, her voice firm and unwavering. "You can steal our horses, but there are other men coming right now who will help us. Here, take this!" She angrily tore off an emerald ring from her finger and threw it at the man nearest her. "That's all I have. Now leave before my *vaqueros* get here and there is more bloodshed."

The man who had caught the ring laughed shortly. "We saw you racing ahead of your escort, *señorita*. You have left them far behind. You made our job easy for us."

"Your job? You mean your thievery!" she snapped, her eyes damning him.

She was not frightened. She was furious. And most of her fury was for herself, for riding into the trap. They had seen her coming and hidden behind the hill. And she had not even looked over the hill as she reached the top. And then to let him take her gun!

The man in the serape was shaking his head at her. He was a young man, with a short black beard and dark, piercing eyes almost as black as his long, shoulder-length hair. There was a thin scar across one cheek, but that took nothing away from his swarthy good looks. By comparison, the man with the rifle seemed a vicious beast, with a long, thick black mustache and a gap-toothed, ugly grin. The third man, still at the top of the hill, was almost unnoticeable, with dark brown hair and no outstanding characteristics. He seemed distant, reserved, and he did not join in the joking of the other two.

The handsome one spoke again, his voice still amused. "We do not wish to rob you, *señorita*." And he tossed her ring back to her.

"What then?" she demanded impatiently. "Can't you see my friend needs help? Tell me what you want and be gone."

The two men looked at each other and laughed. The ugly one, gripping his rifle, remarked in guttural Spanish, "She likes to give the orders, eh? She will not like taking them, I think."

Samantha did not let on that she had understood, but her heart began a rapid beat. She dreaded to imagine what the Mexican meant. She needed to gain control of the situation, and fast.

Ramón began moaning, and she turned back to him. His eyes were closed and he seemed barely conscious. But she saw his hand moving slowly toward his gun. His gun! It was still in his holster. As quick as lightning, she went for it.

"Do not, *señorita*."

Samantha stopped, her hand on the grip. Could she take the chance? Would they shoot her? Yes, they would. Slowly, with the greatest reluctance, she let go of the gun.

"What do you want?" she shouted in frustrated anger.

"You, *señorita*," the man with the serape said quietly, and then he turned to his companion. "Take the foolish one's gun, Diego, and give him the written message to deliver." He looked at Samantha again and explained. "Our job was to find you and take you with us."

She stared, wide-eyed, as the one who had shot Ramón took his gun and put a folded piece of paper inside his jacket. A message. Oh, God, El Carnicero left messages.

Samantha shook her head in disbelief. "Who told you to take me?"

"*El jefe*."

The leader. But who *was* the leader? she asked, and the Mexican grinned. "El Carnicero. It is his wish that you be his guest for a while, Señorita Kingsley."

Hearing him speak her name confirmed her worst fears. They knew her. El Carnicero had not left the area after all. Her father had been right. Why couldn't she have listened to him?

"No," she whispered.

"*Sí*," he countered calmly.

At that, Samantha jumped to her feet and started running down the hill, frantic. The Mexican caught her easily, and they both fell, sliding several feet before they stopped.

"Damn you!" Samantha screamed, spitting dirt. "I won't go with you!" she cried. "I refuse!"

"We waste time here, *mujer*," he replied curtly, and jerked her to her feet.

His grip on her arm was relentless; she couldn't pull away. He dragged her back up the hill, passing Ramón, who seemed deathly still. At the top, the third man guided her to a magnificent white stallion and told her to mount.

Samantha held back. "I'll ride my own horse, thank you," she said caustically.

In response, he whacked El Cid on the rump, sending him racing down the hill. "*El jefe* has sent his own horse for you, Señorita Kingsley. You will ride El Rey."

The King. It was fitting. The stallion looked like a king. His coloring reminded her of Princesa. He would have made a fine mate for her. He was too beautiful for a butcher.

"Mount now, or I will have to put you in the saddle myself," said the man with the serape.

Her head snapped toward him. "I don't see why I couldn't have ridden my own horse," she said angrily.

"Your father will understand better when your horse returns without you," the man replied, then grinned. "Besides, it is an honor for you to ride El Rey. El Carnicero prizes this horse. He cost a fortune. You understand, *el jefe* is being most generous in offering him for your use. He wishes you to know of this honor, so you will not be afraid."

Samantha managed a derisive laugh. "I am not afraid." She mounted the big horse, snatching the reins away from the man. "Why should I be?" she added confidently. "When you give me the means to escape you?"

She reined the horse up, forcing the Mexicans back, and then dug her heels into the animal, charging down the hill. But she didn't even reach the bottom before a shrill whistle stopped the stallion in his tracks and she nearly went flying over his neck. Then the Mexican was beside her, laughing as he took the reins and led her back to the top of the hill.

"You see now why El Rey is so highly prized?" he pointed out proudly.

"I see now why I am to ride him," she replied bitterly, her eyes shooting daggers at him.

The other two men were mounted and waiting by that time, and the one with her mounted, as well, but they did not ride off. She groaned as she saw why. Her escort had finally caught up with them. Each of the bandits leveled a rifle at the approaching *vaqueros*.

Samantha was enraged. "You shoot any of my men," she warned them, "and I swear I'll manage somehow to break this animal's neck. You think your boss will be pleased when you return without his precious horse?"

The bandit in the serape glared at Samantha with angry black eyes, but he turned his rifle away from the *vaqueros*—pointing it at her instead. The four men of her escort had just reached the bottom of the hill, and they halted in a cloud of dust when they saw her and her captor.

The bandit leader shouted down the hill now. "The *caballero* has a message on him for Señor Kingsley. Deliver it!" He added, "If you follow—she dies!"

Samantha was led down the opposite side of the hill, the leader holding her reins. The *vaqueros* were afraid to follow, to risk her life. She knew she was alone now, with no hope of help until the ransom message was given to her father.

They rode south, keeping to a grueling pace. At noon they suddenly changed direction, riding west, toward the mountains. The horses were tiring by then, and they slowed a little but didn't stop to rest, even though the midday sun was beating down mercilessly.

Samantha knew for herself how many hidden canyons and valleys there were in the Sierra Madres, places to hide where a large group of men would never be found. She was being taken to one of those hidden places. Would *she* ever be found? Oh, God, she couldn't think about what lay ahead. She had heard too many terrible things about El Carnicero.

They stopped late that night, right out on the open plain. The men tended the horses before they broke out dried food for themselves. Diego brought Samantha some dried beef, several cold, greasy tortillas, and a flask of wine, of all things. She knew they were probably drinking tequila, and the fact that they had brought wine for her showed a measure of consideration. She was surprised and grateful.

Her hunger was appeased quickly, and she realized how exhausted she was. She ached all over and needed sleep desperately, but she resisted it with all her will. If the bandits slept, she might be able to escape.

There was no fire, but a half-moon lit the plains and allowed her to watch the three men as they sat talking together in soft whispers. She waited for them to settle down, praying they would leave her alone. As she waited, watching them, she fought to keep her eyes open. She waited what seemed like hours, but it was really only ten minutes or so before the three men stood up. Serape, as she had begun to think of him, went to the horses and produced a blanket. He brought it to Samantha. She held her breath as he approached, fearful.

He set her fears to rest by saying, "Sleep while you can, *señorita*. We will not be here long."

He then lay down near her, as did the man in the poncho. But Diego did not lie down. He squatted on his haunches with his rifle across his knees and lit a *cigarrillo*. He was only a few feet away, but he was between her and the horses. He finished the small cigar, but he still didn't lie down, and she knew he would not. He was going to keep watch.

She couldn't escape. But at least they weren't going to molest her. Realizing that, Samantha gave in to exhaustion and drifted into sleep, telling herself that tomorrow she would escape. Tomorrow, somehow.

Chapter 17

TOMORROW came too quickly. The moon had hardly traveled at all when she was jarred awake by a rough hand on her shoulder. During the rest of that night, they rode hard. Once the sun rose, they slowed down. That way, they wouldn't have to stop and rest the horses every few hours. They ate while riding, traveling during even the hottest time of day.

That night was a repeat of the previous one. Samantha was growing quite desperate. The mountains were getting closer and closer, which meant that they were getting closer to El Carnicero. She began to think about him more and more. She couldn't stop herself. She knew that the bandit hated *gringos*. Would he hold her for ransom? Or *was* this only a kidnapping? She allowed herself to think the unthinkable. Did he mean to kill her?

No! She couldn't let herself think that way. But the thought wouldn't leave her, and she admitted to real terror. She didn't want to be handed over to the infamous Butcher. He killed women and children when it suited him. And he hated *gringos* most of all.

That night, Samantha tried to run. She knew she wouldn't succeed, but she had to try. The short man with the poncho kept watch, and she waited until Diego and Serape seemed to be sleeping. Suddenly running at him, she charged the short man, knocking him over. His rifle fell, and she dove for it, then turned to face him.

The other two were up then, grinning at her. Serape said smoothly, "It is empty, *señorita*."

She gasped. "Empty?!"

He shrugged. "We are in the open and can easily see anyone coming. There would be plenty of time to load the rifle if we needed to. Inigo does not like weapons. He never loads his unless he has to." Inigo was the short man, then.

Samantha stared at them, incredulous, then pointed the rifle at Serape's leg, squeezing the trigger.

Nothing. The rifle was indeed empty.

"Coward!" she shouted at Inigo.

"Come, *señorita*," Serape said in amusement. "You waste time when you could be sleeping."

"Go to hell!" she yelled and threw the rifle at him.

She ran for the horses, intending to take one of theirs, one that might not be stopped by a whistle. But she didn't reach the horses. An arm went round her waist, and she was abruptly toted back to her blanket and dropped onto it. She jumped up instantly, swinging her fist at Serape. Her fist struck his cheek with a resounding crack, and she heard Diego's laughter nearby.

Serape didn't flinch. He simply caught her hands and brought them together, then whipped the red scarf from around his neck and began tying her wrists.

"No!" she protested, trying to pull away, but his fingers were quick, and the knot was tied.

"It is not rope, *señorita*. That would cut your pretty skin," he said softly. "You will thank me for that?"

"I will thank you for nothing!" she spat.

"But it is you who made this necessary," he reminded her.

"Do you plan to tie my feet, too, coward?" she hissed, thoroughly enraged.

"Now that you mention it . . ." He grinned. "That is a very good idea. We have little enough time left to sleep. I would not like to be awakened again to find you attacking poor Inigo."

Samantha glared at his back murderously as he left to get a rope. He returned, and, after her futile efforts at kicking at him to keep him away, he caught her feet and wrapped the rope around her boots.

"Damn you!" she cried in frustration. "Tell me your name so I can curse you properly!"

He sat back on his haunches beside her, a bemused look on his face. "Why do you wish to curse me, *señorita?* I only follow orders. I am paid to do a job. I do it. Save your curses for El Carnicero."

At the mention of the dreaded name, she lost some of her anger. He saw this and smiled knowingly.

"You do not wish to meet him?"

"No," Samantha replied. When he stood up, she pleaded. "Wait. Tell me what is going to happen to me when we get where we're going."

"You will be *el jefe*'s guest for a time."

"His prisoner! Can't you give me some idea what to expect?"

"You will not be harmed, if that is what worries you," he said kindly.

But Samantha mistook his tone for condescension. "How would you feel if I had kidnapped you? You'd damn well be asking questions, too!"

He laughed. "I do not think I would mind being kidnapped by you, little one," he said softly.

Samantha blushed. "Can you at least tell me what was in the message you left for my father?"

"That I do not know."

"You're lying."

He frowned. "And you are a bother, *señorita*. Go to sleep."

He moved away. He had told her nothing, and she couldn't believe his assurance that she wouldn't be harmed. But he was most congenial, this *bandido*. He had tied her up, but she grudgingly admitted that she had brought that on herself. He was friendly, and he looked at her with admiration. Perhaps she could make use of that, somehow. It wouldn't hurt to be less hostile toward him now.

Chapter 18

THEY reached the foothills of the Sierras late that next day, having stopped to rest in the early afternoon. Apparently they no longer worried about pursuit but were just eager to return to their camp. They rode hard after their rest, traveling until they left the flat lands.

Late that night, camping by a mountain stream near a small plateau, Samantha looked longingly at the water, wanting desperately to wash off all the grime that had accumulated on her. Her hair was the only thing not matted with dirt, for she had kept it pinned tightly under her hat, but it was still sticky. She knew she looked a mess. But she wouldn't attempt a bath. She didn't trust the men, not even Serape. She settled for washing her face and hands in the cool mountain water.

There were trees here, and it was a little colder. They hadn't been heading up into the mountains after all, but were just skirting the lower edges and, surprisingly, riding north. Samantha didn't question the new direction. She was just glad to be heading back toward her home, whatever the reason. But the bandits had only been looking for a particular trail, she soon discovered, and they found it the next day. The sun had yet to rise when they found the path and turned southwest, making a gradual yet steady upward climb.

Samantha had a new worry. Why didn't the men try

to hide the trail from her? Didn't they care if she knew where their camp was? Either they had no permanent camp...or it didn't matter because she would not be leaving it. Ever.

The air grew colder that evening as they continued to move the horses along, up a narrow path on the side of a steep canyon. She grew nervous glancing down the side of the cliff. They were close enough to the edge that she could see the long drop below.

Once it was full night, Diego, in the lead, held a torch high. Even so, it was dark, and the path was treacherous. El Rey was exhausted, but still he held up better than the other mounts. It was cruel to treat the animals that way. Three and a half days of constant hard riding! She supposed the other horses were from her father's herd and considered expendable.

Soon the path widened considerably, and Samantha sighed with relief. But then they took a sharp turn around the side of the canyon wall, and what lay ahead turned her blood cold.

It was another canyon, wide enough to be a valley, which stretched into the center of the mountain. To the right on the flat, barren land between the cliffs was a small village, a half dozen old houses spread around the ruins of a church. Was this their destination?

Lights shone in several of the houses, but the place was quiet. Not a soul stirred—until Diego, ahead of them, began shouting and whooping, calling out that they had returned. Soon lights brightened more windows. Doors opened. She tensed, fearful.

She didn't want to face the Butcher, but the unknown was terrifying, as well.

She nudged El Rey, forcing him up alongside Serape. "Is this it, then, *señor*?"

"*Sí.*"

"Will—will he be here?" she asked hesitantly.

He glanced at her, raising the brim of his hat so he could see her better in the faint moonlight. "If you mean *el jefe,* I cannot think why he would not be here."

"Is there any reason why I *have* to meet him? I mean, if I'm to be held for ransom, then I don't really—"

"He will want to talk to you, to learn certain things," Serape replied.

"What things?"

He shrugged. "He will want your opinion on whether your father will agree to his demands."

"My father will agree to anything to get me back," Samantha assured him.

"El Carnicero will be glad to hear that. But you do not know what was in the message. You cannot know for sure if your father will agree, not until you hear the demands yourself."

"Someone else could tell me about it," she said brightly, but he cut her off. "Why do you still have fear?" he asked. "I hear fear in your voice. I have told you that you will not be harmed here. He has sworn this to me."

"And you believe him?"

"*Sí,* I believe him," he answered without hesitation. "If I did not, I would never have brought you here. Do you understand me, *señorita?* I do not hurt women."

Samantha let the declaration sink in. Then she spoke up. "You must not have ridden with this bunch very long." She was remembering Manuel's story of the massacre of women and children.

"No, I have not," he replied honestly, thereby dashing her hopes all over again.

"Lorenzo!" called someone from inside the camp. "We are waiting. Bring in the prize!"

Samantha stiffened. The man was speaking Spanish. They wouldn't know that she understood Spanish, and she decided not to let them know. It might be useful to her if they talked freely in front of her.

"Was that man calling to you?" she asked innocently.

"*Sí*. They wait for us."

"Your name is Lorenzo? I liked Serape better." At his bewildered look, she added, "Never mind. I'll explain another time. But tell me, what do you call your boss besides *el jefe?*"

"Rufino."

"Is that his real name?"

"Not likely. Not many who choose this life use their true names. But it is the only name I know him by."

"And your real name?"

"Is not Lorenzo," he acknowledged.

"Lorenzo!" The call was impatient this time, making Samantha wince.

"Come, Señorita Kingsley." Lorenzo started up their horses, heading toward one of the houses. Many men were gathered in front of the house, and torches had been placed on the narrow porch. "There will be hot food and a comfortable bed for you. And it will be better to meet Rufino now. You will see for yourself that you need not fear him."

Lorenzo dismounted as he reached the porch steps, and Samantha did the same reluctantly and nervously. Inigo led their horses away. The other men all gathered around her and stared openly.

A few men were sitting on the steps, and there were at least ten in the yard. Samantha felt surrounded, suffocated, and terrified. They were too close, and she was weaponless. She was not used to feeling so helpless.

Someone reached out and touched the embroidery on her vest, and Samantha swung around to slap away the offending hand. She stood, her back to the house, cringing from their leering, grinning expressions, hoping her fear didn't show.

"*La gringa es muy bella!*" she heard. "*Magnífica,*" said another, and there were whispers that made her more and more uncomfortable. And then they were talking about her outfit, how mannish it was, about the empty gunbelt on her hips. They threw rapid questions at Lorenzo while she stood there in their midst, not knowing what to do, waiting. Waiting for what? Was El Carnicero there? she wondered. Which of these dark, rough-looking men was the cold-blooded killer she so dreaded facing?

She grew more and more frightened, standing there under inspection. She was about to turn away when a deep voice boomed above all the other voices, coming from behind her.

"Are you sure you have brought his daughter. Lorenzo, and not his son?"

Samantha turned to face the speaker, as the question brought a chorus of laughter from the men. As she swung around, she expected to see El Carnicero, a short, barrel-chested man. But the owner of the mocking voice was tall, his lean figure silhouetted in the doorway of the house. He was entirely in shadows because the torches lit only the yard, and only a little of it.

Samantha was grateful that the brim of her large hat hid her face. At least no one could see the fear in her eyes. But she found the fear giving way to temper. She was exhausted. She was hungry. She hadn't had a real meal in days. She was being kept out here in the cold, suffering humiliating examination by a bunch of ragtag bandits. And now one of the bandits was mocking her, as well.

Samantha dismissed the man on the porch and turned to Lorenzo. "You promised me food and a bed," she reminded him. "Must I stand out here until every man in your camp has had a look at me? Where is your leader? I wish to get this over with."

"So you have lost your fear, eh?" He grinned.

Samantha bristled. "There are limits to what I will stand for, *señor*. I am reaching—"

"Oh, *shit!*" The curse exploded from the porch. Everyone else went silent.

Samantha was jolted by the vehemence of the voice and turned slowly back to the porch. But the tall man was gone, probably back into the house. She stared at the empty doorway, her eyes widening as memories echoed. The voice...no! It couldn't be.

There were curses and shouting from inside the house, and Lorenzo shook his head. *"Por Dios!* What has caused this temper?"

But Samantha didn't hear him. She was listening to the voice raging inside the house. That voice, first mocking, then angry...But it couldn't be!

She started up the porch steps, drawn like a magnet, but Lorenzo caught her arm. "No, *señorita.* Something is wrong. I do not understand it. Come, I will take you to another house."

But Samantha shook his hand away without even looking at him and moved to the doorway. She went no farther than that. She didn't have to. The room was brightly lit, and she could see everything clearly. The man was stalking back and forth like a caged angry beast.

"Señorita, por favor," Lorenzo whispered urgently at her ear. "Come away quickly. For some reason, the sight of you has angered him."

Samantha turned to Lorenzo suddenly and surprised him by putting her arms around his waist. Before he could get over his surprise, she pulled back, his gun gripped firmly in her hand.

"Madre de Dios!" he gasped.

But even as he spoke, Samantha was leveling the gun at the man in the room. The gun exploded, smoke curling in the air, but the bullet hit the ceiling because Lorenzo had knocked her arm upward as she fired. He caught her wrist and tried to pry the gun away.

"No!" she screamed wildly, fighting him with all she

had. "Damn you, let go! I'll kill you if you don't let me finish this!"

Quickly the gun was yanked from her hand—but not by Lorenzo. Hank Chavez stood before her, his eyes a dark, turbulent storm. But Samantha didn't care how angry he might be. He couldn't possibly be as furious as she was with herself for failing to shoot him.

Samantha twisted in Lorenzo's grip and kicked him squarely on the shin, freeing herself. She struck Hank's cheek, but his head was turned and the damage was slight. He caught her wrists and twisted them behind her back. The pain shooting through her shoulders effectively stopped her from kicking at him, and she went still.

"Damn you!" she cried.

"Shut up!" Hank hissed. Then he called furiously to Lorenzo, who was still standing in the doorway looking utterly amazed, "You have brought the wrong woman! How could this happen?"

Lorenzo was utterly lost by then. "The wrong woman?"

Hank could barely contain his fury. "Can you not see for yourself that she and I are acquainted? She is Samantha *Blackstone!*"

"Sí," Lorenzo agreed, speaking slowly now. "Samantha...Blackstone...*Kingsley.*"

Hank whirled Samantha around, his fingers biting into her shoulders. "Is this true?"

"Go to hell!"

He shook her. "Is it?"

"Yes, damn you! Yes!"

He let go of her, and she fell back. "Take her into the other room. See that she stays there."

Lorenzo grabbed Samantha's shoulders. "You intend to keep her here in this house?"

"I know her, Lorenzo. I know what she is capable of. I want her where I can keep an eye on her."

"No!" Samantha turned fiery green eyes on Lorenzo. "You told me I wouldn't be harmed," she reminded him. "But he nearly broke my arm just now and has left bruises on my shoulders. You can't leave me here with him! I demand to see your boss!"

Hank laughed, a cruel, taunting laugh. "And just what do you want to see me about, *niña?*"

She caught her breath and swung around to face him again. "You—El Carnicero? I don't believe it. He's short and ugly and—"

"And you feared him?"

"No, of course not." But she knew how unconvincing she sounded, and admitted, "The stories about him are terrible."

"Perhaps," Hank conceded in a level voice. "Most people do fear him, and it served my purpose to use that fear."

"But you're not El Carnicero."

"No," he admitted.

"Is there really such a man?"

Hank nodded. "He is still in his territory to the south, unaware that I have borrowed his name. I needed the man's reputation."

"So you're a bandit." Her voice was heavy with contempt. "I should have realized it before, after what you did to me."

"Any man would have been driven to do what I did, *niña,*" Hank said.

Samantha's face burned. She wished she had never brought the subject up at all. Lorenzo was looking at her so strangely.

"Is he really your boss, Lorenzo?" she asked.

"*Sí.* I follow his orders."

"But are you loyal to him?" She placed a hand on his arm. "Or can your services be bought? I can pay you a great deal of money to take me out of here—more than he will give you from the ransom."

"That is enough!" Hank growled.

"What's the matter—Rufino?" Samantha mocked Hank. "Are you afraid he might accept my generous offer?"

"Tell her, Lorenzo," Hank snapped curtly.

"I cannot help you, *señorita*," Lorenzo said almost apologetically.

"He has your complete loyalty then?"

"*Sí.*"

"Perhaps someday you'll tell me why," Samantha replied in a deliberately sarcastic voice.

Hank's eyes narrowed, turning a dark slate gray. He had managed to bring his fury under control, but he was having difficulty with it.

"Get her out of my sight, Lorenzo. I have heard more of her bitchy tongue than I can bear."

"And I cannot bear another moment in the same room with you!" Samantha managed the last word before she dragged Lorenzo across the room to the only other door. She threw the door open and stepped through it without another look at Hank.

The room was very small and contained only a narrow bed against the far wall, an old trunk, and a washstand. The floor was bare, as was the single window, closed now against the cold mountain air.

"Does he sleep here, Lorenzo?" Samantha asked quietly, staring at the rumpled bed.

"This is his room, *sí*."

"Was," she corrected, and went to the bed to tear off the blanket and sheets, throwing them on the floor. "I won't sleep on the same bedding. I refuse."

Her back was to Lorenzo as his voice came to her softly. "You hate him. Why?"

But she would say no more about Hank Chavez. "Will you bring me clean bedding?"

"*Sí*, and hot food."

"Never mind the food now," she said curtly. "I'm too upset to eat."

"As you wish."

He started to leave, but she caught his arm and said desperately, "Stay with me, Lorenzo."

"Here?"

"Yes, yes, here. I don't trust him."

"But I cannot stay in this room, *señorita*."

His eyes were drawn to the narrow bed, and she said, "Stay in the other room, then. Please, Lorenzo. You can't leave me alone in this house with him."

"He will not hurt you."

"How can you say that? You saw what he just did to me. He would have done worse if you had not been there. I know it."

"What I saw was *you* attacking *him*," Lorenzo replied unsympathetically. "I do not think I would have been so lenient with you if you had tried to kill me, *señorita*."

"You men stick together, don't you?" she returned bitterly. "He wasn't hurt, was he?"

"Yet you did try to kill him."

"Oh, get out of here and leave me alone!" she cried miserably. "How could you understand? You're just like him!"

Samantha turned her back on him, and after a moment he left, closing the door quietly. Hank was standing in front of the fireplace in the outer room, leaning his hands on the mantel, staring at the fire he had just lit. When Lorenzo approached him he turned, then chuckled.

"What? *La princesa* must have clean sheets? Those were changed yesterday."

Lorenzo shrugged. "Since you have slept in them, she will not. Why does she want to kill you, *amigo*?"

Hank turned away. "I do not think you would care to know the answer to that," he said coldly.

"You hate her, too?"

"*Sí*, I hate her, too."

Lorenzo shook his head. "Myself, I have never seen such a beautiful woman," he said sincerely.

"How can you tell, as filthy as she is?" Hank muttered.

"I can tell. And I do not think I could hate such a one, not for any reason," Lorenzo remarked reflectively. "I do not understand how you can."

"You let her beauty cloud your judgment, Lorenzo. Do not be deceived," Hank said coldly. "That one uses men. She tramples on their souls and then casts them aside without another thought."

"So." Lorenzo grinned with sudden understanding. "You loved her."

"Perdición! I could never love such a vixen. Do not mention it again!"

Lorenzo frowned at Hank's sudden show of temper. "She wants me to stay with her. She does not trust you, and I begin to see why."

Hank laughed humorlessly. "Your job is over. You have brought her here. Now she is my responsibility."

"You will not hurt her?"

"Not as long as she behaves."

"That is little reassurance, *amigo.* You saved my life, and for this I owe you. I hope you will not make me regret giving you my loyalty."

Hank grew impatient. "Will you stop worrying? She is not worth your concern, Lorenzo, and I assure you she can take care of herself."

"I would not see her hurt."

"Leave it alone, Lorenzo," Hank growled. "You have let her fool you. She is as calculating and scheming as any man—and just as deadly. And I warn you, I will hold you responsible if she gets her hands on a weapon again."

Lorenzo reddened at the reminder of his humiliation. He could not believe all the things Rufino said about the girl, not really. True, she had meant to shoot Rufino tonight, but this was a desperate situation for her. She had been kidnapped, at gunpoint.

What could he do if the girl angered Rufino again? Lorenzo left reluctantly, without the reassurance he wanted.

Chapter 19

THE door opened without warning, and Samantha sat bolt upright in bed, pulling the covers up with her. She had on only a short laced camisole and the tight bloomers she wore under skirts. She had not expected anyone to barge into the room or she would not have undressed that far. And for that someone to be Hank...

"I want a lock on that door," she told him in a scathing voice.

He looked pointedly at her dirty clothes, lying over the trunk. He grinned as she pulled the covers higher. "You shall have it—but I will keep the key."

"Never mind, then."

"No, I insist. It will be done this morning. And so that no one can break in through the window to harm you, I will have that boarded up, as well."

"Damn you," she hissed through clenched teeth. "Why don't you just tie me to the bed!"

He grinned, his eyes laughing in the old familiar way. "If you give me reason, *chica*, it will be a pleasure."

"I'm sure it would be," she grumbled, and then her voice rose. "Oh, why did I have to miss you that day by the stream? Why did my hands have to shake?"

Hank stiffened, and his eyes turned a stormy gray. He clenched his fists, making an effort to hold them at his sides. He wanted to wring her neck. But more than that, he wanted...no, he would not touch her again. It had not helped to get her out of his system when he had touched her before.

"You did not miss," he told her. "One of your bullets found my side."

"A lot of good it did," she said hotly. "You're still alive."

"You are the most bloodthirsty—"

"No, I'm not!" she cut him off. "Until I met you I never wanted to kill a man! And what are you doing here anyway? I prayed I would see you again—but in jail, not like this! Why are you waging war on my father?"

"It is not a war."

"You're trying to drive him out of Mexico! Why? What has he ever done to you?"

Hank debated what, if anything, to tell her. Because she knew him, knew his name, and knew he wasn't El Carnicero, she might ruin his plans. There was supposed to be no connection between the *bandido* and the stranger who would soon buy the Kingsley land. But Samantha would know that the *bandido* and the new owner were both himself—if she ever saw the new owner. But why should she? She would have to leave Mexico with her father.

"Your father has done nothing to me, Samantha," he said in a reasonable tone as the idea took root in his mind. "It is my cousin he has wronged."

"My father never hurt anyone!" She was quick to deny the charge.

Hank shrugged. "You do not wish to listen, so I cannot explain."

She glared at him. "All right then. What has my father done to your cousin?"

"Antonio went to your father recently and offered to buy your *rancho*."

"Antonio is your cousin?"

"Yes. Antonio de Vega y Chavez," Hank replied. "But your father would not listen to his offer and would not name a price, any price."

"Why should he?" Samantha demanded. "He has no wish to sell our land."

"But it is not your land, Samantha. It is my cousin's land."

"You're crazy." She laughed at him. "My father bought that land. He paid for it. He—"

"He paid cheaply for it. He bought it from government officials, who claimed it was church land. In those days, any church land sold could be easily given back to the church with the next change of government and, therefore, lost to the new owner. That's why it was cheap."

"But you admit that my father paid for the land. How can you say it's not his?"

"Because the officials who sold the land to your father had no right to sell it. It was *not* church land. It was Vega y Chavez land, stolen from my family during the revolution."

"I don't believe it!"

"Did no one ever tell you of the previous owners? Your neighbors, the Galgos, the Barojas? They knew of the massacre at the Hacienda de las Flores."

"Massacre?"

"Yes, massacre," Hank repeated, his voice cold. "Some Juárez *guerrilleros* came to the *hacienda* and claimed it as church property, which gave them the right to confiscate it. Antonio's father was killed for protesting. His grandmother died in his arms, too old to stand the terrible shock." Hank paused, the memory as painful as it always was. "All the men were forced into the army—or shot for resisting. I will not tell you what happened to the women and the young daughters of the *hacienda*."

Samantha was sickened, for she could guess. "And your cousin? What happened to him?"

"He was forced into the army, and later he was thrown into prison for continued resistance. It was while he was in prison that his land was sold to your father. He could do nothing to prevent it. The old deed to the Hacienda de las Flores had been burned by the *guerrilleros*. There was only the word of people who knew Antonio that the land was his. This was not enough for the corrupt officials who were making profits from the sale of 'church property.' There was nothing Antonio could do except hope to buy back his land one day. He has dreamed of nothing else...all these years."

"Are you a close cousin to Antonio?" Samantha ventured. "A first cousin?"

"No, but you have been in Mexico long enough to know that all family here, no matter how distantly related, are considered close. Antonio is like a brother. I feel his frustration as if it were my own."

Samantha was, of course, unaware of his irony. "I'm sorry, Hank, I really am," she said in a moment of real compassion. "But surely you must see that my father is not at fault here. *He* didn't steal your cousin's land. He bought it in good faith. He has the deed, too."

"You are saying my cousin should just forget about the land that has been in his family for generations?" he asked harshly. "He lived on that land for more than half his life. How long have you lived there?"

"That is beside the point," she told him tightly. "My father owns the land now, and you have no right to try and force him to leave. You're not being fair."

"My cousin has lived with his dream too long to give it up. He will pay your father more than it is worth."

"But my father won't sell it!"

"He will if he ever wants to see you again."

She gasped. "You bastard! So that's why I'm here. Of all the terrible, stinking—"

"Enough, Samantha!" Hank cut her off sharply. "I do not like the way this has gone any more than you do, but your father has been so stubborn. And my men were very angry when he sent the *soldados* after them."

"He had good reason to ask the soldiers for help."

"Perhaps," he agreed. "But that did not make them

less angry. In fact, one of the men who saw you suggested the kidnapping."

"Saw me?" she said, uneasy. "Are you saying I was watched?"

"Of course. Everyone was watched. We did not even know Kingsley had a daughter. You were first seen with your large escort going to the ranch, and then again each day after that. It was not difficult to go to a neighboring ranch and find out who you were. But believe me, if I had known it was you, you would not be here now. You were the last woman I wanted to see again, Sam."

"Don't call me that! I told you—only my friends call me that!"

"Of course, and we are not friends," he said with mock seriousness. "But I would rather not call you Señorita Kingsley. I have come to dislike that name a great deal. If you had been honest with me when we met and told me your real name, I would have made the connection later, when I learned who was the owner of the Hacienda de las Flores."

"When *you* learned?"

"From Antonio," he quickly amended.

"It wouldn't have made any difference, though, would it?" she retorted. "You would still have harassed my father."

"Yes, but you would not have become involved. Tell me. Why did you not use your real name?"

"Blackstone was my mother's maiden name. I always traveled under that name. My father and I thought I should avoid using the Kingsley name whenever I was traveling, so as to avoid being kidnapped. Ironic, wouldn't you say? And you're a fine one to talk about assuming false names—Rufino."

He grinned, amused by her taunt. "You have me there, Samina."

Samantha's eyes flashed, and she started to tell him how much she hated his calling her that name, but

Hank held up his hand, the crinkles around his eyes deepening.

"You protest too much." He grinned. "You may as well know now that I will call you whatever I want, be it Samina, *gata* . . . or *puta*."

"You—oh!" she fumed, and her covers quivered. "Get out of here!"

He quirked a brow. "You order me, in my own house?" His voice was deliberate.

"Why did you come in here? I didn't invite you in! I may be your prisoner, but I don't have to suffer your loathsome company!"

"I came to see if you were hungry. You did not eat last night."

"Of course I am hungry. Of all the stupid excuses! You really wanted to humiliate me by catching me in bed. Did you hope to find me unclothed as well?" she hissed. "You're disgusting!"

Hank's mouth thinned to a hard line. He had believed that he could be with her and keep his anger under control, but he was finding that he couldn't. Her disdain enraged him. He would not take her contempt. Damn her, he would not!

Samantha screamed as he took a step toward her, murder in his eyes. She scrambled to the top of the bed, trying to take the covers with her. But the covers caught at the end of the bed, and she let them go. It wasn't important. All that mattered was getting as far away from Hank as she could.

She cowered there in the bed, her eyes wide with fright. Because of that terrible fear, Hank moved no closer. Her anger could elicit his own anger, but afraid, she moved him differently.

"It is well you fear me, *niña*," he said, and his voice was controlled. "It is well you remember what happened the last time you angered me."

"I don't fear you—I hate you. I just can't bear to have your hands on me!"

Hank stiffened but managed to laugh derisively. "Perhaps you do not know what you look like, Sam. I have never seen such a bedraggled woman. I certainly do not intend to dirty my 'hands' by touching you."

"I know how I look, damn you!" she shouted. "And I know whose fault it is for having me dragged up here, riding day and night, never getting a chance to rest or to wash. What the hell do you expect? Should I be wearing silk and smell of roses?"

"What you are wearing now is not so bad." Hank chuckled.

Samantha gasped and quickly crossed her arms over her chest where the nipples had been pressing against the thin linen camisole. But her hips and legs were still revealed by every curve in the skin-tight bloomers, and she couldn't really hide herself.

"Oh! *Will* you get out of here and leave me alone?" she cried, the humiliation more than she could bear. "And don't come back. Someone else can see to my needs."

"Perhaps you have not truly considered your position here. You will not be giving the orders. I have not given it much thought either, but it is time I did. *Sí.*" He grinned. "I think I might enjoy having you at my mercy. After all, Samina," he added, rubbing his side at the place where she had shot him, "I owe you." And he turned abruptly and left.

Samantha threw herself down on the bed to cry out her frustration. This was not the way she had planned for them to meet again. She was supposed to be the one in control, not him! At his mercy? Ah, God, it just wasn't fair!

A little while later, Inigo brought her a large breakfast. The food did not comfort her, however, for while she ate she had to watch her only window being nailed up with sturdy boards. Then a dark little man came in and secured her door with a lock.

After the meal was over and the door shut and locked,

Samantha sat staring at the four walls and the boarded window. Only thin slivers of light came through. As the heat in the tiny room increased, her frustration mounted. She felt sticky and grimy, and she was working herself into such an angry state that she could hardly breathe.

Finally she pounded on the door, screaming that she needed a bath. But no one came. She gave up after hammering at the door on and off for an hour without any response. There being nothing else to do, she lay back down on the bed and fell into an exhausted sleep.

Chapter 20

SCREAMING woke her, a woman's crying and pleading. What were they doing to that poor woman to make her scream and beg like that? Was Hank making her scream?

The screams finally stopped, but the crying continued. A while later that stopped, too, and all was quiet again—too quiet. Samantha could hear her heart pounding. It was the only sound she heard, a maddening sound. She was putting herself in that woman's place, imagining all kinds of horrible things. She was finally beginning to see just how dangerous her situation really was.

At his mercy—*his* mercy! Samantha squeezed her fists until her nails stung her palms. She hated her fear. She had to conquer it, either conquer it or shame herself. Anger was better. Anger was strong. Anger! She would make herself recall all of her fury.

"Hank!" Samantha shouted. "Hank, if you're out there, you damn well better answer me!"

She shot off the bed and began pounding on the door again, the anger propelling her.

"Hank!" she called, her voice strong and unwavering.

Hank sat on the porch steps, listening to the racket Samantha was making. A satisfied grin curled his lips. Let her wonder. Let her stew.

The sun beat down on his legs, stretched out comfortably on the steps. A light breeze teased his black curls, sending a long lock down into his eyes. He brushed it away as he watched two of his men getting their gear ready to leave. They were returning to their villages, returning to their lives, their mission over with.

All the men had been paid handsomely from the sale up north of the stolen cattle and horses. He no longer needed so many men. They had served his purpose, this group of peasants and bandits, and he had been lucky to find them so quickly. But he didn't need them any more. He had all he needed—Kingsley's daughter.

His smile deepened as he considered the little hellion inside the house. It just might prove satisfying after all that she had turned out to be Kingsley's daughter. He had thought about her much too often in the last two months, wanting to get her out of his system but unable to do it. She had haunted him, and his anger had been matched by bewilderment. Why, he had asked himself again and again, did the woman mean so much to him? Why couldn't he simply forget the vixen? She needed to be punished for what she had done to him, what she was *still* doing to him.

He didn't know what had happened between Samantha and Adrien Allston after he left, but he couldn't help wondering about that. Did she still love the man? Did she believe what Hank had told her about Adrien? He had thought about it all during that torturous ride to Santa Fe, where he had finally stopped to have the wound in his side attended to. He still had the bullet in his possession. He carried it with him as a harsh reminder to himself never to fall prey to a woman's deadly charms.

He had stayed in Santa Fe for two days, getting his strength back after losing so much blood. There he found the white stallion and couldn't resist buying him. El Rey and his other horse made it possible for him to reach Mexico in record time, and he had felt better then, believing that his luck was returning. Then, meeting Kingsley, Hank had reached a dead end. How that man infuriated him, refusing even to listen to Hank's story.

Hank, raging, left Kingsley and sought out the nearest *cantina*, losing his rage in a three-day drunken stupor. Coming out of that drunk, he got the idea to force Kingsley into selling the land.

The scheme surfaced as he was remembering Lorenzo and his parting promise that if Hank ever needed him for anything, he could find him in Chihuahua. Hank had thought, I could use you now, *amigo*, to help me change someone's mind. Lorenzo was indebted to Hank for saving his life. It had happened just outside El Paso, where Hank had come upon Lorenzo as he was about to be lynched by four drunken cowboys who claimed he was a cattle rustler. Hank never asked about the accusation. He simply couldn't see a man being hanged for anything less than murder, especially not a countryman.

He had risked his life getting Lorenzo away from the four men because they were too drunk to realize the danger of his rifle pointed at them. There was shooting, and he had lost one of his horses, but he and Lorenzo and El Rey managed to get across the border.

A week later, when Hank located Lorenzo in Chihuahua, his new friend was not opposed to Hank's idea. He had no great love for *gringos*—not after four had tried to lynch him—nor did the other men Lorenzo enlisted. Hank and he had to break three men out of jail. Friends of those three joined Lorenzo and Hank, until there were a dozen.

The plans did not go smoothly. Kingsley was not easy to intimidate. But when the men learned that he had a daughter, they knew Kingsley could be forced to give in.

Hank would approach him again, saying he had heard of Kingsley's troubles and thought perhaps he was ready to reconsider. Kingsley would jump to it. He would sell, leave Mexico, and await the return of his daughter. There was nothing else he could do, not if he wanted her back.

That would be the end of it. Kingsley would have sold his land to Hank, in Hank's real name. Samantha might want to return one day to question the new owner about his cousin, but Hank would just have to avoid her. There would be nothing to connect the respectable new owner with the bandit who had kidnapped Samantha Kingsley.

Kingsley would not be cheated, for Hank intended to pay a fair price for the land. Of course, he would be making his offer based on Patrick McClure's promises, but he doubted that Kingsley would mind if he had to wait awhile for the money. He would be more concerned about his daughter's safety.

It was time he sent word to Pat, to let him know he would need the money quickly. Diego would be the best man to take care of sending a wire. After what had happened just a little while ago between him and his woman, it would be better if Diego left camp for a while. He was too good a shot to let go completely yet. There was still the matter of delivering Samantha to her father, and that would be dangerous if Kingsley had any tricks planned.

"Hank, you miserable wretch! I know you're out there. Open this door!"

He flinched when the pounding suddenly grew louder. What the hell was she using to bang on the door? But he wasn't quite ready to go to her. She could make all the noise she wanted, no one would respond. Lorenzo was the only one who might protest, and Lorenzo was not there. Hank had sent him back down the mountain to make certain they were not followed, and to cover any signs Samantha might have secretly left behind to show their way.

Lorenzo wouldn't be back until the next day. It was just as well. Hank liked Lorenzo. He would hate to see the younger man hurt by Samantha's duplicity. And he had no doubt that she would try to use him. She would use every weapon at her disposal to get away.

"Rufino!" Samantha tried, and Hank grinned. Several moments passed before she called out, "Lorenzo!"

Hank frowned. The pounding became distant then, and he knew it was the window she was banging on. He jumped to his feet angrily.

Hank unlocked the door and threw it open, startling Samantha. She whirled away from the boarded-up window, holding the boot she had been banging with. She was wearing the other one, and the rest of her clothes, as well, except for the gunbelt, which was still lying over the trunk, useless. Her hair was a tangled mass, and her cheeks were flushed. Her eyes were green fire. He stopped, startled.

Angry, she was magnificent. And the sight of her, dirty, wildly disarrayed, yet still undeniably beautiful, made Hank forget his anger.

"I think I will take those," he said mildly, indicating her boots. "I did not have boards put over your windows so you could pound them loose."

"You can't have them."

Samantha stepped back, holding the boot possessively against her chest. Even a boot could be a weapon. She wouldn't give them up.

"Just where have you been?" she demanded. "I have been calling for you half the day!"

He shrugged. "I was busy." Some of the stiffness left her, and he asked courteously, "Did you want something, Sam?"

"I want a bath."

"There is a stream at the end of the village. I will be happy to take you there."

Samantha glared. "I want a decent bath, a hot one—here."

"What you suggest would involve too much trouble. It would be simpler just to take you to the stream."

"I don't care how much trouble it would be!"

"Of course not. You would not be the one to carry the tub in here, to tote and heat the water."

"You refuse?"

"Perhaps if you ask for the bath nicely, instead of demanding it," he offered, "I might consider it."

Samantha stood frozen, tight-lipped. Nicely? She would rather throw the boot at him. But she wanted that bath desperately, wanted it badly enough to demean herself this one time.

She swallowed hard. "Could I have a bath in here— please?"

"Ah! I knew you could be agreeable as long as you had the right persuasion." He smiled.

Samantha waited a moment, holding herself in check. "Well?" she finally asked.

"You will have your bath—if I can find a tub in this miserable village."

He left, locking the door behind him. It was nearly an hour before he returned with a small round tub that looked so old she was sure it would leak. He had the water ready and brought it in. There was only enough to half fill the tub, but he had found her soap and a towel, even a brush and a change of clothes, for which she was grateful, though silently so.

But he didn't plan to leave. As nonchalantly as could be, Hank sat down on the bed, leaning back against the wall, obviously prepared to stay.

"What are you doing?" Samantha demanded.

"I have never watched a woman bathe before," he said smoothly. "I think it will be amusing."

"Amusing?" she gasped and pointed to the door. "Get out of here!"

But Hank shook his head, that slow, maddening grin beginning. "I will stay."

"Then I won't bathe," she said stonily.

"Suit yourself."

Hank bounded off the bed in a single lithe movement and picked up one of the empty buckets he had left on the floor. When he began scooping the water back out of the tub, Samantha caught his arm.

"Leave it!" she snapped, furious. "You enjoy humiliating me, don't you?"

"*Sí, gatita.* I must admit I do."

She turned her back on him, so angry she wanted to scream. Suddenly she began to yank off her clothes, and though she heard him sit down on the bed, she went right on. He hoped to humiliate her, but she just wouldn't let him. There was no need to remove everything. She would just have to wash herself as best she could with the camisole and bloomers still on. They needed washing anyway. Still keeping her back to Hank, Samantha stepped into the little tub.

She shrieked as she felt him at her back, his hands at her waist. Before she could stop him, he had pulled the camisole over her head. Covering her breasts, she faced him, screaming her rage. But that left her unguarded, and in the next moment her bloomers were falling down her hips. She swung a fist at Hank, but he caught it and pushed her down into the water.

"You son of a bitch! How dare—" He bent over, reaching into the water, and she panicked. "No! Don't you touch me, damn—"

But Hank only wanted her bloomers, and he tugged them off. Samantha was bright red when he finished undressing her. She had never been so shamed—well, once before, and *that* had been because of him, too!

Hank dropped her wet bloomers into the empty bucket and said matter-of-factly, "Bathe properly." Then he sauntered back to the bed and sat down again.

He hadn't touched her. Thank God for that. But she wasn't going to entertain him, either. She gave him a look of utter contempt, turning her back on him. Scooping up the soap, she began to wash.

"You are no fun at all, little one."

Hank chuckled, and she muttered, "You haven't a shred of decency in you, Hank Chavez. I used to think you were such a fine gentleman—"

"And so I can be, when there is a lady present," he pointed out cruelly.

"You're a savage!"

"You keep calling me names, Sam, and I will be obliged to do the same. I do not think you will like the sting of the names I have for you."

She ignored the warning and continued, almost conversationally, "You know, I wanted to see you horsewhipped before I had you shot. I used to dream about seeing you bleed."

"You have already made me bleed."

"Not enough. You hurt me!" she shouted. "I may have flirted with you, even encouraged you, but those are harmless things, things every woman does. What you did to me was unforgivable."

"So you do not forgive me," he replied coldly. "I will not lose sleep over it."

"Perhaps you will, when the bounty hunters start catching up with you. I have wanted posters out on you. Did you know that?"

"It will not be the first time," Hank said. He sounded unconcerned, but the fact was that he hadn't known.

"You won't shrug it off so easily after I raise the price, *amigo*," she gloated. "I will make the reward for you so tempting that every bounty hunter and gunslinger in the country will be looking for you."

Hank's gray eyes narrowed, focusing on her back. "That is, *if* you leave here."

Samantha tensed. Had she gone too far? Then she recalled the woman screaming earlier, and a chill overtook her.

"There's another woman here in this camp, isn't there?" she began.

"There are several. Those of my men who had women brought them along."

"I heard a woman screaming," she said hesitantly. "Is she here with one of your men?"

"Yes," he said, deciding there was no reason not to tell her.

"What happened to her?"

"She was beaten."

"But why?"

"She was unfaithful. The whole camp knew it. She was with another man last night, before Diego returned, and that wasn't the first time. But Diego did not find the other man's boots under his bed until today."

"Diego? She is his woman?"

"Was. He has cast her out."

"Oh!" Samantha said in disgust. "He beats the poor woman, *then* he wants nothing more to do with her."

"You approve of unfaithfulness?"

"No, I—I just don't approve of women being beaten."

"Even when they deserve it?"

She didn't answer. That argument would get them nowhere. "If he was going to beat her, he shouldn't have thrown her out. Or vice versa. He should have done one or the other, not both. Is she all right, the woman?"

"She will mend."

His casual answer raised Samantha's ire. "You have no pity, do you? I suppose you didn't even try to stop Diego?"

"I did not interfere, no," he answered honestly. "I would have done the same thing."

"And to think you asked me to be your woman. You would have beaten me, too, wouldn't you?"

"Most certainly," he replied coldly. "Your eyes follow any man."

"That's not true!"

"No?" he asked innocently. "Then you are still faithful to Adrien?"

"You bastard!" Samantha hissed. "You had to say that, didn't you?"

Hank chuckled.

She stopped talking and concentrated on her bath.

Washing her hair in the confining space was nearly impossible, but she finally managed to scoop water onto her head with cupped hands. Angrily, she lathered in the soap.

Samantha didn't hear Hank come up behind her again. All at once the full bucket of cold water splashed down on her head, and she gasped and sputtered, enraged, but his cold voice stopped her from saying anything.

"Get out, Sam," he ordered. "You have been in there long enough. It is nearly dinner time, and I think you will prepare it."

He walked out of the room, leaving the door open, and Samantha sighed with relief. She had intended to stay in the tub until she got some privacy.

She left the tub immediately and, after dressing in the clean, low-cut peasant blouse and full cotton skirt that Hank had provided, she quickly scrubbed her underclothes and blouse, then cleaned the leather vest and skirt with the towel. She left the room, carrying the wet clothing over her arm.

"Can I hang these on the porch to dry without their being stolen in the night?"

Hank was sitting at the rough table near the fireplace, a glass in his hand. "You can hang them on the porch as long as you go no farther than that."

The front door was open, and she stepped onto the shaded porch. There wasn't a thing on it, not a plant, not a chair. The room she had just stepped out of was nearly as bare, with only the table and four chairs, a saddle in a corner, and a bedroll next to it. Open cupboards ran above a long counter by the fireplace. They held a few dishes and pans and some food, but there was no stove.

Samantha laid her clothes over the railing. The sun had disappeared below the high cliff behind the houses, but it was still light outside. She tried to see what lay at the other end of the narrow valley, but another house blocked her view.

A man crossed in front of the house, and Samantha quickly went back inside to escape his curious gaze. But, inside, Hank's eyes followed her, and she began to feel self-conscious in the loose, flowing clothes. The white blouse was much too low, falling just above the curves of her pointed breasts, and the green sash she had tied around her waist only served to emphasize her breasts. The skirt was too short.

"I'll help you empty that tub now, if you're ready?" Samantha offered.

"It can wait."

She turned toward the cupboards. "What is it you want for supper?"

"There are some beans you can refry, and one of your father's plump chickens ready to roast. There will be more supplies coming in a few days, but we are low now."

Samantha tensed, but she did not say anything about the stolen chickens. It wouldn't serve anything to argue with him about his thievery.

After a while, Hank got up and emptied the tub. Samantha didn't offer to help, as she had her hands full. After she had put the food on the table, Hank produced a bottle of wine, pouring them each a glass.

When they were almost finished eating, Samantha finally asked, "Why hasn't Lorenzo come by to see me today?"

"He is gone."

"Gone?" Her voice held dismay. "You mean he left? Why?"

"You give yourself away with so much concern," Hank said drily. "Is he to be your next conquest?"

"I'm not looking for a conquest," she retorted. "But if I were, I would certainly prefer Lorenzo to you. Where did he go?"

"He will be back, but I do not think I will let you see him."

"You intend to keep me locked up in here with only your company, then?"

"You grow bored with my company already," he chided her. "When I am enjoying the thought of having a woman in my house—even you."

"Just don't get any ideas, Hank," Samantha warned him. "I don't mind cooking for you, but that's all I intend to do."

"We shall see, *niña.*"

"I mean it," she said flatly, refusing to be drawn into an argument.

He grinned. "You know, you are beautiful when your eyes flash like that," he said softly, his grin devilish. "And you have the body of an angel. I wonder how long I can withstand the temptation you present."

Samantha rose from the table and walked stiffly to her room, slamming the door shut without another word. Hank's brow creased in a thoughtful frown. He had said those last words in Spanish, for no particular reason beyond his own amusement. Yet she reacted as if she had understood completely. Was it possible? Had she only pretended, before, that she didn't know Spanish?

Hank sat there thinking, long into the night. The bottle of wine was empty when, finally, he rose and, after locking Samantha's door, bedded down on his cold floor and slept.

Chapter 21

HANK didn't allow anyone near Samantha for two days, and Samantha spent those days in an agony of wariness, wondering what he would do next. She hadn't known that she still tempted him. Appalled by his admission, she pinned her hair up in a severe knot and wore her own old clothes, without tucking in the blouse or wearing a belt. She meant to look as dowdy as she could, but she knew her efforts were failing when Hank continued to watch her, his gaze much too admiring. And he continued to lord it over her, reminding her that she was at his mercy.

So she should have been thrilled when he informed her on their fourth night together that he was leaving the next morning. She should have been delighted—but, for some reason, she was alarmed.

"Why? Where are you going?" she demanded. "How long will you be gone?"

Hank laughed heartily. "You sound as if you will miss me, *querida*."

"Don't be ridiculous!" she snapped, getting hold of herself. "You just took me by surprise, that's all."

"Now you disappoint me. I had hoped you had come to enjoy my company."

Her chin jutted upward. "Stop teasing and tell me where you are going."

"You demand answers," he sighed, shaking his head. "When will you learn to ask nicely? The lesson with the bath was not enough?"

Samantha clenched her fists. "Oh, I hate you when you get like this!"

"And here I thought you hated me *all* the time." He chuckled, his eyes dancing, enjoying her rage.

"To hell with you!" she shouted in uncontrolled fury. "Don't tell me, then. I don't care anyway. I only hope you never come back!" She stormed into her room, slamming the door.

But she didn't sleep well that night. Why was he leaving? It made her uneasy. She hated not knowing what was going on.

That next morning, Hank came in to tell her good-bye. He hadn't meant to, had intended just to go. But something drew him. A last look? He shrugged it off.

She was standing by the window. Sunlight filtering in through the cracks in the boards touched her hair with red fire. She was lovely. Even dressed in silk she wouldn't have appeared more beautiful.

She turned, slowly, and faced him.

"You're leaving now?" she asked lightly.

"Yes."

He waited, but she wasn't going to ask questions again. But he no longer wanted her to worry, and he knew how stubborn she could be.

"I should be back in a week," he explained. "There is an old man here, Inigo's grandfather, who will look after you while I am gone."

"How thoughtful," she murmured.

"Do I hear bitterness? Perhaps you will miss me ... just a little? After all, without me, who will you fight with?"

"Why can't Lorenzo stay with me?" she demanded.

Hank came a few steps toward her. "You would like that, eh? Then you would have a whole week to work on him, to get him to help you?"

"Don't you trust him?"

"It is you I do not trust, Sam," he said quite seriously. "And do not look for Lorenzo to visit you while I am gone. He is coming with me."

"Fine! Leave me with strangers. I don't care," she snapped. "When can I leave this place?"

"That depends on your father. I go now to see if he is following my instructions."

Her heart stopped. She had known this was coming.

"Then you're going near my home?" she asked hesitantly.

"Yes."

"Could you find out how Ramón is?"

"Ramón Baroja?"

"Do—do you know him?" She was surprised.

"I knew him when he was little. Through my cousin, of course," Hank added in an offhanded manner. "Why the concern for Ramón?"

"He was with me that day. Diego shot him. Didn't they tell you?"

"They said a man was wounded when he tried to draw on them. That was Ramón?"

"Yes. I must know if he is all right."

"What is he to you?"

"If you know him, then you know he's my neighbor. We grew up together. He is a very close friend."

Hank's eyes narrowed. "No man can be just a friend, not to you, Sam."

Samantha gazed down at the floor, unwilling to meet his eyes. "Will you find out about Ramón?"

"It would be too much risk," he replied tightly.

His callousness infuriated her. "I'm only asking you to do this one thing for me. It was your man who shot him. He could be dead. I must know."

"Very well. But in return, I want your word that you will not try to escape while I am gone."

"I . . ."

She couldn't possibly make that promise. Hank added, "I can have you locked in your room at all times if you prefer."

"All right!" she cried, her eyes glittering. "I give you my word."

He nodded. "Then I bid you *adiós,* Samina."

And without warning, he caught her in his arms and kissed her fervently. It was what Samantha had dreaded. She remembered so clearly the effect Hank's kisses had on her, the way she lost herself to the power of the man. She had been afraid it might happen again, and it *was* happening. She didn't even try to push him away. She just melted, letting him hold her.

After a long time, and with great effort, Hank released her. How pleased she would be to know the torture it was to let her go!

He said huskily in Spanish, "That was so you will know what to expect when I return."

As he left the room, he was grinning. He had seen the comprehension in her eyes, and he was certain that she understood Spanish very well. Why not? She had lived in Mexico long enough to learn the language. He was on to her now, and there were ways he could use what he knew. Yes...there were ways.

Chapter 22

"MR. . . . Chavez, isn't it?" Hamilton Kingsley asked, shaking Hank's hand and motioning him to a seat in the living room.

"You are correct, *señor*. I was not sure you would remember me."

"It hasn't been all that long since you came to see me before, though that meeting was brief and a lot has happened since we met."

Hank took in the man's haggard, almost defeated look. Hamilton Kingsley was not the confident, arrogant rancher he had met before. The ordeals of the last weeks, the worrying over his daughter, those things had taken their toll. Yet he was a strong man and would probably need only his daughter's safe return to restore his vigor. Hank firmly buried the twinge of conscience that had surfaced.

"I certainly didn't expect to see you again, Mr. Chavez," Kingsley was saying, smiling drily. "You were rather, er, upset, when we met before."

"Disappointed," Hank corrected smoothly.

"Yes, well, I hope there are no hard feelings?" Hamilton asked. "You can't blame a man for refusing to part with something of such value."

Hank frowned. "You have a great love for this land?"

"Oh, no. I've always been a nomad. I've lived all over the States and in Europe. I can take a place or easily leave it, I'm just that way."

Hank's frown deepened. They had not gone into this before. Hank had made his offer and had been flatly refused. Kingsley had given only the explanation that the land was priceless to him. But now he was saying that it didn't really matter very much.

"Why, then, did you refuse to sell it to me at a substantial profit?" Hank demanded harshly. So the land didn't matter to Kingsley? Well, it mattered to Hank.

"Here now, we're not going to have another argument, are we? I must say, Mr. Chavez, you should learn to leave emotion out of your business transactions. I have invited you into my house for the second time when the first time proved distasteful. I hope you won't make me regret my hospitality."

Hank was duly contrite. "I am sorry, *señor*. I am not known for a quick temper. If anything, I roll with the punches, as you *americanos* say."

Kingsley laughed. "You could have fooled me."

Hank grimaced. "It is just that this matter is so important to me."

"I gathered that."

"And you say this land means nothing to you," Hank pointed out. "I don't—"

"Hold on now," Kingsley interrupted. "I didn't say that at all. This place is priceless to me because it represents permanency to my daughter. I never settled down until she came to me. But I brought her here to live, so this place is her home. She's the one who loves it here."

"I was not aware that you had a daughter."

"She wasn't here when you came before. She isn't..."

There was an uncomfortable silence. Hank knew exactly what Samantha's father couldn't bring himself to say—that she wasn't there, and why. The love he had counted on was there. The man would do anything for his daughter.

"You speak as if she did not always live with you," Hank said, trying to keep the conversation light.

"Ellen, her mother, took her away from me when she was just a baby. I won't go into that. I didn't see my daughter again until she was nine. I brought her here the year after I finally got her away from her grandparents."

"Her mother?"

"Died soon after she left me."

"I am sorry. I know what it is like to grow up without a mother. Mine died at my birth. My grandmother took her place, but it was not the same."

"I hope she was a sight nicer than Samantha's grandmother. That old woman was a bitch."

Hank laughed. "My *abuela* was a kind woman, if a little forgetful and testy in her old age. She died here in this house."

"Good Lord!" Kingsley gasped. "You didn't tell me your family had lived here!"

"You did not give me a chance to," Hank reminded him. "I am afraid we both lost our tempers before."

Kingsley looked quite uncomfortable. "Yes, well, I can see now why you want this place so much. But I hope you understand now why I won't sell it."

Hank tensed. "You have not asked why I came to see you again," he said.

Kingsley smiled. "I'm sure this is not just a social call."

"I will be frank and admit I had hoped to take advantage of your misfortune," Hank returned in a grave tone. "You see, I have heard of the trouble you are having with *bandidos*. You seem to be the only one in this area whom they are harassing."

"Harassing no longer describes it, Mr. Chavez." Kingsley's voice rose. "The bastards have kidnapped my daughter!"

Hank managed to look shocked. *"Dios!* I was not aware of this, *señor*. You must be mad with worry."

"Worried sick one minute, furious the next. I've never wanted to kill anyone so much in my life as I do this El Carnicero, the leader. And so help me, I will do more than that if he dares hurt my little girl!"

"But how did they manage to take her? Surely she was always with an escort?"

"Yes, she was heavily escorted, but a lot of good it did when she got it into her mind to race ahead of them," Kingsley said angrily. "She's just too damn hard-headed. She knew the danger, yet she still challenged Ramón to race."

"Ramón?"

"Baroja, a neighbor. Possibly my future son-in-law," Kingsley explained. "The two of them raced away from Samantha's escort and were taken by surprise."

"Was anyone hurt?" Hank asked tightly.

So! Ramón Baroja was a possibility for son-in-law? Samantha had lied to him, then, calling him a childhood friend. What else had she lied about?

"Ramón was shot, but he's recovering. The poor boy is devastated though, blaming himself."

"As well he should, if he was foolish enough to let your daughter leave her escort." Hank remembered Ramón Baroja well. He had never been a child to take responsibility seriously.

Kingsley frowned. "Yes, well, you don't know my daughter. I've never been able to control her, so I can't blame Ramón for being unable to."

"Forgive me, Señor Kingsley," Hank said quickly. "I did not mean to judge. I sympathize with you. I cannot imagine what you must be going through. It must be agony. I pray these *bandidos* will not harm the girl. They probably want the ransom and nothing more."

"They don't want money," Kingsley said brusquely. "I wish they did! These scum demand I leave Mexico! Can you believe it?"

"I have heard of such things before," Hank replied smoothly. "Perhaps you have angered this *bandido* in some way?"

"I've never met him!"

"Then why?"

"They say he hates *gringos,* but thousands of us have

settled in this land. It makes no sense that he should single me out, unless it's my land he wants. We're ideally located here, near the border."

"That is possible," Hank agreed. "What will you do?"

"Leave. This afternoon, I will go. Another day and you wouldn't have found me here, Mr. Chavez."

"Surely you have not found a buyer already?" Hank was alarmed.

"A buyer? No, I—"

"Then you will be willing to accept my offer?"

"You misunderstand. I'm not selling this land."

"But you are leaving."

"Yes, and I won't be back until my daughter is returned to me. But, as I said, this is my daughter's home. I won't disappoint her by selling it."

Hank was seething, and it was all he could do not to show it. How could he have made such a mistake? Kingsley intended to come back, despite all the harassment, despite the kidnapping.

"I do not understand you, *señor.* You profess to a great love for your daughter, yet you will bring her back here? Put her in the same danger? What if the *bandido* feels you have tricked him and kills her?"

"Once I have my daughter back, El Carnicero is a dead man. I have already hired the best manhunters in the country. He will never touch my daughter again."

Hank asked stiffly, "Is your daughter so young that you expect her to go on living here with you for many years?"

"No, she's grown up, but what—"

"That is the impression I got when you mentioned your neighbor as a possible son-in-law," Hank continued quickly. "Why then do you insist on holding on to this land for her? She may marry soon and leave it."

"That is neither here nor there," Kingsley said with a touch of annoyance. "The property will belong to her completely when she does marry, deeded to her as a wedding present. That was arranged long ago. Whether she lives here or with her husband somewhere else, she will always have this place to come home to."

"And you will be here waiting for her?" Hank said drily.

"No. It will be hers alone, as I said. I have land across the border I plan to retire to. This is why I am hoping for an alliance between Samantha and the Baroja heir. That will combine the two properties here, and I will be less than a week's ride from either one of them." Kingsley brought himself back to the present.

"I am sorry, Mr. Chavez. I realize this land means a great deal to you. Tell me, how did it pass from your family?"

"That would not interest you now, not under the circumstances," Hank replied in a level voice. "But your daughter, do you think she would consider selling, once the land is hers?"

"That would be up to her and her husband, Mr. Chavez. But I doubt it. Samantha loves this land."

"Perhaps I should court your daughter and marry her then."

Kingsley missed the sarcastic tone and laughed, relieved that Hank was accepting defeat gracefully. "I can't say I'd want you courting my daughter, not with that ulterior motive. But then, you haven't met her, Mr. Chavez. You could very easily lose your heart to her, and this land would be only a bonus—if she would accept you, that is."

Hank left while he still had his emotions under control. To think that if Samantha had accepted him before, he would have come to Mexico to find that he had the woman he wanted and his land as well! And without spending a penny to get back his own land! If only he had won Samantha! If only she had not loved another man. If only she had understood about Adrien.

There were too many ifs. Now there was only hate between them, and a kind of twisted desire on his part.

Yes, he could admit now that he still wanted to possess her even though he hated her.

But he wouldn't. He would fight temptation to the bitter end. He would frighten her with it. He would make her wonder. But he wouldn't give her the satisfaction of knowing he cared.

And her father? *Perdición!* The man intended to leave, get his daughter back, and then return. Hank had not even considered that. He should have demanded that Kingsley *sell* and leave, not just leave. What the hell could he do about it now?

Chapter 23

THE sun was setting behind the mountains as Hank and Lorenzo neared their abandoned village, two and a half days later, in record time. Hank's mood had not improved with the hard riding.

They began the climb up the narrow ledge of the canyon that led to the opening and the village. The light was dim, but they would make it home before it was completely dark, so there was no need for torches.

Indeed it was light enough to see the lone rider who came around a turn far ahead and started down the ledge at a reckless pace.

"Por Dios!" exclaimed Lorenzo. "It is *she!*"

Samantha stopped, seeing them halfway down the canyon, blocking the path. For several moments she didn't move, and neither did the riders below. Then she frantically urged her horse to move backward. But the animal was not trained to that and wouldn't budge.

The ledge was wide, but not wide enough for what she attempted. Hank gasped as she made the horse rear up on his hind legs, forcing him to turn around. The ledge was not as wide as the horse was long, and if he brought his forelegs down, both horse and rider would plummet hundreds of feet to the rocky canyon floor.

"She is *loca!*" Lorenzo cried.

But Hank was thinking that she was more than crazy, she was an idiot to risk her life like that. But then, in a moment, she succeeded. A second later she was riding back to the opening in the cliff wall as though the devil were on her trail. And she *would* think the devil had found her when he caught up with her, Hank vowed grimly.

Beyond the village, at the opposite end of the valley, a mountain stream wound down a boulder-strewn surface and, eventually, found its way to the base of the mountains. It was not an easy exit, but it could be used if one was careful, and it was a way out of the valley.

Did Samantha know about it? Hank started after her, careless of the narrow path he raced along.

Samantha sped past the village, praying desperately that the valley was not a dead end. Pasqual saw her as he stepped out of one of the houses, but she didn't care. It was the man behind her on that powerful white stallion she worried about, the man who wasn't supposed to be here.

God, why had he returned so early? Her plan had been perfect, but had hinged on his being gone for as long as he'd said he would. What was he doing back here so soon? She had been so close! It wasn't fair to find Hank blocking the only exit she knew. She had thought to have another day for sure, maybe even two.

The valley was narrowing. Gnarled trees were closing in on both sides, casting great shadows, making everything dark. She didn't dare look back. She would die if she saw El Rey charging close behind her. The mustang she rode was already winded. She would never have a chance to outrun the white stallion.

Samantha screamed as a rope bit into her breasts. She looked down to find a lasso around her. She tried to pull it off quickly, but the rope tightened, nearly pulling her off the horse.

"Ease up now, Sam, or I will unseat you."

The voice was so close, so loud that it thundered inside her head. Tears filled her eyes as she slowed her mount to a standstill, but she wouldn't let him see her cry. Wiping her eyes, she turned and glared as he walked El Rey slowly up to her. He wore a poncho and a wide sombrero that did not hide the dark stubble on his chin.

He looked more like a dangerous *bandido* than ever. He also looked furious, and she saw that Lorenzo had not come with him. They were alone here, hidden by the trees and bushes, far from camp.

"Get down!" he ordered curtly.

"I will not."

He didn't ask again, but started to tug on the rope. Samantha quickly threw a leg over her horse so that she could land on her feet.

"What are you going to do?" she demanded angrily, more than a little nervous.

"I will take you back to camp."

"Then why must I get off the horse?"

"That horse is not for your use," he said sharply, and she could tell that he was making an effort to keep from shouting. "You exhausted him and frightened him cruelly with that stupid maneuver on the canyon ledge. You could both have died."

"I knew what I was doing," she retorted.

His voice rose steadily as he said, "You risked your life and the horse's after you gave me your word you would not try to escape!"

Samantha paled. She had forgotten her promise. She had never broken her word before. But this was different, she told herself stubbornly.

"My word to a bandit does not bind me," she said with icy disdain.

"You may feel that way now, *mujer*, but you will wish you had not!" he warned darkly. He tugged her to him and held out a stiff hand. "Get on!"

"I will walk."

Hank accepted her pronouncement without trying to dissuade her, not even once. He turned El Rey around, and the rope bit into the place just above Samantha's waist, where it had slipped to. El Rey began a slow trot, and she had to run to keep from being dragged across the ground.

Hank made her run for more than a mile. She had

gone several miles before he had caught up with her. Would he make her run the whole way back to camp? She wasn't sure she could make it. Already her legs felt like dead weights. But she wouldn't ask him to stop. He knew very well what he was doing to her. Damn him! He knew, and he was showing no mercy. Well, she would die before she would beg.

Then suddenly she tripped, falling facedown on the hard ground. She didn't have strength enough to get up and was dragged several yards before a rock jabbed her ribs and she cried out. Hank stopped. She rolled to a sitting position, moaning, and at last the tears spilled down her cheeks.

"Will you ride now?" he asked, but she couldn't allow herself to give in.

"I cannot bear to be near you," she hissed, pushing herself to her feet even though her trembling legs nearly gave out. "I will walk!"

He yanked on the rope, making her stumble forward, but he kept the spirited El Rey to a slower pace. All Samantha needed to do was keep walking, not attempt to stop, and she would be able to keep up without being dragged.

She was raging. He didn't have to refuse her the horse, insisting she ride with him. He had known she would refuse to do that. He was forcing her to walk, using her pride against her.

Her legs were killing her. And her breathing was getting so ragged she thought her lungs would burst. She fell once more before they reached the village, but this time Hank didn't stop, and she had to force herself back to her feet or be torn to shreds on the rough ground. Her clothes were ruined. Two buttons on her shirt had been ripped off, exposing the lace camisole. The skin above her breasts was scraped a vivid red. She had managed to get her arms out from the loop around her, but there was not enough slack in the rope to slip it off. Her hands were burning from holding onto the tight rope to steady herself. But she wouldn't cry. She would rather hate Hank for doing this to her.

When the rope finally loosened, Samantha dropped to her knees, gasping for breath. She stayed on her knees while the men stared. They were in front of Hank's house. Pablo stood on the porch holding a lantern that cast a bright, unwelcome light. The old man was speechless with shock at Samantha's broken appearance. Others soon appeared, including Lorenzo, who was shocked—but not speechless.

"You dare to treat her this way!" he growled furiously, catching Hank's arm as he dismounted. *"Madre de Dios!* Why?"

"Stay out of it, Lorenzo."

"Not this time. Look at her!"

Hank did, and in the bright light he saw at last what he had done to her. But through her tear-streaked eyes Samantha was glaring murderously at him, and the remorse he might have felt didn't surface because of the fury being directed at him.

"She is a trifle worn out," Hank said carelessly. "She brought it on herself."

"She only tried to escape," Lorenzo replied heatedly. "You cannot blame her for that."

"Can't I?" Hank hissed. "She gave me her word that she would not."

"You ask too much."

"No, I expect better of her. You forget I knew her before this."

"But did you have to do this to her?" Lorenzo's voice was quieter. "You had caught her. She could go no farther. Did you have to drag her?"

"I offered to take her on my horse, but she refused. As I said, she brought this on herself."

"I cannot believe—"

"Ask her!" Hank snapped.

Lorenzo did, but Samantha stubbornly shook her head, refusing to corroborate Hank's version.

"She lies," Hank said darkly, a black storm gathering in his eyes. "As she lied to me when she gave her word to stay here. As she has lied about many things."

Samantha tensed, wishing she had not tried pitting Lorenzo against him by denying the truth. She had only succeeded in making matters worse.

"Pablo, set water to boil," Hank was saying. *"La señorita* will need a bath."

He tossed the reins of El Rey to Inigo and dismissed the others standing around with a glance. But Lorenzo would not let it go at that.

"We are not finished here, Rufino," he said bitterly.

"Sí, we are." Hank turned to him menacingly. "I will not be questioned about her, *amigo*. If you do not like the way I treat her, you can leave now."

"Let it be, Lorenzo," Samantha said in a barely audible whisper. "Please."

"But, *señorita*—"

"No, he was right—I lied. He...he did offer me a ride, and I refused."

Lorenzo's shoulders fell. He faced Hank, his expression contrite. "I will bring Nita to see to her."

"No."

What now? she wondered miserably.

"But she will need help with her bath and salve for her scratches," Lorenzo persisted.

"I will tend her," Hank replied coldly, turning his back on Lorenzo.

"But you cannot!" Lorenzo protested, anger rising again. "A woman should help her. You cannot—"

"Basta ya!" Hank cut him off sharply as he swung around, his eyes glassy silver with suppressed rage. "The woman is known to me. I will not see anything I have not seen before. Do you understand, Lorenzo?"

The shock, the embarrassment on Lorenzo's face shamed Samantha. He did indeed understand. No one was to have learned about that—ever. But now Lorenzo knew, and probably thought the worst of her.

"Tell him *why* you know me so well!" Samantha cried furiously, wishing she had the strength to slap Hank's hateful face.

"You tell him, *querida*," Hank replied in a deceptively quiet tone. "But be sure to include the before and after."

Samantha was crestfallen. She could only stare at Hank, damning him with her eyes. She knew exactly what he was implying. How could she cry rape after she had let him do all those passionate things to her first? And, as far as he was concerned, he had paid for everything when she shot him later. It was not a story that made her look like an innocent victim.

"I do not understand this quarrel between you two." Lorenzo broke the tense silence.

"It's none of your business, Lorenzo," she snapped.

With a desperate effort, she tried pushing herself to her feet. She managed to stand, wobbly, and when Hank and Lorenzo moved to help her, she screamed, "Don't you touch me, either of you!"

She used the railing to pull herself up the steps to the porch. When Hank came up behind her and scooped her up, she wasn't grateful.

"Animal!" she hissed. "I don't want your help."

"You will have it anyway, *niña*," he replied, gently this time. He carried her into the house without another word between them.

Samantha would always remember that night. She was forced to accept Hank's tender ministrations, too tired and sore to struggle against him. He bathed her, stripping her down to nothing and carrying her to the tub. And all she could do was cry. The water was scalding, and he made her sit in it for what seemed hours. Then he carried her to the bed and toweled her dry all over, taking an undue amount of time at it.

"My arms don't hurt," she protested.

But her hands did hurt, and she couldn't stop him. And all the while he tended her, his face wore a closed look. She couldn't tell what he was thinking, and she was too tired to wonder if the sight of her so weak and vulnerable was affecting him. He was gentle when he applied salve to her chest and hands, but he could have been treating a stranger for all it showed on his face. When he moved to her bare legs to massage her aching muscles, she moaned beneath his touch, not because of the intimacy, but from the pain his fingers were causing.

Then he was finished, and she opened her eyes despite the shame she felt. She found him staring down at her, his expression no longer shuttered. She recognized the burning look in those gray eyes, and what she saw wasn't anger.

His eyes traveled slowly down the length of her exposed beauty, as if weighing her condition against his desire. Then he took the blanket from the foot of the bed and covered her.

"Sleep well, little one," he murmured softly, speaking Spanish.

The Spanish words rang in her ears as Hank shut the door, closing her in darkness. Why did he so often do that? He didn't know she understood Spanish. Did he hope to make her wonder what he was saying? Oh, why couldn't she just leave this place and forget about him?

Chapter 24

"WHY do you never wear your gun when you come into this room, Hank?"

Samantha was sitting up in bed, leaning back against the wall, her legs bent and hidden under her peasant skirt. She had spent all day yesterday in bed, though it hadn't been necessary. Her legs hadn't hurt nearly as badly as she had expected. Perhaps it was the hot water. Or Hank's gentle massage. But she had stayed in bed, forcing him to wait on her.

She felt fine today, but she was in a testy mood. She had not forgiven Hank.

"Are you afraid I might try to take it from you?" she goaded, when he didn't respond.

Hank set the tray of food down on the trunk and crossed his arms over his chest. He was comfortably dressed in a shirt and trousers, the dark shirt opened halfway down his bronzed chest. Samantha looked for the scars she had left on his chest but couldn't see any, and she wondered bitterly if they had gone away.

"Why should I wear my gun in here? What is there in here for me to fear, *niña?*"

"Oh, you always twist everything around," she said petulantly. "Can you never answer a simple question?"

"But I always answer your questions—when you ask me nicely."

" All right! Tell me right now how much longer you intend to keep me here. It's been almost two weeks."

"A week and a half."

"That *is* almost two weeks! And don't quibble with me. Just answer the question."

"You do not like it here, Sam?"

She glared at the grin curling his mouth. "I'm in no mood for teasing, Hank Chavez."

He shrugged. "I have no answer for you. You must wait...just as I must wait."

She frowned. "But the trip you went on. It was to see if my father was following your instructions, wasn't it? Didn't you find out anything?"

"I found out many interesting things, one of which is that your father thinks he can fool me."

"What do you mean?" Samantha bounded off the bed. "Didn't he leave, as you instructed?"

"Yes, he has left Mexico."

"Well, then, take me to him," she demanded. "What are you waiting for?"

"He left, Sam, but he has every intention of returning. That will not do."

"What did you expect?" she hollered at him. "I told you he wouldn't give up the land."

"And I say he will," Hank rasped. "Or he does not see you again!"

Some of the spark went out of her eyes. "So what will you do now?" she asked softly.

"I have sent another message."

"Saying?"

"That I am aware of his game, that either he sells or he will not get you back."

"It will never work, you know," Samantha said with a touch of humor. "My father won't be browbeaten into anything."

"Then you will stay here indefinitely."

"Oh, no." Samantha was smiling now, delighting in his scowl. "Father will sell, all right, and probably to that cousin of yours. That is how you have it planned, isn't it? Your cousin will be there to make an offer my father is forced to accept? But it won't work, Hank, not by a long shot."

"Antonio will have a signed deed."

"A deed my father can break in any court," she taunted. "That deed won't be worth a damn, Hank, because it will have been signed under duress. And my father will have your message to prove that he was forced."

"You are only guessing. Antonio is not involved. The deed will be good."

"*They* don't know he's involved, my friend, but *I* do." Samantha grinned.

"I told you he knows nothing!" Hank shouted.

"Do you think anyone will believe that? I don't, so why should anyone else?"

"It is the truth!"

"Perhaps. But it doesn't really matter. Just linking your name with your cousin's will do the trick. And I will be there to do just that."

He caught her arm so suddenly that she cried out in surprise. His eyes blazed with dark fury. Samantha cringed, damning herself for goading him.

"You cannot link me with Antonio if you are dead," Hank hissed through gritted teeth.

Samantha paled, but somehow she realized he was bluffing. "You wouldn't kill me."

"You are sure?"

"Yes," she said flatly. "You might rape me like a savage, as you did before, but you won't even hit me. I've hurt you many times, but you've never struck me."

"There is a first time, *chica*," he warned her.

"No. You just don't have it in you."

He shoved her away from him. "Perhaps you are right in this. I do not have the stomach to kill a woman— even you. But a man, Samantha Kingsley—a man I would have no compunction in killing."

"So?"

He walked over to her slowly and raised a finger to

trace along her jaw line. Samantha twisted her face away from his hand, but she stood her ground. She wouldn't be intimidated by him.

"Do you love your father, Sam?"

"What kind of question is that?" she snapped. "Of course I love him."

"And you would grieve if he died suddenly?" he asked softly.

She gasped. "You bastard!"

Samantha flew at him, intending to scratch his eyes out. But Hank's arms circled her, sealing her in a grip that left her breathless.

"You vile, despicable animal!" she gasped furiously, squirming to break away. "You'll never get near enough to him to kill him. Never!"

"You think not? If I can steal noisy chickens, and leave my mark on doors with twenty *vaqueros* nearby, then I can easily reach one man. It would solve this new problem you have made for me, would it not?"

"You can't do it!" she stormed. "You will accomplish nothing if you do!"

"On the contrary, *niña*. I can kill him after he sells the land."

"As his daughter, *I* can still take it to court. You won't win."

"Perhaps," he conceded. "But your father will already be dead, and as a direct result of your stubbornness." He released her abruptly. "Is that what you want?"

"Oh, damn you!"

She fell back against the bed. "Just remember, Sam. *If* I let you return to your father, I can still kill him anytime. And I will, if he goes anywhere near a court. If you love him, you can convince him not to cause me any trouble."

After he left, Samantha stared at the tray of food, too upset to eat. Lord, why did she always have to open her big mouth? If she had just kept quiet, she would have been returned to her home, and Hank would have found out too late that his scheme wouldn't work. He would never have thought of killing her father. Now he held the ace card. But she couldn't let him get away with all this. There had to be some way she could turn the tables on him. There just had to be.

Chapter 25

DIEGO was invited to dinner that night, and Samantha was uncomfortable being near him. She didn't understand why he was there. She couldn't stand being near the woman-beater.

She hoped to avoid eating with them, but when she tried to take her own food to her room, Hank pulled out a chair and insisted she stay. She didn't understand it, for after that, he ignored her completely, and she was excluded from the conversation.

They switched to Spanish after a while, and Samantha's cheeks burned, for the talk was of her. Diego was complimentary in a vulgar way, but Hank was insulting. She wanted to curse him, to ridicule him in turn, but she couldn't say a damn thing because she wasn't supposed to understand Spanish. But Hank was pushing her, pushing her to her limit. She didn't have to sit there and take it.

Without a word she left the table and went to her room. Hank followed, and when she turned to close the door, his hand held it open.

"Why leave so early, Sam? I was enjoying your company."

"I wasn't enjoying yours—or his!" she snapped. "I won't sit there and be talked about behind my back!"

"And how do you know we spoke of you?"

"Because you couldn't say two words without your eyes falling on me. I'm not that dense."

"Perhaps I like looking at you."

"Liar!" she hissed.

His eyes were laughing at her, gleaming with dev-ilry. "You do not think you are worth looking at?"

"I know that you hate me as much as I hate you," she fumed. "And if I can't stand the sight of you, then I know the feeling must be mutual. So stop playing with me. I won't have it!"

"It is only fair that it should sometimes be my turn to play games, Sam. Is that not so?"

"No, damn you, no!" she cried. "You have already had your revenge." Then she lowered her voice to a whisper so Diego couldn't hear. "You took from me what I would never have given to you. You were a savage animal!"

Hank caught her shoulders to pull her close, and his voice was low and threatening. "That is not so. You were the little savage, *chica,* and I have the marks to prove it. Perhaps I should refresh your memory of how it really was."

"You do and I'll mark you up worse!" she cried on a rising note of panic. "I swear I'll tear you to shreds!"

He laughed and let her go. "I do not think so, *querida.* I think next time I will make you purr like a kitten."

"A kitten has claws, Hank. Now go away. I'm sick to death of your threats."

She pushed the door shut on him, then waited to hear the lock turn. But it didn't. She heard him laugh as he walked away, and soon the two men were talking again. Samantha continued to wait, pacing the floor nervously. She wouldn't be able to sleep until that door was locked. She couldn't trust Hank not to bother her, and she wasn't going to let him find her in bed.

Hours passed. She could hear low conversation, an occasional loud laugh, a bottle slamming against the table. Were they getting drunk? She chilled. What would a drunken Hank be like? Would he forget that he hated her? Would he come in here and...no!

She sat down on the bed, then jumped back up again. She looked for a weapon but already knew there wasn't anything useful except the candle holder, and it wasn't heavy enough to do any real damage.

Looking at the candle burned down to only an inch made her realize how late it was getting. She moved to the door to see if she could hear what was being said, but the voices were mumbled. It must be near midnight. Were they never going to sleep?

Just then, she heard the door in the other room close, and she stepped back, startled. Was Diego finally gone?

She ran to the bed and snuffed out the candle, then slipped quietly under the covers, careful to hide the fact that she was still clothed. If Hank opened her door, he would think she had long been asleep. *Lord, don't let him open the door.*

She was stiff as a board, waiting, hoping to hear the door being locked. But no sound came from the other room, and she began to wonder if Hank had fallen into a drunken stupor. And then it hit her. If he was in a deep, drunken sleep, she could easily slip past him. She could escape!

Throwing the covers off in sudden excitement, Samantha rushed to the door again. Very slowly she opened it, holding her breath. Her heart sank. Hank was still sitting at the table, his back to the outside door. Two empty bottles were before him, but he didn't look drunk. The candles on the table had gone out. Only the logs burning in the fireplace lit the room with a dim yellow glow.

"Were you going someplace?"

She jumped.

"Come and join me, *gatita*," he continued in a lazy voice. "I have been waiting for you."

He didn't sound drunk, and Samantha asked hesitantly, "What do you mean, waiting for me? What makes you think I haven't been sleeping?"

He chuckled in a grating manner. "Because the candle in your room has burned all night. The light could be seen under the door, along with your shadow as you passed back and forth, back and forth."

She blushed and replied stiffly, "So I wasn't tired."

"Be truthful, Sam."

"All right," she said with a touch of anger as she came forward. "I was waiting for you to lock the door."

"You could have slept with the door open."

Samantha reached the table, standing across from him, her chin tilted at a defiant angle. "In order to do that, I would have to trust you. But I don't."

Hank's gray eyes lit up with amused laughter. "Why does my locking the door make you feel secure, Sam? I can open it at any time."

"But you never have before," she pointed out. "Not after you shut me in for the night."

"True," he conceded.

"So why didn't you lock the door?"

"You were not going anywhere, nor was I. There was no...hurry."

His casualness annoyed her. "You could have got drunk and passed out."

"And you would have taken advantage of that? No, *mi gatita,* I do not get drunk on a little tequila. At any rate, Diego is the drinker. I have simply kept him company, listening to him talk. You see, he misses his woman, now that she is gone."

"I'm afraid I can't manage any pity for him on that score," she replied drily.

"That is because you have no heart."

She ignored that. "Is that why you invited him here, to listen to his problems?"

"No, *querida mía,*" Hank said in a too soft voice now. "He was here to distract me from a problem I have, to keep me from doing anything about it."

Samantha blanched, wishing she didn't understand. But she did. Diego was supposed to keep him from her. But Diego was gone now.

"I had thought you would go to sleep," he continued

in that same soft tone as he rose slowly from his chair. "I had hoped I would then have the decency not to disturb you."

"Then you should have locked the door!" Samantha cried, in the grip of something she didn't quite understand.

"Perhaps, after all, I did not want you to be asleep," he murmured.

Samantha stared at him for a moment, then shook her head. "You can just get those thoughts out of your head right now!"

"I wish I could. Truly, Sam."

He took a step around the table, and Samantha turned and walked to her room. She got there first and closed the door, but he pushed it open, shoving her into the room as he did. The back of her legs hit the bed, and she lost her balance, falling onto it. She sat up and stared at him as he stood framed in the doorway, the dim glow of the fire behind him. Her heart began a wild hammering beat, and she tingled from the racing of her blood.

He started forward, leaving the door open, pulling his shirt from his pants as he moved toward her. Samantha moved back on the bed as far as she could go, trapping herself in the corner as she had done before.

As she watched Hank remove his shirt, she was aware of a quick rising in her spirits. All that he had implied about his leaving the door unlocked was, she told herself, quite true. Of course she hated the man. Of course she despised this kidnapper, this bandit. But she would not deny the strong feelings she had for Hank, wouldn't deny it to herself now as she had refused to deny it to herself on that other occasion, under the tree. If there was one thing Samantha never did, it was lie to herself. She wanted Hank, and he would see to it that she was not disappointed.

Fearing that he could read her thoughts, she turned her face to the wall, feigning indifference. He would have to make the first move... and the second. He would have to woo her. She would never let him know outright that she desired him as fully, perhaps, as he desired her. Never!

He removed one boot, then the other. The sound of them hitting the floor was so final, it seemed to be sealing their fates. His pants dropped, and he kicked them aside.

"Why?" she demanded. "Are you so starved for a woman that you can't wait for one who truly wants you?"

He lay down beside her, and soon she found her blouse discarded. She could see now the four faint scar lines on each side of his chest.

"As a matter of fact, you were the last woman I touched," he admitted frankly. "You set a fire in me then. You have set another in me now. Wait for another woman? No, my sweet one. You will put out the fire."

"You... you're a disgrace," she gasped, but there wasn't much strength in the protest.

"I will not do anything I have not done before."

"That—"

"Are you ever going to stop talking, Samina?" he breathed softly.

After that, neither of them said another word. She lay across the bed, and he moved to lie on top of her, gently, not pressing with his whole weight. He looked deeply into her eyes, and she gazed directly back without looking away. There were no clothes between them. She could feel the heat of his body down the length of her.

When Hank's face came close to hers she closed her eyes expecting to be kissed, but his mouth moved to her neck instead, and quickly that sensitive area was shivering with gooseflesh.

When his mouth closed over the fullness of one breast and his tongue danced circles around the erect nipple, Samantha began squirming closer to him. She had indeed set a fire in him, and he was kindling one in her. Her mind fought it, but her body was responding to his touch, his lips burning, searing her flesh. And when he forced her legs apart to slip between them, the hardness of him caused deeper heat, making her gasp.

She could feel that hard shaft against her, probing, but he didn't enter her. The smooth round tip of him rested, teasing her, torturing her with waiting, with wanting that first plunge.

She wanted him. He had made her want him despite herself.

His mouth moved back to her neck. "Your skin is satin," he breathed by her ear. "I have not forgotten, *querida*. I have remembered—everything."

Her resistance had faded completely, and he knew it. Her hands grasped his neck, pulling him closer. It was time to end the torture, and as he thrust deeply into her, her body arched, wanting more of him. She was equal to his movements, her passion wild. It was love in its most primitive state.

Hank only barely felt her nails biting into his neck as she reached her peak, for he was in the grip of his own exquisite release. But when the pleasure subsided, the burning sting of her nails took over, and he knew she had drawn blood again. But it was worth it. Damned if this woman wasn't worth anything.

Her breathing was slowing gradually, and her fingers were moving in his hair as he rested his head on her shoulder.

He leaned on his elbows to look down at her. Her eyes opened, and, in the faint light, he saw dark, shimmering pools of green that he would lose himself in if he was not careful.

He touched her cheek with a feathery caress. "You have marked me again, *gatita*," he murmured.

"I know," she replied softly, her hands moving to those scars on his chest, her fingers tracing them gently.

"I will mark you every time in some way. Remember that."

"You do not seem angry," he remarked.

"I don't have to scream all the time," she answered, and the hint of a smile touched her lips. "It's enough that you know I speak the truth."

"Yes." He grinned. "But these new scars I will gladly accept, for they were given in—"

"Don't say it!" Her body went stiff, and her fingers turned into claws that pressed warningly against his skin. "Don't you dare!"

"Very well." His eyes narrowed, angry at the sudden change in her. "But whether you wish to forget it or not, *I* will remember."

"Oh, get out of here!" she snapped then. "You got what you wanted. Go on!"

He left the bed, and Samantha shivered as the cool air touched her where his warmth had so recently been. She quickly covered herself. Hank was staring down at her, furious. For several long moments he just stared at her, and then he left. She turned over, sighing as the door was slammed and locked.

Chapter 26

THE iron plate of food was dropped on the table with a resounding clang. Hank looked sideways at Samantha as she went back to the counter for the *chilis* and *salsas*. These, too, were dropped heavily on the table before she sat down.

"You slept late, Sam," Hank remarked casually, looking at her under the rim of his brows. "Perhaps too late, eh?" She didn't look at him. "There must be something to explain your mood. Should I guess?" he added suggestively.

"What did you expect, a truce? You've only made matters worse."

Her voice was low and bitter, and Hank cringed.

"I am sorry, Sam."

"No you're not. Don't be hypocritical."

She just wanted to forget last night, but she knew she wouldn't be able to, any more than she had been able to forget their first time. He had said that she was in his blood. If only he knew that his handsome face haunted her, as well. Thoughts of him would come to her when she least wanted them to. Was he in her blood, too? No! Then what was this power he had over her will? How was it that he could make her want him, hating him though she did?

"You have not asked about your friend."

She looked up at him, noticing for the first time how smooth his cheeks looked when he was freshly shaven. His long sideburns just touched his cheeks, and he had short black curls that turned upward on his temples, giving him a boyish look. He was all man, this Spanish-American half-breed, boyish-looking or not.

"Sam?"

Samantha met his questioning eyes, then lowered her own. "My friend?"

"Ramón Baroja. You have not asked about him."

"Oh. No, I haven't."

"Why, when you begged me to find out about him? It has been three days, and you have not asked."

"I was afraid to," she lied, unwilling to admit that she had often forgotten for long periods. "Afraid you would have bad news."

"I can see why you might be afraid," he said cryptically, sitting well back in his chair, his eyes intent on her.

"Why?"

"Because you lied to me. The boy is more than just a friend to you."

"He's not a boy," she protested. "He's a man. And I have no idea what you're talking about."

"The very likely possibility of his becoming your husband is what I refer to."

"Who told you that?"

He shrugged. "The rumor came to me."

"A rumor is only gossip, not fact. But what difference does it make? It's certainly none of your business."

"Let us say I have an interest," Hank replied levelly. "Is it true?"

A grin turned Samantha's lips. "What if it is?" she asked evasively, her eyes challenging him.

"I would not like it, *niña*," he said darkly.

She laughed. "You wouldn't? Perhaps you'll tell me why it could possibly matter to you."

"You seem to forget in all of this that I wanted you for my own, Sam."

Her expression sobered. "You don't anymore."

"But I did. You may hate me now, and I accept that.

But you professed to love Adrien. I would not like to think your affections turn so quickly. Do they, Sam?"

After the mention of Adrien, Samantha's temper came to the fore. "I don't give a damn what you do and don't like!"

"Do you love him?" Hank shouted.

Her eyes widened in surprise. He was furious, but why?

"Look at yourself, Hank. Your pride is showing. You just can't stand the fact that I turned you down and might have quickly found another. That's it, isn't it?"

He stood up, and so did she. They glowered at each other across the table. Then Hank suddenly shoved the table aside and crossed the space between them, before Samantha could think to run.

He caught her arms and pulled her roughly to him. "Perhaps you are right, Sam. If I had not wanted you so, it would not matter. We could have been good together. You know that now as well as I do."

He kissed her, his lips rough and demanding. She fought against it for only a few short moments before she was responding, her arms moving up around his neck. His anger had excited her, as did his closeness, and the memory of pleasure in his arms. She couldn't fight all of that.

"Mi querida," he breathed, his lips moving to her cheek, her neck. "I can still make you my woman. I can keep you here and never let you go."

"No!" She shoved him away, shocked. "It's too late for that!"

Hank ran a hand through his hair in a weary gesture. He gave her a long, confused look before he turned and crossed to the open door. He stopped there, looking out at the dirt yard, at the brush-covered cliff a hundred yards away, looking really at nothing in particular.

Samantha stared at his back. "You didn't really mean that, did you—about keeping me here?"

"No."

She moved to pull the table back to where it belonged and straighten the chairs, needing something to do.

"Hank, why did you say that?"

He sighed. "Just words spoken in a moment of passion. Forget them, Sam."

Samantha stood staring at his strong back. "But you don't still want me, you admitted that. You *do* hate me...don't you, Hank?"

He turned and faced her. "Would it make you feel better if I said yes?"

"I want the truth."

"The truth, *niña,* is that being close to you like this is affecting me. When I look at you I—" He stopped, smiling at the bewilderment in her face. "But that is not what you wanted to hear, eh? You like it better, my hating you?"

"It's much simpler that way. And you do, don't you?"

He reached out and cupped her chin in his hand. "Feelings change, *gatita.* When I took you by the stream, I hated you. You know why."

"Because I had scorned you, you said."

"No, because you used me, to further your cause with another man. That angered me more than I could bear."

"You took that all wrong, Hank. *I* never believed that you and I were anything more than friends."

He shook his head. "In your scheme to make your Adrien jealous, you gave *me* cause to think otherwise. My feelings grew deep, until I knew I wanted you for my own. I have never wanted another woman quite as much."

Samantha jerked away from his hand. "What about Angela? You said you wanted her."

"It is surprising that you should remember that." He grinned.

"Answer me!" she snapped.

"I did want her. But I knew where I stood with her. You, *mi belleza,* made me forget her."

"Did you force her, too?" she asked bitterly.

His eyes turned steely gray. "She did not play me false, as you did." And then he laughed. "She also had a man who would have killed me if I had touched her. It is too bad the one you loved would not avenge you, eh? But, then, you did pretty well all by yourself."

"Not well enough," she replied huffily. "Nor am I finished yet."

"Ah, yes, the hordes of killers you will send after me. Let us not forget them. Nor the fact that I will have to kill any who get too close. There will be many deaths for the sake of your revenge, Sam."

"I was not referring to that."

"No? What then? You wish to shoot me?"

"Yes, but you will die knowing your scheme against my father failed. Your cousin won't be able to keep the land you have gone to so much trouble to get for him. I will see to that."

Hank stiffened. "I thought we settled this. You don't believe my warning?"

"Oh, I believe you. But you can't do anything about it if you're dead, now can you?" she taunted.

"And if I do not die, *niña*? If you or your paid killers cannot find me? What then?"

"I can wait," she said implacably. "Eventually I will get our land back."

"How?"

"You can hold me to silence only as long as my father lives. When he dies, your cousin will have the fight of his life on his hands. And I will win, Hank."

"Too much time will have passed," he scoffed. "Your claim on the land would be invalid."

"Not if I pave the way beforehand. Lawyers can do a great deal, you know. I can put it on record now that you blackmailed me to keep me from getting what is rightfully mine."

There was silence, then Hank asked suddenly in a deadly soft whisper, "That land means so much to you?"

"Yes. And I don't care how long it takes. I'll get my

land back." Her eyes gleamed with triumph as she saw how her words were shaking him, and for spite, she added, "Your cousin's sons will never inherit that land, Hank—but mine will. I promise you that." And she turned abruptly and went back to her room before he could find a reply.

Chapter 27

SAMANTHA'S mood improved a hundredfold in the next two days because Hank had believed her, was enraged, and could not hide it. He had no more threats, no means of stopping her. Everything he had done by kidnapping her would be for nothing.

The immediate future would not change. That was the drawback. For the time being, Hank had won. His cousin would have the land—for many years, Samantha hoped, for she wanted her father to live to a ripe old age. But Hank's victory would last only that long.

Samantha gloated. It relieved her boredom very nicely. It made her anger over her confinement subside quite a bit. She forgot to count the days and was surprised to realize that she had been in the valley for two weeks.

If Hank had been on her mind before, he was soon in her thoughts continually. Whether she was in the outer room with him, or alone in her own tiny room, he haunted her. And she did not always think of him with anger.

She was curious about this man who had become the focal point of her life. He had once wanted her to go to Mexico with him. What would it have been like if she had said yes? The circumstances all might have been different. If she had known about Adrien sooner. If Hank had asked her to marry him instead of just to live with him. Things might have been quite different. After all, he was an extremely attractive man—*muy guapo*—as Froilana would say. He had excited her from the first.

Nor would she deny the strange power he had over her when he took her in his arms. What would it be like to be his willing partner instead of having to fight herself.

She would never know. She would always fight him. It couldn't be any other way, not after all that had happened.

But that didn't stop her from wondering. There was that other side to him, the side she couldn't understand. He could be the most winsome, likable man! When those gray eyes of his shone with laughter he could make anyone smile.

And then there was the Hank who was risking his life for his cousin. All of this, for his cousin. Hank would get nothing out of it. Why was he doing all this for Antonio Chavez? She would like to meet the man who inspired such devotion. Or was that, maybe, all lies, too? Perhaps Hank wasn't really so selfless. Perhaps he *would* be getting something out of it, after all. But what?

Samantha leaned back on her hands and stretched her legs out on the porch steps. The morning sun had yet to find its way over the roof to the steps, and it was cool there, but it promised to be a hot day, even at this altitude. She looked around. Her beautiful mountains. She had never thought she would be living in them, tucked away in a hidden valley. And for how much longer?

Times like this, she didn't mind the waiting. She could sit on the porch alone and think. It gave her the only sense of freedom she had. She knew she couldn't wander off. She knew that even now Hank's eyes were on her. He was inside, sitting at the table with his morning coffee, watching her through the open door. But she didn't mind.

She could feel his eyes on her back. He would be scowling. She laughed softly to herself. Yes, he would definitely be scowling. She had burned his breakfast that morning. Not on purpose, but of course he thought it was intentional and blew up about it. Such a grouch! But then she knew what was really eating at him— her and the doubts she had planted in his mind.

Stretching lazily, Samantha rose and crossed to the open door. She stopped there, leaning against the frame, staring boldly at Hank. He caught her eye, and his face darkened. It was amusing to see how easily she could upset him.

"You have something on your mind, Sam?" he asked curtly. She didn't look away.

"Nothing in particular." She shrugged. "I was just wondering about you."

"Oh?"

"Tell me something. If I had agreed to be your woman, just supposing, would you still have taken up your cousin's cause?"

Hank leaned back and, for the first time in two days, grinned. "If you were my woman, Sam, my first loyalty would be to you."

"You're not just saying that to make me think I brought this whole thing on myself by refusing you?"

Now he shrugged. "Think whatever you like."

Samantha frowned. "Would you have brought me here, to live in this shack? Is this the kind of life you were offering me?"

Hank laughed humorlessly. "Believe me, things would have been very different. But it is pointless to speculate. You refused. We are here now under quite different circumstances."

"Of course," she said offhandedly. She sighed. "Don't you get bored, sitting around here doing nothing?"

"There is nothing to be done until I know the last message has reached your father. It is a waiting game we all play. I do not like it any more than you do."

Samantha walked slowly into the room, stopping across the table from him. "You could give it up, you know," she said casually.

"Why? Because you say you will win in the end? You

are not guaranteed a long life, Sam. People die. Your father could outlive you, and then it would be my cousin who won."

"That's a long shot, and you know it."

"Possible though."

"Go right ahead and hope for that if it makes you happy." She smiled.

Hank cleared his throat and went on. "There are two things I can do yet, *niña*, to assure that the land stays in the Chavez family. But you will not like them."

She looked at him warily. "What?"

"Well, you and I could make a baby—if we have not already done so."

Samantha gasped.

His eyes danced with laughter. "I have not given it much thought, but the fact is that you have sworn your sons will inherit that land, and if one of your sons should be mine—"

"Never!" Samantha shrieked, planting her hands squarely on the table to lean forward and glare at him. "Do you hear? Never!"

"It was... just a thought." He grinned.

Her eyes gleamed like emerald fire. "I would never bear you a son!"

"You may not have a choice."

"Don't even think about it!" she warned furiously. "Of all the insane ideas. It's your cousin who wants the land, not you. Why would you think of such a thing?"

She turned away from the table in anger, but she was too upset to leave it alone and turned back to look at him narrowly. "What makes you even think I would keep a son of yours? You know how much I hate you."

"*Sí*, I know your heart is cold where I am concerned. But we speak of a baby—your baby. I do not think you would hate your baby simply because I was the father."

"I can't believe I'm even discussing this with you." She threw her hands up in frustration. "I will *not* have your baby! I didn't conceive the first time you...raped me. This last time will be no different!"

"It only takes once, *querida*," he said softly. "The possibility is there."

"The odds are against it!" she snapped, hating his confident tone.

"I could improve the odds."

Her eyes widened. She understood all too well.

"You really are crazy," she whispered. "Your lust is one thing. But wanting to create an innocent child for such a despicable reason...."

Hank rose, and Samantha backed away slowly. "Don't you come near me, damn you. I'll tell you right now that if I had your child, I might raise it, but I would disinherit it anyhow. Do you understand? You still won't win! I won't let you!"

"I will gamble, Sam, that when the time comes, you will not do so. You will have forgotten me by then, and you will love your child. You will never disown it."

He took a step toward her, and she screamed "No," shaking her head and backing away. "No!"

She was out the door and down the steps before Hank could stop her, running without direction. She wanted only to outrun him, to hide, anywhere.

"Whoa, *muchacha*."

Samantha's feet left the ground as an arm gripped her waist and she was spun around.

"*Caramba!* What has come over you, woman?"

She stopped, recognizing the voice, and nearly cried with relief. "Thank God it's you, Lorenzo. I thought—" And then she stiffened and grasped his shirt. "Don't let him catch me! Please! Don't let him take me back into that house!"

"Rufino?"

"Of course Rufino!" she shouted, wanting to shake him. "Who else would be chasing me?"

"But he is not chasing you."

Samantha looked behind her to see Hank on the

porch, leaning lazily against a post, watching her. She stared at him hard, damning him for making her so frightened, and he stood there as if nothing had happened, making her seem ridiculous.

"Where were you running to, *señorita?*"

She sighed irritably, letting go of him. "I don't know. And don't call me *señorita* anymore. Formality is out of place here. Call me Sam. *He* does."

"Sam! No, no—"

"You call me Samina and I swear I'll break your nose!"

Lorenzo stepped back, his dark eyes confused, and Samantha groaned. What was the matter with her, taking her anger out on him?

"I'm sorry," she said. "I had no call to snap at you like that. He's got me to where I don't know what I'm doing or saying anymore."

"What has happened...Sam?"

"He..."

She looked at the house again. Hank was still there on the porch, waiting confidently, knowing she would have to come back.

"I can't be alone with him anymore, Lorenzo," she said softly, and she turned pleading eyes on him. "He...he's crazy."

"What has he done?"

"What hasn't he done!" She gripped his arms. "Please, Lorenzo, let me stay with you."

"But he has said you must stay with him," Lorenzo reminded her gently. "We have already been through this, little one. I will not go against him simply because you do not wish to be near him."

"It's more than that, damn it!"

"Come. We will straighten this out."

He took her arm, holding tightly when she tried to jerk away. "Lorenzo, for God's sake, don't take me back to him!"

"You are being silly," he said impatiently.

"Silly!" At that point, Samantha lost her temper completely. "He raped me!" she shouted, not caring that her voice carried to Hank. "And he would have again, just now, if I hadn't run away!"

Lorenzo's fingers bit into her arm painfully, making her wince. "That is a harsh accusation, *mujer!* If you lie, to have me fight your battles—"

"Do you think I would admit such a degrading thing unless it was true?"

Lorenzo's grip tightened more, and then, abruptly, Samantha held her breath, watching rage taking over his expression. He swore vehemently and started toward the house with an angry stride.

Samantha stayed where he had left her, staring after him. Lorenzo was going to fight for her! She hadn't expected that. Nor was she relieved. Could he win? If he couldn't, she would still have Hank to deal with, and he would be furious with her for turning his man against him.

Hank was ready for Lorenzo, standing on the porch with his legs apart, braced and waiting. Lorenzo charged up the steps, swinging furiously at Hank, but Hank ducked and threw himself at Lorenzo. They landed in the dust at the foot of the steps, Hank on top, straddling Lorenzo, but throwing no punches.

Samantha stared. Nothing else happened. Where was the fight for her honor? Hank was saying something to Lorenzo, and she moved toward them to find out what lies he was telling. But when she reached them, they were standing up, dusting off their clothes, and she heard only the last of it.

"She will agree?" Lorenzo asked Hank.

"She will."

"She will what?" Samantha demanded, hands on hips, her emerald eyes shooting daggers at Hank.

"Ah, so you have come back on your own, eh?" Hank said. He spoke calmly enough, but there was a message in his eyes.

Samantha saw the anger he couldn't hide. She didn't care. "What lies did you tell him, Hank?"

"No lies."

"You denied raping me?" she yelled.

"Rufino did not deny it." Lorenzo spoke up, uncomfortable. "But he will make it right."

She stared at Lorenzo, aghast. "Would you explain *that* ridiculous remark?"

But Lorenzo said nothing further. He couldn't meet her angry gaze any longer and moved off quickly, leaving her with Hank.

"What the hell did you tell him, Hank?"

"You will find out soon enough," he replied curtly.

"I want—"

"Silencio!" He cut her off brusquely. "We leave this place now. There is no time for your questions, nor do I wish to appease your curiosity."

"Leave?" she gasped. "But you said we had to wait until—"

"I have changed my mind."

"You're taking me to my father, then?"

"Más adelante se lo explicaré," he snapped impatiently.

Samantha stared angrily at his retreating back as Hank bounded up the steps and entered the house, apparently expecting her to follow. He wasn't going to answer any questions.

She knew she ought to be delighted to leave, but instead she was worried. This was too sudden, and Hank's refusal to explain anything made her wary.

What was the man up to now?

Chapter 28

THEY camped out on the open plains that night, making no attempt to conceal their presence. Not even the large boulder they stopped near could hide all of them and the horses too, and Hank seemed not to care.

Over the fire, Inigo cooked a delicious meal of roasted chicken with *frijoles* and *quesadillas,* good enough to rival Maria's fare. Samantha sat near the fire, feeling more secure close to the light. The same three men who had brought her to the mountains were with her again, but Hank was there, too. It made a big difference. Even with the others around, she didn't feel safe with Hank.

He hadn't spoken a word to her since going into the house that morning to gather his gear. She had, heaven knew, little to gather. She wore the peasant blouse and skirt he had provided for her and left her ruined leather skirt and vest behind. Her empty gunbelt was strapped to her hip now—useless, but she wouldn't leave it. Above the holster the gold buckle of her belt worn over the blouse gleamed in the firelight. Fine leather boots poked out from beneath her skirt, and she had put on her silk blouse to use as a jacket. It would provide little warmth if a strong wind picked up, but it was better than wearing the short-sleeved, low-necked cotton blouse alone.

She had been forced to ride El Rey with Hank all day, since no horse was provided for her. Her body was stiff and sore. Hank had made her sit before him in the saddle, and she had determined not to relax against him, for which she was paying already.

She looked at him. He sat across the fire, finishing his meal. He had never got around to telling her the second alternative, but she wouldn't ask, not when his first idea was so shocking. Of course, he might have been bluffing, meaning only to scare her.

Samantha finished the last of her wine and set the cup aside. She watched Diego as he picked up his bedroll and moved off behind the boulder, and Inigo as he cleared the frying pan. Lorenzo was taking a swig from a flask of *tequila*. When he put it away, turning toward her, he wouldn't meet her gaze. He hadn't looked at her all day. Why had Lorenzo suddenly been so pacified by whatever Hank told him? She wanted to question him, but he seemed so disturbed, no, embarrassed by the whole affair. But embarrassed for whom? For her?

Inigo finished cleaning and moved off around the boulder as Diego had done. Then Hank got up and began spreading out his bedroll by the fire.

"Did someone bring a blanket for me?" Samantha asked hesitantly.

But neither man looked at her or answered. Lorenzo was watching Hank, and then he rose, too, and left the area.

"Lorenzo, where are you going?" She jumped to her feet. "Lorenzo!" She did not want to be alone with Hank!

"Leave him be, Sam," Hank said so softly she hardly heard him.

Lorenzo had not gone around the boulder, but was walking away. After a while she couldn't see him anymore.

"Where is he going?" she asked Hank, the suspicions growing and making her voice rise.

"They will all sleep away from us."

"Why?" she cried.

"*Cálmese.*"

"Speak English, damn you!"

"I said calm yourself."

"Give me a reason to!" she demanded, her eyes wide.

Hank came around the fire toward her, but she backed away. "What is it you fear, Sam?"

"You know."

He shook his head. "Tell me."

"You and your crazy ideas about babies!"

He stopped as Samantha continued to retreat. "Ah, so you took me seriously, eh?" he asked, amused.

"Of course not." She tried to sound convincing but failed. "I just don't like the fact that the others are giving you this...privacy. They stayed near me when I traveled with them before. Why have they gone off?"

"You have me to watch over you now. It takes only one man to see that you do not escape."

"But—"

"I want to sleep, Sam, and I can't until you settle down."

"Are you going to tie me up?"

"Do I have to ?"

"No."

"Then I won't," he said agreeably. "I have a blanket for you."

He went to his bedroll and picked up a blanket, holding it out to her. Samantha hesitated. Instinct told her not to trust him. She couldn't run, though. She was still in his power, even out here on this vast plain. As much as she hated it, there was nothing she could do about it.

But she didn't have to seem cowed. Raising her chin, she walked forward purposefully, ignoring the twinkle in his eye. When she reached him, she snatched the blanket away. His deep chuckle grated, but she didn't let it show. She turned away, intending to bed down on the other side of the fire, as far from him as she could.

She was startled when his hands caught her shoulders and he pulled her back, forcing her down onto his bedroll.

"You lied," Samantha said bitterly when he fell down

beside her and put his hand on her skirt. "You said you wanted to sleep!"

"And so I will—afterward."

"After you make a baby?" she cried, her eyes riveted on his face.

"After I give you pleasure, Sam."

"You're crazy if you think I get pleasure out of being raped!"

Hank chuckled. "Now who is lying *dulzura?* There was never any rape."

"Bastard!"

She went for his face. Hank slapped her hand away, then quickly caught both wrists and held her hands above her head.

His eyes were cold steel, his mouth fixed in a hard line. "I like my face the way it is," he said icily. "You scar it with your nails as you did my chest and I swear I will give you equal scars. Think about that, Sam, before you use your claws again."

Tears sprang to her eyes. "You're cruel, Hank. You leave me nothing."

"And what did you leave me when you stole my heart?" he asked softly.

She stared hard at him, searching his eyes, seeing only naked honesty.

"You have your heart back. It's whole and hard and vengeful. Besides, you stole my innocence, which I *can't* get back. You came out ahead, and still you want revenge."

"This is not revenge," he whispered. "You make me ache with wanting you. Does it not satisfy you to have such power over me?"

"No! I suffer because of you!"

"You do not know what it is to suffer, Samina. Even when I took you in anger, I never hurt you. You were more upset that day with the truths I told you about Adrien than with me."

"But you do not take into account my feelings. I hate you."

"But when I make love to you, you forget that."

"I don't!" she gasped.

He grinned at her and with his free hand caressed her cheek. "I am not blind to what happens to you when I touch you, *querida*. Why must you pretend so hard?"

She looked away from him, and a deep flush spread up her neck.

"There is passion in you," he continued huskily. "You cannot fight it. You feel it with me. I strip your pride away, and that is the only thing you suffer. But your pride returns later, so you need not lose it if you do not wish to."

He kissed her and she had no retaliation. He had got inside her, discerned all the truths she had thought hidden from him. He made her feel weak, vulnerable— not because of his strength, but because of his knowledge of her. How had he come to know her so well?

She kissed him back, and he made her seek his lips, leaning back, forcing her to strain for him. Not until she had reached her limit and her shoulders were trembling with effort did he move her head back to the ground and cover her lips with his. He was relentless in passion, fiery and wild, and her desire matched his. She stayed with him, movement for movement, her body drawn by strings he pulled, until at last there was sweet, pulsing release.

The first thought that entered Samantha's mind when clear thought returned was that she hadn't marked him this time. But then his movements caught her attention. He was rubbing his left shoulder and wincing.

"*Gata!* Your teeth are as sharp as your claws. It is not safe making love to you!"

Samantha burst into laughter, and Hank's expression darkened as she laughed harder. She had marked him after all, bitten him and not even remembered it.

"I would remember the position I was in if I were

you, before you amuse yourself at my expense," Hank warned softly.

She sobered instantly. "I'm sorry." She touched his shoulder. "You want me to have a look at your wound?"

"I will see to it myself, thank you, just as I have seen to all the other wounds you have given me."

"Well, if you don't want my help, then how about letting me up?"

He grunted and moved to the side, but threw an arm over her so that she couldn't rise. "You will sleep here."

"Don't be ridiculous," she scoffed.

"I am quite serious, Sam. You will share my bedroll. It is softer than the hard ground."

"I don't care how soft it is," she replied haughtily. "I would rather sleep in a bed of cactus than be near you."

"I do not give a damn what you prefer," he sighed. "I want you next to me, and there will be no more discussion of it. I won't have you slipping off while I sleep."

He fastened his clothing, then bent to fix hers. She tried to stop him, to do it herself, but he shoved her hands away.

"You're impossible!" she hissed, and turned away from him as soon as he finished.

Hank drew the cover over them and settled down behind her, curving his body to hers and dropping one arm around her. "When you are angry, you are like a jewel. You sparkle and shine—for me, eh? You are my *alhaja*."

"You say these things to annoy me, don't you?" Samantha asked stiffly.

"*Si*." He chuckled. "It delights me to stir your temper. But do you know what delights me more?"

"I don't want to know!" she retorted coldly, then asked, "What?"

His fingers brushed a nipple as he answered, "It delights me to see your eyes smolder with passion when—"

"Oh, shut up, damn you!"

She put her hands over her ears, but she could still hear his voice as he continued to taunt her. "Next time I want you, you will not put up so much fuss, eh?"

She didn't answer, wouldn't let herself be goaded. To hell with it. Tomorrow would see her one day closer to her father and to the time when she would see the very last of Hank Chavez.

Chapter 29

SIX days before, they had left the mountains. They had passed the Kingsley ranch—if it still was the Kingsley ranch. For all Samantha knew, her father had sold it already. She felt so dismal with that thought as they circled well around the ranch, to the east, then rode on toward the border.

Hank was in no apparent hurry. He seemed to be dragging his feet, slow to rise in the mornings, making camp early at night. Nearly two days had been wasted through slow progress. Nor did Hank appear to worry about running into anyone looking for her.

They were only a day's ride from her home when they rode into a small village. Samantha had long since given up her stiff posture in the saddle, but she was still tired. She didn't know anyone in this village, but there was a church, so they were probably decent people. The possibility of finding help entered her mind. It would only be a matter of speaking to one person without Hank's knowing, so when Hank pulled up before a *cantina* and dismounted to go inside, she took hope. She waited outside with the others, who were all still on their horses. The street was dark that night, though scattered lights issued from a few houses, and a torch burned in front of the church down the street. This was a small working *pueblo*, and most of the people would be in bed already.

It was twenty minutes before Hank returned and lifted Samantha off El Rey. Lorenzo and Diego followed them into the *cantina*, while Inigo led the horses away to shelter.

It was dim inside the small saloon. A candle flickered at the end of the serving counter near a stairway, toward the door, while at the other end of the room a fire burned under a large pot of food. A woman of indeterminate age bent over the fire, adding fuel. There were only a few tables in the room. A white-haired man slept at one, unaware of the travelers' arrival.

The Mexican woman at the fire turned when they entered, smiling. She motioned them to a table and said that food would soon be ready. Diego and Lorenzo sat down, removing hats, setting saddlebags and rifles aside. But Hank took Samantha to the stairs, taking the candle at the end of the counter to light their way.

His hold on her elbow was firm as they climbed the narrow stairs.

"Will we stay the night here?" she asked before they reached the top floor.

"Yes. There are only two rooms, but Señora Mejia has kindly given us her own."

"The woman downstairs?"

"Yes. She runs this place herself. A widow."

Señora Mejia was the one Samantha would need to talk to, then. How could she manage it if Hank shut her up in a room?

"Don't I even get dinner before you lock me up?"

Hank chuckled at her sharp tone. "I thought you would like a bath. Then you can come down to eat."

They were at the top of the stairs. The two rooms were right there, and out of one came a young lad bearing two empty buckets.

"Your bath is ready," Hank said, thanking the boy before he steered Samantha into the room.

There was ample light from an old lantern. The tub awaiting her was small, but steaming, and there was a fragrance of roses. Samantha smiled. Her favorite scent had been added to the bath. There were clean clothes, too, lying on the narrow bed.

"Are those for me?" Samantha pointed to the white skirt and blouse flounced with delicate lace, and the beautiful *mantilla* next to them.

"Yes."

"The *señora's?*"

"No, a friend of hers has a daughter your size. The clothes are new. They are yours to keep."

"You bought them?" He nodded. "And the rose water was your idea, too? My! You were quite busy while we were waiting out in the street. Will you get me someone to help with my bath?"

"I will be happy to help you."

"Never mind," she snapped.

He grinned. "Then I will see you downstairs when you are finished."

He closed the door, leaving her alone. She ran to the window first, to see if it would offer escape, but there was no overhang, and the drop was straight down. There was nothing to do but take her bath and hope that she still might be able to arrange a word with Señora Mejia.

In less than an hour Samantha descended the stairs, feeling much better after the bath. She had washed her hair, too. The lacy skirt and blouse fit well. They were finely made, probably a special gift for the *señorita* they had been intended for. She hoped the girl would get something just as nice with Hank's money.

But why had he gone to all the trouble? There were sandals, too, and the *mantilla* that was draped over her damp hair was of the same delicate white lace that adorned the skirt and blouse. Samantha felt like a young girl on her way to meet a favored *caballero*. But the only man she was going to meet was Hank.

He was in the *cantina* with Señora Mejia. The others had gone. They were talking by the fire like old friends. Hank, too, had changed clothes. He was wearing the black suit he had worn when he took her to dinner so long ago, the first time he had kissed her. That was when she had understood she had to stop using him to make Adrien jealous. How utterly idiotic that scheme had been, and look what it had led to!

Hank came forward and took Samantha's hand. He led her to a table where a tall candle was burning. There were two place settings, as well as a bottle of wine and a basket of fruit. The *señora* brought *bistec guisado,* a thick stew, and rice and bread.

"Hank, where are the others?" Samantha asked.

"They have already eaten."

That was all he said. He poured them both wine. Samantha frowned. She didn't like this one bit. Why was he being so formal? And why the intimate dinner for two?

Hank noted the frown. "Is something wrong, Sam?"

The questions she wanted to ask would only have amused him, so she stubbornly refused to do so. "No. I was just wondering why you feel safe stopping in this town. All it would take is for me to tell someone here that you've kidnapped me."

"No one here speaks English." He grinned.

"How would you know?"

"I know all these people, Sam," he replied. "They used to live on the Hacienda de las Flores."

Samantha gasped. "Your cousin's people?"

"Yes. The old ones and the women and children came here to live after the Don was killed and all the young men were taken away from the *hacienda.* The men who survived the revolution returned to their families here later. There was nothing for them at the *hacienda* anymore. Your father was there by then, and he had his own hands and even his own house servants. Even the *padre* here served the Chavez family."

Samantha was speechless. And she had expected to find help here! No wonder Hank felt safe. These people would all hate her if they knew she was the daughter of the man who kept their *patrón*'s son from his land.

She flushed, realizing what would have happened if she had asked Señora Mejia to help her.

"Why didn't you warn me about this?" Samantha demanded bitterly.

Hank pretended bewilderment. "For what? It was not something you needed to know."

She glared at him but fell silent. She attacked her food angrily, but soon the anger wore away. After her third glass of wine, she became resigned to spending another week or so with Hank, until they reached the border. She couldn't have him captured here, but there would come a day when he would pay.

"Come, Sam. We will go for a walk now."

Hank stood up and held out his hand to her, but Samantha shook her head. "I would rather stay here and get drunk."

She reached for the bottle of wine, but he moved it away. "No. We will walk first. Then you can come back here and drink all you like."

"But I don't want to go anywhere with you," she replied sullenly.

"I insist. And that is sufficient reason, is it not?" He grinned.

"Oh!"

She stalked out of the *cantina* without letting him take her arm, but stopped outside when she was met by total darkness. There was no moon, there were no stars. It was cool and hushed, as though before a storm. There would probably be a storm before the night was over.

"This way, Sam."

Hank took her elbow and led her to the street. They passed the general store next to the *cantina*, the blacksmith's, a few houses. These cast a little light out into the night, and there was more light ahead, where the church towered at the end of the street. Two men stood

out in front of it, talking together. The door was open,
and candles burned inside.

Samantha let Hank lead her. She was light-headed
from the wine. It was a pleasant feeling.

He walked slowly, and she kept pace with him, his
grip on her elbow steadying her. He said nothing.

"Are you taking me somewhere in particular, Hank?"

"Sí, casarse."

Samantha stopped dead, feeling the wind knocked
out of her.

"Married? *Married!* To—*you?*"

"Hable un poco más bajo."

"I will not lower my voice!" she stormed, wrenching
her arm away from him. "You're crazy!"

"And you understand Spanish very well," Hank replied calmly, the slightest grin curling his lips.

Samantha caught her breath. "You were joking? Of
all the dirty tricks!" she spat furiously. "To say something like that just to get me to admit I speak Spanish.
Yes, I speak it! And you knew that all along, didn't
you?"

"Sí."

"Well? What difference does it make?"

"None."

"Then why trick me like that?"

"There was no trick, Sam. What I said was true. We
will be married. Tonight. Now, in fact."

She could only stare at him, the seriousness of his
tone telling her he meant it.

"You...you can't mean it, Hank."

"But I do, *gatita.*" He shrugged then. *"Lo exigen las
circunstancias."*

"What circumstances demand it?"

"The ones you have created. I do not like it any more
than you, but you force me to drastic measures with
your schemes to ruin my plans."

"Is *this* your other alternative?"

"It was. I was against it. Do you think I really *want*

to marry a vixen like you? No, Sam, you and I could never have a true marriage. We could not live together as normal people. One of us would kill the other."

"Then why?" she cried but then the answer came to her. "You came to this decision at the mountain camp, didn't you, when Lorenzo attacked you? That's what calmed him down, isn't it? You told him you would marry me!"

"Yes. You forced my hand. I like Lorenzo. I did not want to hurt him. Though I had considered marriage to you and rejected it, I reconsidered. And it does solve the problems you have thrown my way. I may not like it, but I do come out ahead because of it."

Samantha stiffened. "Aren't you forgetting something—*amante?*" she said contemptuously. "In order for you to marry me, I have to agree."

"You will."

"Not on your life!"

"No, Sam, on your father's life. If we are not married tonight, Diego will ride for the border. He will find your father and kill him."

"You...you're..."

"Determined."

"—despreciable! Culebra! Tiránico diablo!"

"Sam—"

"Vil pícaro! Pillo! Sucio—"

"Basta ya!" Hank snapped. "We hate each other equally, but we will still be married."

"But it's insane!" she protested frantically. "You think you can control me if you are my husband. You won't! I won't live with you!"

"I do not expect or want you to," Hank replied. "I will still return you to your father."

Samantha quieted. "I'll divorce you. You will have accomplished nothing."

"I suggest you wait a month or two—you may be glad to have the title of *señora.*"

Samantha blushed hotly. "In case I find myself with child? I don't care. I would still divorce you."

Hank shrugged. "It will not matter then."

"Why?"

"Come along." He ignored the question and caught her wrist. "They are waiting for us."

Samantha saw who *they* were. The two men in front of the church were Lorenzo and Inigo.

They reached the church steps all too quickly, Samantha feeling as if she were being led to slaughter. Lorenzo avoided her damning look. She supposed that, to him, raping was unimportant as long as Hank married her. That was supposed to make it all right!

"Todo está arreglado," he told Hank.

"Good," Hank replied smoothly. "We will get it over with, then."

Over with? Yes, Samantha told herself. Get it over with and soon forget it. Marrying Hank Chavez would make no real difference in her life. She was being forced into this. She wouldn't think of herself as being *really* married. Just as soon as she was back with her father, safely away from Hank, she would get a divorce. It would be that simple. She would not battle with him now.

It did not take long. In just a few moments a little old *padre* was speaking sacred words over her, binding her in the eyes of God to Enrique Antonio de Vega y Chavez. She didn't even listen. The words meant nothing to her. She had to be nudged when it was her turn to speak. She spoke. She agreed. When all was quiet, she knew it was over.

"Dios le bendiga," the priest said, and Hank kissed her, a short, dutiful brush of the lips that left her cold.

And then Hank was escorting her out of the church, and the priest remarked on what a handsome couple they made. Lorenzo's reply was, *"Se detestan mutuamente."*

Samantha imagined the priest's face as he heard that

she and Hank detested each other. The old man wouldn't understand. *She* didn't understand any of this anymore. She was weary.

But she was married.

Chapter 30

"SAMANTHA CHAVEZ." The name rolled off Samantha's tongue experimentally. "Señora Chavez." She frowned. "I don't like the name. It's the hateful name of a hateful man."

"You are drunk, Sam."

"So I am."

She giggled and fell back on the bed, her arms flung wide. A little wine from the bottle she was holding sloshed onto the floor, but she didn't notice. Hank was staring down at her, shaking his head, his eyes dark, unreadable. It made her giggle again.

He had brought her back to this room directly from the church. She had expected the worst, but he left her there. Two bottles of wine had been placed in the room, and Samantha had quickly finished one, hoping to drown the confusions of this night, to drown what might still happen. She had just started on the other bottle when Hank returned.

She closed her eyes to try and stop the spinning in her head. When she opened them again, several minutes had passed, and Hank was bent over the bed, leaning toward her. She first noticed his bare chest, then started to look lower, but blushed and quickly met his eyes instead. He was smiling at her, and she closed her eyes against it.

"Go ahead, Hank," Samantha said thickly. "I won't remember anyway."

"Remember what?"

"Your raping me again."

"Rape?" He chided her with a click of his tongue. "We are married now."

"Ha!" Samantha laughed. "That ceremony you forced me into didn't change anything. I am no more willing for you to touch me now than I was before."

"Then relax, *chica*. I only meant to remove your clothes so you can sleep comfortably."

"Truly?"

Hank was lifting her to a sitting position and her head went crazy, throbbing, spinning dizzily. She couldn't focus on Hank. He was a blur, rocking from side to side, making the dizziness worse.

"Will you be still!" she demanded testily.

Hank grinned but said nothing. And as Samantha closed her eyes, her thoughts became coherent. She knew what was happening.

She didn't delude herself, however. She knew she was drunk. She knew Hank was undressing her. She felt the cool air on her body when she was laid back down on the bed. Even her underclothes were discarded. Then came the tugging, as the bedding was pulled out from under her, and the warmth when she was covered.

But Samantha couldn't believe that Hank was really going to leave her. After all, she had drunk so much wine in order to prepare herself. She had wanted to be so drunk that she wouldn't remember anything about her wedding night. Was it for nothing?

The bed was too still.

"Hank? Hank, where are you?" Samantha asked, her voice slurred.

"Right here, *querida*."

His voice was by her ear, and she turned to find his face next to hers on the pillow. He slipped an arm under her neck and drew her head over to his shoulder. Good! She knew he had been lying. He wouldn't let the opportunity pass. She was just too vulnerable.

"Just be...quick," she mumbled.

Hank laughed. "As my wife, you now deserve my consideration."

He sounded more as if he were talking to himself than her, and it took several moments for what he said to sink into Samantha's muddled thoughts.

"You won't force me?"

Hank chuckled softly. "On the contrary, little jewel. It will do no good to seal our marriage if you can say later in all honesty that it was not done because you do not remember it. I will wait until you are sure to remember."

"I don't want to wait. Please, Hank."

"Do you at last plead for my love, Samina?"

His teasing tone made her stiffen as she realized she was indeed begging him. She dug her nails into the tender side of his chest.

"You call waiting until I can remember being considerate?"

Hank didn't answer. Her nails left him slowly, leaving behind the sting of tiny cuts. And then her hand was slack against him, her breathing even, if a little heavy.

Hank sighed. Samantha's soft breasts pressing against his left side burned as much as the cuts. He ached to love her. This crazy marriage, the reasons he had insisted on it . . . he didn't think of those things just then. Her warm body cuddled close to him blocked out all thought, created a fire that would not die down until he could brand her with it.

But not now, not when she was besotted with wine. That was not how he wanted this special joining to be.

Hank cursed himself. He had left her alone after the ceremony in order to increase her fear, to make her wait and wonder. But he had managed only to spite himself. He hadn't known Señora Mejia would leave wine in the room for their private celebration. He hadn't known that his temper would cool off, that he would change his mind and want this night to be special.

He had come back to the room meaning to make Samantha want him—for the right reasons. He meant to make her want him as much as he wanted her.

Samantha stirred and slid one leg over Hank's. He groaned and, quickly disentangling her limbs from his, shot off the bed. He looked back down at her. She did not awaken. She was not aware of his turmoil.

Her hair was spread out over the pillow, and he marveled at the rich auburn color tinged with red, silken and soft. One stray lock curled over her breasts, rising gently with her breathing. He had not seen her this way before, so at peace, so beautiful. He had to clench his fists to keep from touching her.

"She is making me crazy!" he swore, then grabbed his pants before leaving the room. It would be a long, torturous night—not unlike many other nights he had spent since meeting Samantha.

Chapter 31

"THIS is not the wedding night, Hank," Samantha protested sleepily. "You missed your chance."

"What does daylight matter between lovers?"

"Lovers? Lord!" she said, and tried unsuccessfully to push his hands away.

Hank laughed. He had awakened her with his hands. She had come out of her deep sleep to find them caressing her all over. She had thought she was dreaming, the sensations were so delicious. She had been shocked to find the hands real.

"Go ahead then." She tried to put as much boredom into her voice as she could manage. "I know there's no stopping you when you get like this. I'm tired of trying."

"Do you hope to wound me with indifference?" Hank asked softly.

She met his gaze levelly, a frown creasing her brow. "Would it wound you? Would it really make any difference to you?"

Hank grinned down at her knowingly. "You would like to think so, eh? But it is pointless to speculate, *querida*. Your indifference cannot last. You know it as well as I."

His lips caressed her softly. A few moments later, she thought she was being devoured by the ardor of his kiss. When the kiss ended, she was left wanting. Hank lay on top of her, his hands tight at her shoulders, his chest pressed to hers, his lips moving maddeningly down her neck.

She couldn't fight his power. What was the point?

Somehow, he always managed to make her respond to him. He always managed to win. She let reason take over. After all, he was her husband. They were married. Her husband...husband.

She repeated this over and over in her head until Hank entered her and she moaned. She locked her legs over his hips, and met his thrusts wildly.

"Mi marido," she was saying aloud, barely aware of it.

And then she clasped his head and bit his ear, not hard, but enough to make him aware of her. "You wanted me to remember," she whispered before she thrust her tongue into that ear and felt him tremble in reaction. "You, too, will remember, *querido!"*

She kissed him with abandoned passion, and his increased wildly. He was a virile beast, and she loved it. She joined him in climax and descended with him, savoring everything.

But Hank was not finished. He took her again, as savagely as he had before, and as tenderly. She joined him, her nails caressing this time. Her hands were just as gentle as his, because at last she wanted to give pleasure as well as receive it. And she did.

It was not a time for wonder. Wonder would come later. Now Samantha only felt, felt and responded to Hank's tenderness.

He was an amazing man, this handsome *bandido*— her husband. She slept with that thought, languorous, sated, with Hank half on her, half at her side, his head resting on her breast.

"It is time we moved on, Sam." Hank woke her with a gentle shake.

He was dressed, and he turned away to gather her clothes. She gave silent thanks that his eyes were not on her, for she blushed, remembering, and she didn't want him to see her embarrassment. Why, he was acting as if nothing unusual had happened. Could he really think nothing of it?

She felt so different. She hadn't realized Hank could be such a tender man. It shed new light on him and made her uncomfortable about her old animosity. That was dangerous, extremely so. She *had* to forget their union, forget about that marvelous joining. *He* obviously had.

"I will take you to your father now," he finally spoke.

He handed her the clothes she had ridden in, which had been washed by some kind soul. The lace skirt and blouse, her wedding clothes, were gone. She wouldn't ask about them.

She swung her legs over the bed, turning her back to him. "So, you marry me, and now you give me back to my father?"

"At least you will never be a *solterona*, eh?" He chuckled.

"An old maid!" she cried indignantly, and glared over her shoulder at him. "No chance!"

"You think your Ramón would have married you when he saw you grow big with another's bastard? There are not many men who will take soiled goods."

"You're despicable!" Her eyes flashed green fire at him. "And you're assuming something that will—not—happen! I didn't need you to save my reputation. And I certainly won't thank you for it."

Hank smiled, his gray eyes dancing. That face, those eyes, the way he looked at her...She backed down. Lord, what was he doing to her?

"You still haven't told me why you really married me," Samantha said in a much calmer tone. "And I won't believe this nonsense about saving me from scandal. Why, Hank?"

"You really cannot guess?"

"Would I be asking if I could?"

She was dressed by then and turned to him in time

to see him shrug. "Perhaps it will be clear to you one day."

"Why don't you make it clear now? There was no purpose. You can't control me. You hand me over to my father and I divorce you. So? What have you accomplished? None of this will help your cousin keep my land."

"You do not want to know, Samina," he replied mysteriously. "Truly, it would ruin your day."

"You have already ruined my day!" she screamed at his retreating back.

He was gone, leaving her in a rage. "God, what a teasing, aggravating bastard he is!" she told the walls.

The others were waiting outside the *cantina* in the bright morning sun. Many people were gathered there to bid Hank good-bye. They called him Don Enrique. Had she heard that name before? It sounded familiar, but she couldn't place it just then. All those people, so happy for him, had surprised her.

Samantha stood by stiffly until Hank offered her his hand and helped her to mount El Rey. The people waved her good-bye. They knew her to be Hank's wife—his lawful wife. Lord, she couldn't stand much more of this, and the smiling faces made her feel worse than she had in some time.

Chapter 32

IT was a short but grueling ride to El Paso. Whereas Hank had dragged the pace before they were married, he now drove them mercilessly, as if he couldn't wait to get to the border and get her off his hands.

He never gave Samantha a chance to talk to him. As they rode, he flatly refused to answer the questions she threw over her shoulder at him, and when they camped, she had no further desire to speak to him.

He didn't demand his rights, not until the last night, when they were camped a mile from the Rio Grande and El Paso rivers, where Hank assumed her father would be waiting.

That night, once again, Hank was tender. And Samantha, knowing this would be their last time, very nearly matched his tenderness.

When she woke the next morning, he was gone. The other three men were still with her, lazing about the camp as if they wouldn't be going anywhere anytime soon. Samantha was bewildered. Hank hadn't even said good-bye.

When Lorenzo brought her coffee and some dry food, she asked him to sit, smiling, hoping to draw him out. "Where has he gone so early?"

"To El Paso."

"Alone? Is Antonio there? Is he supposed to meet his cousin?"

"Antonio?"

Samantha sighed. "You don't even know Antonio? Lord, don't you know why I was kidnapped?"

"I follow orders for which I get paid. I do not ask questions."

Samantha's anger surfaced, but she didn't want to antagonize Lorenzo. "What did Hank tell you when he left? Did he leave a message for me?"

"*Sí*, he said to tell you to watch for him in six or seven months."

She frowned. "What does that mean?"

Lorenzo shrugged. "He said you would understand."

After a moment, she did, and blushed. In six or seven months, if she were pregnant, she would be very obviously so. Even on leaving he had to taunt her!

"Then he's not coming back here?" she asked. "I mean, if he left that kind of message, he doesn't intend to see me again soon."

"No."

"But when do I get taken to my father? How will you know if everything has been arranged?"

"We are to wait here, Sam. Your father will come for you here."

"When?"

He shrugged again. "Perhaps today—or tomorrow. Be patient, little one. You will soon be with your father again."

As he rode toward El Paso, Hank worried. Would he be able to meet Kingsley as if by accident? It had to appear accidental. He would say he had come to El Paso to visit a cousin. He would be completely surprised when he happened to run into Kingsley.

Dios, it was such a gamble. If only he hadn't had to change his plans halfway through all this. Meeting Kingsley a second time after the kidnapping was dangerous. The man might begin to suspect, or at the very least wonder about Hank's involvement. He had meant to wait longer, to take the chance that Kingsley might sell to someone else before Hank got there, rather than appear too soon after the last message was delivered.

But here he was. His plans had been changed—because of Samantha.

There had been too many ifs where she was involved. She was too damned clever. Even now he couldn't be completely sure that marrying her had covered all possibilities.

As her husband, Hank had full control of everything that belonged to her. Divorce would not change that. Samantha could dissolve the marriage, but she could not get back what had legally become his the moment they wed—the Hacienda de las Flores for one thing.

But Hank still wanted the deed in his hands, paid for and entirely legal. In effect, he would be paying for what he already had control of. He didn't want the land for nothing, though. That had never been his intention. He insisted on paying for it.

But that raised another consideration. His offer was based on Pat's promises, and if they didn't pan out, he would be unable to buy the land. With Samantha as his wife, though, he no longer had to worry too much about that, he reminded himself.

So why wasn't he counting his blessings? Why was there that underlying regret, an insane desire to turn around and take Samantha back to the mountains, to make up to her for all the hurt, to forget about her father and his land, to make Samantha love him, somehow?

Dios mío, he was crazy to even think such things. She was making him crazy!

Chapter 33

SAMANTHA would have been climbing the walls if there had been any to climb. Four days had passed and no one had come. The May heat was sweltering. The water, fetched during quick trips to the river, was warm and rusty tasting. The food supply was dwindling, and the men were feeling her impatience as well as their own.

By that fourth afternoon, she was sick of the waiting, dirty and sticky, and, though it irked her pride to admit it, she smelled as bad as the men did. She was burned brown by the sun, and if her father were to come now, he probably wouldn't recognize her. But he didn't come. Why?

"Something has gone wrong, Lorenzo," Samantha accused after pulling him away from the others so they could talk alone. "You said one or two days. Why hasn't my father come?"

But Lorenzo knew as little as she did. "Perhaps he was not in El Paso."

"Hank would have returned if that were so. Besides, my father has a ranch only a few hours' ride from town. He would be in one place or the other. Anyone looking for him would have found him by now."

"We can only wait."

"Without food?" she pointed out. "No, I demand you take me to town. We will see for ourselves what is going on."

"I was told to wait."

"Forever?" she snapped. "Damn it, *you* go then. No one will know you. Find out where my father is."

When Lorenzo shook his head, Samantha itched to hit him. "Why?" she cried. "What if something has happened to Hank? What if he wasn't able to let my father know that I'm here? We could be waiting for nothing." She saw his frown and pressed her point. "It would be a simple matter to find out if my father sold his Mexican land. He was to sell it to Antonio Chavez, Rufino's cousin. You would only need to ask around. Please, Lorenzo. We can't just wait."

He gave in. They needed food, and he used that excuse with Diego and Inigo.

While Lorenzo was gone, Samantha was a bundle of nerves, the waiting and the apprehension of bad news closing in on her. Something had gone wrong, she was certain of it.

If that wasn't enough, Samantha had to contend with Diego and the leering grins he turned on her at every opportunity. It was the first time she had been left with him in charge of her. The fact that Inigo was there with them did not lessen her nervousness. She still thought of Inigo as a coward. If Diego decided to attack her, he would be no help.

So her relief couldn't have been greater when Lorenzo returned, before dark, just as the sun was setting. He seemed tired and troubled, however, and she held her breath, waiting for him to speak.

He stared at her for several unbearably long moments, as if debating what, exactly to tell her. At last he said simply, "We will go now."

"Go? Just like that?" Confusion and anxiety were making her anger rise.

"Por Dios!" Lorenzo exclaimed, impatient. "Is that not what you wanted to hear?"

"I want to hear why my father didn't come for me! What has happened to him?"

"Nothing—that I know of. He was in town, but he is at his ranch now."

Samantha wanted to cry. "Then the land wasn't sold? I'm still to be kept prisoner?"

"The land *was* sold, two days ago. The new deed is recorded in the court house."

"How do you know?"

"I located the clerk. He remembers Señor Kingsley— and the new owner. The sale was also announced publicly. I suppose your father thought one of us would be there, watching him and waiting to hear of the sale."

"But Rufino *was* there," she reminded him. "Why didn't he tell my father where to find me? My father did his part. Lorenzo, I don't understand."

"I don't either," Lorenzo sighed.

"You didn't find Rufino?"

"No," he replied reluctantly.

"Then—" Her eyes widened suddenly. "He didn't sell to someone else, did he? I mean, oh, Lord, Hank would have been furious if someone other than his cousin bought the land. That would explain—"

"No." Lorenzo interrupted her speculations. "The clerk I questioned remembers the buyer. It was Antonio Chavez."

"I..." She started to voice her confusion again, but suddenly she wasn't confused anymore. "That son of a bitch! He did this on purpose!"

"Who?"

"Hank! Rufino!" she stormed. "He never intended to let my father know where to find me. Don't you see? He's done this for spite. He's probably long gone, with his cousin, laughing because he's left me and my father waiting."

Lorenzo shook his head, frowning. "I cannot believe that of him."

"Why not?" she asked furiously. "You don't know him the way I do!"

"But you are his wife."

"What has that got to do with it? He didn't want to marry me any more than I did him. He had to force me to agree to it."

"I cannot believe that," Lorenzo replied stubbornly.

Samantha lost all patience. "Lorenzo, he's not the man you seem to think he is. He may have saved your life, but that doesn't make him honorable. He threatened to kill my father if I didn't marry him. Do you really think I wanted to? Do you really think marriage made all right everything he did to me? He gets what he wants in whatever way he can. *That's* the kind of man he is."

"Basta ya!" Lorenzo snapped angrily.

"It's not enough! You still don't believe me, do you? But Hank's got what he wanted and he's gone. You can't deny that. I should have been released two days ago. But I'm still here—you're still here. He's left you in the lurch just like me—and without a care!"

Lorenzo's eyes narrowed darkly. "Get your things! We go now!"

"Where?"

"I will take you to your father," he replied brusquely.

"And the others?"

"They will go their own ways now. It is over."

It *was* over, really over. She was going home to her father. In just a few more hours, she would be with him....

The water splashing up his nose choked Hank back to awareness. A bucket of it had been thrown in his face. It was not the first time, but he forgot and tried to shake the water out of his eyes. The pain stopped him, shooting through his head like the explosion of a thousand tiny lights. *That* made him remember—everything.

One eye was shut tight, the other blurred from the water and stinging as his sweat ran into it. He hated to think what the rest of his face looked like. He could

barely open his mouth. Both sides of his jaw were probably puffed out grotesquely from repeated blows. Blood
was caked to his lips.

There were things he could be thankful for, however...so far, at least. His nose had bled but it wasn't
broken. And he still had all his teeth, though they had
shredded the inside of his mouth.

He wasn't sure about the rest of him. There were
two ribs he knew for certain were cracked, but the pain
in that area was deceiving. His whole rib cage felt
crushed. His whole body felt crushed for that matter—
except his hands. There was no longer any feeling in
his hands at all, not even in the first two fingers of his
right hand, which had been pulled back until the bones
snapped.

How long had he been strung up now, rawhide cutting into his wrists, causing the numbness in his hands?
A day? Two? It was night. He could see that much
through the blur of his one open eye. Lanterns were
burning brightly inside the old barn and it was dark
outside the open door. It was left open because of the
stink—his stink. He had not been fed, or let loose to
relieve himself. But the shame of that was the least of
his worries. For Hank could see no way out of this.

How could things have gone so wrong so suddenly?
He had met Hamilton Kingsley, as hoped, the second
day in town. He hadn't seemed to suspect anything at
all, and had accepted Hank's reason for being there.
Hank hadn't even offered to buy the land. He had waited
for Kingsley to broach the subject. He had soon enough,
and the deal had been settled, the papers signed late
that afternoon. Hank had the deed, had it on his person
right then, in his coat pocket. The land was his, legally—but a damn lot of good it was doing him just
then.

He had asked himself over and over again if it was
worth it, and was slowly deciding that it wasn't. There
was little patience left. His tormentors were getting

tired of his continued resistance, and who knew what
was next?

And Kingsley? Was he still here? How that man had
fooled him, up until the deed was in his hands. Then
he had seen the rancher talking with two of his hired
men and felt the first inklings of uncertainty. Shortly
after that, those two men had come to his room at the
hotel. They had invited him to join Kingsley at his
ranch. When he refused, they insisted, at gun point.

It was early evening. No one had seen him being
escorted out of town. He hadn't even had the chance to
have the message delivered to Kingsley, to let him know
where he could find Samantha.

But that wasn't what Kingsley was interested in. He
took it for granted that his daughter was on her way
back to him, now that he had done exactly as instructed.
No, Kingsley wanted El Carnicero—or the bandit he
thought was El Carnicero. He was as hell-bent on revenge as Samantha had ever been, and he was convinced, or had let his men convince him, that Hank
could lead them to El Carnicero.

Hank's only consolation was that no one had even
hinted that he might be El Carnicero. Everyone knew
that bandit was a short, fat Mexican. But Hank was
assumed to be one of his gang.

He couldn't really blame Kingsley for this. If he were
in the same position, he would do everything in his
power to keep what was his. And the old man wasn't
even aware of the lengths his hired thugs had gone to.
Kingsley had been disgusted when he saw Hank's condition, but Nate Fiske, the spokesman for the men, had
defended the treatment.

"You want a confession, don't you? Evidence that'll
get you back your land?" Hank had heard him asking
Kingsley. "And El Carnicero? If we don't get him, he'll
be doing things like this again. This Mex is one of them."

"But what if he isn't?" Kingsley had revealed the
doubt he still harbored. "What if he's telling the truth?"

Nate Fiske laughed. "You didn't feel that way yesterday, Mr. Kingsley, when you turned over your land to him. You were sure then that he was involved."

"I let you convince me, but—"

"Maybe I need to point out certain facts again," Nate had said impatiently. "Your trouble didn't begin until after this fellow came to see you, wanting to buy your land. You refused and suddenly you had bandits after you, demanding you get out of Mexico. When that didn't work, they took your daughter and *he* showed up again. By chance? Maybe. Except you made the mistake of telling him your plans. The bandits made a new demand then. You either sell or kiss your daughter good-bye. And who should conveniently show up in El Paso, *still* eager to buy your land?

"It don't wash, Mr. Kingsley. Chavez either hired those bandits himself or he's one of them. Either way, he'll tell me where to find El Carnicero. And that's what you're paying me for. Getting your land back, through a confession, will cost you more, but you'll be willing to pay for that. Won't you?"

Hamilton Kingsley had reluctantly nodded. And he had said nothing further, giving Nate Fiske silent consent to do whatever was necessary.

The only thing that might help Hank was to hold out, continue to insist on his innocence, and pray that one of these hardened men might finally believe him. Or Kingsley might relent and stop them. That was a long shot, though. Kingsley had showed his sensitivity. He would probably stay away until it was all over.

Escaping was out of the question. There were seven of them, the worst sort of brutal men. Hank knew their kind, men out for easy money, capable of anything, even murder. He had come to hate every one of them—Nate, who had seen through Hank's scheme, and Ross, the big Texan who had cracked two ribs with only one blow of his fist. Then there was the one called Sankey, who had laughed as he snapped Hank's fingers, and who kept insisting that more torture was the only way to get a confession.

Hank didn't know all their names. Three of the men stayed in the background, keeping watch while the others slept, not taking part in the beatings and questioning.

There was one man Hank found himself hating the most, and that was Camacho, the flat-faced Mexican. A short, two-faced, weaselly son of a bitch. He was the worst, whispering Spanish words, pretending concern, his voice working soothingly when Hank was in the most pain.

His bearded face moved in front of Hank now. "You awake, *amigo?* The *gringos* grow impatient. I cannot help you unless you tell them what they want to know."

Hank tried to shut out that wheedling voice, but he couldn't. He could see more clearly now. A few of the men were sleeping, but Sankey wasn't one of them. He squatted by a fire in the center of the barn, holding a long-handled knife over the flames. Wondering what he would do with that knife was torture itself.

"Confiesa Usted Sufatta?"

"What—guilt?" Hank managed to grit out stubbornly.

"Estúpido hombre!" Camacho said in disgust. "Nate, he grows angry. He will let Sankey have his way with you soon. Why not confess now? If old man Kingsley can get his land back through such a confession, that means more money for these desperados. *Comprende?* They want more money. So?"

Hank did not reply, and Sankey called out, "Has he had enough, Camacho?"

"I do not think so, *amigo.*" The Mexican shook his head wearily. "He is very foolish."

"Then get away from him." Sankey stood up. "It's my turn now."

"Hold it, Sankey." Nate stepped in front of him. "I

told you that was out. There ain't no way he could survive."

"Hell, they do it in them eastern countries all the time. The men survive—they just ain't men no more." Sankey chuckled. "Shoot, Nate, I wouldn't really have to do it. I guarantee he'll spill his guts the second this hot blade touches his skin."

"There are other ways. The old man don't want him dead, and we do it his way if we want to get paid. Understand?"

"Then how about this?"

Sankey pulled his gun and fired before Nate could stop him. Hank jerked as the bullet knifed through his thigh. But he didn't cry out. After a moment, the pain lessened to a dull burning and his body relaxed, getting heavier and heavier, his mind losing its grip, playing tricks. He saw the miner from Denver before him, bullet-riddled, crawling away, but surviving. He saw Samantha with a gun in her hand, ready to pump more and more bullets into him, smiling triumphantly. He wouldn't survive as the miner had, not at her mercy. It was his last thought before both visions dimmed into blackness.

Chapter 34

SAMANTHA slid off Lorenzo's horse before he brought it to a complete halt, tripped running up the porch steps, then swung around. She had almost forgotten Lorenzo.

"You'll wait, won't you?"

"I think not, Sam. Here. Rufino asked me to give you this before we parted."

Samantha caught the bundle he threw at her. Even in the dim light she recognized the white lace skirt and blouse. A lump caught in her throat. Why would Hank want her to have these clothes? A reminder? Damn him, he was still getting his little thrusts in.

Well, she wouldn't let it affect her. These clothes had no sentimental meaning for her. She tucked them under her arm and stepped back to the edge of the steps. Pale moonlight fell on her.

"You can't just ride off, Lorenzo. Give me a chance to see my father, and then I'll come back and bid you *adiós*. We've been through so much together."

His horse stepped nervously, sensing Lorenzo's tension. "It is not safe for me here."

"Nonsense," she scoffed. "You don't think I'd let anything happen to you, do you? You brought me to my father. He will be grateful."

"No, Sam."

"Very well, Lorenzo." She sighed, and then added impulsively, "You know, whether you helped me or not, your presence gave me courage at times. For that I thank you."

"Adiós, amiga." His parting carried to her in a whisper.

"Hasta la vista, Lorenzo."

For several seconds, Samantha stood there, watching him ride away. He was her last link with the ordeal. Her chest felt tight. But she wouldn't think about it now. Her father was waiting.

She turned and quickly entered the old ranch house. It had been years since she had been there, but she remembered the place quite well. It was dark inside. Empty. She hadn't expected it to be quite so empty, but then her father hadn't been there long. The furniture probably hadn't arrived yet. She wondered absently whether her father even had a bed to sleep in.

She approached his old room, her boots clicking and echoing over the wooden floor. This certainly wasn't how she had pictured their reunion. But no matter. Once he was awake...

The door to his old room was ajar. "Father?"

Samantha stepped inside. This room was lighter, catching the moonlight through back windows, even though they were filthy. He wasn't there. A blanket, a candle, and an old crate were in a corner, the only things in the room.

She frowned and called out again, going to the next room quickly and throwing open the door. It was empty, as was the next room.

Her heartbeat picked up tempo as she went to the front room. The whole house was empty. And Lorenzo was gone. Had she stranded herself here?

The gunshot made Samantha's hand fly to her mouth to stifle her startled cry. The bundle of clothes fell to the floor. She held her breath, her eyes wide. Lorenzo? Oh, God, was this a trap? Had her father shot Lorenzo?

The gun Lorenzo had returned to her when they crossed the river was in her hand before she ran to the front door and threw it open. She strained, trying in vain to see into the darkness. There was nothing. Clouds now blocked the moonlight, and she couldn't see beyond the front yard.

She started to call out, but stopped herself. She hadn't been able to tell where the shot had come from. Her first assumption faded away. Her father wouldn't have set a trap for her kidnappers, not here. And if he was out there somewhere, wouldn't he have come to the house by now? Hadn't he heard Lorenzo's horse?

She didn't know what to do. The ranch was deserted, yet someone had fired that shot. Lorenzo? But why?

And then she heard a horse galloping toward the ranch, slowing as it came closer, as if hesitating. Soon the sound stopped, and when no one appeared, Samantha wanted to scream.

"Are you all right, *chiquita?*"

She jumped a foot. "Damn it, Lorenzo, you nearly scared me to death!"

"I am sorry, Sam. But when I saw you alone on the porch, I was not sure if I should come forward or not."

"But I *am* alone, Lorenzo," she said. "My father isn't here."

"Is that why you fired the gun?"

"*I* didn't. Didn't you?"

"It came from here, Sam. I thought you were signaling me to come back."

"No. I...I think it's time we searched the rest of the place. If I remember right, there's a barn and a storehouse out back, and some other houses beyond that." And then she was stricken by a realization. "Maybe my father found one of the workers' old houses more inhabitable than this one. He could be here. You said he wasn't in town today."

"He could have returned there, Sam."

"Well someone's here!" she snapped, but then quickly changed her tone. "Will...will you come with me to find out?"

He nodded reluctantly. "I suppose I must. But I will tell you, Sam, I have no wish to meet an angry father."

"You can always quietly disappear once I find him," she suggested, much relieved.

"Believe me, I will."

Samantha led the way around the house, feeling better with Lorenzo beside her.

The yard was run-down, overgrown, and they had to skirt around a crop of trees and thick bushes that she didn't remember being there. Before the barn was even in sight, they heard voices arguing. Then they saw light spilling out of the barn, light she hadn't been able to see from the back of the house because of the dense growth.

Lorenzo clamped a hand on Samantha's shoulder to stop her, but she shook him off. Her father had to be in that barn. But something was wrong. Who was fighting?

She reached the open door and stopped cold, feeling bile rise in her throat. Quickly she moved out of the light, gesturing behind her to Lorenzo.

Her father wasn't there. He couldn't be! That poor man strung up, bleeding—Hamilton Kingsley wouldn't be a party to *that*. Never!

"Is your father there, Sam?" Lorenzo whispered.

"No, no."

"Then—"

She shivered as the voices inside the barn carried to them clearly.

"*Amigos,* you fight over nothing. He is not dead. He has only fainted."

"You sure, Camacho?"

"*Sí.* He breathes."

"You see, Nate, I told you he weren't dead. But now he knows what to expect."

"Shut up, Sankey!" Nate growled. "I've had it with you! You pull any more stunts like that and you're out."

"You won't get anywhere unless you put some fear into the bastard," Sankey defended himself.

"That's enough," Nate ordered harshly. "Count yourself lucky the old man went back to town tonight and didn't hear the shooting. If he had—"

"So what? I didn't kill him."

"Shit!" Nate turned away from him. "Camacho, get that wound tied up before he bleeds to death."

"I say we wake him up again," Sankey put in. "Now's the time to show him we mean business."

"Does anyone agree with Sankey?"

There were several moments of silence, and then the Mexican spoke up. "There is only so much he can take. It would be best to let him recover a little. A dead man will not tell us anything."

A new voice spoke up. "I agree, Nate. Let's give it a rest until morning."

"Ross?"

"I think I'd like to get some sleep myself."

"That settles it."

"And what if he don't break tomorrow and tell us what we want to know?" Sankey wouldn't let it rest. "How much time are we going to waste here?"

"However much we have to," Nate replied in a harsh, quelling tone that put an end to the argument.

Outside the barn, Lorenzo nudged Samantha. "I do not like the sound of this at all," he whispered. "What did you see?"

"There . . . seems to be some sort of interrogation going on. I saw six, maybe seven men and . . . and the one they were talking about, he's tied up between two posts, hanging. I've never seen anyone so badly beaten—swollen, bruised, and shot. Bleeding from the leg. He must be in terrible pain."

"And the men, they work for your father?"

Samantha turned on Lorenzo in sudden rage. "Don't you dare think those thugs work for my father!" she hissed. "He would never allow such brutality!"

"But they mentioned the old man going back to town," Lorenzo pointed out gently.

"They meant someone else, that's all," she said. "Not my father."

"Yet they are on his ranch," he persisted.

"No!" she bit off angrily. "I'll prove it!"

Lorenzo couldn't stop Samantha before she stepped back into the open doorway, clearly in view if anyone should look that way. But no one did. Samantha took a hesitant step inside, only one. Lorenzo wisely stayed out of sight.

Most of the men had settled down to sleep, but two were sitting by the fire, and one looked up and saw her standing there.

At first he said nothing. Surprise registered in his dark, *mestizo* features. He just stared at her, taking in her disheveled, dirty appearance, the gun in her hand.

"Camacho, you take the watch first," the man beside the Mexican said as he rose. "Wake me in a few hours."

Camacho grinned, revealing decayed and missing teeth. "I think your rest will have to wait, Nate," he replied without taking his eyes from Samantha. "We have company."

"What the..." Nate fell silent, following Camacho's gaze. His eyes narrowed. "Who the hell are you?"

"It would be more appropriate for me to ask you that," Samamtha replied calmly.

The sound of a woman's voice roused the others who had not fallen asleep. Grins appeared on grizzled faces. Nate still glowered, however.

"You alone, girl?" someone asked.

"What's she doing here?"

"The Lord's answered my prayers!"

There was laughter, and Samantha stiffened. "You men are trespassing," she said coldly. "And what you've done here is despicable."

Her eyes fell on the beaten man, his head hanging to the side against a raised arm. The barbarity! She turned away, taking in all of them at a glance, disgust and revulsion in her expression.

"You got some interest in this man?"

The question caught her by surprise, and she looked back at Nate with contempt. "Only a humane interest. No one should be treated like that."

"Maybe she's a friend of his, Nate," a fat, beefy man remarked. "Maybe she can tell us what we want to know. Just give me a few minutes with her—"

"Stay out of this, Sankey!" Nate barked, uncomfortable under Samamtha's condemning regard. "And you, girl—explain what you're doing here right now."

"This is my father's ranch, and I'm ordering you off it immediately."

"Your father? You're Samantha Kingsley?"

She gasped. "Do you know my father?"

Nate relaxed a bit. "We work for him. You're all riled up about nothing, ma'am. We ain't trespassing. We're doing a job."

"You're lying!"

Nate tensed, his eyes darkening. "I could say the same of you, girl. Maybe Sankey was right and you're one of the kidnappers come here to help this one escape."

Samantha's stomach turned as the implication hit her. "Kidnappers? My God, is that what this is all about? You...you..."

"We were hired to find the bandits who took Kingsley's daughter and forced him to sell his land to that fellow there."

She went cold suddenly. "Who *is* this man?"

"Calls himself En—En—oh, hell, one of them long Spanish names, something or other Chavez."

"Antonio!" she gasped.

"You see, Nate, she does know him."

"No, I don't." She shook her head slowly. She wouldn't look at Antonio again—she couldn't. Hank's cousin! "Why have you done this to him? I can't believe my father would tell you to torture a man!"

"Kinsley wants El Carnicero. He don't care how we

go about finding him. And Chavez there is going to lead us to him."

"No, he won't," she said calmly, though her anger was rising steadily. "And you're going to let him go or I'll have you all fired. I know my father, and I tell you he won't condone what you've done here."

"Now hold on—"

"Don't listen to her, Nate. She ain't Kingsley's daughter. Look at her. You think his daughter would look like that? She's one of them, just like Chavez."

"I don't give a damn who she is." A big giant of a man spoke up. "I ain't taking orders from no woman."

"Look, girl," Nate said now. "You better just take yourself on into El Paso, and leave us to our business. If you really are Samantha Kingsley, you'll find your father waiting there for you."

"I'm not leaving here until you let that man go," Samantha said firmly. She knew she was taking a stand she might regret, but she was compelled. "He needs a doctor. I'll take him to one."

"Like hell you will!" Sankey shouted, and started toward her.

Without a thought, Samantha shot him. Quickly she turned the gun back on Nate. He was white-faced, as were the others. But she was still calm, in control. As usual, men had underestimated her.

"Now will you let him go?" she asked Nate quietly.

"There's too much money at stake here. And you can't shoot us all, girl."

"Can't I?"

It was bravado, by then. The shot had woken the two sleeping men, there were six of them against her. She couldn't shoot them all at once. They all knew that. And Lorenzo? Was he still outside?

Samantha thought quickly, but didn't know what to do next. Men like these wouldn't think twice about shooting it out with a woman. But could she back down now?

"Dios mío!"

Samantha started at Lorenzo's exclamation.

"I've never been so glad to see anyone, *amigo*," Samantha said as he came in and moved to stand behind her. "I was afraid you had left."

Lorenzo looked at her sharply and said furiously, "How can you stand there so calmly while he hangs there in torment? Do you not recognize him?"

She was shocked by the uncalled-for attack. "I've never met Antonio Chavez. How could I recognize him? And I'm hardly calm."

"Por Dios. Look closer, little one." Lorenzo realized his mistake and spoke softly. "It is Rufino."

Her eyes flew to the man. "No," she gasped! The black hair, the unrecognizable face. "No!" She ran to the man, forgetting everyone else, her gun limp in her hand. "It's not." The black clothes, bloodied, were the clothes Hank had worn when he married her.

She reached him, unaware of the smells, unaware of her heart's wild beating, of her stomach twisting. *It's not him. It's not him.*

The words beat a tattoo inside her head as Samantha slowly, fearfully opened his shirt to find proof. Yes, the chest scars were there. The color drained from her face, and a scream tore from her throat. The scars were barely discernible beside the blackened, bruised skin across the whole of his stomach and rib cage. She collapsed on the floor, retching, the vision haunting her even with her eyes squeezed shut. Hank, oh, God! No!

Samantha was moaning, oblivious to her surroundings. Lorenzo had not moved from his position by the door. No one watched Samantha. It was Lorenzo, alone, who held the men at bay. Two six-shooters in the hands of a man ready to pull the triggers was a different story.

"What the hell got into her?" Ross grumbled.

"Talk to this one, Camacho," Nate ordered, ignoring Ross. "You speak his lingo. Explain we got a job to do here."

"There will be no talking," Lorenzo said sharply before Camacho could open his mouth. "We will wait until *la niña* recovers. What to do here will be her decision."

"Well, I ain't gonna stand here and dance to no woman's tune," Ross said in a quarrelsome voice.

"Don't push it, Ross," Nate warned. "You want to end up like Sankey?"

"Hell, this one ain't no crazy woman. *He* knows he can't stand up to us all."

"Do I, *señor?*" Lorenzo asked dangerously. "Perhaps you would like to find out what I think?"

Camacho grabbed Ross. "Ease off, *amigo*. This one is like me. He will not back down from a fight."

"You think I'm afraid of a skinny—"

"Of course not," Camacho said agreeably. "But his guns are not so skinny, eh?"

"Just what is your interest here?" Nate demanded.

"I will see the man released," Lorenzo replied.

"And then?"

Lorenzo understood his anxiety and smiled darkly. "You need not fear me, *señor*. Chavez is my *amigo*, but I am not a vengeful man."

"What about her?"

"That is a different matter."

"But she said she did not know him," Camacho pointed out, casting an uneasy glance at Samantha, who was sitting on the floor, shaking. He could face a man anytime. But he knew nothing about women, especially a woman who carried a gun. And this woman frightened him. She had already shot his friend without flinching. "Is she *loca?*"

"No. And it is no wonder she did not recognize him. You have changed his appearance," Lorenzo replied coldly. "And, by the way, *señor*, she is who she claims to be. And she does know this man—very well. But her feelings for him..." Lorenzo shrugged. "I cannot—"

"Shut up, Lorenzo! You talk too much."

He grinned and looked over to find Samantha glar-

ing at him in the old familiar way. His grin widened.
He had been afraid that he would have to handle the
men alone, that she had completely broken down. He
knew it would be better to keep her riled. That way,
she would not lose control again. And he knew how to
keep her riled.

"I was merely speculating, Sam," he said innocently.
"You see, I am confused. You claim to hate him and
yet—"

"Damn you, shut up!" Samantha shouted, pushing
herself to her feet. Her face was colorless, her eyes wild
and glazed as she turned them on the men by the fire.
"Bastards!" she hissed. Then she seemed to crumble
again. "I wanted to see this happen to him. I wished it
on him long ago."

"Sam, are you all right?" Lorenzo called sharply.

She spun toward him with flashing eyes. There was
relief in anger, and Samantha let it flow through her.
It made her guilt less tormenting. "Just keep them away
from me, Lorenzo. I'm going to cut him down, and if
one of them makes a move to stop me, you shoot him."

"You gonna let her get away with this, Nate?" Ross
demanded belligerently.

Samantha turned and leveled her gun at the big
Texan. His eyes widened, and someone whistled in surprise at her slow deliberate action. But Ross was goaded
and drew his gun. She let him pull the long-nosed Colt
from his holster, and then she shot it out of his hand.

"You open your mouth again, mister, and it will be
the last words you ever speak," Samantha told him
icily. "The same goes for the rest of you. And you, *señor*."
She motioned Camacho with her gun. "You will assist
me." He stared at her and she snapped, *"Comprende?"*

The Mexican moved forward carefully. It was the
last thing he wanted to do, getting close to a crazy
woman.

Samantha stepped back, indicating that Camacho
should cut Hank down. She kept her gun on him, ready

for anything he might do with the knife he pulled from his belt. But he simply cut the rawhide, bracing Hank with his body, then lowered him gently to the ground.

"His horse. Where is it?" she demanded.

"In the back. I will get it."

"No. You stay here where my friend can watch you."

Samantha moved to the back of the barn, her legs like jelly. She found El Rey still saddled and led him to where Hank was lying half on the ground, half in the barn doorway. She looked down at him, mesmerized by a face she didn't recognize.

"How will we get him to town, Sam?"

She looked up at the dark, inquiring face before her and slowly let the question bring her back to clarity of mind. "I don't know. There's no wagon or time to make a litter. He'll have to ride with you, Lorenzo. El Rey can carry you both—if you can manage to support Hank."

"I will manage."

"You'll have to hold him up," she warned. "I think he has broken ribs. All . . . all those bruises. I don't want him lying on them and bouncing."

"I will see he has a gentle ride."

"I know you will. I just . . . Look at him, Lorenzo." She started losing control again, choked on a sob, but Lorenzo caught her arm and shook her.

"Not now, little one. Do not give in now. Let us get him safely away from here first. Then you can cry."

"Cry? I'm not going to *cry!*" She jerked away from him, took a deep breath, and turned to Camacho. "Help us get him onto his horse. And be careful. I don't want him waking up until I get him to a doctor."

She stepped to the side to keep watch on the men so Lorenzo could turn away. Lorenzo and Camacho managed to get Hank into the saddle. There was a groan, and her eyes flashed. Her fingers tightened on her gun.

"*Vámonos ahora,* Sam."

"Wait just a moment."

"Sam—"

"I have a few words for these gentlemen," she said in a carefully controlled voice. "Go! I will catch up."

Reluctantly, Lorenzo urged El Rey forward. Samantha kept her gun on the men while El Rey moved away. After the horse had gone far enough that they could barely hear its hoofbeats, she spoke.

"You have wasted your time here, but I will see that you are paid." Her eyes locked with Nate's. "Only there will be no reward for El Carnicero. I will see to that, too. As of now, consider yourselves fired." She didn't flinch from the look in Nate's eyes.

"Now, look—" he began.

"You had better let me finish, mister." She cut him off smoothly. "Because I dearly wanted to kill you tonight. The night isn't over, and I'm not gone yet, so I'd be holding my breath if I were you." When he clamped his mouth shut, she added, "Now I'm not asking you to believe me. You'll find out soon enough that everything I've said is true. I'm Samantha Blackstone Kingsley, and when I get through with my father, he'll wish he never had a daughter. But that doesn't concern you."

She waited to see how her words were being taken. Not one of them moved, but she didn't relax her guard. It seemed the two troublemakers were taken care of, Sankey lying on the ground, possibly dead, and Ross holding his hand, murder in his eyes. She knew his type. He wouldn't try anything further.

She set her gaze on Nate again. "Now, I'll be going to El Paso—you can even follow if you like. Only you stay away from my father until tomorrow. I don't trust myself to see him tonight. If you don't do all I say, I will probably hire men just like you to track you down and do to you what you did to my...friend. You can doubt that, but you're advised not to."

She slipped out of the barn, running around the tangled brush to the front of the house. Lorenzo was waiting there with his horse, Hank before him in the saddle of El Rey. Lorenzo had fooled them and had doubled silently back to guard Samantha.

Without a word to him, she mounted, and they rode toward El Paso. She didn't bother looking back to see whether the others were following.

Chapter 35

A CANDLE flickering on the tall round table lit the narrow hall. Against the wall were two wooden benches reserved for patients waiting to see the doctor. Samantha sat on one bench, Lorenzo on the other, across from her. She had declined the use of the comfortable parlor in the front of the house. The sky would be lighting with the dawn soon. They had waited for hours.

Finally the doctor came out of his office and stood above her, listing all of Hank's injuries, going into great detail. Samantha gripped the bench for support. She had prayed for a learned doctor, not some country horse doctor who treated people as a sideline, and this man was certainly knowledgeable.

Finally she couldn't stand any more details. "Doctor, will he mend?"

"There's no way of knowing that, miss. You can never tell about bones, whether they will set straight or not."

His tone was reproving, as if she were questioning his abilities. He was tired. They had awakened him to tend Hank, and he had been at it for hours.

"But will he be all right, doctor? Can you just tell me that?"

"It's too soon to say."

"I believe *la señora* wishes to know if he will live," Lorenzo put in quietly.

The doctor frowned. "Of course he'll live. He's taken a bad beating, but I've seen worse."

"But his leg. It bled badly on the way here."

"Not enough to matter."

"Are you sure?"

"Look, miss, right now the worst that could happen to that young man is if infection set in, causing blood poisoning. I might have to take the leg off if that happens."

"No!"

"I said that was the worst. And even if it were necessary, he seems healthy enough. He would survive it. But that's not likely to happen. The wound was clean. I don't foresee any trouble there. His fingers were in worse shape. They should have been seen to sooner."

"It shouldn't have happened to begin with," Samantha said tiredly.

"Well . . . but things like this do happen. Why just last week—"

"Doctor, is it all right if we see him?"

"I wouldn't advise it right now. He didn't come to while I worked on him, which was a blessing. He's resting quietly now. His breathing is normal. And rest is the best medicine at this stage. Tomorrow will be soon enough for you to see him. I suggest you get some rest yourself, miss, or I'll end up treating you, too."

Samantha sighed and nodded. She was drained. Sleep would be heaven. It might wipe away this nightmare. If only for a little while.

Lorenzo walked her to the hotel where her father had once stayed. A quick word with the night-clerk proved he was there now. But the haggard-looking young man behind the counter wasn't at all accommodating. When Samantha asked for a room, he gave her a quick look, then insisted on being paid in advance. But she had no money, nor would she accept Lorenzo's.

"My father is registered here. He will pay for my room."

"I will need verification," the clerk insisted. "If you'd care to wait until a decent hour, I'll be happy to inquire of Mr. Kingsley—"

"The hell you will!" Samantha cut in sharply.

"This is not necessary, Sam," Lorenzo said calmly as he placed a few bills on the counter.

But Samantha snatched the money and stuck it back in his hand. "No. I've had my identity doubted once too often tonight. I'll pay for that room myself, or I'll sleep out in the street. Besides, I want you to stick around—if you will—to stay with Hank until he's better. I want you to be my guest while you're here."

"I will stay, Sam, because he is my friend. I will not take pay for it."

A tired grin came slowly to her face. "Suit yourself, *amigo*. But with pride like that, you'll never get rich."

"Look who talks of pride," he chided, waving the money she had thrust at him.

She turned once more to the clerk and pulled her gun out of her holster. "As for you, I want a room and I want it now."

The young man backed up so quickly he slammed into the key board behind him. "Take any one you want!" he gasped, and scrambled to grab a room key.

"No, you jackass," Samantha said. "I'm *giving* you my gun. Here." She shoved it across the counter. "It's worth a good deal more than a night's stay. If I don't reclaim it tomorrow, or rather, later today, you can throw me out and keep it. Now. The key."

He picked up the gun before tossing the key down, then resumed his insolent manner. Samantha ignored it this time. What did it matter what he thought of her?

Lorenzo bid her good-bye. He wasn't going to stay in the same hotel. "There are cheaper places," he pointed out when she started to protest. "As you said, I may not get rich, but I do not live beyond my means, either."

She was too tired to argue and let him go, promising to meet him at the doctor's house in the afternoon.

It was full dawn by then. Pink light spilled in through the windows of the room she entered on the second floor. Somewhere in this hotel was her father, sleeping. She was no longer eager to see him. She felt betrayed. That was illogical, of course, and one-sided. What her father had done, he did for her. She was reacting with confused, battered feelings.

Where was the Samantha Kingsley who had sworn to see Hank horsewhipped, tracked down and killed? She should have been jubilant to see Hank beaten, and instead she had crumbled like a pathetic, spineless woman. Why did it tear her apart? And what could she say to her father, knowing what he had allowed to happen?

Samantha fell on the bed, pressing her palms to her temples. Soon enough, she would find answers. Soon enough.

Chapter 36

SAMANTHA had only just fallen asleep when there came a persistent knocking, then hammering. She covered her ears, but the pounding continued. A voice was calling her name.

She knew the voice.

"Come in!" she shouted, so her father could hear her over the noise he was making.

The door flew open, and Hamilton Kingsley stood there, dressed in an impeccably tailored gray suit, looking splendidly well despite the tired lines under his eyes. She saw surprise register on his face, then delight, and then a smile that made the lines under his eyes seem to disappear.

"I didn't believe it was you, Sam! The way they described you— You're all right? I mean—"

"Yes, of course! Don't I look just fine?"

Her sarcastic tone stopped Hamilton cold, and, after a moment, he stood back to look her over.

"As a matter of fact, you look terrible. What did they do to you, Sam? I want the truth."

"Don't you dare change the subject!"

He was baffled. "What?"

"How could you, father? How could you let those men torture him!"

"Him?" Hamilton stood back, frowning. Everything Nate Fiske had just finished telling him was apparently true. He hadn't believed it.

"So you do know Chavez." This was not a question,

but a continuation of his thoughts. "He was one of El Carnicero's men, then. I was right about him!"

"And what if I say you were wrong?" Samantha demanded.

"I would feel mighty damn guilty. In fact, I *was* feeling mighty damn guilty on the off chance that he was really just an innocent party. But not anymore, by God!"

Samantha stared at her father incredulously. "I think you'd better leave my room, father."

"What?"

"I—said—leave!" she ground out slowly. "I'm not up to talking to you now. I'm tired, and I'm going to say something I'll regret."

"Oh, no, you don't, Samantha." Hamilton shook his head sternly. "You're not going to avoid this. You're going to tell me why you helped that man. Now I've called off my men for the time being, but—"

"Your *men?*" she shouted, her eyes sparkling with the fury she had tried to bottle up since first realizing it was Hank tied up in that barn. "Your paid killers, you mean! Do you realize I was in more danger last night facing those men of yours than I was the entire time of my kidnapping? I told them who I was, but that didn't matter. I had to shoot two of them."

"You *what?!*"

"Oh, did good old Nate forget to mention that, father?" she asked cuttingly. "Perhaps he also forgot to mention the condition of the man you let them torture? That you would allow them to do such a thing..."

The venom in her voice shocked him. "Now, Sam, nobody was tortured."

"What do you call shooting him while he's bound and helpless? Breaking his fingers and ribs? My God, I didn't even recognize him!" she cried, tears springing to her eyes. "I looked right at him and didn't know who he was."

"Damn it, Samantha, I didn't know they would go that far," Hamilton protested.

"That's no excuse!" she stormed. "You should never have turned him over to them. You must have known what they were."

"All right," Hamilton conceded uncomfortably. "So I made a mistake. But Nate assured me he could make Chavez talk. Don't you see, Sam? I had to find El Carnicero. I had to make sure this never happened again."

"You could have waited. I could have told you El Carnicero would never bother us again."

"How can you be sure?"

"Because there is no Carnicero."

"Now, wait a minute—"

She cut off his protest impatiently. "Oh, there is a bandit by that name, but the real Carnicero never even heard of us. Hank only assumed that name."

"Who the hell is Hank?"

"Chavez."

"Antonio?"

"No, his cousin, Enrique."

"But that *is* Antonio, Enrique Antonio de Vega y Chavez, the man I sold the land to."

"No, father..."

Samantha stopped. She had heard that name before, but where? And then it hit her suddenly, too suddenly, and she paled. The priest! That was the name he had used when he married her to Hank.

All at once the pieces came crashing down on her as they fell into place. There was no cousin. It was Hank who wanted the land!

Why hadn't he told her the truth? Looking back, she knew the answer.

"I'm glad he has the land, father."

"Glad? You can't be serious!" he gasped.

"I'm afraid I am. Oh, I love the land and I'll miss living there. But it means more to Hank. It belonged to his family. It was his, really."

"You're saying the fellow I sold the land to is the one who kidnapped you? The leader of those bandits?"

"Yes."

"Then why in blazes did you help him?"

"I don't know," she said quietly.

He waited for her to go on, and when she didn't, he threw his arms up in disgust. "Well, that settles it. There's no way in hell he'll keep that land now, not with you able to identify him."

"But I want him to have it."

Hamilton shook his head. "I paid good money for—"

"He paid you didn't he?" She cut him short.

"An IOU is all I've got!" Hamilton shouted.

"Then you honor it, and give him time to pay it. He obviously wants to pay for it. He didn't have to. He didn't have to come in here at all, risking himself. The land was already his."

"A long time ago, maybe—"

"Now, father. It's his now. He got it through me." Samantha saw his confusion and reluctantly explained, "He's my husband."

They stared at each other for several long seconds before Hamilton turned on his heel. He was so disgusted that he had to leave the room or else strike Samantha. All these weeks of worrying, crazed with fear, while she went off and got herself married. Married to the man who kidnapped her!

But at the door he turned back to face her. The sight of her sitting on the bed, shoulders slumped, her head bent forward in utter dejection, dissolved his temper.

"Why, Sam? Just tell me why."

Her head snapped up. "He forced me to marry him."

"I'll kill him!" Hamilton growled.

"No, father, let it go. I plan to divorce him. It doesn't matter anymore."

"But the land will still be his."

"I told you, damn it, I don't want you to do anything about that."

"What can I do? Whether you get a divorce or not,

he'll still have control of anything that came to him through the marriage."

She started to laugh suddenly. Of course. That was why he had married her. And why he had said it wouldn't matter if she divorced him.

"I don't find this at all amusing, Sam. The man should be horsewhipped."

"Yes, well, I've thought the same thing many times," she admitted.

"He deserved what Nate and the boys did to him!" he continued, working up a fine rage.

Samantha sobered. "No, he didn't deserve that," she said sharply. "I'm sorry, father. It's my own remorse I'm taking out on you."

"What is that supposed to mean?"

"I hated him, hated him so much I was going to pay to have him beaten and killed. I would have, too, only—"

"Then all this is because I beat you to it?"

"No!" she cried painfully. "Don't you understand? It tore me apart to see Hank like that. I don't *know* why. I can't explain it."

"Just what are you saying, Sam?"

"I didn't know I would feel this way. I could have been the one responsible for his suffering. *That* is my sorrow, father. And it doesn't make it any easier that it wasn't me, but you. It's nearly the same thing. He'll still blame me."

"Do you think he'll want revenge, then?"

"No. He has what he wanted. He had to pay a little extra for it, but the doctor said he should recover. He had better recover." Her voice rose warningly.

"Why do you care, Sam? Just what has gone on between the two of you?"

She sighed. "A lot of fighting, father."

"You said you hated him. Why? The kidnapping?"

"There were many reasons."

"Damn it, Sam, do I have to spell it out?"

"All right, yes, he...seduced me," she shouted. "But he married me, too. Only that's just one of the reasons. I met him before I came home. I loved Adrien then, or I thought I did. But Hank revealed some ugly truths about Adrien, and I hated him for it. He took me, because I had used him to make Adrien jealous. He wanted me, and I used him. So he used me. I shot him, though. And I hated him." She stopped as she realized her words were pouring out in jumbled confusion. "What does it matter: I don't want revenge anymore. I just want to forget it all. Leave it alone, father. And leave Hank alone, too. He's suffered enough—and so have I."

Samantha curled up on the bed, then, turning her back on her father. She was utterly drained. She couldn't explain any further. She would go crazy if she had to explain—or think—about Hank, and why her feelings were suddenly so different. Why, damn it, why?

Chapter 37

HANK threw down the cards and leaned away from the table. "I am through for tonight, *amigos,* and probably for some time to come. I cannot afford these little pleasures."

He said it with a grin, yet young Carlos, who had come with the other *vaqueros* and their families, was uncomfortable hearing his *patrón* admit to being in dire straits. It was hardly a secret that things were bad, yet to hear Don Enrique speak of it.... Carlos finished off his tequila and left the room.

Hank reached for the bottle on the table and filled his glass once again. "I suppose you think I should have kept my mouth shut?"

Lorenzo shrugged. "It is not for me to say."

"Then get that frown off your face."

They were alone in the room. It was only when they were alone that Hank felt free to drop all pretenses. Lorenzo grinned. He was getting used to these black moods.

"I think I will retire, *amigo,*" Lorenzo said lightly. "There is no talking to you when you get this way."

"What way? There is nothing wrong with me."

"You see." Lorenzo made his point. "You cannot even admit a simple truth."

Hank sighed. "What would you have me do? Complain constantly that things are not going as I expected? Or should I smile and pretend I have not failed miserably?"

"It might help if you stopped considering yourself to

have failed. You have not. You have won, *amigo*. You have your *hacienda*. You have your people back."

"I have them, but no means to pay them!" Hank replied irritably.

"Have you heard one complaint? No. They are happy to serve you, to be a part of a *hacienda* again, this one, where many of them were born, where most of them served your father. Things are not as they were in your father's day, but it has only been two months since you came. Two months is not enough time to count your efforts a failure."

"It is enough time to know that I am getting nowhere, Lorenzo. The old man left nothing, not one piece of furniture, not a single head of cattle, not even a bag of salt. It took all I had to buy basic supplies. I have my land, but I did not consider the thereafter."

"The mines are producing," Lorenzo reminded him. "And the gardens supply food. No one is starving."

"It is not enough. And how long can I ask these people to go with less, when they are used to more? The mines may be producing, but a scant quantity, and at back-breaking effort, since Kingsley took the mine equipment, too. What profit there is goes to pay for the animals and wagons to transport the men to the mines. It will be a long time before I can buy proper equipment, longer still before I can get cattle. In the meantime—"

"In the meantime it is rough going, as it would be for anyone who starts from scratch. No one thought it would be any different, Hank. You are the only one dissatisfied with the progress you have made."

Hank finished his drink, and a grin slowly curled his lips. "Why do you put up with me, *mi amigo?*"

Lorenzo smiled back. "I have nothing better to do."

"But you work for nothing. And on top of that, you have to listen to me cry over my troubles. I am grateful for your help. I just do not understand why you give it. You paid your debt. You owe me nothing."

"Ah, but there is a pretty *muchacha* here, Carlos's *hermana*..." At Hank's doubting look, Lorenzo gave up. *"Está bien."* He shrugged. "I promised I would stay with you until you no longer had need of me."

Hank gripped the empty glass. "You did not promise me, so I suppose you mean her?"

Lorenzo nodded.

"I will not believe that, Lorenzo, any more than I believed the other things you tried to tell me about her," Hank said coldly. "Now, if you had said she paid you to spy on me, I would believe that."

"It is me you insult with those words, not the woman," Lorenzo replied quietly.

"I did not mean it that way. I just cannot believe what you say about her."

"You cannot, or you do not want to?"

"I know her! That woman hates my guts!"

"Perhaps," Lorenzo agreed, adding, "only it did not appear that way to me."

"What would you call her shooting me, then?" Hank asked angrily.

"When? That night?"

"Yes, that night!"

Lorenzo shook his head. *"Amigo,* she was not in the barn when you were shot. I had only just brought her to the ranch."

"But I saw..."

Hank paused, trying again to remember. He had seen Samantha, gun in hand, not a speck of mercy in her fiery green eyes. He carried that memory, the last vision he had had before he woke up in the doctor's house. Was it only a vision? He had seen the miner there, too, and that surely was a vision.

"All right, maybe I only imagined she shot me," Hank admitted grudgingly. "But there is no way in hell I will believe she helped you get me out of there."

"It was I who helped her. I would not have had the courage to go into the barn alone."

"You are being modest," Hank insisted sharply. "Why will you not admit you did it alone?"

"*Dios mío*, because I did not!" Lorenzo replied in exasperation. "If Sam had not faced those men, you would probably be dead. We did not know it was you they had. I had no reason to interfere."

"But you did."

"Because she shot one of them, and I went in to help her, to see if I could get her out of there before she was jumped. Then I saw you, and told Sam. You see, she did not know the man she was attempting to help was you."

"Now if you had told me *that* before, I might have believed you," Hank returned. "I can see her helping some poor fool, but not me. I suppose she was delighted to see me strung up?"

"When she realized it was you," Lorenzo explained fast, because Hank had never let him get this far before, "not even I expected such a reaction. She collapsed at your feet and was sick."

"Damn it, Lorenzo—"

"No. This time you will hear it all. I have no reason to lie to you, Hank. I have no reason to tell it differently than the way it happened. I admit freely that I was as frightened when Sam broke down as I was when I was nearly hanged. She lost control completely, leaving me to hold them off. I knew I could not do it alone. My courage had come from her. But I quickly saw that they were even more frightened of her as she bent at your feet, mumbling and moaning. It showed that you meant a great deal to her."

"Nonsense."

"I am only saying what I believe went through their minds, for it is surely what I thought. She was a woman with a gun in her hand, a dangerous woman with reason to kill them all.

"She goaded one of the men. He drew, and she smoothly shot the gun from his hand. There were no more protests after that. She was in complete control, giving orders, seeing that you were cut down. She even ordered me to leave with you, to go on ahead, but I came back for her, of course."

"All right, Lorenzo, why? Why would she do this?"

He shrugged. "I did not ask. She is your wife. It seemed natural to me. It is not my business."

"Marrying her did not change how she felt about me," Hank returned, but his friend changed the subject.

"She waited with me for hours that night while the doctor worked on you, until he said you would live. Then she came to see you late the next day, but you were still unconscious. She left when you began to mumble in your sleep."

"What did I say?"

"A name," Lorenzo replied, grinning. "Another woman's name."

Hank frowned. "Did you talk to her after that?"

"Not for long."

"Did she say why she did not have me arrested?"

"No."

"Damn it, what *did* she say?"

"Only that no one would contest your right to the land. And she made me promise to stay with you."

"She knew the land was sold to me?"

"*Sí.*"

"*Dios*, now it all makes sense," Hank said quietly, anger surfacing again. "She pitied me."

Lorenzo kept quiet.

"She knew the land was stolen long ago. She felt sorry for my 'cousin,' and now she feels sorry for me. *Perdición!*" Hank swore. "I do not want her pity. I will give this land back before I let that woman pity me!"

Lorenzo was amazed. "What does it matter? She has gone her way, and you have gone yours. You have what you wanted."

"This is more important."

"Why?"

"Because it is!"

Lorenzo watched as Hank stormed from the room. He knew the root of his friend's discontent. It was not the hardships they were having, but Samantha Kingsley Chavez, his wife.

Chapter 38

"WHO in hell let you in here?" Hamilton Kingsley demanded. He rose from behind his desk, his face reddening. "Never mind. Just get out, Chavez. Get out!"

Hank ignored the order and moved closer to Kingsley's desk. "I come for a purpose, *señor*."

"Revenge? I should have guessed."

"No." Hank cut him off. "Not for revenge. I have chosen to forget the time I spent here."

"Why?" Hamilton asked suspiciously.

"As you can see, I have recovered," Hank answered, his tone level. "And I am a fair man. I will concede that you were justified."

"More than justified, considering the true extent of your crimes. If I had known then what I know now—"

"That is neither here nor there, *señor*. The fact is, you had the opportunity to have me arrested, but you did not take advantage of it. I can only conclude that you have decided to forget the whole affair, as I have."

"Not by choice, mister," Hamilton returned coldly. "If I'd had my way, you'd be rotting in prison for the rest of your miserable life!"

"Then why?"

"Because that's the way Sam wanted it."

"Why?"

"Who the hell knows!" Hamilton blustered. "What does it matter to you? You're free. You got what you wanted."

Hank frowned. Both this man and his friend Lorenzo thought he should be satisfied. Neither of them knew how important it was for him to find out why Samantha had taken his side.

"You are saying, *señor*, that you let your daughter have her way without giving you an explanation? I find that hard to believe."

"Oh," Hamilton waved at Hank with disgust, "she claimed the land meant more to you than it did to her. She felt... you'd suffered enough."

Hank's eyes narrowed. "So. As I suspected, she conceded out of pity."

"Pity?" Hamilton laughed. "You don't know my daughter."

"It is the only thing that makes sense."

"Think what you like. I'm not going to stand here arguing with you about it."

"Then I will see Samantha."

"No, you won't," Hamilton said with cold finality.

Hank gazed at him levelly. "Has she divorced me?"

Hamilton sat down wearily. "No, I'm sorry to say. She hasn't."

"Then I have a right to see her."

"Not in my house you don't. In case it's not clear to you, Chavez, you're not welcome here. State your business and get out."

A muscle twitched in Hank's jaw. He was up against a brick wall and knew it all too well. He had come alone, not wanting to cause additional hostility by a show of force. He didn't really know what he'd expected.

"I am here to reclaim my IOU," Hank said stiffly as he dropped a bank draft on the desk.

Hamilton picked up the check with a good deal of surprise. "Well, now, I never thought I'd see this. You strike it rich all of a sudden?"

"As a matter of fact, yes."

What Hamilton had meant as sarcasm stuck in his

craw as fact. "From my mines?" he fumed. "By God! You're paying me off from my own mines!"

"That would be ironic—if it were true," Hank said wryly. "But no, *señor*, the copper mines hardly support themselves. This money comes from Colorado silver."

"A big strike?"

"So my partner tells me."

"Well, if that don't beat all," Hamilton replied, disgusted. "Hell, Chavez, you could fall in a shit pot and come out smelling like a rose. You got it all, don't you— everything you wanted?"

"Not quite, *señor*."

"Oh? You mean there's still some justice in this world?"

Hank could barely contain his own temper. The brick wall was growing.

"The IOU?"

"By all means." Hamilton opened a drawer, searched through it quickly, then tossed the note across his desk. "And that ends your business here, Chavez. You may be married to my daughter for the time being, but it's not a marriage *I* recognize. Don't come again."

Hank stared hard at his father-in-law, debating whether to force the issue. He desperately wanted to see Samantha. But he was alone. All Kingsley had to do was call a couple of his *vaqueros*.

"I will go, *señor*. Will you tell Samantha that I was here? That I wish her to get in touch with me?"

"I'll tell her, but it won't make any difference. She doesn't want to see you." He chuckled drily. "The last time she mentioned your name, it was to curse you. No, Chavez, she definitely has *no* wish to see you."

Hank turned on his heel and left, his anger growing as he went around the back to get El Rey. Samantha was here, somewhere. Here, yet unavailable. He wanted only to talk to her. Did they think he would kidnap her again? *Dios,* she was his wife! He had not intended to take advantage of that fact, yet the fact remained. And Samantha had done nothing to change it, not yet.

"Mi caballo, por favor," Hank asked the old *vaquero* standing just inside the barn.

He wouldn't enter that barn. Just the look of the place brought back the pain, the fear. It also made him think of what Lorenzo had told him about that night. He could envision Samantha here, magnificent in her fury. But helping him? Saving him? He still couldn't picture that, not without knowing the reason. He *had* to know the reason. If he kept on wondering about it, he would go crazy.

"Your horse, *señor.*"

"Gracias."

Hank mounted, but did not ride away. He looked around, looking at the house in particular. Was Samantha inside, or out riding?

The ranch had been cleaned up, and it looked as if the Kingsleys had always lived there. His own ranch looked just as good since Patrick McClure had dumped a fortune on his doorstep. As Lorenzo was always saying, Hank should be satisfied. He had reached his goal. He had his family estate back, and it was prospering. It was everything it had once been. But there was such a lack. Hank wasn't enjoying his triumph. Even his new wealth made no difference to him.

"She will not suddenly appear, *señor.* You have wasted your time coming here."

Hank looked sharply at the old Mexican. "What do you mean?"

"Did you not come here to see Sam?"

"I came to pay a debt," Hank replied coldly.

The *vaquero* grinned, raising Hank's ire. "There are many ways to repay a debt. You did not have to come all this way just to do that."

"Who are you?"

"Manuel Ramirez. I have been with the *patrón* since before his daughter came to him. Nothing goes on in this family that I do not know of."

"You know where Samantha is, then?"

"Of course. Just as I know you are her husband, Señor Chavez."

"Then tell me, Manuel, will you not agree that a man has a right to see his wife?"

"Certainly," Manuel replied, but added pointedly, "if that wife had married the man willingly."

Hank scowled. "Damn it, I just want to talk to her!"

"Why, *señor?* You did not even want to marry her. You told her she was free to divorce you."

"Qué diablos!" Hank swore. "How do you know all that?"

"Sam confessed many things to my wife and daughter while she was here, some things that she did not even tell the *patrón*."

Hank eyed the man thoughtfully and said softly, "Then perhaps you can tell me why she helped me that night."

"Sí. I know why. But it is not for me to tell you, *señor*. It is not something you should hear from anyone other than Sam."

"Por Dios! But if I cannot see her..."

Manuel shrugged, saying nothing further. In a rage, Hank jerked on the reins and rode off. But something Manuel had said struck him, and he stopped suddenly, pulling El Rey around to trot back to the barn. *"While she was here,"* he had said.

"Ramirez! Sam is not here at all, is she?"

Manuel grinned. "Ah, so you caught my slip of the tongue. I thought you had missed it."

"Is she?"

"No, *señor*. She was not happy here. She has been gone for several months. If you wish to see her, you will have to travel a great distance."

"To where?" Hank asked impatiently.

"To the land where she was born."

"She's in England?" Hank was stunned.

"*Sí*, England, where her *hermano* lives."

Chapter 39

"SAM, you must hurry or you will not be ready on time."

"Oh, leave me alone, Lana," Samantha grumbled, pressing the warm, wet cloth against her brow. "I have a terrible headache, and I feel a cold coming on, too."

"I think you just make excuses because you do not wish to leave that warm bed."

"Nonsense. So what if it's a little cold in here? It's the middle of winter. I'm getting used to the cold."

"You are used to it no more than I am," Froilana scoffed. "And if you are catching cold, it is because you insist on taking morning walks in the park."

"I have to get out of this house sometime, don't I?"

"In good weather, *sí*. But we have not had decent weather for a month. And as for a headache, you have been in bed all afternoon. It is impossible for you to have a headache."

"Well, if I didn't have one before, you're certainly giving me one now! Honestly, you're worse than your mother ever was. Do this, do that. If I had known how bossy you were going to be, I would have left you at home."

"And who would take care of you if not me?"

"Damn it, Lana, I'm not a child!" Samantha snapped.

"Then do not act like one. And get out of that bed."

"No! Don't argue with me anymore. Just give my brother some reason why I'm not dining with him." She sighed then, relaxing into her plump pillow. "Really, Lana, I just can't face getting all dressed up for a simple dinner. Shelly's formality drives me *loco*. He'd have me wear a ball gown to breakfast if he thought I'd do it."

"You forget this is not a simple dinner, Sam. His *novia* comes to meet you tonight."

"Oh, Lord!" Samantha groaned. She threw off her warm covers and sat up wearily. "I did forget. Why didn't you say so to begin with? Get me a gown—the bright yellow velvet—and the yellow slippers. And a shawl—don't forget a shawl, a heavy one. I'm not going to sit down there in that big, cold room and freeze just to please my brother. Oh, damn, how could I forget?"

"Perhaps you had other things on your mind."

Samantha scowled as her friend moved off to the wardrobe. "I haven't been brooding, Lana, and I wish you would stop insinuating that. I hardly think about him at all anymore." Froilana's silence was eloquent, and Samantha didn't try to argue further. She was tired of that subject. Her arguments were all lies anyway, and Froilana wasn't fooled. Samantha did think about Hank. She thought about him all the time.

"She is late then?" Samantha asked as she entered the drawing room and found Sheldon there alone.

"Women usually are, my dear."

She let the remark pass, though she had just spent a frantic half hour rushing through her toilet so that she wouldn't be late. Remarks like that were typical of Sheldon. He could be so irritating at times, and he was so utterly snobbish that she wasn't even sure she liked her brother.

He certainly hadn't been what she had expected. Their reunion had been a surprise to both of them. Sheldon thought her too animated, too outspoken, too American. She thought him just plain dull.

Sheldon was everything their grandmother would have wanted, the perfect aristocratic snob. But he was her brother, the only family she had besides her father. And she had to make allowances, too, had to be understanding of his life with their grandmother. Their lives had taken completely different courses. They spoke differently, they thought differently, they had absolutely nothing in common. They did not seem related at all, except for their physical similarity.

In fact, Samantha still had to remind herself that Sheldon was her brother, for he was a stranger to her even after all these weeks together. There were no questions from him. Anything Sheldon knew about her, she had volunteered.

She had been willing to bare her soul, but quickly changed her mind when his lack of interest became all too apparent. He didn't ask why she had come to England, how long she meant to stay with him, or even why her husband hadn't come with her. She was relieved not to have to talk about Hank, but it did astonish her that he never even asked a single question about their father—not even about his health!

She supposed it was breeding that made him that way. She could even be generous and put his lack of curiosity down to discretion. His feeling that one's life is one's own affair went both ways: he never mentioned anything out of his past, either. What she did learn about him was from her own observations.

In that way she learned about Teresa Palacio, Sheldon's bride-to-be. He announced one morning over breakfast that he would be married in the spring. Not one word had been mentioned of the young Spanish girl before that moment, not for the entire month of Samantha's visit. Samantha was anxious about the meeting. She wanted to make a good impression for her brother's sake.

"Would you care for some wine before dinner?" Sheldon offered in a dull, lifeless voice.

Samantha shook her head, wondering how any woman could fall in love with this cold, unemotional man. Oh, he was handsome enough. Very handsome, in fact, and rich—their grandparents had left the entire estate to him. But he was just so... so damn boring. Lifeless. But, then, maybe Teresa was like Sheldon.

"Some tea then?"

"I'll wait until your *novia* arrives."

Samantha moved about the room, restless. The truth was, she felt uncomfortable alone with Sheldon. She wished it weren't so. It shouldn't *be* so, but it was. She tried to remember their childhood together at Blackstone, but the more she thought of it, the more she realized that they had hardly ever been together then, she under her grandmother's thumb, and Sheldon virtually raised by a score of male tutors. They hadn't had a typical childhood, and they couldn't have a normal relationship as adults.

"*Novia.* Such a quaint word, that," Sheldon remarked, surprising Samantha. "Teresa calls me her *novio.* She would like me to learn Spanish, but I don't see the point in our both learning a new language."

"She doesn't speak English?"

"Not very well yet."

Samantha grinned. "Then how did you two ever get so far as to discuss marriage?"

As soon as she asked, she realized she shouldn't have. Sheldon's look was clearly disapproving, although anyone who didn't know him wouldn't have guessed, the change was so subtle. But she had seen that look many times. It angered her. She couldn't even ask a simple, spontaneous question without his getting all out of sorts.

"You needn't answer, brother," she said stiffly. "I suppose this, like everything else, is none of my business."

His milk-white complexion took on a good deal of color very suddenly, and Samantha was delighted. What she really wanted was to see her staid, unemotional brother lose his temper once, just to prove he was human. She sighed. That was probably asking too much.

"Actually, my dear, we did need a translator when we met. Jean Merimée proved quite adequate. Remember Jean? You met him at the races when you had only just arrived, before..."

Samantha burst into laughter as Sheldon's face darkened even more. He couldn't finish. "Before I chose not to join you anymore on your rounds of amusement? It still embarrasses you, doesn't it?"

"Now, Samantha, it was your choice."

"My choice! Oh, it doesn't bother me. It's perfectly natural for me to look the way I do. But I knew how uncomfortable I made you, so I declined your invitations. Look! You can't even speak of it! I pity your new wife, Sheldon, I really do. You'll probably lock her in her room when she gets—"

"Samantha! Really!"

She grinned up at him innocently. "Don't you plan to have children?"

"Yes, of course," he replied uneasily.

"Then I must warn Teresa about your attitude. She would do well to keep any tidings of that sort to herself as long as possible."

"Good Lord, you wouldn't say anything to Teresa!"

Green lights danced mischievously in Samantha's eyes. "Teresa would thank me for it, don't you think?"

"I certainly do not."

"Why, Sheldon, have I upset you?" she asked solemnly. "You actually look quite angry."

"I am not angry," he sighed, shaking his head. "I just don't understand you, Samantha."

"You never tried to," she replied, truly serious now. "If you had, if you knew anything about me, you would know that I was only teasing you."

"But your bluntness—"

"—is part of me. I've had the freedom to speak my mind ever since I left England. You can't imagine what a blessed freedom that is, Sheldon. But I won't embarrass your *novia* with it. I do know how to be tactful. Just don't expect me to curb my tongue with you. You're my brother, and if I can't be frank with you—" She stopped, grinning as the front door knocker sounded. "Well, your *novia* has saved you from your brazen sister. I'll go let her in."

"Samantha, no."

But she moved out of the drawing room into the hall, stopping the butler on his way to the door. "Wilkes, I'll get that."

"Samantha!" Sheldon followed her into the hall. "For God's sake, it's not proper for you to—"

"Nonsense." She cut him off. "It's much nicer to be informal this way."

Sheldon couldn't say any more without raising his voice, and he would never do that. Samantha glanced back to see him standing in the drawing room doorway, gazing at the ceiling as if to say, *What next, Lord?* She grinned, thoroughly satisfied with herself. She couldn't remember when her spirits had been so high. Sheldon had almost lost his temper—almost. She would have to work just a little harder to see him angry, really angry, at least once before she left. She would prove to them both that Sheldon could be human.

A knock sounded once again just as she reached the door, and she composed her features. She would have to show their guest how gracious and proper she could be.

"Bienvenido, señori..." The welcome died as the lamplight revealed the man on the doorstep. "Lorenzo?" Samantha gasped.

"Sam," he said simply.

"Oh, Lord." She laughed. "What in heaven's name are you doing here?"

"When I was offered the chance to see Europe, I could not refuse," Lorenzo replied smoothly as he doffed his hat. The top hat seemed so odd on Lorenzo. He grinned, his gaze drawn to her belly. "You have put on a little weight, I see. It becomes you."

But Samantha didn't hear. She had finally noticed the carriage, and the man on the curb paying the driver.

She panicked and slammed the door shut, the sound drawing Sheldon and Wilkes back into the hall.

"Samantha, are you mad?" Sheldon demanded, coming toward the door.

"It's . . . not Teresa."

Before he could speak again, the door knocker rapped loudly.

"Samantha—"

"No! Don't open it, Sheldon! They'll go away."

"This is absurd. Wilkes, kindly see who it is."

"Damn you, Sheldon!" Samantha cried, and she moved as quickly as she could toward the stairs. "At least let me leave the room first," she called over her shoulder. "I don't want to see him."

"Who?"

"My husband!"

"Good Lord," Sheldon exclaimed. "She slammed the door on him, Wilkes. Can you imagine what the poor man must think of us?"

"No, sir," Wilkes replied drily.

"Well, let him in, man. We're keeping him standing out there in the cold."

Chapter 40

"YOU cannot hide up here forever, Sam."

"Yes, I can. And I shall."

Froilana shook her head sternly. "Your brother has invited him to stay. You must face him sometime."

"No."

"But the *novia* has come, and they are holding dinner for you."

"Tell them not to."

"Madre de Dios," Froilana said in exasperation, her hands on her hips. "You wish your husband to think you a coward? You shame yourself and your brother, as well. How will the *señor* explain to his *novia?"*

"He'll think of something." Even as Samantha said it, she sighed angrily. "Oh, all right! Damn! I'd rather face him than listen to you all night. But you'll wish you hadn't forced me to go down there, Lana," she warned. "My absence won't shame my brother as much as my presence will. I can't be in a room with Hank without losing my temper."

Her maid chose that time to become silent.

Samantha entered the drawing room ready for a fight, aching for one. But with one look at Hank, all the words she had rehearsed took flight. She wasn't even aware of all the eyes turned her way, or of her brother's relief. She missed the surprise on Teresa's face. Sheldon hadn't warned Teresa of his sister's condition. Jean Merimée was there, but she saw only Hank.

He looked strikingly handsome, his hair combed back

on each side and curling down to his neckline, his face clean-shaven, his dimples deep as he grinned, his eyes sparkling in that special way. He was dressed in formal elegance, the black dinner jacket setting off a burgundy vest and white silk shirt with diamond-studded buttons. Fine clothes suited Hank.

Samantha became fully aware of her own appearance the moment Hank's eyes left her face and moved down to her large belly. She blurted out the first thing she could think of.

"So, Sheldon, where is your *novia?*"

"Here."

Samantha turned toward the sound of his voice, tearing her eyes from Hank's. "Yes, of course." She crossed to Sheldon and greeted the young Spanish woman by his side.

Samantha was struck by her beauty, the dark, liquid eyes, the almost blue-black hair coiled and tucked behind a short *mantilla*. She had a strikingly sensual face, with full, rounded lips, feline brows, and high, narrow cheekbones.

"Teresa." Samantha blushed. "You must forgive me. I have not seen my husband for a very long time."

"That was—*evidente*," Teresa replied with some difficulty, before she turned to Jean and switched to Spanish. "Dearest, explain to this one that I am not familiar with her language yet. I doubt I will ever grasp their vulgar English."

"You wish me to tell her *that?*" Jean asked, obviously aghast.

"No, dearest, just—"

"That will not be necessary," Samantha cut in in Spanish. "You will not need a translator with me as you do with my brother."

Teresa's mouth formed a small *O*, and her olive complexion brightened, but she recovered quickly. "I am sorry, Samantia. I meant no disrespect."

Samantha smiled, but there was no warmth in her eyes as she looked at Jean, whom her brother's intended had addressed so intimately. Teresa was lovely, but Samantha was less prepared to like her. She had to wonder if Sheldon was so fortunate after all.

"You must not give it another thought, Teresa," Samantha said congenially, managing to keep her smile fixed. "My brother mentioned that you are learning English. You really should study harder. It pays to know what others are saying—especially when they are talking about you."

Jean Merimée moved uncomfortably, and Teresa stepped closer to Sheldon, as if making a point. "I quite agree."

"Would it be too much to ask for a little English?" Sheldon ventured.

"Of course," Samantha replied sweetly. "I was just telling your *novia* that she and I must get better acquainted. After all, you've told me so little about her, Sheldon."

At that moment Wilkes announced dinner, and Sheldon almost sighed with relief. "Shall we? Jean, if you would be so kind." He turned Teresa over to the short Frenchman who escorted her from the room.

Samantha stared after them, thinking that Jean Merimée was what was called a ladies' man. Dashing, debonair, he was not quite handsome, yet there was an appeal about him, probably because of his remarkable blue eyes. Samantha had disliked him the first time she met him, and she still did. He had made a pass at her, and after she rebuffed him, she had watched him move smoothly to another woman and make the same overture. To hear him and Teresa talking as if *they* were the engaged couple...

"What is he doing here?" Samantha asked Sheldon, nodding toward Jean.

"He was good enough to escort Teresa here."

"You trust him alone with her?"

"Of course," Sheldon gasped indignantly. "He is one of my counselors. And he is a very close friend, as well, Samantha."

"Close to whom?" she muttered.

"Samantha," Sheldon implored, not really hearing, "I must ask you to behave for the rest of the evening. Gad, you haven't even spoken to your husband yet."

"Nor do I intend to," she said so casually that he didn't know what to reply.

Quickly, he approached Hank and Lorenzo, who were across the room. "Mr. Chavez, Mr. Vallarta, if you will join us?"

Samantha watched Hank's leg as he walked forward, but there was nothing wrong with it, not even a limp. With that concern out of the way, she gave him a chilling look before taking Lorenzo's arm and walking with him.

"So, *amigo.*" She smiled, determined to put Hank out of her mind. "Have I finally learned your last name?"

"*Si,* I am now proud to bear it."

"May I take that to mean you have given up your lawless ways?" she teased, in a strange, reckless mood.

Lorenzo grinned and nodded. "I am completely respectable now. Your husband pays me well, now that he is rich."

"I'll thank you not to mention him if you wish to continue this conversation," she replied sharply.

"Ah, Sam." He chuckled. "You have not changed. Most women in your condition are serene. But you are still the little spitfire, eh? Shall I tell you what he did when I explained why you slammed the door on us?"

"How could you explain?" she retorted. "You couldn't possibly know why."

"Ah, but I do. You did not want him to see you in your present condition."

"Nonsense," she said calmly enough. "*I* just didn't

want to see *him*, that's all." She waited for him to continue, and when he didn't, she demanded, "Well, what did he do when you told him I was as big as a cow?"

"I did not put it that way."

"Lorenzo!"

"He laughed," said Lorenzo.

Samantha stiffened. "He would! Yes, he would."

"You misunderstand, Sam," Lorenzo hastily assured her. "He is delighted."

"Of course!" she hissed. "He was so damn sure this would happen. Now he can gloat."

"I tell you he is happy that he will be a father," Lorenzo insisted. "I know him well, Sam, perhaps better than you do. I am not mistaken in this."

"I don't care what you think, Lorenzo. I know differently. Didn't he say I should watch for him in six or seven months? You gave me that message yourself. Well, it's been seven months. Why do you think I came here? So he wouldn't find me. So he wouldn't know. But he came anyway—and didn't I warn you not to speak of him to me?"

As soon as they entered the dining room, she left Lorenzo's side. She was furious. So Hank had laughed? Damn him!

Samantha sat down in a huff, but almost got up to leave when Hank took the seat on her right. The table was huge, and there were six empty seats, yet he sat next to her.

Fortunately, dinner was served the moment Sheldon took his seat at the head of the table. Samantha concentrated on her plate. It gave her the chance to gather herself, to put anger aside and consider what Hank's presence here really meant.

The conversation around her broke into Samantha's thoughts. Lorenzo, across from her, was describing Mexico to Jean Merimée. But it was her brother's words to Teresa that caught Samantha's attention.

"...and ten years passed rather quickly. This is the first visit she has made in all that time."

"Then she was no here when you dear *abuela* die?" Teresa ventured.

"Abuela?"

"Grandmother," she explained.

"Oh, no, Samantha was not here then."

"A pity. She was such a fine woman, so kind."

Samantha almost choked. For the moment, Hank was forgotten as she looked aghast at Teresa Palacio, and then turned questioningly to her brother.

"Is she talking about *our* grandmother, Sheldon?"

"Yes. Teresa tells me she met her several years ago, long before she met me."

"She was a wonderful woman," Teresa added, her dark brown eyes on Samantha. "It was my pleasure to know her before she die."

"Henrietta Blackstone?"

"Sí."

Samantha was surprised, to say the least, but decided to give Teresa the benefit of the doubt. "Sheldon, you should have written to me, to tell me that grandmother mellowed in her old age. Then I might have come back to make amends."

Sheldon cleared his throat awkwardly. "Actually, my dear, there was no mellowing, not that I could see. Nor did she...well...she never—"

"Forgave me for going to America?" Samantha supplied with a grin.

"I wouldn't have put it so bluntly," Sheldon returned with a warning look.

"You never do."

"So this is why you were disinherited?" Teresa asked pointedly.

Samantha wanted to laugh as Sheldon's dark scowl turned from her to his blunt bride-to-be.

"How did you know?" Samantha asked. "I find it hard

to believe that my brother spoke of my being disinherited."

"You *abuela* spoke of you to me," Teresa explained. "Not Sheldon."

Samantha sat back, eyeing the slightly older woman across from her. She was finding it difficult to believe what Teresa was saying. Henrietta Blackstone, a kind, wonderful woman? That description was so laughable it was ridiculous. And that her grandmother should talk about her to a stranger when she had sworn never to speak Samantha's name again? But why would Teresa lie?

"It's true, of course, that I was disinherited," Samantha admitted without any inflection in her tone. "My grandmother and I never agreed on anything. She disowned me when I chose to live with my father, rather than stay with her. It's something I have never regretted doing."

"Then you do not regret your loss?"

"It didn't matter to me. My father isn't poor, Teresa. I have everything I could possibly want."

"She also has a rich husband," Jean put in suddenly. Samantha turned to Hank and saw him shrug.

"My husband's wealth is irrelevant, Monsieur Meriméer." Samantha's gaze was coolly disdainful. "And I do believe this subject is in rather poor taste."

"Forgive me, Samantia," Teresa said contritely. Her demure smile lacked even a measure of remorse. "I worry you begrudge your *hermano* his inheritance. It is no good to have envy in a family."

Samantha was speechless. And *she* had expected to rile her brother with bluntness! He sat staring at Teresa, his mouth a tight line, his eyes furious. He must be making every effort not to show his emotions, Samantha thought.

"Your concern for my sister's feelings is ... touching, Teresa," Sheldon commented after the uncomfortable silence. "But you needn't have worried. Her first-born child receives half of the Blackstone estate."

"What?" Teresa demanded, her voice just a bit anxious.

Samantha looked at her sharply. Jean Merimée appeared disturbed, as well.

"I do not understand, Sheldon," Jean said. "Your grandmother's will, I handled it myself. There was no mention—"

"No, there wasn't." Sheldon cut him off drily. "But there wasn't any reason for you to know about my grandfather's will, which you did not handle. He was not as stubborn as his wife. He would not see his only granddaughter cut off completely, so he made provision for her through her children. My grandmother never knew."

Samantha repressed her grin, wanting to applaud her brother. He had coolly ruffled a few feathers and was satisfied with releasing his anger in this way. Now he was as calm and composed as ever. How did he do it? Perhaps she could learn from her brother.

She should have been furious that she hadn't known of this sooner, but somehow she wasn't. Still, she couldn't resist baiting Sheldon a little.

"Is this one of those little tidbits you like to wait until the last moment to reveal, Sheldon dear?" Samantha asked sweetly. "I'm surprised you let this one out before my firstborn arrived."

Her taunt scored. She received a quelling look from Sheldon but ignored it. She devoted her attention to her plate once more.

"Why do you purposely anger your brother?"

She had heard that deep voice so often in her dreams. Samantha wouldn't look at him. She steeled herself.

"That's none of your business."

"Look at me, little one." Hank spoke softly in Spanish, so near she could feel his warm breath by her ear.

She couldn't stand it. She rose stiffly, made her excuses graciously, and left the room. Her condition allowed for an early exit. She wouldn't have been able to bear hearing one more word in that soft, persuasive voice. She couldn't talk to him, not yet. She wanted to hit him, to scream at him—to kiss him. Damn him!

Chapter 41

HANK opened the bedroom door without knocking, but instantly regretted the impulse to barge in. Samantha was in the process of being undressed, and the look she turned on him was murderous. The girl attending her quickly pulled Samantha's gown back down to cover her, then stepped back, wide-eyed.

"Forgive me, Sam," Hank offered lamely.

Of course, Samantha wasn't having any of it. "Forgive you? After you come in here uninvited, knowing you're not welcome? How dare you?"

"I could say I have every right to enter my wife's bedroom," Hank replied coldly, and Samantha drew in her breath sharply. "You start in on me about your husbandly rights, and I'll divorce you so fast you won't know what happened!"

"*This* is your husband?" Froilana gasped, drawing Samantha's angry attention.

"Don't pretend you didn't see him earlier, Lana, when my brother invited him in. You told me yourself what happened between them."

"But I did not actually see. I was at the top of the stairs. I only overheard them talking. *Caramba!*" Froilana exclaimed in fascination. "How can you be angry with one so handsome?"

Hank chuckled, and Samantha cringed. "Oh, Lord," she said. "If you find him so irresistible, Lana, you can have him. Just get him the hell out of my room first!"

"I would be glad to have him," the girl said shamelessly, "but I think it is you he wants."

"You're impossible! Just get out, both of you," Samantha shouted in exasperation. *"Dejadme!"*

"Go on, *chica,*" Hank said persuasively to Froilana. "Let me have a few minutes alone with her."

"Don't you dare, Lana!" Samantha snapped, but the girl looked from her to Hank, then grinned and left the room, closing the door after her.

Samantha wanted to scream, to throw something, but she knew better than to exert herself. She glared venomously at Hank and his laughing gray eyes.

"I suppose you think it's amusing that you won her over like that?"

"Considering I never had such luck with you, yes, it was very amusing."

Emerald eyes flashed. "Well, you can just turn around and follow her out that door."

"We will talk first."

"No we won't! I know exactly what you have to say, but I don't have to listen to it. I'll scream first. This isn't the mountains, Hank. Someone will come."

"You would cause a scene?"

"Yes," she replied stonily. "I've been through enough. I'll have you thrown out before I stand here and listen to you gloat."

"Gloat?"

"Spare me the innocent look," she said derisively. "You came here to say I told you so. There—I've said it for you. *Now* will you get out of here?"

Hank shook his head. "You remember too much of the past, *gatita.* You should forget the unpleasantness, as I have tried to do."

"Forget!" Her eyes widened in amazement. "I remember everything. Everything, Hank!"

"I wish you did not." He sighed deeply. "Ah, Samina, I hoped it would be different. I did not come here for what you suggest. I came only to ask you a question."

She was skeptical, but he seemed so genuine, so sincere.

"What question?"

"I wish to know why you did not seek the vengeance you swore you would have. You had the chance."

Samantha stared hard at him, bewildered. "You came all this way just to ask me *that?*"

"Yes."

"I don't believe it."

"Ask Lorenzo. He will tell you how this has bothered me. It was not like you to give up," he said. "Did you pity me?"

"Pity?" she laughed, amazed. "How could I pity you? You got everything you wanted, and now you're rich."

"You could have had me arrested, thrown into prison," he went on. "You could have left me to your father's men that night. Instead you took me to a doctor. You took my side against your father. Why?"

She turned around, unable to face the very questions she had never been able to answer honestly for herself. "I was tired, Hank, tired of fighting—of the anger. I felt we had both suffered enough."

"Truly, *querida?*" His voice was closer.

She swung around. His nearness made her weak, made her remember things best forgotten.

"I've answered your question," she said as coolly as she could. "You can go back to Mexico now and leave me alone."

His eyes caressed her face, then moved to her belly. "No. I will stay awhile, at least until the little one is born."

Samantha's expression turned stony. "You're not welcome here."

"Ah, but your brother *has* made me welcome." Hank grinned. "He is more generous than you."

"Only because he knows nothing about our real relationship," she said hotly, her temper at the fore. "You're my husband in name only. If you try changing that—"

"Stop it, Sam. Why are you fighting now? You say

you are tired of fighting, yet you bare your claws the moment you see me."

She couldn't meet his probing gaze. "Because of why you came here."

"But I have told you that was not why I came," he reminded her. "I wanted answers. However, I am not so sure that I have them all."

"Of course you do."

"Then why, if we have both suffered enough, do you make this meeting so difficult?"

Samantha was near tears. He was right, of course. She was being unreasonable and she didn't even know why. Was it her condition that made her so defensive? Oh, she hadn't wanted him to see her this way!

"There shouldn't have been another meeting, Hank," she said, trying to sound calm. "I never expected to see you again. I came to England so I wouldn't have to."

Hank looked away. His voice was but a whisper as he asked, "You still hate me that much?"

Samantha was startled. Did she? She had thought about him so often these last months. But, oddly enough, never with hate.

"I...I'm not sure what I feel anymore. I just can't be with you now, when I'm...when I look...oh, just go away, Hank."

Samantha looked away, but he turned her face back to meet his eyes. "What is it, Sam?" he asked softly. "Are you embarrassed for me to see you like this?"

"Certainly not!"

He grinned. "You lie, *querida*. You are embarrassed. But there is no reason. Do you not know how beautiful you are?"

Samantha tensed. "Will—you—get—out!"

"Ah, you are as stubborn as ever, and as maddening." He sighed. "I will go, Sam. I leave this house, as well, since my presence so upsets you and that is no good at this time. I will leave an address with your brother, in case you need me. But before I go, I will do what I wanted to do from the moment I saw you tonight."

Before she understood, Hank scooped her gently into his arms and kissed her. His lips were like wine, a taste to be savored, so long denied. The power he always had over her when she was in his embrace was there, the same as ever. She was oblivious to everything but his kiss, the magic of it, the wonder of it.

After a long while, Hank broke away with a sigh. The look he gave her was full of longing. Yet, true to his word, he turned and left.

Samantha stared in amazement at the closed door. He could still leave her breathless and trembling. Why? Why only with him?

Chapter 42

THE sweat was dripping from her. "Is the doctor coming?" Samantha gasped, trying in vain to control the increasing pain, unable to stop its rise.

"Sí, sí, he is on his way," Froilana assured her as she added more wood to the already blazing fire.

The labor pains had started that afternoon. At first, Samantha had thought nothing of them. There had been so many little discomforts this last month. The dull ache seemed unimportant. But Froilana had noticed the frowns crossing her face. Sure enough, the time was at hand.

Lying in her bed, Samantha wanted to cry or curse. She had never dreamed it would be so bad. She had been told it would be painful but worth every minute of the pain. Ha! Who had told her such nonsense? Lana? What did Lana know? She had never been through *this. This* was unbelievable. She was going to make it her mission in life to warn other women not to have babies.

"Are you trying to roast me with that fire!" Samantha shouted.

"Cálmese, Sam."

"I'd like to see you be calm in my place," Samantha retorted.

"You want them to hear you downstairs?"

"Who?"

"Your *hermano* and—"

Samantha moaned. As soon as the pain subsided, she looked sharply at her friend. "And?"

"Did I say and? *Cielos,* what am I thinking of?" Froilana replied evasively.

Samantha let it go, too exhausted to care who else was downstairs. Teresa probably. She had come often since that night nearly two months before when Hank had suddenly come back into her life.

She had never asked Sheldon about the address Hank was supposed to have given him. Nor did Sheldon mention it, or anything else about Hank's visit. She imagined he just wanted to forget that night.

Well, here she was, about to have Hank's child. It wasn't fair for revenge to be carried so far. Samantha bit her lip as the pain came again.

"When does this end, Lana?" she asked in despair. "I really can't take much more."

"You are fighting the pain," Froilana scolded gently. "You must relax."

"Oh, certainly. That's fine advice—when you're not the one suffering. The doctor isn't even here yet. He's going to be too late."

"You worry over nothing," Froilana admonished. "There is plenty of time. The doctor will be here long before the baby comes."

"Oh, God." Samantha groaned. "That's the last thing I needed to hear. Plenty of time! I won't last plenty of time. There's no way I can last. I'm going to die!"

"You only make this more difficult for yourself, Sam. Do not resist the pain. This is your first child. Naturally, this one will give you the most pain. You will forget it though, and the next one will come easier."

"The *next* one! Have another child? Never!"

Samantha collapsed back onto her pillows. She didn't know which was worse, what she was feeling now or what she had felt when she first went to stay at her father's Texas ranch. The first thing she had found was her wedding clothes, laid out over the bed in her new room. What she had felt that day, such terrible emptiness, was the beginning of feelings to come.

Oh, the *vaqueros* and their families had all come, bringing with them everything from the Mexican ranch. The place had been fixed up; there were still open plains to ride on, mountains in the distance. It was much the same as her old home, but still she hated it because of that one night. The barn was a constant reminder of that night. She was troubled, miserable, plagued by memories. She wasn't sure what she wanted out of life. Her old amusements were no longer satisfying at all, and the future looked grim. She was miserable without knowing why.

But when Samantha had realized she was pregnant, she came to life, hating Hank all over again. He had wished a child on her, and he had gotten his wish. She was furious. Yet somehow she was relieved, too. It gave her an excuse to leave the place that was driving her crazy with memories. And she could leave the country, too, so that Hank would never know about the baby.

She had thought she would feel better once she was gone, but she hadn't. She began to think of the child and raising it alone and was miserable all over again. What she began to feel for the child helped a little, though. And so had Sheldon, wondering about him, trying to understand the anger he aroused in her. Then, Hank had arrived.

The pain rose unbearably, and Samantha screamed just as the doctor entered the room. She didn't care anymore that the doctor had come. It was Hank who ought to be there. He was responsible. But, no, she didn't want him here, to know how much she was suffering. No, she didn't.

Sheldon had promised to send for him when Samantha's time was near, and Hank was more than delighted when the message came. All the way across London, he was ecstatic. Lorenzo came along, but Hank didn't hear a word he was saying. Samantha was giving birth to his child. Her child. Their child.

Moments after he arrived, he heard the screams from upstairs, and he was sick. With a drink in his hand, he sat in a far corner of the drawing room, as far as possible from the closed door. Shaking the ice in his glass helped muffle some of the sounds from upstairs, but every once in a while all the color would drain from his face. He sat there in a daze on his third drink, agonizing over what was happening upstairs.

"You shouldn't be here, Hank," Sheldon remarked as another scream died away, leaving the room eerily silent. "Nor should I, for that matter." He was the only one pacing the room, and he was doing that quite briskly. "Good heavens, man, this is no place for men!"

Hank focused on Sheldon. It was several seconds before he spoke. "You will not throw me out?"

"Of course not."

"Then I will stay."

"My club is near here. Why don't we...?" Sheldon offered.

"No."

Lorenzo shook his head, watching the two other men. "He is right, Hank. This is no place for you now. Leave for a while."

"My place is near her," Hank replied.

"She does not know you are here," Lorenzo said pointedly. "You cannot help her."

"Leave me be, Lorenzo. This is where I want—" The loudest scream yet tore down the stairs and Hank's glass slipped from his hands. "Christ! She is dying. I have killed her."

"Nonsense," Lorenzo chided.

Hank turned on him. "Can you swear to me she will not die? Can you?"

"Oh, Lord," Sheldon broke in. "I can't take any more of this. It's highly improper and...and *it's driving me crazy*. Stay if you must. I'm leaving."

He grabbed his coat and strode to the door. But as

he reached the hallway, a baby's cry joined with Froilana's delighted exclamation. "It's a boy!"

Sheldon came back to the drawing room, the slightest of grins on his lips. "I have a nephew."

But Hank was already out of his chair. He passed Sheldon, ran up the stairs, and opened the door to Samantha's bedroom.

Steam was thick from the boiling water, and the heat was terrible. Froilana tried to protest Hank's presence, but the doctor nodded his approval and she went back to cleaning the baby.

"You are the husband?"

Hank didn't hear the question as he stared down at the large bed, unable even to see Samantha's face. "Is she all right?"

"Do you not wish to see *el niño?*" Froilana asked him proudly.

But Hank ignored her, too. "Is she all right?" he repeated forcefully.

"Why don't you ask me?" Samantha said softly.

Hank approached the bed. Samantha could barely keep her eyes open, but she managed to look hard at him before she closed them. He had never seen her so worn out.

"Sam?"

"What are you doing here?" Her voice was hoarse.

"I made your brother promise to send for me," Hank explained quickly. "And, Sam, you cannot deny my right to be here."

"Yes I can. You didn't want me, remember? It didn't matter to you if I got a divorce. So what is your interest here?"

Hank stiffened and answered defensively, "The child, of course."

"Of course," she replied.

"I am not up to fighting with you, Sam," he sighed. "Christ, I thought you were dying up here!"

"Absurd," she scoffed tiredly. "It was unpleasant, but

all women who have children go through it. I don't
...even...remember..."

Her eyes closed again, and her voice trailed off. Hank
just stood there and stared at her, unwilling to move
from her side. Samantha Blackstone Kingsley Chavez,
his wife, the mother of his son, the woman who drove
him crazy with wanting her. This woman always amazed
him, with her pride, her daring, her temper, her passion. If only she had truly hated him, hated him con-
sistently, he might not be confused. But in passion she
had showed him what it could be like for them. It would
have been better not to know. Then he would never
have accepted that he loved her. For even when he
hated her, he loved her.

Chapter 43

THE coach and four moved through the park at a sedate pace. A cool night breeze with the scent of spring blew in through the curtained windows, causing the coach lamp to flicker and distort the features of the two people inside.

"Do you think Sheldon was angry that I asked you to escort me home, Jean?" Teresa asked, her voice tense.

The Frenchman shrugged. "Who knows, *chérie?* Who knows if that Englishman has ever been angry in his life? Truly, I do not think he feels very much. *I* would never leave my fiancée in the care of another man so often, friend or not."

"Do not underestimate him!" Teresa cut in sharply. "Men who are cold like that can erupt into great violence."

"Then you should have left well enough alone and let him take you home."

"I could not bear to ride with that woman again. He takes her everywhere with us now. If I had to listen to one more of her catty remarks, I would scream. You have not heard some of the things she has said to me. When she got her figure back, a sharp tongue came with it. I fear she knows about us, *caro.*"

"Nonsense, *ma chère,*" Jean chided. "Samantha can only guess. And you should not mind her. If she is bitchy, it is no doubt because of her husband. They cannot be in the same room without sparks flying, and now Chavez has moved into the Blackstone townhouse because of his son. Samantha hates it but can do nothing about it. Sheldon has taken his side in that marital war."

"I do not care about that. Her insinuations make me nervous. So far she makes her remarks in Spanish, so Sheldon does not understand. But..."

"She takes her frustration out on you, Teresa, that is all," Jean soothed.

"But why must I suffer her?" Teresa snapped. "I hate that woman!"

"Come now."

"You dare to take that condescending tone with me?" She cut him off. "Oh, I hate you when you treat me like a child!"

"What is all this fuss?" Jean asked, used to her fits of temper. "You will be married soon, and we will have no more worries."

"But will I be married, Jean?" she demanded. "Did you find this other will?"

"No," he admitted, his voice grave. "But I'm afraid I did find out what we wanted to know. My senior partner handled the old man's estate."

"Afraid?"

"It's what I feared, Teresa," he said solemnly. "If Sheldon dies without issue, everything will go to Samantha's child."

"Even if I am his wife?"

"Yes. The old man made sure the estate would go to the blooded heir."

"Curse that woman and her child!" Teresa hissed. "She is ruining all of my plans. I have worked too long on this, Jean. I cannot afford to give up on Sheldon and find another man. I have gone through the last of my family jewels. I have no money left to catch the right husband with."

"Calm yourself, *chérie*. We have not lost yet."

Teresa glared at him. "Our plan was to kill Sheldon after a few months of marriage. Now you say I will have nothing if he dies!"

"Exactly. But it was better to learn this now, before we got rid of Sheldon. The terms of the will are indefinite. Whether Samantha had the child now or five ... ten years from now, the estate would still go to that firstborn. If we killed Sheldon first, we will have lost everything. There will be no way to recover the estate once it goes to the boy."

Teresa's eyes lit up. "You said first, *querido*. Have you solved our problem?"

"There is only one solution. Samantha and the boy must die first. His half of the estate will not be turned over until he is a year old. If he does not reach one year, we will have it all once we get rid of Sheldon. For with Samantha gone, there will be no other Blackstone to claim the estate."

"But she plans to return to America right after our wedding. How can we kill her in that country? She will have her father's protection there. It is too risky."

"We will take care of it before she leaves."

"But the wedding is two weeks away."

"The sooner the better, then. Your wedding to Sheldon might be postponed a few months because of the tragedy, but then our worries will be over and it will be back to the original plan."

"How?"

He shrugged. "I haven't given it much thought yet. Have you any ideas?"

"Suicide. After all, she is very temperamental—and estranged from her husband."

"You mean she kills the baby and then herself?" Jean laughed drily at that. "No, no, *chérie*, suicide will never do. She adores that boy. No one would ever believe she killed him. Herself, maybe, but not the boy."

"The husband could be blamed, then. It is no secret that she plans to return to her father, and Chavez is not welcome there."

"Yes, but he would not kill the boy, either."

"What do you suggest then?" Teresa asked petulantly. "The only time she is alone with the child is in the townhouse, and they must be killed together."

"I agree. And since we can't kill them there, we must get them away from the house together."

"But that Mexican servant always goes with them when they go out."

"I am not talking about just going out. We will get them out of the house somehow, perhaps when all others are sleeping. Yes, I have it now!" he said, excited as the idea came to him. "It will appear Samantha has run away with the child. She can leave a note to that effect. The reason will be the husband. She fears he will try to take the child from her, and so she must go where he will never find her—disappear."

"But Sheldon must know they are dead. They must be declared dead."

"Yes, a simple matter of a run-in with highway robbers. The country roads here are not safe." He grinned. "Do we not hear of robberies and killings all the time? Of course, she does not know this, and she will be fool enough to take Sheldon's best carriage. What robber can resist a rich carriage that travels unescorted?"

"Oh, you are brilliant, *caro!*" Teresa exclaimed. "No wonder I love you so."

"And I you, *ma bien-aimée.*"

"But will you do it yourself?"

Jean's bright blue eyes narrowed. "I do not think so. She is too lovely."

"Jean!"

He chuckled. "Do not fault me for appreciating beauty, Teresa. If I did not, I would not have fallen in love with you. But do not worry. I know a man who will kill anyone for a price."

"But can we afford him?"

"Oh, it will cost nothing. When he is through, I will get rid of him. I have no trouble killing scum."

"When?"

"Tomorrow night, I think. She is joining you for the charity ball?"

"Yes."

"Then she will be worn out afterward and will sleep soundly. The only difficulty will be getting her and the boy out of the house without being seen."

"But how will you get into the house undetected?"

"No problem. As far as Sheldon knows, I am unaware that he won't be home tomorrow night. I will stop by on some pretense after Sheldon and Samantha have gone to the ball. Wilkes will offer me refreshment even though Sheldon is not home. When he leaves to get it, I will leave a note saying I couldn't wait, and then go upstairs and hide myself until the time is right. Wilkes will think I have left the house, and Sheldon won't think anything of it when Wilkes tells him I stopped by."

"You will be careful, won't you, *querido?*"

"Of course, *chérie*. Our future and the Blackstone fortune depends on caution and good planning."

Chapter 44

"YOU dress to entice, eh?" Froilana remarked as she brought out Samantha's rose-colored shawl that matched her gown.

"Of course not," Samantha scoffed.

"But this gown is cut so low—"

"It is fashionable, Lana, and that's all." Samantha cut her off. "And do stop picking on me. This is an important ball. You want me to look nice, don't you?"

"Nice? I think you dress for him."

"And I think you presume too much!" Samantha snapped, whirling away from the mirror. Her toilet was complete, and she looked stunning. "Besides, he isn't coming."

"He always refuses to join you and your *hermano* because he knows you do not want him along. But he usually shows up at the parties anyway because he cannot bear to be away from you."

"What utter nonsense. Hank doesn't care what I do. He has insisted on staying here only because of Jaime."

"La, how you deceive yourself, Sam."

"Oh, stop it! I am tired of listening to your fairy tales, Lana. Hank has only one interest here, and that is his son."

"When you enter a room, his eyes do not leave you. What is that if not—"

"You don't know what you're talking about!"

"And you refuse to see what is obvious!" Froilana shouted back.

"Oh!"

322

Samantha stalked out of the room. She and Froilana seemed always to argue lately, and always about Hank. And he no doubt overheard many of those arguments, his room being across from hers. How that must amuse him! How frustrating to have her own servant be his staunchest ally.

Froilana was simply enthralled by his good looks, that was all. But Samantha knew him for what he was, a man who would do anything to get what he wanted.

And now he wanted his son. Why? That was the perplexing part. He had taunted her with this child before it was even known to them. He had said it would be her child, that she would raise it, she would love it, without his having any part in it. Now suddenly that was all changed. Since the night of Jaime's birth, she had lived with the fear that Hank would try to take the boy from her.

It was a constant fear, and it made her distrust Hank's every action, every word. It made her always defensive, always antagonistic. It was a shield, too, that she used to block out her own feelings. It was simply easier to hate Hank than to accept her other feelings.

They stood on the edge of the room, watching as young couples and older ones swirled past on the parquet ballroom floor. The large room was aglitter with lights and the dazzling colors of exquisite ballgowns. Teresa was unusually quiet. Jean Merimée was absent, for once, and Samantha wondered if that was the reason for Teresa's subdued mood, for she was usually quite vivacious when the Frenchman was around. It was appalling to see the amount of attention Teresa devoted to Jean. And Sheldon didn't seem to notice, to know he was being cheated. But Samantha did. She had tried making excuses for Teresa's behavior toward Jean, but it was no good. The looks, the intimacy of feeling between them, it was too obvious. Why couldn't Sheldon see it?

Sheldon left to get refreshments, and Samantha stood stiffly beside Teresa. She didn't feel like sparring with the Spanish woman. She was in a bad mood to begin with, and if she got started, she might come right out and accuse Teresa of infidelity. That wouldn't do. She had no proof, and there was already enough animosity between them.

Several of Sheldon's acquaintances asked Samantha to dance, but she declined. She would have accepted if Hank had been there, but he wasn't. She wished she hadn't come. She wished she were home with Jaime. The only reason she attended these parties and dinners with Sheldon was to spite Hank, to show him that she could go out and have fun without giving him a single thought. But when Hank had stopped coming along to witness all the supposed fun she was having, the spice went out of it. It all became boring and tedious, and she often took her discontent out on Teresa. Not that the woman wasn't deserving, but Samantha didn't like to be quite so bitchy.

It was all Hank's fault. If he would go away, if she could just stop thinking about him...

Sheldon returned with their refreshments, bringing some friends of his Samantha hadn't met before. She didn't pay particular attention to the introductions, but she couldn't help staring at the tall man and his beautiful wife. They were such a handsome couple, and, noting the closeness between them, Samantha was struck with envy. Her attention picked up when Texas was mentioned.

"...one of the Maitland holdings was a ranch there, and Angela and I decided to make that our home."

"What a coincidence," Teresa remarked. "Samantia is from Texas, as well. You do not know each other?"

The man grinned. "Afraid not, Miss Palacio. Texas isn't exactly a small state."

"What brings you to England, Bradford?" Sheldon asked. "Just a visit?"

"A delayed honeymoon, actually. I wanted Angela to see England in the spring, but we couldn't make it last year because we were too busy building a new ranchhouse."

"You didn't tell me you had American friends, Sheldon," Samantha couldn't help pointing out. She knew his aversion to what he called her "American habits," and was quite surprised to see him so friendly with this man. "You haven't been to Texas, have you?"

"No, my dear. I met Bradford here quite a few years ago. His family owns an estate not too far from Blackstone."

"And how do you like it here—Angela?" Samantha asked the lovely brunette with the violet eyes.

"It's a bit colder than I'm used to." Angela smiled.

"I know what you mean. I spent the winter here for the first time in eleven years and like to froze my—"

"Samantha!" Sheldon exclaimed.

"Oh, relax, Shelly," Samantha chided, receiving an even darker look for using the nickname.

Bradford Maitland burst out laughing, his golden-brown eyes alight. "A girl after my own heart, Sheldon old man. You should have told me you had such a spunky sister. I would have called on her when I returned to America."

Angela jabbed Bradford in the ribs. "Just remember you're a married man now, Bradford Maitland," she said sternly. He drew her closer and whispered something that made her giggle.

Samantha grinned. She liked these two. They were open, not afraid to show their affection or their tempers in public. It must be wonderful to be that happy, she thought wistfully.

"Well, look who has decided to join us after all," Teresa purred.

Samantha turned, expecting to see Jean Merimee. But it was Hank walking toward them. The blood suddenly raced through her as she thought of her daringly cut gown. She would ignore him, of course. Now she would have to dance with other men.

She watched his approach. His eyes were not on her, but on Bradford and Angela Maitland, who were watching him closely, the young woman smiling in delighted amazement, the handsome man scowling.

"I don't believe it!" Angela cried with undisguised pleasure. "Hank Chavez!"

"Angelina." Hank grinned, taking both of her hands. "Still as beautiful as ever. And still with this one, eh?" He nodded to her husband.

"Damned right she is!" Bradford replied stiffly. "She's my wife, now."

"Ah, well, I did not think otherwise, *mi amigo*," Hank said softly, his eyes twinkling. "Though, what she sees in you I will never understand."

"Just keep your distance," Bradford warned, and Samantha was shocked because he was perfectly serious.

"Both of you stop it," Angela broke in, and the men looked away from each other. "Is this any way to act with old friends?"

"He is still as jealous as ever, eh?" Hank whispered to Angela, and Bradford glowered. Hank chuckled. "Relax, *amigo*. You have met my wife, have you not? How can you think I have eyes for another woman when I have a wife as lovely as Samantha?"

"She's *your* wife? Well, I'll be damned." Bradford began to relax. "Congratulations."

"I'm so happy for you, Hank," Angela added.

"I would be happy, too, if she would not shoot daggers at me with her eyes," Hank replied with mock gravity. "I think we both have jealous spouses, eh, little one?" He winked at Angela. "I had better attend mine now, before she thinks I ignore her too much."

Samantha was so furious that she actually saw red. Angela...Angelina...this was Hank's love, the woman he had spoken of so often, the woman he had called out for when he was beaten and delirious. And here Samantha had been, standing and talking to her, actually liking her—oh! And to listen to them, and *him*, calling her jealous! How utterly preposterous. Jealous?!

"Dance with me, *querida?*"

"No!" she hissed, but Hank ignored her refusal and swung her out onto the dance floor.

"I think our friend there has a definite problem on his hands," Bradford remarked to Angela, drawing her onto the dance floor, as well.

"No more of a problem than I have," Angela returned meaningfully.

Bradford grunted at the reference to his own jealousy. It had nearly cost him the woman he loved. "He's lucky, though. She's a beauty."

"Oh, I think she's just as lucky."

"Do you?"

"But not nearly as lucky as I am."

Bradford beamed proudly and pulled his wife closer. "How I love you, Angel."

Samantha saw Bradford and Angela twirl past on the dance floor and her eyes glittered green fire. "Let go of me, Hank. I'm warning you." She tried once again to break loose but couldn't.

"You would not cause a scene, would you, *gatita?* Your brother is watching."

"I don't care!"

"Why are you so angry?"

"I'm not angry!" she retorted furiously, and then hissed. "How dare you embarrass me like that? How dare you accuse me of being jealous?"

He raised a brow, amused. "You were not?"

"No!"

"Then why do you kill me with your eyes?"

"You embarrassed me, damn you!" Her voice drew surprised glances, but Samantha didn't care, so blind with fury was she. "What must Teresa think, seeing you fawn all over that woman, and with her husband right there?"

"Since when do you care what Teresa thinks? You are not even civil to her."

"Well—my brother, then!"

"I only greeted an old friend, Sam. You make more of it than there is."

"An old friend, my foot! You think I don't know who she is? That's your Angelina! You loved her!"

"I wanted her."

"You still do!"

"No, Samina, it is you I want."

"Ha!"

"It is time I proved it to you. Tonight, when the house is quiet, I will come to you."

Samantha gasped. "You do and you'll meet the point of my gun," she said stonily.

Hank drew back, surprised. "You brought your gun to this civilized land?"

"It goes wherever I go."

He sighed. "You disappoint me, Sam. I suppose you would shoot me as you did that miner in Denver?"

She stumbled as the words took hold, and he caught her. "How did you know about that?"

"I was there. I've always wanted to know why you shot that man so many times."

"Because he wouldn't leave me alone," she replied, adding, "Just like you."

"Is that a threat?"

"Take it however you please," she retorted stiffly.

Hank leaned closer and whispered, "I think I would not mind a few bullet holes if it meant having you again."

The softness of his voice unnerved her. His proximity had weakened her, as it always did. Suddenly Angela was forgotten.

"Hank..."

"It has been a long time, *querida*."

"Hank, don't."

"Have you forgotten what it is like?"

"Stop it! Don't think I don't know what you're up to. You're just using me so you can get Jaime. You said yourself that we could never have a normal marriage."

"I was angry when I said that."

"Yes, angry because you were about to marry me but you didn't want to. You never wanted to. You may want me—but you hate me."

"Sam—"

"Just leave me alone!"

Samantha kicked him squarely on the shin, and he released her. She walked quickly to her brother's side, wanting desperately to leave. But it was too early. Hank left Samantha alone for the rest of the evening. She told herself to feel relieved. After all, it was what she wanted—wasn't it?

Chapter 45

HANK woke with a start, grabbing the clock on the bedside table. He couldn't make out the time and reached for matches but couldn't find them in the dark. What had awakened him?

He got up and opened the door cautiously, but the hall was dark and quiet. He closed the door, wide awake. He was surprised that he had slept at all, troubled as he was. Was she sleeping?

Absently, he moved to the window, leaning against the ledge. What was he going to do about Samantha? She wouldn't listen to him. She wouldn't let down her guard for even a moment. She was so damned obstinate, so damned infuriating. Things could be different between them, if only she would let them.

The Blackstone carriage pulling out onto the street drew Hank's attention. He frowned, watching it drive away at a fast pace. Where would Sheldon be going in the middle of the night? Hank straightened suddenly. If Sheldon was away, he couldn't come to his sister's rescue when Hank entered her room. Would she really shoot him? Not if she was sleeping and he entered quietly. What had Bradford told him tonight?

"If you love her, you'll find a way," Bradford had said. "Swallow your pride if you have to, but speak from the heart."

He would do just that. He would make her listen to him. He would admit to her that he had never hated her, that anger and hurt because she had used him had made him pretend. Yes, he would admit that her rejection of him was what hurt the most.

Hank wasted no time crossing the hall to Samantha's door. But when he opened it, he found an empty room. Had she moved to another room because he had warned her he might come? But that wasn't like Samantha. She would have preferred holding him off at gunpoint in order to have the upper hand.

Hank swore. What did she hope to accomplish by hiding from him? Was she with Jaime?

But the child's room was empty, too, and Hank's blood chilled at the sight of the empty crib. Remembering the carriage moving away from the house, Hank dashed into Sheldon's room.

He did not hesitate to enter. It didn't lessen his growing alarm to find Sheldon asleep. Hank quickly nudged him awake.

"Your sister, where has she gone?"

"What?"

"Samantha has left the house with Jaime and her servant. Where would she go in the middle of the night?"

"For God's sake, man. How should I know?"

"She did not tell you she was leaving?"

"No." Sheldon got up and quickly pulled on his trousers. "Are you certain she left the house?"

Hank nodded curtly. "The rooms are empty, and one of your carriages left a little while ago."

"Did you look for a note? Or see if she took any clothes?"

"No."

Sheldon lit a lamp and carried it as they went to Samantha's room. A note was on the bedside table.

"She says she won't be back, that she has to get away from you." Sheldon's face was tense with bewilderment.

"*Perdición!* She sneaks off in the middle of the night! I do not believe it. This is the coward's way, and she is not a coward."

"I admit this is foolish, but the fact is she's gone. She's probably at the docks by now."

"The carriage did not drive toward the docks."

"What?"

"It went the other way."

"Lord, what is she thinking of?" Sheldon murmured. "The country roads are not safe at night. Some aren't even safe by day."

"Do you have any idea where she could be going?"

"No."

"Perhaps your country estate?"

Sheldon shook his head. "She hates Blackstone. Always has."

Hank ran his hands through his hair, his frustration growing. How long had Samantha planned this? Or had it been planned? The open wardrobe caught his eyes. It was full of gowns. But of course she would want to travel light. She had probably taken only a few things. Her vanity table was cluttered with powders, combs, pins, and fragrance bottles. A small chest was there, as well, and Hank moved to it.

"What are you doing?" Sheldon asked.

Hank opened the chest and frowned. "She has left her jewels behind."

"All of them?"

"This chest is full."

Hank moved to the bureau and opened drawers urgently. He stopped when Samantha's gun stared up at him and her words echoed in his mind. *"It goes wherever I go . . . wherever I go."*

Chapter 46

IT was pitch black in the carriage. What little moonlight there had been was gone because of all the overhanging trees. Samantha couldn't begin to guess what road they were on.

Froilana was crouched on the seat next to her, holding Jaime to her breast. Jean Merimée sat across from the two women. They had no idea who was driving.

There had been nothing she could do when Froilana woke her and she saw Jean holding a gun to Jaime's head, the baby cradled in his left arm. He had ordered Samantha to gather a few clothes. She ought to have gone to the bureau first. She had a gun there. But as soon as she had grabbed a few dresses, Jean had ordered her and Froilana from the room. She couldn't argue. He was extremely nervous as it was, nervous and angry because Froilana had surprised him by sleeping in Jaime's room. He was forced to bring Froilana along, which he hadn't counted on.

They had moved through the silent house without alerting anyone, Samantha praying every moment that someone would awaken. But no one had heard them, and soon they had reached the carriage house to find a tall, pathetically thin man waiting for them and the carriage ready to go.

Jean would answer no questions. He was a different man then, curt, perhaps frightened. He kept watching the road behind them until they had left London behind. The horses slowed to a moderate pace because of the darkened road. How the driver could see at all was a mystery to Samantha.

She pulled her robe tighter over her nightgown. Jean hadn't let her change. How embarrassing it would be if, come morning, they arrived someplace with her and Froilana both in their robes and nightgowns! And what on earth was she doing worrying about that when she didn't even know why Jean had kidnapped them?

A kidnapping—again. But this time she didn't have only herself to worry about. She tried to see Froilana's face, but couldn't. Miraculously, Jaime had slept through it all. Her little angel, looking so like Hank except for the vivid green eyes. Their baby.

She wished desperately that Jean had not brought Jaime. He could have demanded ransom for her alone from either Sheldon or her father. But maybe Jean wanted some of Hank's money, as well. Hank might not ransom her, but he would give all he had for Jaime. Damn Jean! How could he be so despicable? And how long before this would be over and she could go home?

As if in response to her silent question, Jean rapped on the side of the carriage with his cane, and they slowed to a halt. "Get out," he ordered tersely.

"Where are we?"

"Just do as you're told, Samantha."

His tone didn't leave room for argument. It was a little lighter outside the carriage, but not much. They were in a forest, and a quick look in all directions revealed nothing else. No houses, just more trees. Where were they?

"Sam, there is nothing here," Froilana whispered to her, standing nervously by her side, holding the baby.

The terror in her voice was catching, and Samantha steeled herself. "I know, Lana. Don't worry." She tried to soothe her, but her heart was beginning to race. Suddenly their clothes were tossed at them.

"Put something on," Jean said curtly. "You can't be found in your night clothes."

Found? "Why have we stopped here, Jean?"

"This is as far as we need to go."

"I don't understand."

"Of course you don't. But soon you will." Then he shouted to the driver. "Peters! Hurry up before someone comes this way!"

Peters was climbing down from the carriage, and Samantha began shaking as a deeper fear took hold of her.

"Jean, for God's sake! What is this about?" she cried, moving closer to Froilana and Jaime.

"It really is quite a shame, Samantha," Jean sighed, sounding genuinely regretful. "I don't want to do this, but I really must."

"Must do what?" Samantha cried.

"No need to get hysterical. Peters has promised to do it quickly and painlessly."

"What?"

"Kill you, of course."

"Madre de Dios!" Froilana shrieked.

"You can't be serious, Jean," Samantha said, suddenly calm. She had passed the point of fear. "For what reason?"

"Money," he stated evenly.

"But I don't..." She stopped, understanding dawning. "You mean the money coming to Jaime? You would kill us just to get Teresa half the money from the Blackstone estate?"

"Not half, my dear, though we could have lived comfortably on half, I suppose."

"We?"

"Now don't pretend you haven't guessed, Samantha," he said with a degree of impatience. "Sheldon is too naive to be suspicious, but you're not."

"You and Teresa?"

"Exactly."

"But where do you fit in, Jean?" Samantha asked.

"She is to marry my brother. Will you be content to be just her paid lover?"

"Teresa was right. You are a bitch. But, no, your dear brother will meet with an accident later on. That was our plan all along. It's too bad you and the boy got in our way. This wouldn't have been necessary if not for your grandfather's will. If we had known about the will sooner, we never would have picked Sheldon for Teresa's husband. Peters—"

"No, wait!" Samantha cut him off frantically. "Jean, there's another way. My husband is rich. So is my father. You don't need to kill anyone."

"Come now, my dear, you know it's too late for that. You know our plans now. Besides, the Blackstone estate is worth a great deal, and Teresa is a greedy woman. She is used to wealth. When her family lost their fortune she became quite desperate."

Samantha well understood desperation. She was on the verge of panic, for Peters was just standing there, waiting for Jean to give the order.

"Jean, please. Jaime is just a baby. Give him to another family. No one will *ever* know. You don't have to kill him, too!"

"It won't work. The money will be held up somehow unless he is reported dead."

"You can't kill my baby!"

"Do you think I like this any more than you do?" he shouted back. "I have no choice now. It has gone too far. So no more..."

He fell silent as they heard the sound of hoof beats.

Jean swore. "We have wasted time, and now someone is coming. Peters, go over by the horses—quickly! If someone asks, pretend one is lame. I'll take the women into the woods until the rider is gone."

But Peters didn't move. "Let me kill 'em now, Gov. There's time."

"No, you fool!" Jean snapped. "We can't take the

chance of there being any witnesses. This must look like simple robbery and murder."

"But I'm quick," Peters protested nervously, his eyes darting to the road. "I don't want to be talkin' to no bloke who might be a robber himself. We can be gone before he gets here."

Samantha backed up, nudging Froilana to move with her while the men argued. Then she shouted. "Run, Lana!"

She threw the clothes she was holding at the men and pulled Froilana into the woods. The two ran for dear life as they heard Jean cursing again. Peters shouted foolishly for them to stop.

"Go after them, Peters!" Jean ordered frantically. "I'll stay with the carriage. Find them, damn it, or you won't get paid a farthing!"

Samantha broke into a clearing, but it was too bright, so she pulled Froilana back into the dark of the forest. They ran to their left for several yards, and then she yanked Lana down behind a bush. Her heart was pounding painfully, her breath coming in gasps.

"I don't hear him following," Samantha whispered.

"I...I am frightened, Sam."

"I know. Hush. And please, Lana, don't let Jaime cry. If they hear him—" A shot rang out, stunning them both. "My God! Jean shot whoever that was!"

"Madre de Dios, now they will both look for us." Froilana's voice rose fearfully.

"Don't get hysterical," Samantha whispered sharply. "Stay calm. They won't find us. It's too dark."

"But should we not run? Leave these woods?"

"No, they'll hear us no matter how quiet we try to be. Right now they've lost us. Stop talking now. Stay quiet."

They squatted on the damp ground, listening fearfully for every little sound. The foliage was thick, and it was a good hiding place as long as no one came near. The minutes ticked by agonizingly. There was a shout from a distance. Samantha's name was called, but the women kept still. How absurd to think she might answer!

Jaime began to coo softly. Froilana rocked him, and Samantha prayed continuously that he wouldn't cry.

Suddenly twigs cracked nearby, and Samantha held her breath. There was the sound of footsteps approaching, and they soon grew louder.

"Oh, God, he's coming closer to us," Samantha whispered. "Lana, I'll hold him off while you run with Jaime."

"No!" the girl gasped in horror.

"Do as I say."

"No!"

"Damn it, Lana, I can stop him better than you can. Now get out of here and save my baby. Go!"

Put that way, Froilana had to agree. With a quick hug for Samantha, she disappeared into the brush toward her left. It was none too soon, either, for a few minutes later a man appeared from the right. Samantha didn't know whether it was Jean or Peters, but it didn't matter. She leaped for his legs in the way she had been taught to bring down a calf. He crashed down on his back with an oath, and she pummeled him before he rolled over, taking her with him. She went for his eyes, her only hope was to blind him, but he caught her wrists and slammed her arms to the ground.

"I warned you before about those nails, Sam."

"Hank?" she gasped, disbelieving. "Oh, God...Hank!"

She began to sob. Gently he pulled her to her feet and gathered her in his arms.

"It is over, *querida mía*. Ah, *mi amor*, hush now," he soothed. "You are safe. It's over."

Chapter 47

IT seemed a very long ride back to town. Jean had been shot, by Sheldon. That had been the shot they'd heard. He was only wounded, not dead, and Sheldon had him tied to Hank's horse. He was personally escorting him to jail, refusing to let Jean out of his sight.

At long last, Sheldon had showed his temper. He was in a rage after Samantha explained Jean and Teresa's lethal plans. She had waited a long time to see him so angry. She was glad that he wasn't taking Teresa's treachery badly. He was furious at being duped, but he did not grieve over Teresa.

Peters had got away. And it had taken time to catch up with Froilana and bring her back. She was asleep in the carriage, with Hank driving and Samantha holding Jaime close to her. She had come too close to losing him, and to losing her own life. She prayed she would never have another night like this one.

It was gray dawn as they reached the Blackstone townhouse. Sheldon went on into town with Jean. Samantha almost pitied Teresa when Sheldon got hold of her.

Froilana took Jaime to his room, and Hank followed Samantha into her room and closed the door after them. She turned to look at him carefully. She was grateful. If he hadn't found her gun and realized something was very wrong, she would probably be dead. They had, in effect, declared a truce. But only for a while, she thought.

"What do you want, Hank?"

He didn't answer. Samantha looked more closely and

saw the dark look in his eyes. He was angry, seething. Her back stiffened in defense.

"Answer me." Her tone turned aggressive.

He exploded. "Can you even imagine how frightened I was for you? *Por Dios!* You were nearly killed!"

Samantha thrust her chin upward. "Don't you take that tone with me! It wasn't my fault!"

"Like hell!" he shouted. "If you had not kept me from your room that Frenchman would never have been able to get to you. He would have had to kill me first!"

"Oh, fine. A lot of good it would have done me if you were dead!"

They stared at each other furiously, then suddenly Samantha grinned at the stupidity of the argument, and Hank burst into laughter.

"Did you see my brother?" Samantha giggled. "I swear he wanted to shoot Jean all over again when he tried to explain what he'd done."

"And what about you? Pulling me down the way you would a steer."

"Too bad I didn't have a rope."

"You would have liked that, eh? Tie me up and do your worst?"

"I didn't do so badly."

"You lost, however."

"Oh?" She grinned. "I notice you didn't hold me down very long, Mr. Winner. Certainly not like you... used...to."

Samantha sobered. Why had she said that? Bringing up the past broke the fragile truce.

Hank realized it, too. But he wasn't ready for the spell to end. Tonight, he had realized more than ever how much he loved her. Racing to find her, half out of his mind with fear that he would be too late. He had to tell her.

"Samantha."

She backed away, her defenses rising. "No, Hank, I think you'd better—"

He caught her to him and silenced her protests with his lips. She raised her hands to push him away, but before she touched him, her resistance was gone. Her hands curled around his neck. All the long months apart, months of remembering how it was between them, the fiery magic, the incredible ecstasy. Samantha wanted it, needed it again, this one last time.

There was no room for doubt any longer, not when he was searing her with his lips, lifting her, carrying her to the bed.

Her robe was cast aside and nightgown quickly followed. Not for one second did Hank stop the kisses he placed here and there, springing loose Samantha's passion. When he moved away for a few moments to shed his clothing, she waited breathlessly for the touch of his body against hers. Soon enough, it was there. Her limbs curled around him, and she arched her body to meet the drive of his first thrust.

It was almost more than she could bear, that explosion that came only a few moments later. Coming all too soon, still it went on and on as Hank continued thrusting into her until at long last, he reached his own height.

When Hank collapsed on her litterly spent and so very vulnerable, Samantha was filled with sudden tenderness. His desire for her was real, even if nothing else was. She carried that realization with her into sleep.

Hank woke to find Samantha standing at the foot of the bed, her gun leveled directly at his chest. Wearing only her white flannel nightgown, her hair streaming in dark abundance down her shoulders and back, she looked too innocent for the hard anger in her eyes. She moved the gun, indicating that he should get out of bed, and he cursed silently. He had had his chance to talk to her, had it but lost it when she responded to his kiss. Talking was forgotten in favor of their passion. Had he lost his one chance to speak?

He pulled on his clothes, angry. "You do not play fairly, Samantha."

"Don't talk to me about fair play," she snapped. "You took advantage of me."

"No. I only kissed you. Everything after that was done by both of us—together."

"I'm not going to discuss it," she replied stiffly. "Just leave, Hank."

His eyes narrowed at her hard tone. "Damn it, Sam, we have to talk."

"No."

"But we cannot go on this way, and—"

"We can't live under the same roof, or else this will happen again."

"Would that be so bad?" he asked softly.

"Yes," she said evenly.

He shook his head. "The real problem is that we fight when we no longer have any reason to."

"I have reason," she replied. "I don't trust you, Hank. I'm going home. And no doubt you'll return to the Hacienda de las Flores that you fought so hard to get. And that takes care of our problems."

"But you are my wife."

"In name only. That was your own doing, or don't you remember? You married me only to get your land. You never intended to see me again. You didn't care anything for me. Remember, Hank?"

"I said many things then that I did not mean, Sam. You did, too," he reminded her. "You swore you would divorce me, but you haven't."

"If you're worried that I'll tie you up indefinitely with this marriage, you needn't be. I'll divorce you eventually."

"That is not what I want."

"I *know* what you want, Hank." Her voice rose again. "But you can't have Jaime."

"Sam—"

"No! Now get out of here!"

"Are you afraid to hear what I have to say?" he asked, his voice soft. "Is that why you stop me before I can even begin?"

"I'm not slow witted, Hank. I know very well what your plan is. You'll tell me you love me, say we should make our marriage work for Jaime's sake. But it will just be lies, Hank."

"I *do* love you, Sam."

She faltered, hearing him actually say the words. But she wouldn't let herself trust him.

"No, you don't. I know you, Hank. You will say anything to get what you want, and you want Jaime. I don't blame you. But you gave him to me. He's mine, not yours."

"What can I say to convince you I love you?"

"Nothing," she returned stubbornly. "You proved your true feelings long ago."

"That was only anger and pride, Sam, I swear."

"Oh, God!" she cried. "Get out!" She raised the gun. "Out! I can't stand any more!"

Hank stared at her hard for a moment, then slammed out of the room. The forcefulness of his exit signaled its finality, and Samantha knew, deep inside, that she would never see him again. He would leave the house as soon as he could, and that would be the end of it.

Tears sprang to her eyes, and she wiped them away furiously.

Chapter 48

SAMANTHA didn't leave her room for the rest of the day. Froilana came in later to tell her that Hank had packed all his things and gone. She wasn't surprised that he hadn't said good-bye. In truth, she was numb, spent, with nothing left, not even regret.

When she joined Sheldon for breakfast the next day, she told him she would be leaving for home within the week. Characteristically, he took the news without even raising a brow. But his reply surprised her.

"What is your hurry, my dear?" he said drily. "After all, your husband isn't here any longer to elicit any complaints."

She drew herself up. "Do I detect a bit of sarcasm, Sheldon?"

"Well, you must admit you weren't exactly fair to the man," he replied.

Samantha didn't try to keep the anger from her voice. "You always did take his side, and without knowing any of the facts, too. Did it ever occur to you that I might have had good reason to put him off? The man hates me!"

"That is ridiculous. It was plain that he loved you."

"How would you know?" she snapped, then added cuttingly, "You couldn't even see what was going on right under your nose with Teresa and Jean. I'm not impressed by your observations regarding Hank."

"You fight dirty, don't you, sister?" Sheldon's voice was low.

Samantha blushed. "I'm sorry," she replied, truly contrite. "I shouldn't have said that."

"No, it's quite all right, Samantha," he said. "The matter is done with, and I'm certainly not going to mourn the loss."

"But didn't you love her?"

"Yes, I suppose I did."

"You suppose?" Samantha was incredulous. "Why did you ask her to marry you if that was all you felt?"

Sheldon shrugged. "She would have made a suitable wife. It was time I married."

"Don't you think it would be nice to marry someone you love?" she asked, trying to keep her tone reasonable. "Or don't you want love?"

"I could ask you the same thing."

Samantha's eyes sparkled again. "Neither Hank nor I wanted to get married. I told you, you don't know the facts."

"But you love each other."

"Lord! You're as infuriating as he is, Sheldon. We were talking about you—for a change. Can you please stick to the subject?"

"If you must know, I've been looking for a wife for quite some time now."

"And Teresa was the best you could find? I can't believe that, Sheldon. Surely there were others?"

"Yes, actually there were several I could have lost my heart to. But I'm afraid *I* didn't strike *their* fancy."

"I can tell you why."

He looked at her sharply. "I would rather you didn't. You are a bit blunt for my taste."

"And you're not blunt enough."

"There are certain standards a gentleman must—"

"Oh, balderdash," she scoffed. "Where is it written a man can't show a little feeling? That's your trouble, Sheldon. You never run hot, not even warm. You're always cold, cold, cold, like you're made of stone. You know, the first time you raised your voice since I've been here was the other night? You were wonderful!"

"I was angry, Samantha."

"Of course! You had every reason to be. And didn't you feel better afterward? A person has to feel once in a while, Sheldon. If you're amused, show it. If you're happy, show that, too."

"And if you're in love?" he asked pointedly. "You should take your own advice, Samantha."

"We're not talking about me," she said coldly, and at that, they both fell silent.

He was right. She loved Hank, but she had never let him know. When had she stopped hating him and fallen in love? Oh, did it matter? She couldn't go back and do everything all over again. She had made him hate her, and she couldn't change that now or ever. It was done.

"Have you seen Teresa?" Samantha asked, hoping to take her mind off Hank.

"Yes. It was really quite amusing, the way she cried her innocence. She tried to make me believe that Jean acted on his own, and that there was nothing between them."

"You didn't believe her?"

"Of course not. It was obvious that she had expected me to say that you were dead—not tell her that her lover was in jail. Her shock was apparent. I'm afraid I lost my temper. And you're right, I did feel much better afterward."

Samantha grinned mischievously. "You ought to come home with me, Sheldon. Father could *really* teach you how to lose your temper."

"I might just do that."

Her mouth fell open. "Do you mean it?"

"Yes. Why not?"

"Oh, Shelly—"

"For God's sake, Samantha, don't call me that!" he said.

"Oh, shut up." She laughed. "This is wonderful.

You're going to make father so happy. He'll be so surprised! Oh, Sheldon, I could kiss you."

"Let's not get carried away, my dear. I haven't lost all my British veneer yet."

"You will, Sheldon. Yes, you certainly will. I'll see to that."

Sheldon cast his gaze heavenward, as if begging for help.

Chapter 49

SAMANTHA would never forget the look on her father's face when he met his full-grown son. That reunion was a heart-rending time.

After a month, Sheldon seemed a different man altogether, wearing cowboy duds, out on the range each day, learning ranching. He took to it well. And Hamilton was always nearby, watching, teaching, so proud to have his son with him at last.

Samantha felt a little left out, but she was so happy for her father that she couldn't complain. They were a whole family now. But she was missing something, missing a man. Little Jaime meant the world to her, but he couldn't completely fill the void in her life.

She had done a lot of soul-searching on the trip home, and she saw that her life did not present a pretty picture. If only she could change things so the future wouldn't look so grim, so lonely.

The very least she could do was try, she told herself simply. Hank might not love her, and she might end up killing him if he ever looked at another woman, especially Angela, but she would be happier with him than apart from him. That was the truth. She needed Hank. She needed the sight of him. She needed his touch. Damn it, she would make him love her.

Samantha's apathy lifted when she made her decision, but all the way to the Hacienda de las Flores she feared that Hank would not even see her. She might have made him too angry during their last meeting. But she had to try.

She wasn't going to use Jaime to influence Hank, either. She had left him with her father. Hank had to accept her for herself alone. After all, she did have her pride.

She was as nervous as a cat when she finally reached the *hacienda,* her old home. Now Hank's home. Manuel and his son had escorted her for the week's journey, and they were all hot and tired when Lorenzo rode out to meet them. His warm greeting didn't assuage her fears. He didn't ask why she had come, but the two pack horses laden with her clothing indicated a long visit and Lorenzo grinned, seeing that.

Hank was in the *sala* going over his accounts when Lorenzo brought her inside. Samantha stood there nervously, waiting for him to glance up at her. She felt terribly self-conscious, knowing she was not at her best. Her green silk shirt was sweat-stained and wrinkled, and the black riding skirt and vest were almost brown from trail dust. Tendrils of hair escaped from under her wide-brimmed hat.

She had brought along the white lace skirt and blouse of her wedding and the thought of it made her blush. Hank would only have to see it to know why she was there.

Lorenzo's announcement made her feel even worse.

"*Amigo,* look what roamed in off the range."

Looking up, Hank rose slowly, speechless. Tension built as he stared at her, the moments going by.

Lorenzo grinned. "Well, I think I will leave you to... whatever. Just don't kill each other, eh?"

The silence that followed Lorenzo's departure was unbearable.

"This room," she said hoarsely, glancing everywhere but at Hank. "It hardly looks the same."

"The furniture makes a difference."

She couldn't judge his mood from his voice. "I suppose," she agreed hurriedly. "I imagine the rest of the house is changed, as well."

"Would you like to see it?"

"No. Perhaps later." Why were they having this ridiculous conversation? she asked herself.

"Samantha, what are you doing here?" he blurted finally.

The opportunity was there at last, but she could not bring herself to admit why she had come. She had rehearsed words over and over, but, faced with Hank, the words just wouldn't come.

"I just happened to be in the area," she said quickly, then could have kicked herself for the silly excuse.

"Visiting Ramón?"

She detected the anger in his voice, and her back stiffened. "No, I was not visiting Ramón," she replied sharply. "And, for your information, I don't need an excuse to come here. This is my house, too. Or have you forgotten that I'm your wife? If I were to decide to live here, you couldn't do a thing about it."

"You can't be serious!"

His amazement brought her temper to the fore. "Yes, I am! In fact, I think I *will* stay. I'd like to see you try and stop me."

Hank stared at her, confused, then shook his head. "I will never understand you, Sam. You remind me that you are my wife, but I seem to remember you denying that the last time we were together."

"It suited me to do so."

"Oh? And now it suits you to use that title to gain entrance to my house?"

"Our house."

Hank came around his desk and stood in front of her. "Oh, *our* house. Yet you said we cannot live under the same roof. You did say that, remember? I suppose you would like me to move out?"

She couldn't blame him for being angry. This was going all wrong.

"No, I—"

"You what?" He cut her off brusquely, his eyes dark

and stormy. "You think we can live here together? You may like this constant war, but I do not."

"I don't like it either!" she shouted back.

"Then why did you come here? Why have you not divorced me? Why haven't you put an end to it, so I can stop hoping?"

"Because I love you, damn it!"

Hank was stunned, but only for a moment. He stared into her eyes, then began to laugh. "Ah, Samina, how long I have waited to hear you say that."

He reached for her, but she backed away. "Don't you touch me, Hank."

He ignored her warning tone and reached again, coming closer.

"Don't. I mean it. There are things we have to settle first."

"Very well."

He stepped back, grinning with pure delight. Samantha could barely concentrate. But she had to make herself say the things that needed saying.

"You're willing to give our marriage a try?" she began.

"Querida, how could you doubt it?"

"Then we'll give it a chance. But I warn you, Hank. I won't stand for any unfaithfulness."

"Nor will I."

She nodded, then started to pace, ready for the difficult part, afraid of what she might learn. "Nor do I want you to pretend you care for me when you really don't. I'm willing to live with you...but I don't want any pretending."

"Qué diablos!" he swore. "Do you mean to tell me you came here even with those crazy doubts in your mind?"

"They're not crazy. You hated me, Hank, you know you did."

"You felt the same, little one," he said gently. "But there was a difference. I never *really* hated you. There was anger, yes, and hurt. I had found a woman I loved, and she spurned me. But you really did hate me."

"Yes."

"And now you say you love me. Am I to doubt your word, Sam?"

"No," she said uneasily.

"Then why do you doubt mine?"

"It's different."

"Why?"

"You didn't want to marry me," she insisted. "You were furious about it."

"Yes, I was. Because I was marrying you for the wrong reason instead of for the right one."

"To get the land?"

"Yes. I did not want to marry you for that," he said softly. "I wanted to marry you to have you and love you. But you were not willing."

Samantha was not quite convinced. "You never asked me to marry you, Hank. Not once. That time in Colorado, you asked me to be your woman, not your wife."

"You never let me finish."

"You said you had no intention of offering marriage," she reminded him.

"Ah, Samina, could you not tell that was only pride talking? Of course I meant to marry you. I loved you then—I love you now."

"What about Angela?"

"*Por Dios!* Can you not just accept what I say?"

"But you loved her."

"I have told you before, she was a beautiful woman and I wanted her. As soon as I met you, she was forgotten."

"Really?"

He sighed. "Yes, really. Are you satisfied now?" Slowly she nodded, and he grinned. "Then will you get over here and kiss me?"

She ran into his arms. "Oh, Hank! I'm sorry. I just had to be sure. You do understand, don't you?"

She was showering his face with kisses, giving him no chance to answer. Finally he caught her head, held her still, and kissed her soundly.

"Yes, *mi amor*, I understand. With all that has happened between us, there was reason for us both to doubt. But no more, Samina. No more doubts. Please. You came to me, and now I will never let you go. For the rest of our lives, you will never again doubt my love."

She held him close. Her smile was beatific. "For the rest of our lives. How wonderful that sounds. *Mi caro, mi querido,* I hope you know I will hold you to that promise. And if we fight again—or, rather, when we fight again—I think you know how to make it right. I think you've always known."

"Yes," he murmured, and those gray lights danced in his eyes. "Like this," he said, and kissed her again.

Epilogue

SAMANTHA, dressed in buckskins, leaned forward in the saddle, resting her arms lazily on the pommel. They were on the north range, viewing the large herd of cattle there, a herd twice as big as her father's had ever been. She looked sideways at Hank, but he didn't see her. He was proudly looking over his land, their land. But she was looking him over, gazing openly at this husband of hers.

She would have to get used to thinking of him in that way. For so long she hadn't. For so long she had been such a fool. Now she knew she had been deluding herself all that time.

How could Hank still love her after what she had put him through? But he did. She didn't doubt it, not anymore. She glowed, remembering the previous night. She had wondered long before what it would be like to be his willing partner, and now she knew. It was wonderful beyond imagining.

"Lorenzo comes, and about time, too," Hank observed as his friend came galloping over to them.

"You were expecting him?"

"Yes."

"But I thought we were going to ride alone."

She couldn't keep the disappointment out of her voice, and Hank grinned at her. "It was to be a surprise, *querida*. If I had told you before we left the ranch that we would not be returning, you would have delayed, perhaps even refused to go."

"Go? Where?"

Lorenzo approached them and silently handed over two heavily filled horse packs. "To the mountains. These supplies will last until we get there. I sent others ahead last night with more," Hank explained.

"You mean the three of us are going back to that camp?" Samantha gasped.

Lorenzo chuckled. "As much as I would like to join you, Sam, I was not invited. And this one"—he indicated Hank with a bemused grin—"makes me waste my time coming out here with the supplies, just so he could delay telling you."

She blushed as the full realization struck her. "We're going to the mountains, just the two of us?"

Hank replied, "This is not the first I have thought of it, Sam. I wanted to take you back there before, just after we married."

"I wish you had."

"You do not mind?"

"Mind? I think it's a wonderful idea!"

"Well, if you two are set on going, you'd better go quickly," Lorenzo warned them. "We seem to have visitors."

"What the devil—" Hank frowned, seeing the large group of riders and a wagon approaching from the north.

"Why—it's my father!" Samantha exclaimed.

"*Perdición!*" Hank swore. "What is he doing here?"

"Now, there's no reason to get upset, Hank."

"Do you forget his feelings for me?" Hank asked. "Or does he now accept me as a son-in-law?"

"Well, no," she replied uncomfortably. "Actually, he didn't want me to come here. But I did come, didn't I? He couldn't stop me."

"I suppose he is here to rescue you then?" Hank said darkly. "If he thinks he can take you from me—"

"Now, stop it, Hank." She didn't raise her voice, but it was an effort. "He *is* my father."

"And I am your husband."

Hank said it softly, and Samantha's temper dissolved under his gaze. "Yes, you are." She grinned. "And it's time my father accepted that, once and for all."

She rode off toward the group before Hank could say any more. He shook his head, thoroughly disgusted by this sudden turn. Five more minutes, just five minutes, and they would have been well on their way to the mountains, and seclusion.

"Cheer up, *amigo*," said Lorenzo. "It is not so bad."

Hank looked over at him sharply. "Not so bad? I could have had her all to myself, Lorenzo. How would you like to be cheated of that time with the woman you love?"

Lorenzo chuckled. "You will have other times. You will have the rest of your lives."

"I suppose," Hank conceded. "But, right this minute, that doesn't really help."

The two men followed Samantha. When they reached the group, she was standing by the wagon, hugging Jaime. Froilana was sitting in the wagon, looking at Samantha. Hamilton Kingsley was beside his daughter, a sternly disapproving look on his face, because she was ignoring what he was saying to her. Sheldon was standing nearby, as well, and Hank was amused to see the Englishman in trail clothes, a gun strapped to his hip.

Hank greeted the men quickly as he dismounted. His attention, like Samantha's, was on his son. He moved quickly to her side and put his hand lightly on Jaime's head. Samantha smiled up at him, her eyes bright with happiness. "You haven't seen him for months. Here." She handed Jaime over to him. "See how much he's grown?"

Hank laughed as Jaime's tiny fingers caught at the brim of his hat, pulling it off. The brim went straight into the baby's mouth, and Samantha scolded gently as she took it away from him. Hank grinned at them, retrieving the hat. His son. His wife. He dreaded to think what life would have been like if Samantha hadn't come back to him. But she had, and now they would be a family.

One member of her family wasn't too happy about that, however.

"Señor Kingsley." Hank nodded stiffly to the older man.

"Chavez," Hamilton said curtly.

"Oh, honestly," Samantha sighed. "You two had better start liking each other—whether you want to or not!"

"Samantha—" Hamilton began, but she cut him off.

"What are you doing here, father? I told you I would send word when to bring Jaime."

"He missed his mother," Hamilton said helplessly.

"Nonsense," she scoffed. "You must have left home on the same day I left. What are you really doing here?"

"I'm here to talk some sense into you!" he blustered. "And to bring you home."

Samantha stiffened. "I am home." And with that, she turned on her brother. "Damn it, Shelly, you were all for my coming here. You understood. Why didn't you talk him out of this?"

Sheldon looked shamefaced. "I tried, my dear. I suppose I haven't mastered the art of argument yet."

He said it so solemnly that Samantha burst into laughter. She couldn't be mad at him. She couldn't be mad at her father, either. She was just too happy to be mad at anyone.

"That's all right, Shelly. You'll learn," she teased. "And as for you, father...look at me. Do I look like I need help?" She hugged him. "I'm grateful that you still have such concern for me, but it's not necessary." Earnestly she looked up into his eyes, hoping to make him understand, to be happy for her. "I love him. I love him with all my heart. And he loves me."

"But—"

"No. Please don't bring up the past. The past was all...wrong. What counts is now."

"You're sure, Sammy?"

"Very sure."

"Well then." He moved over to Hank and offered his hand. "I suppose it's time I recognized your marriage. Old men act like fools every once in a while. I hope you'll forgive this old fool."

Hank smiled broadly and shook the hand. "With pleasure. And you will not regret giving your approval. I promise you that."

Samantha took Jaime and handed him up to Froilana in the wagon. "The only problem, father, is you've come at a bad time." She caught Hank's hand and grinned. "We were just leaving."

Hank's eyes were dancing with delight as he led Samantha to El Cid and helped her mount. "You are all welcome at the *hacienda*," he added. "If you care to wait until we return."

"Where are you going?" Hamilton frowned.

"You might say, on a honeymoon." Her smile was for all of them.

"Now? But you've been married a year."

"Lots of people take delayed honeymoons." She laughed. Glimpsing Hank's amused look, she knew that he, too, was thinking of Bradford and Angela Maitland. "Ours is long overdue."

"But for how long?"

"Two weeks maybe."

"Or even a month," Hank said as he mounted El Rey.

"Don't frown so, father." Samantha giggled. "You need a little rest. Enjoy the house, visit your old friends in the area. We'll be back before you know it."

"I suppose I don't have much choice," he grumbled.

"No, you don't. *Adiós*." And then she looked at Hank, and her eyes gleamed mischievously. "I'll race you."

"Oh, Lord!" she heard her father sigh.

Hank grinned, his eyes laughing with the challenge.

"You have no chance of winning, *gatita*," he warned her.

"Don't I?"

Riding side by side, they raced away from the others, moving faster and faster until Samantha put her fingers to her lips and let out a shrill whistle. El Rey halted immediately. Samantha rode on, her laughter floating back on the wind to Hank. Shaking his head at her, he couldn't help laughing. With her, he would never win. He hadn't won in the past. He wouldn't win in the future.

But it didn't matter. He had won her love.

Dear Reader:

If you enjoyed this book, and would like information about future books by this author and other Avon authors, we would be delighted to put you on the mailing list for our ROMANCE NEWSLETTER.

Simply *print* your name and address and send to Avon Books, Room 1210, 1790 Broadway, N.Y., N.Y. 10019.

We hope to bring you many hours of pleasurable reading!

Sara Reynolds, Editor
Romance Newsletter

Book orders and checks should *only* be sent to Avon Books, Dept. BP Box 767, Rte 2, Dresden, TN 38225. Include 50¢ per copy for postage and handling; allow 6-8 weeks for delivery.